POLARITY
REVERSED

SUSAN MERAKI

For my sister.

CONTENTS

Chapter 1 – Re-Match

Daniel sat at a wooden table, staring down at a chessboard, his hands embedded in his thick, dark hair.

"You appear tense, Daniel," Father Crane said to his teenage acolyte.

Daniel exhaled and briefly closed his eyes. He put his left hand on the table and tapped his fingers, pondering an appropriate response for his mentor. His eyes meandered aimlessly around the dimly lit, austere, cavernous room. Avoiding eye contact with Father Crane was critical – he always felt intimidated by it.

There was nothing Daniel wanted more in the world at this very moment than to beat him. He had come close nearly three months ago when their match ended in a stalemate. Since then, Father Crane had soundly beaten him each time they'd played – with seemingly little effort. Daniel's eyes shifted up to Father Crane; they rested to a cold, dead gaze.

"Are you okay?" Father Crane asked as he leaned forward, planting his elbows onto the table.

Daniel was unmoved. He was determined to decipher the complexities of Father Crane, the complexities that were cloaked by his humble appearance: black cassock, simple glasses, clean-shaven, and trim, but greying hair. Father Crane never lost at chess. Father Crane never lost at anything and was never wrong about anything. He always appeared to know what was going to happen long before anything did happen – almost as if he had the ability to predict events far in advance. He was too perfect, but Daniel was convinced that every man has a flaw – a vice that would expose his weakness. Daniel was determined to find that flaw in spite of Father Crane's commentary. Father Crane was clearly trying to distract him.

Father Crane rested back in his chair and folded his arms across his body. Daniel realized that his silence could be seen as disrespectful – this was his only worry. Father Crane had been kind and insightful during his nearly eight years at the monastery. Daniel gravitated towards him.

Conversely, Daniel avoided the monastery's other residents. He wrote them off as useless – they were always too busy memorizing scripture, chanting, and walking annoyingly slow. They never gave Daniel any advice beyond regurgitated Bible verses and they were quick to chastise him without any meaningful explanation.

"It's God will... You must rest... You should be humble... You cannot speak... Learn to forgive...," they would tell him.

They weren't human to him. Father Crane, on the other hand, was the parent that Daniel never had. He believed Father Crane was the only inhabitant at the monastery capable of thinking for himself. Father Crane didn't question anything because he unequivocally knew everything. When Daniel asked a question, Father Crane didn't give a parroted response – Father Crane somehow knew precisely what to say.

"Daniel, these chess matches are intended to be a friendly learning experience. We are not in a competition," Father Crane said.

"I'm… I'm sorry, Father. I must admit that I feel that I cannot speak to you while we play."

"Why?"

"Well… I don't want to lose my focus. I don't want to be distracted. I need to keep my train of thought," Daniel answered.

"Ah, yes. So you see, the monastery's rule about maintaining silence does have some value in everyday life," Father Crane responded with a brief smile.

Daniel couldn't help but quickly smile back at him. Father Crane was undoubtedly his best friend; he was the only person Daniel trusted. It frustrated him that Father Crane wasn't always available, so he was frequently alone. Father Crane would unexpectedly take trips – sometimes for many days. Daniel's only true mental excursions were during his time with him. Time spent with him was an instant vacation away from the monotonous, boring, and unnecessarily lengthy rituals that he was beholden to daily.

"Father, may I ask a question?"

"Please," Father Crane said, gesturing with his hand.

"What is the purpose of the monastery?"

Father Crane raised an eyebrow.

Daniel shifted back in his chair. "I mean… I don't question our faith… I…," Daniel stammered.

"Daniel," Father Crane interrupted, "We are here to be a bastion of God's will to the best of our ability. We are to live humbly before God so we can be in tune with His will."

"Yes… yes, I know this," Daniel said, blinking a few times.

Father Crane pushed his glasses further up on the bridge of his nose. The rest of his body remained perfectly still. He calmly crossed his arms once more, maintaining stern eye contact with Daniel.

"I just wonder why we can't go out there and make God's will happen. We just sit here hoping it will happen. We are passive. We do nothing when we should be doing something."

Father Crane's face stiffened slightly.

"I'm sorry Father Crane. I didn't mean to offend..."

"You did not," Father Crane responded firmly. Father Crane stood up and walked to a nearby lamp. "Come," he said, motioning his hand.

Daniel got up from his chair and walked to Father Crane. The two of them stood before the lamp – the only source of light in the room.

"This lamp just sits here. It does not do anything, right?" Father Crane asked.

"It gives us light," Daniel responded.

Father Crane turned the lamp off. The room went completely dark.

"How useful is this lamp?" Father Crane asked.

"It's... It's the most useful object in this room."

"Yet it is only noticed when it is needed. It is only noticed when it is gone," Father Crane turned the light back on and continued, "It allows us to be us. It allows us to be useful. It allows us to see danger. It allows us to enjoy each other's company. It allows us to see our enemies and our friends."

"Then our monastery is a very dim lamp," Daniel said with hopelessness latched to his face.

"A very dim one, yes, but the small amount of light that it gives is enough to provide guidance even in the darkest times. Our purpose is not to push our will onto people. Our purpose is to be there for them when they need us. People have the

4

freedom to do whatever they please. We are forgotten about – or scoffed at – until we are needed. It is only then that people realize that we have always been there for them, that we were always on their side."

Daniel looked at the ground and thought about Father Crane's words. Father Crane returned to his chair at the chessboard. Daniel remained standing in front of the lamp, well behind Father Crane.

"But there is so much bad that happens to people and we are just sitting here letting it happen," Daniel said, shaking his head slightly.

"That is the natural course of life. Mankind will naturally improve at the fastest rate that it can tolerate."

Daniel smirked, "That's because the world is filled with people who believe that everything's fine. While others die, they believe everything's fine. If that same pain was forced on the people that believe everything is fine… then I'm certain that something would be done about it. World pain would end faster."

"Daniel, look at the callouses on your hands. Did you get them overnight?"

Daniel looked at his leathered hands. He shook his head.

"You grew your callouses through hard work in our fields. Your hands are tough, resilient because you let your hands grow their callouses at the fastest rate they could naturally tolerate. If you had worked faster, they would have blistered and bled. So, you see, there is a natural limit towards change that we humans can tolerate; that limit is frequently exceeded by our own doing. Mankind has never tolerated forceful pushes – even if the intent is for good. Force of any kind will always have negative residual effects that may not be immediately apparent."

"But there is so much bad out there."

Father Crane turned his chair towards Daniel. "Until the world is happy with status quo there will always be pain out there; the world will never be happy with status quo. There is always someone somewhere unsatisfied enough with their life that they must act on it with some degree of anger or violence. It does not matter if it is because their favorite TV show was cancelled or if it is an empire they want to rule."

"I think... I think understand now," Daniel said, beginning to pace. "If the world was happy with status quo then there would never be a reason for mankind to improve. There would never be a reason to cure diseases, to learn how to work together more effectively, to find more efficient ways to farm and so on. The best thing to do is make sure status quo never happens. The best thing to do is to keep people pushed so they will keep improving. Mankind gravitates towards being at rest and we must keep them in motion."

"Daniel, you are missing the point," Father Crane said.

Daniel stared blankly towards the ceiling, still caught up in his thoughts for a few seconds. "Hmm? Oh... what was that?" he asked.

"Status quo will never mean happiness. Status quo does not mean that mankind cannot improve on its own. Status quo is simply the rate of change mankind can naturally tolerate. It ebbs and flows on its own with no intervention required. It is by divine design," Father Crane said.

"But Satan is the greatest contributor to strife. In a way, Satan guides status quo. It's Satan's influence that sets this limit that mankind can naturally tolerate. If God wanted Satan destroyed, He could do so at any moment He chooses, yet He lets him live on... for a purpose."

Father Crane locked his eyes onto Daniel's eyes.

"Father Crane... I'm sorry... I stepped over my boundaries. I'm still a student trying my best to learn. I know this takes time."

"Think about what you have said after we finish the match," Father Crane said, waving his hand back towards the table with the chessboard.

Daniel bowed his head obediently and walked back to his chair. He sat down, putting his elbows on the table. A few seconds later, Daniel moved his queen one forward space. His eyes slowly lifted up to Father Crane.

Father Crane clasped his hands together at his chin. His breathing was slow, steady, and heavy. A minute later, Father Crane moved his pawn one space forward – exactly as Daniel had hoped.

I'm so close. I can feel it, Daniel thought.

Daniel quickly moved a pawn forward one space.

Father Crane's eyes opened a slight bit wider. Daniel perked up – he'd never seen Father Crane show even the slightest iota of surprise during any of their matches. Father Crane carefully moved his knight forward, taking Daniel's pawn. Daniel looked down, stricken with disbelief; Father Crane's king was exposed. All he had to do was move his queen forward to seal the match.

"I think I have you checked," Daniel said as he moved his queen in place.

"Checkmate, it appears," Father Crane said, gradually looking up at Daniel. "You have won."

"Yes!" Daniel popped up and shouted, "Yes! Yes! Yes!"

Father Crane sat steadfast, his whole attention seemingly affixed to the aftermath on the chessboard. Daniel's joy frenzied into hops and skips.

"Daniel," Father Crane finally spoke up.

Daniel ignored him and continued buzzing around. "I can't believe it!"

"Daniel."

Daniel continued to ignore him. Father Crane slammed his fists to the table and yelled out, "Daniel! Calm down!"

Daniel immediately stopped his celebration. He turned towards Father Crane and wiped all signs of joy from his face, sitting back down at the table. He sank into his chair and began to fidget with his hands. "I don't know what came over me... I was filled with elation," Daniel said.

Father Crane stared him down, deadpanned. Daniel couldn't make eye contact.

"Is it wrong to celebrate... just a little bit?" Daniel gulped.

"Will this be our last match?" Father Crane asked firmly.

"No. I hope not."

"Then nothing has ended."

Daniel lowered his head, "No... I guess not."

Father Crane stood up. "Now then – how did you beat me? What did you do differently this time versus all of the other times?"

Daniel tapped the side of his cheek. "I did what you didn't expect me to do," Daniel finally said.

"What was that?" Father Crane asked, folding his arms.

"I let you make the moves. I let you be aggressive. I let you believe that you were ahead and that caused you to lose focus on making the right move."

"Yes. Many times doing nothing is all of the *something* you need to do. It is natural for people to interpret inaction as action – and then overcorrect for something that was never there."

Daniel's attention turned back towards his victory – he was nearly in tears. This was the best day of his life. Beating Father Crane was his crowning achievement in a life that started very dark and without hope. He beamed, knowing he would wake up the next day as if there were no other bad days that were ever behind him. After all, he had beaten the venerable Father Crane – the man who was once thought to be unbeatable. God finally favored him.

"Are you still gloating inside?" Father Crane asked, leaning forward.

Daniel dropped his eyes toward the ground. "Yes, Father, I can't help it. I'm just so happy. I haven't felt this good in... in as long as I can remember."

"It is God's gift to allow you to be joyous, but to revel in the presence of your defeated foe is mocking one of God's own creations."

"Yes, you're right. After all, you have beaten me many more times in the past... and... and..."

Daniel abruptly stopped speaking. A few seconds later, sadness draped his face and his eyes drifted listlessly.

"Are you all right?" Father Crane asked.

Daniel tucked in his lips and clenched his fists, brimming with anger.

"Daniel, are you all right?" Father Crane asked again.

Daniel's breathing picked up. He wanted to lunge at Father Crane and punch him in the mouth.

"Daniel?" Father Crane asked again.

Daniel grabbed his head in a vain attempt to wring out all of the anger that was wholly consuming his body. "Do you remember?" Daniel asked and quickly inhaled. "Do you remember our 54th match?"

Father Crane's face fell flat. "I remember many matches," he said.

Daniel winced. "THIS!" he shouted. "This match is the exact setup of THAT match except you didn't move your knight forward. Instead you moved THAT PAWN," he said, pointing at a pawn, "And then thirteen moves later you slaughtered me."

"Calm down, Daniel," Father Crane commanded.

"No... No... Something told me that this looked awfully familiar and then – like a brick falling on my head – it was clear. Not only did you let me win but you planned this!" he yelled and then calmly put his hands over his face. "You planned from the very beginning of the match."

Father Crane was silent. Daniel waved his arm through the pieces on the chessboard, wiping them off the table, scattering them across the floor. He stormed out of the room, slamming the door behind him.

* * *

"Interesting – I did not predict that," Father Crane said softly as he got up from his chair. This was the first time that someone without full Polarity made something unpredictable for him. Daniel's Polarity was nearly full – he was getting better at seeing into the future and into the distant past. Father Crane had to make a choice: He had to kill Daniel or keep trying to turn his Polarity back. Allowing Daniel to become one of *Them* was unacceptable – killing someone that was on the cusp of becoming one of *Them* was a protocol of *Us*. Father Crane needed advice.

Father Crane left the room and walked down the weakly lit adjoining hallway. He reviewed his actions of the chess match. He certainly didn't want Daniel to know that he let him win; he hoped that he would find some part of joy in his otherwise joyless life. Letting him win might help his Polarity to reverse. He further worried about Daniel's emerging need to leave the monastery – it was clear that Daniel couldn't be bottled up any longer within its confines.

He did not ask for this life. He experienced too much death, too much pain, Father Crane thought.

Father Crane briefly stopped and looked at a portrait of Jesus Christ suffering on the cross. He knew that some people pay the ultimate price to change humanity, that anyone can change humanity if they're willing to pay whatever price is required.

Father Crane continued walking and made his way to the front door of the monastery. He turned the heavily worn iron doorknob and slowly opened the large, creaking wooden door. The star-filled sky dominated the backdrop. He closed the door behind him and walked down the small, stone set of stairs. The air was brisk and cool, but Father Crane didn't care – he was more focused on the meeting he was about to have in two minutes and fourteen seconds.

He walked across the large dirt parking lot in front of the monastery and stepped into a nearby cabbage field. The freshly tilled top soil spilled into his shoes with each step, but he didn't lose any stride – he was never late for anything. Finally, after having walked about one hundred yards, he stopped.

"I am not quite sure what to say," he said loudly.

"You'll have to do your best!" a voice shouted back at him.

About forty feet in front of him in the bright moonlight was a young man – a face full of acne and barely eighteen years old. Father Crane made eye contact with him and gave a swift nod to acknowledge his presence. "Max, I still believe that I can do this," Father Crane said with a hint of lingering defeat.

"You've had many years to reverse his Polarity and you're failing miserably," Max said and then rubbed his nose.

Father Crane looked down at the ground.

"What happens once he gets his full Polarity? What kind of a threat is he gonna be to *Us*? Why take a chance and give *Them* yet another asset? He is razor-close. He is right in front of you. You've had many chances to kill him and – for some reason – you believe you won't have to."

"He is still young and impressionable. It is not impossible to reverse him."

"You don't know that – sixteen isn't that young. Reversing Polarity doesn't happen very often at all – and it isn't worth the risks. Even I'm not sure what will happen to Dan."

"I… I was hoping you would not say that," Father Crane muttered.

Father Crane had come to love Daniel as a son. He knew that Daniel was a risk when he took him in nearly eight years ago.

"Come on – the kid killed his parents. He also killed all three sets of foster parents. He got away with all of it," Max said.

"I can sense he feels guilt about his parents, but he does not feel remorse for what has become of the others."

"Why do you believe in this experiment of reversing his Polarity? *We* can't take a chance of it becoming full."

Father Crane paused, carefully selecting the words to use towards his superior. "None of *Them* know about him. He is isolated here at the monastery and he is completely oblivious of his powers. *They* will not protect him because *They* do not know about him."

"He's a sliver away from getting his full Polarity. His ability to see things in a positive light took a major blow thanks to your little chess match. You've only given him more negative intention – and when his negative intentions are full then so will be his Polarity. He will become one of *Them*," Max said.

Father Crane dipped his head.

Max continued, "Once he's got his full Polarity, he'll become completely aware of everything. He'll know who you are."

"He is not predestined to become one of *Them*. He has a choice," said Father Crane.

"So far he's made his way without much trouble to become one of *Them*. You are, for all intents and purposes, violating one of *Our* three protocols."

"*We* must annihilate those who are on the cusp of becoming one of *Them*," said Father Crane.

Max cocked his head to the side. "However, it's true that *We* could learn something from this. Reversing the Polarity could be easier than killing – maybe."

"Yes."

Max closed his eyes in deep thought. "It appears… It appears that he's still clinging onto his love for you and his guilt in killing his parents."

"His love for me is evacuating, I am afraid," Father Crane said.

"Once that's gone and he forgives himself of his murders then he'll become one of *Them*. I've predicted it."

Father Crane nodded, his face wracked with sadness. "Your predictions are always pristine. He must then be annihilated."

"Yes. We cannot lose the opportunity. You must take care of this before it happens."

"I will."

"I'm willing to give you more time. However, *We* must not forget that Polarity reversal has only happened when something extraordinarily significant happens to that person," Max said.

"Like seeing God."

"Something like that, yes. But it's because of that, a more progressive approach won't work. Dan can already predict many of your moves. You're not able to fully predict Dan. Once Daniel insists on being called Dan, you'll know that he's a different person – he will be seconds away from becoming one of *Them*. You must kill him then."

Chapter 2 – Confusing World

10 years later…

Susie slowly walked up to the front door of her mother's home and stopped. Her body swayed a few inches to her right – her knees were on the verge of buckling. The bright sun and occasional breeze helped keep her awake. She wiped a newly forming tear from her eye and took a deep, quick breath. Her hand reached out towards the doorbell, but she pulled back a few inches from it. The doorbell wasn't going to work, but she wasn't quite sure how she knew this.

Mom will tell me the doorbell doesn't work after I finally knock and she finally answers the door. This doorbell won't get fixed for another three years, six months, four hours, and two…, she thought.

She grabbed her shoulder-length brown hair with both hands and pulled. "Why can't it stop just for one minute?" she pleaded softly, unsure of what abilities this new power, Polarity, had bestowed on her.

Twin boys were born at this very spot yesterday in 1867. This home will be demolished for a new high rise in twelve years. At this very moment, the neighbor two homes down on the left will walk out his front door.

Susie turned her head to the left and – on cue – a man emerged from his front door two homes down.

The man will go to his mailbox and find a notice of lien from the IRS. He will be panicked and run back inside yelling, "Oh my God!" He will lose his house by this time next year.

Susie turned her head forward and closed her eyes, hoping that this wouldn't happen – that this was just a weird, very protracted dream.

"Oh my God!" she heard the man yell, shortly followed by the sound of a slamming door.

Susie pressed her head against her mother's front door and cringed. Her eyes opened slowly and she rubbed her face with both hands, trying to keep a grip on her composure. She hurriedly knocked on the door with what was left of the little energy she could still muster.

KNOCK KNOCK KNOCK

Her arm dropped, falling limp to her side. She leaned heavily against the doorframe, waiting for her mother to answer.

"It will take you another minute and twelve seconds to get to the door," she said, wincing, shaking her head.

Several tears streamed down her cheeks and she slumped to the ground, sitting against the door.

"I know what you're doing right on this very minute, Mom. You're sewing. You heard the knocking but you will keep sewing until you need to change thread… and only then will you get up and open the door," she whispered.

She wiped her face of her tears and slapped the side of her head several times, but her Polarity wouldn't stop. It was the past, present, and future – uncontrollably at the same time.

"Stop… stop doing that… PLEASE STOP," she implored.

Mom will die of Alzheimer's when she's 71, she thought.

"STOP!" she yelled, burying her face in her hands.

Her phone beeped; she received a text message. She reached in her pocket and grabbed her phone.

I will be in contact with you primarily through texts, it read.

"What? Who is…," she said aloud.

This is Father Crane, a new text read before she could finish her question.

She almost dropped the phone, bewildered at the timing of the text. Father Crane is a name that shouldn't be real, but it clearly was. She coughed a few times and leaned her head against the door, trying to piece together whatever reality she could recognize. Her phone beeped again. She looked at its screen.

Lean off the door – your mother is about to open it, it read.

Susie perked up and leaned forward right when the door opened. She looked around the quiet neighborhood – wondering exactly how Father Crane knew what she was doing.

"Oh Susie! What a nice surprise!" her mother said.

Susie looked up at her mother momentarily, but quickly returned her attention towards finding Father Crane.

"Oh, honey… why are you sitting there? Are you okay?" her mother asked.

Susie looked around for a few more seconds and said, "Oh, I knocked because the doorbell doesn't work."

"That's funny," her mother said, closing her eyes briefly. "I was just about to tell you that I'm glad you knocked because the doorbell doesn't work."

Susie grabbed the doorknob and pulled herself up from the ground. "I can pick up some butter at the store," she mumbled.

Her mother scratched her head. "What?"

"You just told me you needed butter for the macaroni and cheese you were going to cook, right? And… I… am a bit confused I think," Susie said, still mostly looking around the neighborhood.

"I didn't ask you anything, honey. I was just thinking about making macaroni and cheese earlier today but I'm sure I have butter... or do I?"

Susie looked at her mother – she felt comforted in seeing her aged, familiar face.

Her mother smiled, "Nope. No I don't. I used it yesterday morning for the pancakes. How did you know, sweetheart?"

Susie grabbed her temples – she realized that she was confusing the future events given to her by her Polarity with the reality of the moment. She was skipping ahead into the evening unintentionally.

"Mom... I need to talk to you about some things... pretty important things."

"Sure. Come on inside. You're letting all of the AC out. Sometimes I wonder why we live in southern California with summers like this," her mother said, opening the door wider.

Susie hugged her mother tightly, her face embedded in her mother's curly, long, grey hair. She let go of her mother, looked into her tired eyes and gave her a kiss on the cheek.

"My, you're full of love today," her mother blushed, putting her hand on her cheek.

"You're my mom. I love you every day."

Susie carefully walked through the small foyer – almost tripping on some peeled away linoleum flooring – and into the living room. She navigated through many over-flowing boxes on the floor, stepped over a few stacks of old magazines, and collapsed on one of the four dingy, hole-ridden couches – it was the only one that wasn't covered with stacks of papers or trinkets one would find at garage sales. Susie caught a bad odor from its cushions.

SNIFF SNIFF

"Mom... what's that smell on the couch?" she asked.

"Oh, it's probably cat pee. Why?"

Susie sat up. The odor definitely caught her attention, waking her up.

"Do you want anything to drink?" her mother asked.

Susie coughed and said, "I've... I've had some really weird things go on the past 24 hours... well, now that I think about it... probably the past eight months or so."

"Oh?"

"I need you to tell me if I'm crazy because you're the person I trust most and I know you'll listen to me," Susie said, hugging a throw pillow, trying her best to keep a grip on her Polarity's musings – it wanted to tug her into the future and then, without warning, well into the past.

"Oh honey – everyone's got a little crazy in them. Your sister Karen has her own form of crazy with all those boys she dates. Well... she drives them crazy. She's twenty-four and acts like she fifteen," she laughed.

Susie shook her head, "No – not like that."

"Okay...," her mother replied, trailing off.

"An airplane crashed yesterday, right?"

"Oh yes... terrible. It's all over the news. Everyone died."

"No... not everyone. I... I was on that flight," Susie said, gulping.

Her mother scrunched her face and a put hand on her hip. She sat down next to Susie and said, "Honey... is this about a boy? Because they can make you pretty messed up in the head, if you know what I mean," she said, circling her right index finger around the side of her head.

"Actually... Actually, yes. Yes, there was a boy involved," Susie said, biting down on the nail of her index finger.

"Oh what did he do?" her mother said, patting Susie's knee.

"He… Dan… He put me on that airplane," she began with increasing anger. "Dan tried to kill me… He tried to kill me. I didn't know it then… but I know it now."

Her mother's eyes drifted downward. "Susie – this is just stress from college. You do it to yourself. Besides, you couldn't have been on that airplane. No one survived."

"How do you know?"

"The TV…"

"The last time I saw you was about a week ago. SO MUCH has happened since then," Susie said, standing up.

Her mother was silent, her mouth opened slightly, but stopped short of saying anything.

"Mom, please. I need you to hear me out."

"Okay," her mother said with a tinge of nervousness.

"I'm not sure where to begin."

"Start stories at the beginning," her mother said plainly. "It helps keep things straight."

That wasn't a bad idea. Susie remembered how Dan introduced her to Polarity several months ago – he did so by predicting simple future events that were about to happen. She snapped her fingers once and said, "Maria will call you tonight and tell you that she won $100 on a scratch-off."

Her mother laughed, "That was last night, honey. How did you know?"

"Exactly – how did I know?"

"I don't understand, dear."

Susie clenched her fists. She knew that Maria won the $100 but she confused the past as the future. "Oh, this is frustrating," she mumbled.

"What's frustrating?"

Her mother's phone rang.

"That's Maria's husband. Maria just passed away," Susie said quickly, pointing at the phone.

"Susie! Don't say such horrible things," her mother said as she picked up the phone and answered, "Hello?"

For the next few minutes, her mother repeated the same phrases, "I'm sorry... She will be missed... I loved Maria like a sister."

During this time, Susie used her Polarity – to the best of her ability – to determine if there was any way she could tell her mother about what she experienced. She closed her eyes to focus, doing her best to concentrate on her Polarity – to attempt to control it to some degree – to look into the future using different approaches with her mother so she could figure out what was the best way to tell her what had happened. Being able to see into the future with some control, she reasoned, would allow her to play out different approaches in advance. She hoped to find an approach that would be effective in telling her mother what had happened to her.

Within a second, everything was completely silent and then her mother's voice returned with an echo to it. Susie opened her eyes and the world had a much brighter tint to it. All objects – from her mother to the magazines on the floor – emanated what appeared to be faint blue sparkles. Susie knew that this wasn't real yet – it was her Polarity showing her the near future...

Her mother finished her phone call. Susie asked, "Mom, do you ever have déjà vu? A creepy feeling whenever you meet someone for the first time? Do you ever use your intuition? Or have you ever had a long string of good or bad luck?" Susie asked.

"Why, yes, of course. I think everyone does."

"Those – and other abilities – are actually one in the same. Everyone has just called them different things without realizing they were all the same thing. It's called Polarity."

"Is déjà vu a French word or a Spanish word? I don't think it translates to Palaria... Pol... whatever that word you said."

Well, that didn't work. She tried another approach…

Her mother finished her phone call. Susie said, "I think I have what's called 'full Polarity'. With it, I can see perfectly into the future and the past in an instant."

"Sweetheart, did you join a cult of some kind? I… I don't like that."

That didn't work. And another…

Her mother finished her phone call. Susie said, "Mom, there are two factions of people who only refer to themselves as Us or Them. These factions use their Polarity in opposite ways. One side uses their Polarity to create chaos. The other side uses their Polarity to maintain stability. Both sides hide, blending in un-noticed with the rest of world. Both sides believe they are helping mankind."

"I always thought the phrase 'plain sight' was a funny phrase… This doesn't sound like the kind of movie I like to see. I like Westerns. You know that."

And another, but more blunt…

Her mother finished her phone call. Susie said, "Mom, there are two groups of people on this planet that are opposites of each other – let's just call these groups Us and Them. These groups subtly manipulate people by the hundreds to do their will. You, I, and everyone else… we just believed we had strings of good luck or bad luck when, in fact, we were just being used by these people."

Her mother stared at her blankly for a few seconds and finally said, "That's fascinating sweetheart. I hope you make friends with these people. They sound like a hoot."

And one last shot…

Her mother finished her phone call. Susie said, "That guy I was dating – Dan. He tried to kill me because he knew I was about to get my full Polarity..."

"Is that what you girls call your periods these days? I lose track of what words the younger generations use."

Susie face-palmed.

Susie snapped out of her Polarity-driven visions and stood up from the couch, her mother still on the phone. Barely a second had past. There wasn't a plausible way to describe to her what Polarity was, who *Us* and *Them* were, or the dangers that came with this ability. It took Dan nearly eight months to slowly build up to it – just to have her marginally accept it as truth. And now that she has her full Polarity, it's still difficult for her to grasp on her own – expecting her mother to understand would be even more of long shot.

"I'll come back later," Susie said, waving as she walked out the door.

After taking a few steps outside, she realized she didn't know where she was supposed to go or what she was supposed to do. Just a week ago, she was a straight-A college student with an overly straitlaced life. Now she wasn't sure what she was. She was lost. She looked around, hoping to see if that Father Crane would still be around.

Across the street, she saw a familiar face – a policeman – who was staring at her. He was easy to spot – the sidewalks were barren of activity. She recognized his blond hair and his somewhat tall, thin stature. She blinked a few times, but he remained there, still staring. He waved at her.

"We should talk!" he yelled across the street.

"I'll be right there, Frank!" she yelled back.

Frank? Yes, that was his name – she remembered seeing him briefly a little over a day ago in the airport right before she boarded the doomed airplane. It felt like months since she'd seen him last.

He was a welcome sight, but she wasn't sure why. She found her second wind and carefully maneuvered through the few passing cars and crossed the street. When she made it to the sidewalk, she turned and walked directly to him – with every step forward, he took a step back.

"Whoa!" he yelled to her, "Whoa! Don't get too close now… get away!"

Susie ignored him and picked up her pace. Frank took a few steps backwards, pinning himself against a parked delivery truck. Susie started to close the gap between them. Susie got within 35 feet of Frank and she immediately collapsed to the ground – dizzy and nauseous. She wasn't sure if it was exhaustion, but she needed to get to Frank.

"Get away!" she heard Frank shriek, almost as if it were an echo.

She looked up towards Frank and crawled a few more feet towards him.

"PLEASE!" Frank gasped – he was on the ground as well, gripping his stomach, writhing in pain. "Please get back! *We…* *WE* CAN'T GET TOO CLOSE. *WE* ARE OF THE SAME POLARITY!"

Susie couldn't move forward any further. Her head was spinning badly and she could barely breathe – it felt as if someone had just swung a sledgehammer into her chest. She slowly inched backwards, almost needing to claw her way on the sidewalk. A few feet later, she quickly re-gained her faculties but remained sitting on the ground. She turned around to face Frank.

"Goodness, don't ever do that again. You're one of *Us* now and you can't just – wait, scratch that – YOU MUST NOT get within forty feet of any of *Us*. That's the limit. If *We* do then *We* get sick… and *We* will die a pretty bad death within a few minutes," Frank said.

Susie rubbed her eyes, "Is this…"

Frank looked himself over and mumbled, "I forget just how much that sucks. I think I peed myself. Note to self: Change underwear."

"Is this real?" Susie asked, sitting upright, tucking her knees to her chin.

"Oh yeah – all of it. This is all real. It's pretty freaky and intense… but it's real," Frank said while he dusted his pants off with his hands.

"I don't know what's real… I have to be hallucinating," she said under her breath.

"I'm so glad you made it. I was worried sick that you wouldn't," Frank said.

"What?"

"Oh, well, 24 hours ago on the airplane you crossed a very important line: You completely rid yourself of all negative intentions. Once someone is completely rid of negative intention then you get your full Polarity… and you become one of *Us*."

"It's true?" she asked, her voice shaking.

"Yup. You have your full Polarity now – just like any other human can, but hardly ever does. It allowed you to perfectly predict the future just enough to save your life on that airplane. Man that was close," Frank said with a trailing whistle. "And now – welcome to your new life," he said, his arms out-stretched.

A few passers-by walked past Susie along the sidewalk, giving time for Susie to ponder. Everything she remembered in the past day was apparently true.

"And what about *Them*? Are *They* real too? Is Dan real?" she asked, after the passers-by were several yards behind Frank.

24

"*They* are real and *They* are terrible people. *They* have no capacity for positive intentions… *They* have the opposite side of Polarity. And, yes, Dan is real and *He* is one of *Them*."

"Dan was trying to… to kill me before I became… before…"

"Before you became one of *Us*. Yup – *He* sure tried to, but you got away by the skin of your teeth."

"Why?"

"Yeah, so, when a *normal* human is about to get his or her full Polarity on the positive side, *They* will do whatever it takes to kill that person. The same thing happened to me, but I had some protection from *Us*. Like you, I was almost killed by *Them*. Like you, I was smacked in the face with massive confusion that follows getting your full Polarity. Actually, I still feel pretty messed up, but it does get easier… sort of. Everyone's different," Frank said, kicking into the ground with the tip of his right foot.

She shook her head. "Why the elaborate ruse? Why did Dan go through eight months of our friendship just to put me on a doomed flight to kill me?"

"Oh *He* wasn't your friend – never was. *He* is one of *Them*. When you first met, *He* didn't sit well with you, right?"

"No. He was… he was too perfect," she said softly.

"*His* Polarity guided his every movement. *He* knew exactly what to do and when to do it."

"I feel so stupid. I was so naïve," Susie said, putting a hand on her forehead.

"Don't feel bad. What happened to you happens a lot – many times with bad results."

"I can't imagine anyone ever being so dumb."

"Really? Do you know who Gilles de Rais is?"

She shook her head slowly.

"Gilles lived in the early 1400's. *He* was a powerful leader in the French army – always made the right decisions. No one questioned *His* decisions. *He* was perfect to everyone around him. But, *He* was also recorded history's first serial killer – particularly children… hundreds of children."

"So."

"*He* was one of *Them*. *He* was once assigned to kill a young French girl named Jehanne – she was about to become one of *Us*."

Susie's mouth opened slightly and she blinked several times – she knew exactly what Frank was going to say.

Frank continued, "*He* gained her friendship, guided her, and sent her to her death in the most roundabout way…"

"Joan of Arc," Susie gasped.

"Yup. She was better known by that name. Of course, history has little meaningful record of his involvement with Joan of Arc – and leaving no trace is always part of *Their* plan."

"*He* killed her… because she was about to become one of *Us*," Susie said.

"Yup – just like Dan tried to kill you. Dan knew exactly what you needed to hear with perfect timing to draw you closer so you'd ignore your intuition – that you now know was actually your Polarity speaking to you."

"There's no such thing as intuition," Susie said, running her hands through her hair.

"Uh uh. Never was. Polarity is responsible for what everyone's called intuition, serendipity, unsettled feelings, déjà vu… you get the idea. Everyone has it – some have more of it than others… like *Us* and *Them*. Your brain is now opened up to see anywhere in the past, present, and future – all at amazing speed."

"I was so… so tired. I still am."

"*He* kept you exhausted to get you out of your comfort zone. It's a clever tactic *They* use."

"I was so… naïve."

"Everyone is naïve, if you know what to say and exactly how to say it."

She closed her eyes, sickened at knowing she was just led along. "Why didn't he just shoot me?"

"Killing someone isn't easy if *We* are protecting you. *He* won't try to kill you if *We* can lead the police or other authorities back to *Him*. Actually, heh...," Frank reflected, "*He* tried on many occasions to kill you but you didn't know it."

"I almost got shot standing in front of that building from that stray bullet...," Susie said, staring forward.

"But you squatted down to pick up a coin right before the shot fired, right?" Frank asked.

"Yeah," she said, placing her hands on her head, interlacing her fingers. Her face froze. "That coin... You put it there?" she gasped.

"Well, truth be known, Father Crane did. Two days before you found it, he slipped it in a laundry basket of a single mother. The single mother found it and gave it to her five-year-old son. Her son dropped it while he was walking by that spot three minutes before you were shot at," Frank said and then shifted his eyes toward the ground. "That Father Crane – he makes all of this Polarity stuff look easy."

"That's impossible. That's just dumb luck," Susie said, aghast.

Frank put his hands out, palms outward, and said, "Oh no, no, no. This is how the battle between *Us* and *Them* goes – everything the rest of the world experiences is written off as luck... good or bad. If something is too lucky to be luck then it was probably *Us* or *Them*. Both sides work with extreme subtly to remain completely hidden from the rest of the world."

"So Dan put me on that airplane," Susie said.

"*He* planted you and seventeen other people on that aircraft – and they were sent to their doom and none of it – absolutely none of it – can ever be traced back to *Him* by the authorities because how subtle *He* made it all happen. *He* didn't leave a plausible trace. Hey, I'm a cop and I'd have no idea even where to begin with that airplane crash," Frank said.

"You're a cop – why don't you do something? All those people died. You can't just...,"

"There's no evidence. I can't exactly just walk into the station and declare that I'm omniscient and, oh – by the way – let me tell everyone about how that plane crashed. Think about it."

She put her head in her hands. "I loved him. I... I fell hard for him."

"Dan... *He* is very good at what *He* does. *He* is one of *Their* best," Frank said.

"I... I don't know what to do now."

"Well that's why I'm here... well, I'll try," Frank said, scratching his head. He began to fidget his fingers. "*We* are protecting you from *Them* because *They* will still try to... well, kill you in... in very round about ways. At some point in the near future, Father Crane will summon you to meet with him. Father Crane will give you further guidance. He's a bit... intense. For now, just get used to your Polarity on your own terms. Remember – like everyone else on the planet – you've always had your Polarity in the form of intuition, déjà vu, instinctive feelings, and so on. The only difference now is that your Polarity is full – and so those same abilities are now perfect. It will take time, but you will be able to tune into it like any other sense... like a newborn unknowingly kicking her legs to become the child learning to walk for the first time... or something like that."

"Sure, I guess," Susie said nervously.

"Susie, I know that your world has been turned upside down," Frank said, exhaling. "It's been about ten months since I got my full Polarity and it still feels like I'm questioning reality. But I'll tell you that it does get easier."

"I don't want it."

"Sorry, but you've always had it – it's just another natural human sense that we've all had since the beginning of time. You just have a fuller form of it now. If you were blind your whole life and then gained sight, how would you react?"

Susie nodded slowly and said, "Thanks, Frank."

"For what?"

"For saying exactly what I needed to hear."

"Well, I already had this conversation with you long ago through my Polarity. Father Crane figured it would be good practice for me."

"You knew I was going to get too close to you?"

"Yes. Admittedly it sucked pretty bad, but its effectiveness was pretty convincing," he said, grinning widely. "It was the best way to make the point."

"Yeah... that really did suck pretty badly," Susie said, smiling faintly. "Oh... what will I do for money? I mean... I have my job in the computer lab on campus... well... I think...," she said, biting down on a knuckle.

"I already left you money," Frank replied.

"What? Where?"

"I left it..."

Susie interrupted, "No wait... if this is real then I should be able to look into the past and see where you put it with my Polarity."

Frank chuckled, "You can try but you're still pretty new. I'm still very new and..."

"I know where it is," Susie announced, her eyes unfocused.

Frank cocked his head back. Susie walked over to a storm-drain pipe that snaked down the side of a nearby building's wall. She slipped her fingers behind a portion of it and grabbed a hold of an envelope.

"$2000? You put this here... ten hours ago?" she asked.

"Yes!" Frank smiled, pointing both of his index fingers at her. "Impressive. The best way to get accustomed to your full Polarity is to accept it, dive right in, and treat it like any other sense."

"How did you get the money?"

"Heh, there's close to $58 billion in unclaimed bank accounts in the U.S. alone. If you know account numbers and PINs – and *We* know all of them – then it's pretty simple."

Susie stared at him stoically.

Frank sighed and said, "Your life is forever different. With all of the problems Polarity seems to solve, it opens up a whole new world of complexity that is very difficult to describe... so you will just have to experience it."

"Will you help me?"

"Yup... Oh, *We* use texting a lot, by the way. It solves problems with getting too close to each other. It allows for more privacy with conversations than a phone call. There will be a lot of texts from me until you get to meet with Father Crane."

"Thank you, Frank. I would give you a hug if I could," Susie said, trying her best to channel some energy for a stable smile.

"Yeah, please don't. I don't think I could stand peeing myself again," he smiled back.

"I don't think *We* want to...," Susie stopped. "Wait – why am I saying *We* like that?"

"*We* don't have a name. *They* don't have a name either. Having a name makes it too easy to be tracked in the future. Let's say *We* went with the name 'The Super Troop'. All *They* would have to do is look into the future, identify everyone who was to be a part of The Super Troop, and kill those people's parents before they had a chance to be born," Frank said.

"So... it's *Us* and *Them*... and *They* use the same terms, but in reverse, right?"

"Yup."

Chapter 3 – Hello Dan

Two months later…

Dan stood alone behind a restaurant waiting for the perfect moment to go back inside. He had finished eating here twelve minutes earlier. The sunlight beat down on his neck and the heat coaxed beads of sweat to appear on his brow. He wiped his forehead and traced his fingers through his neatly trimmed, dark brown hair. He looked at his phone to check the time.

"Time to say hello again," he whispered.

Dan leisurely walked to the front of the restaurant and entered.

"Hello," the hostess said.

"Oh hey… I realized I left here without leaving a tip for my waitress. Laurie was her name, I think."

"Oh – she's way over there in the back," the hostess said, turning around and pointing.

"Thanks."

Dan saw Laurie in the back talking with another waitress. Seeing anywhere in the present was easy with his Polarity – he knew they were talking about how she was just stiffed a tip. It was a tip that she needed badly, a tip that Dan came back inside to give. As he approached, Laurie caught him in the corner of her eye. Her voice became hushed as she uttered something to the other waitress. Dan continued walking, but used his Polarity to observe the conversation the two were having…

"Oh my God…. Heather, there's that guy that left without tipping me. He's walking over here," Laurie said.

Heather briefly glanced at Dan and turned back to Laurie. "He's cute. You think he has a girlfriend?"

"I don't know. Why do you think he's back?"

Heather looked at Dan briefly – whom was now about ten feet away – and then said to Laurie, "Tall, great body, thick dark hair, gorgeous blue eyes – who cares if he has a girlfriend?"

"Shh," Laurie quietly shushed.

When Dan got to Laurie, Heather walked away.

"Laurie, right?" Dan asked with concern enveloping his face.

"Yes," she said, with a slight glower.

"I'm Dan. I'm so sorry – I left here without leaving a tip," he said as he handed her a twenty-dollar bill.

"Twenty dollars?" Laurie asked, mystified. "That's way too much."

"No it's not. Your service was great and… you were fun to talk to… your smile was very nice," Dan said, locking with her eyes.

Laurie grinned and brushed her hand through her hair. Dan liked her type: shoulder-length brown hair, brown eyes, about five foot five, and moderately fit – it made him think about Susie for a split second.

"That's very sweet," Laurie said.

"Well, thanks. I can't help but feel like somewhat of a jerk. I think I just got caught up in the moment of talking to you during lunch and I lost track of things."

"We barely talked at all," Laurie said playfully.

"Now that hurts – after all we've been through together."

Laurie giggled.

"I was also a bit distracted... I lost my dog recently and someone called to tell me they found her," Dan said.

"Oh? What kind of dog do you have?"

"A golden lab."

"I love golden labs! I've had them all my life."

"Well, technically my dog is still a puppy."

"Oh! How sweet! Do you have pictures?" Laurie asked, placing a hand over her chest.

"I do," Dan said as he sat down at a nearby booth.

He patted the spot next to him, motioning Laurie to sit down – she didn't hesitate. Dan pulled out his phone and immediately opened up a picture album filled pictures of an adorable puppy doing adorable things. He talked about each picture as if he took them with his own camera – and not from a dog-lovers website he visited only three hours ago. His Polarity allowed him to know everything he needed to get her – his Polarity showed him that Laurie once had a golden lab named Goldie.

"Her name is Goldie," Dan said.

Laurie lightly slapped him on the shoulder and brightly said, "Goldie was the name of the dog I had when I was little."

"No kidding?" Dan said with boundless enthusiasm.

As his flipped from picture to picture, he and Laurie giggled and gasped at the concentrated cuteness that can only be found in puppies. Laurie inched closer to Dan with each picture. She grabbed his arm several times and talked closer and closer to his face.

I've got her, Dan thought.

And then Dan's face was wiped of emotion, his neck muscles tensed, and he gritted his teeth.

"What's the matter, Dan?" Laurie asked, cocking her head back.

Dan didn't say anything. His interest in Laurie instantly faded. He closed his eyes and slowly opened them. There, now right in front of him, was Susie sitting in their booth on the other side of their table.

"Hello, Dan," Susie said.

Dan didn't say anything. Laurie looked at Susie and then looked at Dan.

"Is… Is everything okay?" Laurie asked.

Susie answered, "Well Laurie, Dan is my husband and he left me at home with the kids. He thought he could go out and pick up more women. Did he show you pictures of puppies?" she said pointing to Dan's phone sitting on the table, "That usually works for him. Well, that doesn't bother me as much as the time he spent in prison…"

Laurie got up and left, horrified.

Dan and Susie stared at each other for several minutes in silence.

"Let's see… *You* were going to keep Laurie out all night so she would be tired at her other job tomorrow – at the fertilizer plant. She would doze off and cause an accident that would kill her and 53 other people," Susie said.

Dan stared at her.

"Well… that won't happen anymore," Susie said.

Dan smirked and shook his head, "The tragedy would have forced new laws to make the materials harder to get. It would have stopped a religious cult from getting a hold of the stuff and killing well over 600 people next year… But why do I bother? *You* won't understand. *You're* one of *Them* now."

"*You* enjoy this too much," Susie said.

"Is it wrong to enjoy what you do? Pain is wonderful – it makes you take action. It's a beautiful thing. Without pain, people can't experience pleasure. Without pain, people lay dormant, wither, and die without ever improving. People need *Us*. The world wouldn't have made it through the Stone Age without *Us*."

"Playing God is delusional. It isn't needed."

"Right before I kill someone, I look into their past at their most innocent moment. It reminds me that whatever God put people here forgot to instill a sense of urgency into them. People are at their best in tragedy – not in innocence. Pain is part of God's plan. *We* are pain. *We* are a part of God's plan."

"Fear is not the most effective way to rule. Fear will eventually end because people will overcome it."

"Fear?" Dan chuckled, "*We* don't scare people – it's a waste of time. *We* hurt people. *We* kill people. *We* act so mankind won't rest. Fear takes way too long and you have to keep it up forever and ever – no thanks. Negativity is *Our* core and, when it's focused, it has amazing results."

"*You* aren't needed."

"Needed? Negativity is in everyone. It has a purpose: Change. Positivity only results in status quo – nothing changes. With negativity, people take action – they break down barriers and then rebuild what should have been," Dan said.

"*You* aren't needed. There have been plenty of tragedies without any of *Your* kind's involvement."

"*You're* so brainwashed. Besides, aren't *You* the hypocrite? Don't *You* want to kill me?" Dan asked.

"If I did then wouldn't I be giving *You* another opportunity to fail?"

"Oh please, do *You* really think *You're* that good?"

"Not at all. I just believe *You're* that bad," Susie shot back.

"Heh… I swear if all of these people weren't here right now it would give me the greatest pleasure to slit *Your* throat and watch *You* choke on *Your* own blood."

"Well, *You* were always better with drama than *You* were with results."

Dan narrowed his eyes.

Susie leaned in, "And to think just now it only took me three lines to get *You* mad."

Dan shifted his body and shook his head. He smiled sarcastically. "Well Susie, *You've* come a long way in a short time. Most of *You* who are so new to *Your* Polarity wouldn't be able to contain it. Opposites do attract and it's not in a pretty way."

"I'm sorry… Are *You* already giving up on mocking me? Did *You* give up that easily?"

"*You're* a nobody, Susie. *Your* existence is insignificant and just sitting here with *You* is a complete waste of time. *You* are a naïve novice who thinks she knows better. I have many years ahead of *You* with my Polarity and there are so many ways to kill *You* that *You* don't even matter."

Susie wobbled her head slightly and said, "I don't know… I just figured *You* could come up with something more creative than that. I used to think so highly of *You*… now it's kind of funny and oddly sad."

"LISTEN TO ME," Dan fumed, trying to keep his voice down, "It was a pleasure having *You* fall in love with me. I laughed every night before I went to bed at *Your* innocence, at *Your* senseless feelings. *You* were just a little girl who couldn't ever get the guy – any guy. *You* thought *You* finally had one and I can tell *You* that it was absolutely hilarious to know that *You* still didn't get one. Getting to know *You* was nauseating. No guy could ever tolerate five minutes with *You* without gouging their own eyes in boredom. *You're* a prude that's painful to hang out with, has nothing interesting to say, doesn't know the first thing about having fun, and gets caught up on losing a dime... a freaking DIME. *You* spent most of *Your* conscious life wondering why people didn't talk to *You* and why *You* didn't have friends. *You* blamed it on the struggles *Your* mother went through. I can tell *You* this, Susie: It was all *You*. People avoided *You* because *You* are the epitome of drama, of holier-than-thou, of you-know-what's-best. No one likes *You* because of *YOU*."

Susie sat motionless, her face devoid of any sign of emotion. Dan waited for her response.

"Speechless?" Dan asked.

Susie shrugged her shoulders with calm indifference.

Dan cackled, "*You* are so pathetic. *You* waltz in here without even knowing what to do or say."

"Well, *You* were always long-winded. *You* couldn't ever keep *Your* mouth shut. *You* always had to talk and talk and talk – *You*'d go on forever if *You* could," she smirked.

Dan narrowed his eyes and said, "Humor me. Why are *You* here?"

"I'm here to distract *You* while Spike takes care of Rich."

Dan's eyes widened. He reached for his phone sitting on the table, but Susie grabbed it first. She quickly slammed the phone into the tabletop, shattering it into many pieces. She got up.

"Good luck in warning Rich in time," she said as she walked away.

Dan pounded his fists once on the table, "NO," he said, frothing at his mouth.

* * *

Spike hopped off his bicycle. He locked it to a chain-linked fence that surrounded a playground in a quiet suburban neighborhood. He wasn't wearing his normal dark Gothic attire. Instead, he opted for a polo shirt, jeans, and a brown backpack.

His trademark Mohawk was covered with a baseball cap. He was just another suburban resident – for as long as it took him to finish his job.

Rich's house was only about a hundred feet away. Spike knew that Rich's Polarity would alert him – they were opposites, after all. Spike had been waiting for this moment for quite some time. It was a moment when Rich would be caught at his weakest moment, when Rich would distract himself to a point that he wouldn't pay full attention to his Polarity. It was a moment when Rich had a victim. His victims were usually little girls. In this case it was a five-year-old girl, a little miss beauty queen regular – complete with an over-the-top obsessed stage mother.

Spike had studied Rich's habits for the past six months – he studied all of his targets with the greatest diligence. Killing one of *Them* required perfect timing.

He picked up his pace, walking across Rich's lawn and straight to his front door. Spike knew that only one of Rich's neighbors was home – the man across the street who worked at night and slept during the day. Spike's Polarity picked up on these facts and the fact that Rich had left the front door of his house unlocked. Rich may have his Polarity, but Spike also knew that Rich was clumsy.

He entered the house. It was filled with mismatched used furniture – most of it appeared to be plastic lawn furniture. There was a giant beanbag chair sitting in front of a large flat screen television. Empty TV dinner boxes and pizza boxes were stacked in random places. Hundreds of candy wrappers were found in piles like naturally occurring snowdrifts. There were air freshener cans found throughout the room, but the stench of rotting food was over-powering.

Spike ignored the mess and quietly walked to a closet found between the living room and kitchen. He opened the door slowly, pushed away some coats, and carefully moved a false wall to the side. The opening created was about three feet wide and it led to a wooden staircase. Spike softly went down the stairs. With each step, he planted his foot where his Polarity predicted it would not make any noise. He got to the bottom of the stairs and put his backpack on the ground. He saw Rich about thirty feet away – his obese figure and short, curly hair was hard to miss.

Spike could see Rich putting red lipstick on the little girl – who was wearing a glistening tiara and a white dress. Her arms were above her head chained to a wall. Tears trickled down her face and she sniffed with each breath.

"Don't cry Vanessa. It won't help," Rich said, smacking his lips.

She closed her eyes as Rich giggled.

Spike spotted a portable stove sitting on the floor. It had a pot of bubbling cooking oil on it. There was a handgun sitting on a table right in front of it. The wall to the left was canvassed with ropes, chains, metal pokers, razors, short swords, and various other instruments of torture – all looked well used. There was a barrel of various sporting goods within reaching distance of Spike; he grabbed a baseball.

Rich took a step towards his cooking oil and stopped. He slowly turned his head towards Spike. Spike grinned.

"How ya doin' Rich?" Spike said with his Australian accent.

"Spike... I... I...," Rich stumbled.

Rich looked at the gun next to him and reached to pick it up. Spike threw the baseball at the gun – a perfect throw already practiced through his Polarity – knocking it into the cooking oil below. Some of the oil splattered on Rich's arm.

"Aaa!" Rich screamed as he scraped the oil from his blistering arm.

The girl opened her eyes.

"Help me," she whimpered.

"Don't worry, lass. Everythin's gonna be fine," Spike said in a bright, but soft voice.

"No it won't!" Rich yelled at her. "You're dead you little whore! I'm gonna cut you up!"

The girl looked at Rich and grimaced, stricken with fear.

"Vanessa," Spike said quietly. "Vanessa?"

She looked at Spike.

"Do you remember the song your mum sings to you every night? The one that goes 'My dear, my dear, my dear Vanessa…'," Spike sang softly.

Vanessa smiled and started singing it. She closed her eyes and happiness overcame her demeanor.

Rich looked at Vanessa, "Do you really think that…"

Spike laughed, interrupting Rich. "Rich, *You*'re about to die and all that comes to *Your* head is the opinion of a lit'l girl?"

"She's a whore, Spike! A whore! She'll grow up to be a whore! Every woman is a whore or wishes she could be!"

Spike sighed.

"What?! *You* don't believe me? How many wars were started over women?! How many people have died because decisions were influenced not by reason, but by lust?" Rich looked at Vanessa, grabbed her chin tightly, and said, "THIS is what the world giggles away as entertainment! THIS is what girls will be taught to aspire to be! When I'm done with *You* Spike, I will rip her apart from the inside out. I will show the world what happens when they say THIS is okay."

Spike put his hand on his forehead and shook his head. "God… I heard *You* say somethin' about giggles, but then all I heard was blah blah somethin' somethin' blah blah."

Rich lowered his eyebrows and spit. "All right Spike, all right. *You* wanna end this now? *You* think *You*'re so tough that *You* can't be beat, huh? *You*'re too cocky. *You*'re in my house, MY domain."

Spike whipped out his switchblade.

Sha-shing

Rich's eyes widened. "*You* would be nothing without that knife."

Spike threw the knife at Rich, missing his right ear by an inch, embedding it in the drywall behind him.

"Take it," Spike said. "Kill me with my own knife."

Spike then grabbed a softball from the nearby bin and rolled it slowly towards Rich. It stopped a few feet in front of him.

The little girl continued singing, her eyes still closed. "Will you shut up?!" Rich yelled at her.

"Sing louder my dear!" Spike yelled back with jubilance.

The girl obliged and sang as loud as she could.

Rich looked down at the softball and then looked at Spike.

"What was that for?"

"I want *You* to step on it, slip, fall on the back of *Your* head, break *Your* neck, and die. It's quite simple really."

"That's ridiculous! That's the best distraction *You* have for me?!" Rich yelled.

"Save *Your* breath for dyin'! Come on now! I'm waitin'!" Spike shouted, sporting a devilish smile, motioning his hands at Rich.

"*You're* dead," Rich said as he turned to grab Spike's knife from the wall.

As soon as Rich grabbed the knife, he was immediately electrocuted – Spike had thrown the knife directly into the main power line of the dungeon; it was just on the other side of the drywall. A puff of smoke came out of the wall and Rich screamed.

"Aaa!"

Rich jumped back with one foot landing squarely on top of the softball, slipping backwards. He landed on the back of his head, causing his neck to break.

Spike pulled a blanket and a thick rubber glove out of his backpack. He unfolded the blanket and placed it over Rich's lifeless body.

Vanessa stopped singing and she opened her eyes.

"Everything's all right sweetheart," he said as he put on the rubber glove.

Spike pulled the knife out of the wall and put it and the rubber glove in his backpack.

"You're a nice man," she said, smiling ear to ear.

Spike swung the backpack over his shoulder and unshackled Vanessa from the wall. "Let's get you 'ome."

"Are you an angel?"

"Do me a favor... keep singin' that wonderful song, huh?" Spike replied.

Vanessa gave him a hug. He picked her up and she started singing again.

Chapter 4 – Questions

Susie was sitting alone on a green, rocky hilltop waiting for Father Crane. Several boulders peeked from the ground in the surrounding area. Her loose blouse kept her cool while a gentle breeze blew steadily across her body. The wind eased her anxiety somewhat – she wasn't sure what to expect with her first face-to-face meeting with him, presumably her first superior as one of *Us*. She was looking forward to whatever guidance Father Crane could offer her in helping her make better sense of her new life with Polarity. She had stayed in contact with Frank for the past couple months. Frank was very helpful and kind – he warned her on several occasions that Father Crane was a bit more direct.

Her Polarity was coming under her control better with each minute, but she would still experience random visions into the future and into the distant past. Many of these visions appeared senseless. She would see the lives of people she never met – some from several hundred years ago. These lives, almost in their entirety, were seen in a matter of minutes. She was able to see the lives of other complete strangers well into the future, to the day they died. She witnessed these experiences as if she were a fly on the wall.

There were some limitations: She didn't know what people were thinking and she didn't understand the foreign languages they used. Anything she could learn was only through what she saw, touched, tasted, or heard – oddly, smell wasn't part of the gift of Polarity. Furthermore, controlling exactly whom she could see and what time period she would see them required careful concentration. Mastering her Polarity would take time.

She focused much on her own past to help her tame her Polarity – the familiarity was critical in keeping the large volume of information manageable. Looking back on her life, she was deeply upset about how she had lived it. Dan was right about her: She was self-righteous, holier-than-thou, and obsessively uptight. She wasn't fun; she was nearly incapable of it even though she thought she otherwise at the time. If people didn't act like her or understand her then they were clearly lost because she knew better. Her full Polarity granted her the ability to replay all of her moments that she once lived – she was mortified. She saw incidents in which people actually avoided being in the same places she was just because they didn't want to get an impromptu lecture or, at a minimum, her judging eyes.

I actually believed that by setting a good example to people that they would want to be around me, she thought.

People wanted to be around other people who were just as flawed as they were – and sharing each other's lives came naturally. There wasn't any empathy for someone like Susie who got hung up "over a freaking dime," as Dan put it.

She looked back on all of the what-if's that she passed up – all in the name of playing it too safe. She was to die 67 years later having never been happy without fully realizing it until she was on her deathbed – far too late to do anything about it. She already missed incredible experiences that would have created lifelong memories because she forced herself to be inflexible in so many ways – she rarely took chances and, because of this, she rarely had a chance to be happy.

Susie clenched her fists, reeling over the precious lost time. She wanted to have friends – just a couple of good friends – and once wondered why the only "friends" she could scrape together seemed to be from study groups at the university. She wanted to get married one day, but it was clear that her own obsessive personality – however difficult this was to swallow – made it near impossible to live with herself, let alone with another person. Her Polarity let her see inside herself from thousands of different angles, through the eyes of others.

She shook her head, trying to shake the inevitable depression that would follow. To distract herself, she focused on the future – on Father Crane specifically. She could see him standing in front of her; he would arrive in the next two minutes.

"Two minutes and ten seconds," she whispered.

She started to look further back in time at his day. She saw Father Crane getting in his car, leaving the monastery. She then saw all of his morning – all in a few seconds. She kept going further back in time. Days of Father Crane's life were seen with little effort, in nearly every detail. Weeks went by. Months went by.

A flock of birds chirped loudly overhead. She snapped out of her vision.

"Whoa!" she gasped, startled.

She closed her eyes. She struggled to take it all in – all of the many things Father Crane was able to accomplish in such a short amount of time. Susie felt it as if she was with him. She saw all of the people he saved – including her, two months ago. She saw all the people he killed or had ordered to be killed. She couldn't make complete sense of all the hundreds of little actions he executed on a daily basis – from faking a sneeze at a pre-planned moment to planting a five-dollar bill into a stranger's pocket. All of these little actions seemed to serve one of three purposes: They were used to stop plots by *Them*, they were used as decoys to distract *Them*, or they were used to kill one of *Them*.

"Susie," Father Crane said.

Susie opened her eyes and saw Father Crane standing about forty feet in front of her. He was holding a bag of donuts in one hand and a folded chair in another. He was wearing a full collar priest's shirt and black cassock, just as she would expect from a Catholic priest.

"Father Crane," she said.

Father Crane stood still for a few seconds. He then threw the bags of donuts towards Susie. Susie's Polarity took over...

"This is our first meeting. I am pleased to see that you are so well composed. Most who are new to their full Polarity are a terrible mess," Father Crane said.

"I was a mess. There's just so much going on that I wasn't aware of."

"No one convinced you to ignore everything. Polarity has always been with mankind as a silent partner. It is so interwoven into humanity's fabric that it is never noticed. It is as if one were trying to find an elephant under a microscope. As Frank told you: Everyone has it. Some have more than others. Much more. It is quite a bit to take in. How are you managing?"

"I feel a bit disoriented, but I feel better each day," Susie replied.

"Excellent."

Father Crane sat down in his chair, crossed his legs, and rested his arms on the chair's armrests. Susie waited, wondering if Father Crane was going to say anything. Instead, he simply sat motionless, keeping eye contact.

"Is it okay if I ask some questions?" Susie asked.

"Please."

"We can see everything that ever happened, right?"

"Yes, but there is a catch."

"We can see it but it doesn't mean that we'll understand it?" Susie answered.

Father Crane nodded his head once.

"The further I look back in time… the harder it is to understand what's going on," she said.

"Cultures are different. You have no context. You can only do your best to infer what is happening. You may have your full Polarity, but you are still human – you still must reason in order to understand. You cannot go back to the time of Christ and understand what was going on unless you understood the language, the culture, and so on. Your Polarity has opened up your brain so you can process everything your Polarity feeds you, but you still have these other limits."

Susie took a deep breath. She felt overwhelmed, knowing that she had visibility of so much that has happened but really didn't understand much of it.

"This is why We do not rely too heavily on the past to guide our decisions about keeping the future intact," Father Crane added.

"The future… Before we talk about the future, I have a question about the past," Susie said.

"Is there a God?" Father Crane asked sternly. "Everyone asks that question once they have received their full Polarity."

Susie wasn't sure if she should say anything or not. She had always believed in God before she had her full Polarity. Now she saw her new powers as a test of faith. She believed it was fair question, but she didn't want to offend a priest.

"Yes, there is," Father Crane began.

Susie's face lit up.

"I believe, but others of Us do not," Father Crane finished.

Susie shook her head. She was puzzled that there could be a difference of opinion with this question. She expected important questions like this would have been definitely settled by those with their full Polarity – Father Crane in particular.

"Spike disagrees with me completely. He is a staunch atheist. He and I have had several minutes a year debating the subject."

"Only... Only minutes?"

Father Crane raised his eyebrows and took a deep breath. "Minutes. Before you had your full Polarity you would sometimes have intuition guide you, correct? Just like everyone else?"

Susie nodded.

"Just like everyone else, your intuition would give you the decision but not the reasoning behind the decision — it felt like a gut reaction. Now that you have your full Polarity, you can clearly see the many, vast lines of logic that guided your once mysterious intuition. You can reason through hundreds of arguments in a matter of minutes — all by using your Polarity with someone else who has their full Polarity. Remember that using your Polarity is playing out what will happen in the future as if you were really there — you play out those events with the other person. And only a fraction of a second is spent — just as it was when you were only aware of your intuition before you had your full Polarity. Intuition gave you answers quickly because intuition is a result of your Polarity."

"I guess — I'm not sure what it's like to debate or converse with someone just by using my Polarity."

"That is one of the first parts of your training."

Susie wondered at the possibilities and what it would feel like to have a conversation with someone just by using her Polarity alone.

"You should also remember that neither Us nor Them are omniscient. You can look deep into the past of the earth's history and summarily waste your time. Our ancestors were very clever about keeping each respective side focused on the future. The past can be pondered for an eternity and, in the meantime, the future is neglected. With each minute you investigate the past because of your selfish curiosity then you are taking away a minute from protecting the future from Them. Our ancestors — from both sides — intentionally set up great disruptions across mankind to ensure that untangling the past would be impossible," Father Crane said.

"Give one example," Susie demanded.

Father Crane turned his head slightly to the right, but kept his eye contact on Susie. He narrowed his eyes a bit and remained silent. Susie realized that she most likely insulted him, but she wasn't going to budge on her demand. She never accepted vague answers for unambiguous questions.

"Well then," Father Crane started, "You are familiar with the Tower of Babel?"

"Yes, everyone was once in one spot with one language. They built a tower trying to reach heaven. God responded by giving them different languages and scattering them across the earth," Susie said.

"Science has told us that mankind emerged out of Africa many years ago. But, somehow, we had entire civilizations evolve in nearly complete isolation – civilizations from China, to the Americas, to Europe, and to Africa. All of them look very different, act very different, have completely different languages, and none of them have any reliable record whatsoever of where they originally came from. Yet, after all of this time, all of them are part of the same species known as mankind; we are somehow all the same."

"I never thought of it that way," she said.

Father Crane took a white cloth out of his pocket and removed his glasses – he cleaned its lenses with the cloth while he spoke, "These different civilizations managed to exist for millennia as different races, cultures, and languages – all with a surprising amount of isolation. Mankind has never dealt with isolation on its own accord for very long – mankind's very nature is to explore and to be curious."

"True," Susie said.

He put his glasses back on, put the white cloth back in his pocket, and said, "The only thing that could contain mankind in such an isolated state for such a long time would be something orchestrated by Us and Them."

"We... We worked with Them?"

"I believe so. With each isolated civilization that was created, mankind was given a separate cooking pot to advance in ways that could not be accomplished if we were all together as one. The Greeks excel in math while the Chinese invent gun powder; the Europeans master navigation while the Africans invented a written language. The diversity and isolation of these people allowed mankind to advance rapidly. It also caused a great amount of confusion of mankind's origins before this scattering of civilizations – this was done deliberately and it could only be accomplished by Us and Them. This, of course, is just a theory but it is the only plausible theory We have. I do not fully understand how We could ever work with Them because They are irrational and cannot be reasoned with."

"Untangling that would be a pain," Susie conceded.

"Yes. It is also a waste of time. Each of Us are too valuable of an asset to waste time on the past. What is done is done. You cannot sacrifice your valuable time thinking about irrelevant subjects of the past. My belief in God is my own."

"What about evolution versus creation?"

"Ah... evolution is a wonderful thing. Over eons it has provided predators with sharper teeth and prey with faster legs. It has continually found ways, through selection, to make all living things survive from other things that will kill them."

"I didn't expect you to say that."

"Why?"

Susie shook her head, "I'm not sure."

Father Crane stood up and paced back and forth in front of his chair, maintaining constant eye contact with Susie. He continued, "Evolution has been praised as being the primary driving force that allows us to survive. If there was ever a threat, evolution found a way to eventually defeat it – with one very notable exception."

Susie tilted her head.

Father Crane stopped pacing and said, "Natural death. Everything dies on its own. Natural death is the one thing that evolution seems to ignore, even though natural death is the quintessential, ultimate, top-of-the-food-chain predator. It is the one thing that happens to every living creature and evolution has never had an answer for it."

"Why?"

"Because evolution has learned that bad people exist. Natural death is the only way to make sure they go away and leave the natural course of things alone. It is the only way to ensure that those who resemble the rear end of a horse will die," Father Crane said, ending with a small smile.

Susie smiled back.

"Evolution, in a way, has a conscious form of knowing how far it should go. It does not occur randomly. It actually knows its limits. Evolution is, in a way, intelligent on its own accord."

"Bad people...," Susie started, but stopped.

"Are We evil or good?"

Susie was motionless. Father Crane nailed it. With everything she had witnessed in the past months, it wasn't entirely clear to her – although she didn't believe she was evil.

"I will give you an ambiguous answer because the complete answer is something you must discover on your own – it makes more sense when you understand it on a personal level. Got it?"

"Yes," Susie mumbled.

"I really detest those words – good and evil – because they are, in reality, just broad labels people use when they cannot come up with anything more creative. They are cop-out terms – and this is coming from the mouth of a dedicated Christian."

"We don't believe in good or evil?" she asked.

Father Crane put his hand to his chin and tapped the side of his cheek in thought. "They are the purest form evil, but They would consider Us to be evil. They are not evil fulltime even by Our definition – even Harold, my counterpart, has a son that he dotes over and loves dearly."

"But They are completely immoral. They cause so much pain and suffering – and They like it. How can They consider Us evil?" Susie retorted, aghast.

"Tomorrow a school bus carrying 29 children in Idaho will plunge into a river. All but two children will perish. We will not intervene."

Susie gasped, "We can stop it."

Father Crane stared at her coldly. "Why?"

Susie scowled, "Really?"

"We let nature takes it course. People die all of the time – if not by accident, ill will, or by the ultimate predator, old age. So then… We let those children die… Are We evil?"

"Yes."

"And They are good?"

"No."

Susie cocked her head back, confused.

"The world is apparently full of evil then."

"No… it's not. My mother is good, wonderful person."

"According to whom?"

"Me."

"Has everyone she has ever come across in her life agree with you?" Father Crane asked.

"I don't know."

"Has anyone ever thought she was evil?"

"I… I guess a few of her ex-boyfriends… but they were violent alcoholics," Susie said.

"So you must be non-violent and sober to be qualified to label someone as evil? What other qualifications would you like to impose?"

"I didn't mean it that way."

Father Crane shook his head and closed his eyes. "My definition of evil is anything or anyone who opposes letting God's creations be God's creations. To change something or someone into your own definition of what good is, in effect, is to change them into YOUR image and thus it's the most insulting form of blasphemy – this is the epitome of evil. We live and let live." He opened his eyes and began pacing again. "However, you will come up with your own definition through your own personal experiences. When it occurs to you – you will know it. I would like to hear it someday."

"But…"

"Now then," Father Crane interrupted, "Back to your training… I need you to focus on me and nothing else. I need you to use your Polarity to have a meaningful conversation with me. This could take a long time for a *novice to master – especially since I will be using my Polarity as well. This will make it difficult for you…"*

Susie caught the donuts that Father Crane threw to her.

Father Crane dropped his chair and took a few steps backwards, almost stumbling. His jaw dropped a tad. "Oh my," he said solemnly.

Susie sat quietly, somewhat puzzled at what could have spooked Father Crane.

"Oh my," he repeated.

"What?" Susie asked.

"No one ever has… No one ever has so early…," Father Crane said while he looked down at the ground, wiping his brow.

Susie leaned forward. She wasn't sure what she had done, but Father Crane was at a clear loss for words. A few seconds later, Father Crane stiffened his posture, standing upright as if he was never rattled. He stared at Susie. Susie didn't move a muscle. Five minutes went by without a single word or movement between them. Finally, Father Crane's face loosened.

"Well, Susie… It appears that you can skip a large portion of your training. You were able to converse so naturally – and convincingly – that even I was not aware of it. Well done."

"Wait… What?"

"*We* will next talk about your most serious flaw: Your lack of allowing flaws to happen."

Susie shook her head and said, "I know. I missed out on life. I missed out on enjoying it because my rules wouldn't allow me to. I missed out on being happy, making friends. I missed out on…,"

Father Crane interrupted, "I could not care less about those things."

Susie froze.

"You are so ill-prepared to deal with mistakes that when you make them – and you most certainly will – you will spend an inordinate amount of time, anguish, and retrospection trying to deal with them."

"I know," Susie said, briefly closing her eyes.

"You do not. How long did you pine over making a C- on your math exam four months ago? How much time did you spend beating yourself up and whining about it when you could have been doing ANYTHING else?"

Susie was silent. She beat herself up for at least a week over it.

Father Crane pointed at her, "By avoiding making mistakes to such an extreme, you have made the biggest mistake of them all: You have no ability to grow through self-improvement. You have no idea what is good for you and what is not because you will not allow yourself to deviate in the slightest. The inability to make friends, get married, and all of the other social activities that you have missed out on are merely side effects. Just because you have your full Polarity does not mean you will be mistake-free... oh, quite the contrary. And you are exceptionally predictable – and *They* love that. *They* will kill you with no problem."

"I've spent too much time trying to prevent mistakes. I kept everything too tight, too narrow. I kept myself in a constant state of fear and I didn't even know it."

"Yes. In some ways you were mature well ahead of your years; however, your constraints stunted your maturity deeply in other areas of your life. Do not waste any more time reflecting on your past. You have beaten yourself up enough. You were not pre-destined to be like that. You did that to yourself and you can change it yourself. It is essential that you allow the opportunity to make mistakes in life – it teaches you how to deal with them quickly and effectively when other mistakes happen. Survival for

Us depends on who can react quickly and most effectively – and so far you are neither quick nor effective."

"I was saddened because I didn't allow myself to have fun. I didn't want to rock the boat. I know that sounds silly."

Father Crane shook his head, "No, it is not. You will find ways for leisure and social time with *Us*. Even *They* do it. Even *They* are humans."

"How do I not be careful and be comfortable with it?"

"No matter how careful you are, you will make mistakes. Give yourself some room – a lot of room – to make mistakes, but do it on your own terms. It will make you stronger. Live a little. *They* certainly will not expect that – and it will actually protect you from *Them* because of it. I expect to see improvements with each time *We* meet."

"I hope so… Oh, why don't *We* just meet through *Our* Polarity? *They* can't see *Our* conversations when *We* do that, right?"

"*They* cannot. However, each of *Us* differ with *Our* ability in using Polarity. That can cause serious problems because information can be missed. Furthermore, conversations through Polarity are unconsciously steered by your own latent desires and curiosity; people tend to talk about what they want and not what they need. When issues are truly important, *We* are better off meeting in person when it is possible. This does come at a cost of *Them* monitoring *Our* dialog, but *We* avoid giving away too much information. *They* will do the same."

"Lastly…"

"Yes?"

"What happened to my father? He disappeared because he was going to be sent to prison. I've tried to look into the past to figure out what happened, but it makes no sense. It's really confusing," Susie said.

Father Crane stared at her briefly and shifted his eyes towards the ground.

"Please."

"I will tell you everything I know."

Susie nodded.

"I only know this: You will find out from another one of *Us*, but it will not be from me. This is what I was told from my superiors – they knew you would ask. I have no other knowledge."

"But...," Susie blurted, but Father Crane already started walking away.

"You are next to meet with Spike and Frank. They will provide you with more insight into Polarity from their perspective!" he yelled over his shoulder.

Susie stood up and watched as he disappeared on the other side of the hilltop.

Chapter 5 – Organization

Susie was standing in the middle of an empty parking lot with Spike, who was about forty feet in front of her. He was standing against a lamppost, smoking a cigarette, wearing all black and sporting a freshly sculpted Mohawk. His hair was highlighted blond, leaving the rest of his hair jet black. The sun was behind a few clouds, beginning its journey to hide below the horizon.

"Father Crane just coldly walked away without saying goodbye. He just told me to talk to you and Frank," she said.

"Ha," Spike laughed, "That's 'im all right. He's the perfect overseer."

"Overseer?"

"Yeah, *We* carry as an organization – *We* 'ave to. There isn't any other way to be effective. *We* are constantly challenged by hiding from the rest of the world while *We* are constantly challenged by eliminatin' *Their* actions. It's gotta be a coordinated effort. Me, you, Frank, and 'bout thirty others… Father Crane is *Our* overseer. It's his role. He gives *Us* direction. He is one of many overseers found throughout the world."

"What's your role?"

Spike looked down at the pavement, puffed his cigarette, and said, "Assassin."

"Assassin?"

He looked up, "Yes. It's my primary duty to eliminate *Them*. I usually don't get involved in any other tasks other than that. It takes a lot of careful plannin'."

Susie became despondent. She disliked the idea of needing to kill anyone. "Was this... your choice?"

"Well – yes and no. I never killed anyone until I became one of *Us*, but it was clear to me that I was best suited," said Spike as he flicked his spent cigarette away.

"Why was that?"

"Well, I grew up on the streets of Brisbane. My mum and dad were violent alcoholics. I was alone and my mates was whoever would accept me. Was the wrong crowd, of course. We always found ways to get into trouble – nothin' too serious at first: graffiti, minor vandalism, and the like. As we got older, the trouble became more risky, more serious. My mates began to rob, sell drugs, rough people up – some were very bloody."

Spike reached in his pants' pocket for a pack of cigarettes and a lighter.

"Somehow I can't picture you doing any of that. You can look the part, but you just don't strike me as someone who would do it."

He put a cigarette in his mouth and grinned, "Well, I never really 'ad it in me. I loved my mates and I'm sure they loved me – in their own distorted way. They saw me as the quiet one and let me be. But I got a lot of exposure."

"What happened to them?"

Spike lit his cigarette, took a drag, and said, "Well, one day they decided to go pay a visit to some blokes who owed them money. I had a bad feelin' about goin' along with them so I faked illness. In short, people died that night. Whoever didn't die was sent off to prison."

"I'm so sorry," Susie said.

"Heh, it's quite alright. But anyway, I already had exposure to the rougher sides of life. It was clear to me and clear to Father Crane that I was best suited to strengthen my strengths – and that was applyin' what I learned to help *Us*."

Susie admired Spike and this surprised her somewhat. She admired him because she could feel the good in him despite his horrible upbringing. She briefly looked into Spike's past and quickly concluded that Spike's description of his past was much worse than he portrayed; he was surrounded with violence, despair, poverty, and hopelessness.

Susie laughed.

"What?" Spike asked.

"Your real name is actually Spike?"

Spike rolled his eyes and said, "Dad was big into volleyball before he got mum pregnant and he thought it to be an appropriate name."

Susie dipped her head, looking toward the ground in reflection for a moment. "I don't get it. Why do you feel compelled to do this? Why don't you just walk away?"

Spike stiffened his postured and took a drag of his cigarette. "That's easy for me. The obligation to do *Our* will is obvious: I wanna help mankind and I feel privileged bein' able to play such a crucial role. The idea that *They* force mankind to go in *Their* direction troubles me. If you don't help *Us*, then you are indirectly helping *Them*."

"Sure... I guess," she said with uneasiness.

"Hey, you don't 'ave to do what Father Crane or any of *Us* do. No one's forcin' ya. You'll find out pretty fast just how terrible *They* can be and you'll see the virtues of bein' able to do somethin' about it."

"I know how terrible *They* are. I want to help, but I still feel uncomfortable with the... violence."

Spike shook his head and said, "Heh, talkin' with *Them* will get you nowhere. And *We* need all the help *We* can get. If *We* don't put *Our* complete focus on *Them* then it gets out of control really quick. *We* put *Our* focus elsewhere then *They* will up the damage considerably. *We* 'ave to act as one to stand a chance, so you need to get over your uneasiness."

"Okay... What about me? What's my role?" Susie asked.

"I dunno," Spike said and then took a drag from his cigarette. "Father Crane will tell you in due time."

Susie and Spike turned their heads towards the setting sun – Frank was walking towards them. He stopped about forty feet away from each of them. He was wearing his police uniform.

"What da ya know, it's Frank," Spike said.

"Hey guys," Frank said with a simple wave of his hand. "Sorry I'm late... I had a few things happen."

"Takin' care of business, eh?" Spike asked.

"Yeah, sometimes I wonder if it gets easier. I was almost killed twice today by *Them*."

"Twice?!" Susie gasped.

Spike and Frank looked at Susie.

Spike said, "Oh Susie, that's nothin'. It's usually closer to four. You 'aven't felt it yet because *We* are still protectin' you."

Susie looked around her. She wondered if she was being too distracted to notice.

Frank said, holding his hands out, "Don't worry Susie. *We* will ease you into it."

"Thanks... I think," Susie said.

"Frank – I was just tellin' Susie about the roles."

"Oh good," Frank said, smiling at Susie.

"What's your role?" Susie asked, smiling back.

"Me?" Frank asked – almost as if he was asking himself. "Oh I'm… I'm an operative… well, I'm trying at least. I feel pretty inadequate to be honest. I'll never be as good with my Polarity as this guy here is," he said, pointing at Spike.

"Frank's responsible for settin' actions into motion. He's responsible for counterin' *Their* actions. Most of *Us* are operatives," Spike said, blowing smoke out through his nose.

Susie looked Frank over. He looked like a gentle man, mild mannered. She wondered how he could be a part of this violent, unseen conflict. Frank's eyes seemed like they never blinked. His lips were halfway sucked into his mouth. Something worried him.

"Is everything okay, Frank?" Susie asked.

"Yeah… yeah, I guess."

"Frank is one of the few of *Us* that still keeps contact with his family," Spike said.

"I have a wife and three small children," Frank said.

"His twin girls are adorable – just turned six," Spike said.

"Well, I still keep in contact with my family," Susie said.

"That's because *We* are still protecting them… it's pretty nuts… nerve-wracking," Frank said, turning his head towards Susie. "Eventually, you'll have to let go because *We* can't protect them forever. The only way to protect your family is to abandon them forever – it's the only protection from *Them*."

"*They* won't waste *Their* time on people you let go of," Spike said. "But you 'ave to truly let go of them – *They* don't waste time on things you don't care about."

Susie choked up. She didn't want to let go of her mother or her sister. They were the only people that she truly had. She couldn't think about what it would do to them.

"Do *We*… Do *We* kill *Their* families?" Susie asked, sickened.

"No," Spike said. "*We* look at it a bit differently. Most of *Them* don't have families because it represents stability of mankind and civilization – killin' *Their* families would actually help *Their* cause to that end. *They* are capable of love, havin' loved ones, and *They* genuinely care about *Their* loved ones – but *They* would gladly sacrifice *Their* loved ones if it drove one of *Their* causes. Besides that, *We* are glad to let *Them* waste any of *Their* time on *Their* families. It helps *Us* offset *Our* disadvantage."

"Disadvantage?" Susie asked.

Frank added, "*We* are roughly out-numbered two to one."

Susie shook her head a little.

Frank continued, "You just got your full Polarity. Something had to push you over that edge to finally get it – you had to rid yourself of all negative intention. For you, it was forgiving your father. However, it's much easier for someone to destroy than to protect, it's much easier to believe force is the way to make people change for the better – it's easier to become one of *Them* than one of *Us*. Then there's also the rush that comes along with destruction – it's like a drug."

"There are many more people becoming *Them* than *Us*," Spike said.

"The odds are against *Us*?" Susie asked.

"The odds seem against *Us*." Spike replied. "*Their* emotions are also *Their* undoin'. *They* get too wrapped up into the rush and thrill to concentrate. *They* innately enjoy destruction, harm, sufferin', pain, and the like because it's easy to see results quickly – and that's what makes *Them* good at what *They* do. But those emotions make *Them* lose focus. *They* are actually aware of this weakness. As opposed to correctin' it, *They* accept it and *They* will take more chances than *We* will because of *Their* numbers."

Frank said, "*Us*… *Them*… it's somewhat balanced on average in the long run. Let's face it: Keeping things stable isn't the most exciting thing in the world. It's thankless because what *We* do goes unnoticed."

"Oh, but what about…," Susie began.

Frank grabbed his head. "No!" he yelled. "OH GOD NO!" he yelled again.

"What?!" Susie yelled.

Frank ran away still yelling, "NO! NO! NO!"

"Frank, wait!" Susie yelled.

"Susie," Spike said as he flicked his cigarette away. "There's nothin' you can do."

"What's going on?" Susie asked.

"Frank's wife and children… They're being killed at this very moment."

*   *   *

FBI Agent Vincent "Vinny" Lagetti, a 38-year-old of average height and build, sat in the front passenger seat of his four-door sedan as it drove through a middle class neighborhood of southern California. His partner, Agent Eddie Kerwin, drove, keeping his face straight ahead. Vinny continuously clicked a pen in one hand and held an open, blank notebook in another. The car's air conditioner roared at full strength, but the monotonous clicking was loud and over-powering.

"You know that clicking is going to drive me nuts, Vincent," Eddie said, tapping the steering wheel.

"You know what I like about you?" Vinny asked, cracking a smile.

"What's that?"

"I know when you're really mad at me because you call me Vincent and not Vinny. You sound like my mother. If it weren't for your crewcut and five o'clock shadow, I could mistake you for her – except you're much taller, way bigger, your hair is darker than hers and a little red, you're 46 and she's 74…"

Vinny looked for some kind of reaction from Eddie but there was nothing – Eddie kept his eyes steadfast on the road. Vinny held out his pen with his thumb on the back end, readying to click it once more. He grew a smile — a smile that got progressively bigger with each passing second. He wanted to see Eddie flinch. Vinny eventually saw Eddie's eyes shift towards him.

"Jeez almighty, Vinny. We're trying to progress on our investigation, remember? Focus, Vinny. Please focus," Eddie implored.

Vinny put his pen away and closed his notebook. "You know what your problem is?"

Eddie barely shook his head.

"You need more fiber. You're too uptight," Vinny said, looking in the vanity mirror and running his fingers back through his nearly black hair, trying to straighten it.

"Christ, Vinny, we've been partners for three years now. I'm still waiting for the day that you will at least show some sign of the professionalism that your older brother had. He was tops. Vinny, you're a smart guy but your work ethic is about as undisciplined as it can get. You may have been an agent for what… nine years now, but you're still acting like you're right out of the academy."

"Hey, we've done great work. Yeah, we've had some issues along the way. I know what I'm doing. So you've got a couple years on me…"

Eddie pulled over and stopped the car. He turned to Vinny and said, "I'm just trying to get through the day. I'm trying my best to concentrate. I don't feel well."

"All right Eddie… all right."

Eddie took out a pill canister from his pants pocket, opened it, and popped a few pills.

"Heart burn again?" Vinny asked.

Eddie closed his eyes and nodded, "It doesn't quit."

"You pop those things like candy. Maybe you should get a second opinion."

"Maybe – but let's focus, huh? Our house is a block away."

The two drove a block forward to a home that was cordoned off with bright yellow police tape. Police cars and ambulances lined its perimeter.

"Whoa, what do you suppose happened here?" Vinny asked.

"Well, this is our house. We're gonna find out," Eddie replied.

Eddie parked their car across the street from the cordoned home. The two got out and approached a group of police officers. They held up their FBI badges and introduced themselves.

"Hello officers, I'm Agent Vinny Lagetti and this is Agent Eddie Kerwin. We're with the FBI."

"FBI?" an officer with a badge that read *GRIFFIN*, asked. "Why is the FBI here? What jurisdiction do you have?"

"Actually we came to interview Officer Frank Moore for a case. We didn't expect anyone else to be here at his house," Vinny said looking around at the many vehicles, "What, exactly, is going on?"

"I'm Lieutenant Griffin. Frank's not here. We don't know where he is. His family...," Griffin choked up, "His family... his wife and kids... they're still inside the house... but they're deceased. That's why... that's why we're here... I'm sorry, but Frank and I go way back. This is pretty emotional for me."

"Oh... I'm sorry," Vinny said quietly.

Vinny's eyes became glassy and tears were on the verge of forming. He turned to Eddie who, as expected, kept a hollow look on his face.

"So, why is the FBI here?" Griffin asked.

"There was a plane crash about two months ago – the flight from Los Angeles to Detroit," Eddie said.

"Yeah I remember that. Everyone died," Griffin said.

"We're not sure if everyone did. When the airlines notified families of the passengers on board, one mother insisted that her daughter was still alive – there is substantial proof that she is. Airport security videos clearly showed her getting on the flight but never getting off before takeoff."

"What does Frank have to do with this?" Griffin asked.

"The security videos showed him talking to this young woman in the airport before she boarded. It wasn't just a passing conversation either. We believe they knew each other and, well, we wanted to know whatever Frank might know," Vinny added.

"You can't find this woman?"

"She's never home when she's expected. We always miss her by a few minutes. It's almost like she knows we're coming," Vinny replied.

Lieutenant Griffin looked towards the house. "Well, this is an active crime scene. I can't let you inside the home. We don't know where Frank is."

"Hey Lieutenant?" another police officer interrupted.

"Yes?" Griffin replied.

The police officer laid out a large diagram on the hood of a car right next to them.

"We believe the perpetrators entered through the front door," he said pointing at the diagram.

Vinny looked inside the car on its dashboard. "WHOA!" Vinny yelled.

"What?" Griffin asked.

"Get off this car," Vinny said calmly.

"Why?" Griffin asked.

"Because it's evidence," Vinny said.

"What?" Griffin asked as he stepped away from the car.

"All VIN numbers are found at the bottom of the windshield inside the car on the dashboard. This car's VIN has been scratched out. No police officer would have a car without a VIN number," Vinny said.

Griffin looked down through the windshield. "Yup, you're right. Okay, everyone please move away from the car," Griffin said.

"You see, Vinny, you're a smart guy. Why can't you be like this all the time, huh?" Eddie asked him.

Vinny ignored Eddie and looked around. He liked the challenge of solving cases – even those that weren't his. Admittedly, finding a woman who committed no crime and didn't want to be found wasn't the most exciting work for him, so he took a few minutes to play detective.

It seemed that everyone in the neighborhood had come out of their homes to take a look at the excitement. The house across the street, however, was an exception. Vinny could hear a dog barking from within it and he could see a silhouette peeking through a slightly parted curtain. Vinny took a step towards the house and the curtain fell back straight, the silhouette disappearing.

"Lieutenant, have you talked to all of the neighbors?" Vinny asked.

Griffin had his back turned, facing Frank's home. He didn't respond.

"Did you…," Vinny started.

"Agent whatever-your-name-is," Griffin turned around and interrupted, "This is my case. I appreciate your intent to help but we'll be okay… okay?"

Eddie tugged Vinny's arm, "Hey, let's go ahead and go."

"Sure thing. Thanks for your time, Lieutenant," Vinny said as they walked away.

They crossed the street and sat down in their car.

"You can't help those that don't want to be helped, Vinny," Eddie said.

"They're missing evidence," he sulked.

"Sometimes you rub people the wrong way. It's not what you say it's... it's... okay, it is what you say and maybe you just shouldn't say it."

Vinny slumped down in his seat somewhat. "Yeah, it seems that no matter what I do, people always find a way to bite into me."

Eddie exhaled and said, "Vinny – you're just a little different. People just don't understand you all the time. You're not serious enough and, because of that, people think you're naïve... a nice guy. That really doesn't suit the FBI too well all the time, that's all."

"The FBI is in my blood."

"Maybe your blood is the only part of you that is."

Vinny idolized his older brother – a legendary FBI agent – when he was growing up. His brother was killed on duty when Vinny was still in high school. Vinny swore then that he would take over where his brother left off. He tried his best to keep focused on his work, but his mind would inevitably wander off at the most inappropriate times. His methods for investigation were seen as ingenuous, but unconventional. The FBI didn't like unconventional; they preferred to have repeatable processes. He was constantly walking on eggshells with the FBI's leadership. He knew that they kept him this long only because of who his brother was.

"Hey Vinny, let's go find that girl Susie, huh?"

Vinny began to punch some numbers into their car's computer, which was positioned within the center console.

"Vinny... what are you doing?"

"I'm looking through the stolen car database to see where that car came from," he answered.

"Vinny, please. Will you please just focus for crying out loud?"

Vinny kept pushing buttons. A few seconds later a report appeared on the computer's screen.

"Well what da ya know... there was a car recently stolen...," he started and he pressed a few more buttons.

Eddie turned off the computer. "Just stop it. Stop it already."

"Sure... Eddie," Vinny said sheepishly.

Their car sped off.

Chapter 6 – Linus

Dan stood with a small crowd of people about a hundred yards from Frank's house, watching Vinny and Eddie drive away.

He received a text from Harold, *Take care of the evidence according to plan.*

Dan groaned. Normally he would have greater respect for Harold. Harold was his overseer, but he felt Harold was reckless a bit too often with the execution of his plans. Harold's plan resulted in too much evidence left behind for *Them* to lead authorities back to *Us*. Killing Frank's family was always an objective, but this was more complex than it needed to be – five men were sent into the home and stabbed his wife and three children. Dan felt it should have been two. Strangulation should have been used – it was far less messy than stabbing. He certainly wouldn't have directed this to be done at their own home.

Dan turned around. A block away was Susie, leaning on a tree. Dan assumed that *They* would have others – not just Susie – working this incident. It was situations like this that Dan disliked the most. *They* would be watching him non-stop, twenty-four hours a day.

They will believe this is too easy for Them, Dan thought.

He debated what it would be like to ignore Harold's directive. He had harbored a growing disrespect for Harold over the past few years, believing that his lavish lifestyle as a mega-corporation CEO distracted him too much. Dan felt that he could be a more effective overseer than Harold ever could. However, Dan was obedient to his leadership because not doing so would result in disownment by *Us*. Disownment meant that *They*, beginning with Father Crane, would have no problem killing him. Dan needed *Us* to help watch his back from *Them* – watching each other's backs was the single most important survival tactic for both sides. Whatever leadership that there was above Harold should be taking note of this – maybe the leadership would do something about Harold.

I understand, Dan texted back.

Dan took a few steps closer to Frank's house. He looked at the parked car, which now had police tape surrounding it – his Polarity predicted it would be towed to an impound lot in a little more than two hours. From there, the car would be investigated at the local police station – the analysis there would be inconclusive and it would be transferred to police headquarters for deeper analysis shortly thereafter. The fact the car broke down in front of Frank's house was very sloppy because using that car in particular was easily avoidable – Harold did nothing to prevent the thugs from using it. Dan wondered if *They* would notice this.

He looked at the home across the street from Frank's house – whose inhabitant was hiding behind the curtains. It was an elderly woman, Mrs. Davis – a widow who kept a stout Rottweiler dog for protection. She saw the five thugs enter, leave, and have to run away on foot because their car didn't start. She never left her house except to play bingo and to get groceries – activities that were each once a week. Having a witness from time to time can happen, but having a witness that never left home and literally lived across the street was overtly careless to the point it looked intentional. Again, Dan wondered if *They* would question why Harold didn't account for such an obvious oversight. In any case, *They* would protect Mrs. Davis until she would gather the courage to contact the police.

Dan next turned his attention, via his Polarity, to a nearby gas station. It had video footage of the thugs waiting in its parking lot, sitting on the hood of the same car that was now parked in front of Frank's house. The video was already in the police's hands. This, too, had to be dealt with. The video didn't bother Dan as much because it wasn't too revealing towards the thugs' identities. However, any one of *Us* or *Them* would know that avoiding video surveillance was exceptionally easy because it was exceptionally predictable through Polarity. It was likely that *They* would see this oversight as an acceptable risk for the reward of killing Frank's family.

Dan put his hand to his chin and thought about the five thugs who murdered the family. Two of them were about to get a conscience and turn themselves in. These two thugs – Tony "Big Dynamite" Williams and Gary "G-Man" Boyd – wouldn't turn themselves in for well over a week. Like Mrs. Davis, *They* would try to protect these two thugs in the meantime.

Dan shook his head and cupped his hands against his mouth and exhaled – usually when *We* killed people, there are many degrees of separation from the crime. However, these murders were so straightforward that Dan felt they appeared too contrived. The car, Mrs. Davis, the two thugs, and the video footage – four remnants of evidence that could all damn Harold – just waiting to be capitalized by *Them*. Dan would have to take care of the video and car first – those objects would be processed by the police first and *They* would certainly be protecting them immediately because of that. Furthermore, witnesses like Mrs.

Davis and the two thugs could wait. When it came to witnesses, there were more options – scaring them was an easy way to delay their testimony and killing them could always come later.

"I will need some help from some of *Us*. But who?" he mumbled.

All of Harold's operatives were too busy doing the will of *Us* – not to be concerned with the mess that Harold created here. He wasn't going to ask Harold for help because he knew Harold wouldn't give it. He needed help from the outside, from someone who wasn't under Harold's direction.

"Linus maybe?"

*   *   *

"Why did *We* let Frank's family die?" Susie asked, digging into Father Crane.

Both were sitting forty feet away from each on the grassy hilltop.

"That is not important. *We* must discuss Linus," he answered coldly.

"I need to know about Frank's family... what will become of my family?"

"They, too, will die. Now, on to Linus," Father Crane said, raising his voice.

"No."

"No?" Father Crane said, leaning forward. "Fall into place young lady. NOW."

"No. Tell me why *We* let Frank's family die."

Father Crane stood up and pointed at her, "You will fall into place!"

"Fine. I will just use my Polarity to get through this conversation to get my answer."

Father Crane opened his mouth, but didn't say a word.

"Don't expect me to pay attention when you tell me my family will die," Susie said.

Father Crane narrowed his eyes and compressed his lips together. A few seconds later, his face relaxed completely. "Yes, I know. I must admit that I am ill-prepared for you. Most that get their full Polarity are not capable of using it with such precision and fluidity as soon as you have. It usually takes well over year to get to your point and by then their obedience is… well… very different from yours."

Susie crossed her arms, but didn't say anything.

"Frank was warned early on that he had to let completely go of his family. When I say completely, I mean he was to have zero thought about them. It was the only way to protect his family from *Them*. Frank dragged his feet. He installed extra security systems in his house. He never left their sight except when he really had to. He could not let go. *We* did *Our* best to give him more time, but eventually *We* had higher needs for *Our* operatives. When a hole was discovered, *They* pounced on his family."

"Why couldn't *We* stop it?"

"Given enough time, it was inevitable. Frank was not going to let go. He could not."

"And what about my family?"

"Susie, very soon you will be tested in ways that you cannot imagine. You will be faced with the decision to kill."

"I won't."

Father Crane planted his right elbow on an armrest and cradled the side of his cheek in his right hand. He remained silent.

"I won't," Susie insisted.

"You will find out," he said with certainty.

Susie frowned. She didn't like the confidence that Father Crane exuded in his assertion. He appeared so certain that she would be wrong, that she would kill one day.

"Now, on to Linus," Father Crane said.

"Okay."

"Linus is one of *Them*. *His* lethality is unequalled – even for *Us*. *He* is *Their* top assassin worldwide. Wherever *He* moves, there will be trouble. *He* travels the world extensively and is fluent in many languages. *He* is very gifted."

"Is *He* coming here?" Susie asked.

"Yes. *His* notoriety means that *We* always track wherever *He* goes. *He* is far too dangerous, too deadly. I believe Dan intends to use Linus as a distraction. Harold has tasked Dan to clean up the mess at Frank's house. It appears that Dan has help. Linus was an extreme choice, but *He* will be effective."

"Okay, I'll be on the lookout for *Him*."

"It is not that simple. Linus reports to no one. *He* does not report to Dan. *He* does not report to Harold. *He* meanders about the earth killing any of *Us* that obstructs *His* path. *We* are not fully sure why *He* is coming to help someone as lowly as Dan. Regardless, if you face *Him*, you will die."

"How can I avoid *Him*?"

"Fortunately, *We* have a few advantages that are unlike any other of *Them*. *His* notoriety has caught the attention of several governments, including the United States. They are curious about *Him*. They try to learn about *Him* without actually coming in contact with *Him*," Father Crane said. "*He* is always trying to shake them off *His* path."

"That's good, I suppose. What does *He* look like? What kind of jobs or disguises does *He* take on?"

"*He* is 47-years-old, bald, badly scarred face. Part of his right ear is missing. *He* is built as well as any body-builder and wears dark sunglasses all of the time – *He* is completely blind."

"Blind?" Susie asked.

"Yes, blind. However, *His* blindness makes *Him* exceptionally sensitive to his other working senses. *He* uses a guide cane although *He* does not need it; it is more of a show, really. The man can navigate any gauntlet just as well as any one of *Us* or *Them*. The blindness makes him a particularly good assassin."

"Why?"

"*He* has been blind his entire life. *He* does not fall victim to the distractions of sight. *His* brain can focus more on its Polarity. However, *His* blindness also means that *His* effectiveness is very localized and limited – *He* cannot do things like drive a car without drawing attention to him. So *He* is a very committed assassin."

*   *   *

Linus sat in an airplane, waiting as everyone else de-planed. He was always the last passenger to get off – it annoyed him to wait, but he knew it was expected of blind passengers.

"Sir, everyone else has gotten off the aircraft. Can I help you off?" a woman's voice asked.

"You must be the flight attendant. You sound nice, dear lady," he said. "Do you mind if I touch your face to get an idea of what you look like?" he asked.

"Oh well, I don't know. I...," she stumbled.

"No worries," Linus said.

He didn't need her permission. He already played out similar dialogs – in slightly different ways – many times using his Polarity. In one of those dialogs, she did give him permission. He knew exactly what she looked like, what she was wearing, what she ate for breakfast, and that she was cheating on her husband – all in less than second.

Linus reached out, feeling around for something to grab onto to help him get up. He grabbed the headrest of the seat in front of him with one hand and held onto his guide cane with the other. He stood up slowly.

"Do you have a carry-on bag?" the flight attendant asked.

"If I do, I have no idea what it looks like," Linus chuckled.

There was silence. Linus could feel her warmth nearby. He could hear her breathe softly. He used his Polarity to predict the outcome of randomly punching his fist forward – it would break her jaw; he knew she was still looking at him.

"It's a joke! It's a small brown suitcase overhead," Linus said.

"Oh, yes, here it is," the flight attendant replied.

"Thank you, dear lady."

Linus exited the aircraft and walked steadily through the airport with his guide cane extended out in front of him. He skillfully maneuvered through the crowds and outside to the taxi stand. He walked right up to an available taxi and got into its back seat – just as the taxi driver was hurrying around to help him in.

"Where to?" the driver asked.

"The Fresh Catch – that seafood restaurant downtown."

"Okay."

Linus could hear the driver sit down in the driver's seat. He could hear him press buttons on his meter. Linus grew flush with anger. He knew the driver was adding extra charges to his fare, taking advantage of his blindness – the fare was to be $38 but it was now $45. This happened frequently to him and his rage slowly built up, but he had ways to take care of these things.

"So, how are you doing today?" the driver asked as they drove off.

Linus didn't say anything. He kept his head forward, biding his time, containing his anger. Nearly twenty minutes had passed. They were a couple blocks away from The Fresh Catch. The taxi hit a pothole. At that moment, Linus started stomping one foot up and down on the floorboard of the taxi, but kept the rest of his body perfectly still – it perfectly mimicked the sound of a flat tire.

THUMP! THUMP! THUMP!

"Oh jeez," the taxi driver said, "I gotta pull over. There's something wrong with the tire back there."

And our semi truck driver is falling asleep, Linus thought.

As the taxi slowed, Linus slowed his stomping to match its speed.

THUMP... THUMP... ... THUMP... ... ... THUMP

Linus stopped once the taxi stopped. The taxi driver opened the door and stepped outside. The instant he did this, a semi-tractor trailer in the far right lane veered into the taxi, sideswiping it, hitting the taxi driver – killing him instantly.

Linus was unhurt. He casually got out of the taxi and resorted to walking the rest of the way. He could hear several cars honking and people yelling towards him, but he ignored them. For Linus, he had accomplished a few things: First, the world was rid of a taxi driver who took advantage of the disabled. Second, the driver of the semi would further the movement of legally restricting how many hours truck drivers could drive each day – something *They* had been working on for several decades. Most importantly, Linus enjoyed the nuances of killing in creative ways; he was a hobbyist.

Linus finally entered The Fresh Catch. The hostess helped him to an open table.

"Can I get you a drink?" she asked.

"Could I have pitcher of water please, dear lady?" Linus answered.

"A pitcher?"

"I'm pretty thirsty. I just figured it would save you the trouble of making lots of trips."

"Sure thing," she said.

A minute later, she came back with a pitcher of water. She filled his glass and put the pitcher down on the table in front of Linus.

"Oh, dear lady?" Linus asked.

"Yes?"

"I'm looking for a group of people that could be here. Two men and one woman. They should be dressed very nicely. One man is bald. The other man has a thick beard and glasses. The woman is wearing a dark blue business suit. Their names are Bob, Raphael, and Cindy. All of them are in their early 40's to early 50's."

Linus knew the hostess was scanning the restaurant because she was about to answer him.

"Oh, I think I see them – they just entered through the front door," she said.

"Wonderful, could you please invite them over to my table?"

"Certainly."

As the waitress walked away, Linus poured a powder into his pitcher of water. He tapped his foot, waiting for them to join him. A few minutes later, he heard one them approaching.

"Please, have a seat, Bob. Invite your friends over," Linus said, facing aimlessly forward.

"Kind sir, I think you've mistaken us for someone else," Bob said.

"You are with the Department of Homeland Security, yes? Let's stop wasting time. I know you're following me."

Bob sat down. Linus knew that Bob motioned the others to sit down with him – he could hear his hand whooshing through air. He heard Raphael and Cindy approaching, finally sitting down at the table with him.

A waitress asked, "Oh, will we have more at this table?"

"Yes, three more," Linus said.

The waitress filled their glasses of water using the pitcher at the table.

"I'll be back to take your order," the waitress said as Linus heard her walk away.

"So, did you guys hear about the baseball game last night? Quite a thriller, huh?" Linus asked them, breaking the awkward silence.

Bob and Raphael both had opposing bets on last night's game – Linus went back in time and witnessed their conversation to this effect.

"Well, I made Raphael $20 richer," Bob sulked.

"It wasn't the money as much as it was the pride, huh?" Linus asked Raphael. "I had money on that game, too. I bet Bob here has been really rubbing it in," he laughed.

"Yeah, he won't leave me alone about it," Raphael responded.

"Cindy, I hope you don't mind the guy talk," Linus said.

"I'm used to it," she said.

"I understand. My niece went to West Point. She says the same thing."

"Oh, I went to West Point."

"What year?" Linus asked.

"I was '93," Cindy answered.

"Ah, my niece was '94," Linus said.

For the next hour, the four of them had an unplanned party of sorts. The three Homeland Security agents drank Linus's water. With each sip, they became more amiable and had less inhibition – thanks to the scopolamine powder that Linus added earlier. Cindy was laughing boisterously at just about anything Linus said. Bob giggled non-stop. Raphael kept telling the same three jokes over and over again but with different foreign accents. Linus knew they were all at point where they would willingly do whatever he asked of them.

"Let's get out of here. I'll drive," Linus said, standing up.

Everyone laughed.

"Let's do it!" Bob cheered.

Later that evening Linus sat in a chair waiting for his three "friends" to wake up – they were tied to metal chairs that were bolted to the floor. They had been unconscious for a couple of hours now and Linus was losing his patience. A long knife rested on a nearby table, waiting to be used. He whipped out some smelling salts from his bag and waved it underneath the noses of Cindy, Raphael, and Bob. The three of them coughed and came to.

"Time to wake up," Linus said sternly.

Linus took off his shirt, revealing his undershirt – and his veiny, bulging muscles. He cracked his knuckles and rubbed his hands together.

Bob shook his head, "What... why... what's going on?"

Linus grabbed his guide cane and whacked the heads of Cindy and Raphael. "Wake up!"

The two of them coughed.

"Now, let me tell you how this will all go down. Your government has sent you to follow me. I don't like that. It's rather discouraging and very annoying."

Linus could hear Cindy's breathing pick up and Raphael wiggling – trying to work his body free from his chair.

"I want you to continue with your investigation for the next two years, but you are to leave me alone. You are to convince your superiors that you are doing your work. At the end of two years, you are to close the case and declare that it was nothing more than nonsense."

The three kept silent.

"Now, you are wondering what will happen to you, yes?" Linus smiled and then laughed maniacally.

He got up from his chair, walked behind them, and began pacing back and forth.

"I am an ardent believer in effective marketing. With the right marketing, anyone can be convinced of anything. Anyone can be dissuaded from doing something they shouldn't. I believe the most effective form of marketing...," Linus leaned over and whispered loudly into Cindy's ear, "...is not to threaten someone directly but to threaten their loved ones."

Linus stood upright, went back to his chair, and casually sat down. He chuckled a little bit and tapped the knife sitting on the table. He turned to Cindy, "Now, dear lady, you have three children. One just left for college, one is in high school, and the youngest – little Milly – just finished middle school. Milly just got her first boyfriend. She plays the trumpet but wishes she played the saxophone. On her way home from school later today, she will be picked up and I will personally sever every tendon in her body. I will record her every scream and I will mail it to you along with her tongue – you won't find the rest of her."

Cindy began to cry quietly.

"Oh and let's not forget about the forgotten child – the one you gave up for adoption when you were much younger."

"Oh God... please... no," Cindy cried.

Linus snickered, "I can start with her first if you like, hmm?"

"No," she cried.

Linus turned to Raphael. "And you...," he started.

"You can't threaten me, you worthless piece of...," Raphael interrupted.

Linus grabbed the knife and slashed it just under Raphael's right knee.

"Aaa!" Raphael yelled.

"I know that!" Linus said. "You don't have anyone to threaten. You are a loner."

Raphael continued screaming. Linus lunged forward with his knife and neatly cut a small slit into his throat. Raphael instantly went hoarse.

"Your screams were irritating me. You've lost your vocal chords, but that's... heh... that's just the beginning, my friend," Linus laughed.

Bob vomited.

Linus lifted his knife up and said, "Now, my people, we have a saying called 'Lingchi'. We will sometimes use it to greet each other. Its direct translation from Chinese is 'slow-slicing' or 'death by a thousand cuts'. The point of Lingchi is to slowly cut off flesh from your victim so that he – or she... I don't want to leave you out, Cindy – lives as long as possible, experiencing as much pain as possible. The goal is to get to a thousand cuts without your victim dying. It's a show of patience... that everything adds up to an irreversible end."

Cindy continued crying. Raphael's breathing was heavy and erratic. Bob was quietly saying a prayer.

Linus smiled widely and stood up, "For you Raphael, I'll make this special because I have patience for this. I have my smelling salts to keep you awake. For you – let's make it three thousands cuts, hmm? Take note, Cindy and Bob: Do as I say and leave me alone."

Chapter 7 – Letting Go

Susie walked out of her home, a place she rarely visited since she gained her full Polarity. She didn't feel comfortable staying there – she felt it to be too predictable for *Them* to harm her. Tonight she was on her way to her mother's house for one of her regular visits. In front of her home in the darkness of her dimly lit street was Old Faithful, her beloved car. It had been sitting there for almost three months. Driving Old Faithful wasn't an option; she foresaw it getting to her mother's house but not starting again.

Going to her mother's house as often as possible was a top priority – she constantly worried about *Them* attacking Mom. For good measure, she frequently invited her sister Karen over, too, just as she did tonight. Susie realized that her family had protection from *Us,* but she felt more comfort in being near them.

She walked to the bus stop a block up her street, worrying each step of the way. Forever letting go of her mother and sister was hard to accept, but she knew she had to do it to protect them – *They* wouldn't hesitate to kill them both. So far, *They* hadn't tried anything, but that's only because *They* appeared too busy with more important tasks at the moment – which were undoubtedly compounded in complexity by the evidence left in the murder of Frank's family. Regardless, she always wondered if each visit she had with her mother and sister would be her last.

Susie opened her umbrella over her head. A few seconds later, raindrops started falling. The rainfall picked up quickly, surprising the few other passers-by in the area who frantically took cover – it wasn't supposed to rain tonight, according to the weather forecast. A few seconds later, her bus pulled up. The doors opened up and Susie took a step toward the bus. She stopped.

"Oh, I may have forgotten something. I'll just catch the next bus!" she yelled to the bus driver over the pelting noises of the surrounding rainfall.

The bus drove off. Although the next bus wouldn't come for another five minutes, she foresaw that this bus would cause her to be even more late: A passenger was going to get sick, vomit, and cause the bus to stop to clean up.

Susie took a step back and three steps to her right. At that moment, a car drove by and sliced through a newly formed large puddle – a formidable wave of water splashed up and canvassed the spot Susie was once standing. Her ability to use her Polarity felt almost as automatic as breathing. It was easy to predict nearly everything that would happen – even somewhat far into the future. What concerned her most was that she found it difficult to predict what *They* were doing. *They* were able to predict the future and *They* were also able to change it.

Susie dedicated most of her time focused on Dan and followed his movements – it was somewhat of an obsession because he tried to kill her. She could see where he was at the present but had difficulty predicting where he would be just a few minutes later. Dan was very good about changing his future on the fly. Susie could see him talking with person after person – male or female. His ability to say the exact words people needed to hear was impressive and this made her feel less stupid for falling for him several months ago. Using people to mask future intent was critical because people were less predictable than a car splashing water, un-forecasted rain, or her car not starting – those objects don't have free will. A person's free will was easy to predict as long as it wasn't influenced by *Them*. Dan's influence, unfortunately, was amazing.

Susie's phone beeped as she walked the few steps back to the bus stop. She received a text from Father Crane.

You are to disrupt Dan from destroying the evidence against Harold. I will help you, the text said.

Susie was a little surprised at this – she didn't feel adept enough at using her Polarity to meet the importance of this task. She debated asking Father Crane to help with something else, something much less important.

She was about to text him back, but he already responded, *All missions are important. There is not a single action that you will ever do that is not critical. No missions are easy. Each mission will always feel like your first.*

A mission? Calling something a "mission" made it feel even more important and added a sense of complexity to what was asked. Father Crane made it seem so formal yet so casual at the same time. Her palms became clammy as anxiety set in. It felt like she was about to take a tough exam at school, but the stakes of failure were far more severe now – her body had no idea how to react to this. She wished she had more time to hone her skills with her Polarity.

Susie still had a few more minutes before the next bus came along. She wanted to think about her family, but she had to think about stopping Dan. She again wondered if this would be the last night that she would see her family and, if it was, what should she say to them? She wanted to be there for them – especially her mother.

Her mother lived in an ever-changing state of hysteria, worry, elation, depression, and confusion – all brought on by her father deserting them many years ago. Susie wanted to tell her mother more information about her father. It would help her cope. She wanted to tell her that he was still alive. Then again, Susie wanted to tell her mother many things that would inevitably bring up the question of how Susie knew so much. Acting natural was still a skill that she felt distant from grasping.

The bus pulled up. Its tire struck the same puddle that Susie had skillfully dodged before; however, this time she was squarely hit by the ensuing torrent of water. From her waist down to her toes, she was soaked. Susie fumed. She wasn't mad because she got wet. She was mad because she wasn't paying attention and she, in effect, let herself get soaked. If Father Crane were here, he would have chastised her for thinking about her family instead of thinking about her mission and her surroundings.

It's that easy for me to lose focus. It's that easy for me to mess up, she thought.

She stepped onto the bus and closed her umbrella.

"It sure is raining out there," the bus driver said as Susie showed her bus card to him.

"Yeah," Susie barely replied, still distracted from her mistake.

She sat down a few feet away from a younger man towards the back of the bus. There were other places available, but she chose this spot to avoid the predicted conversations from other people on the bus…

"Oh my, I didn't think it was going to rain," the retired woman at the front of the bus would say to her.

"I wish I brought my umbrella. I was so close to bringing mine. Something told me I should," the middle aged man would say to her.

"Why are you wet?" a young boy would ask her – only to be followed up with, "Shut up, Johnny," from his mother.

She had roughly three minutes before the 22-year-old man sitting nearby was going to start talking to her. Susie used this time to focus as much as she could on Dan; however, thinking about her family kept interrupting her train of thought. She wasn't going to let go of them yet in spite of what happened to Frank's family – she wasn't ready.

Three minutes went by.

"Boy you're all soaked," the man nearby said to her, as expected.

"Yeah," Susie replied, making brief eye contact.

Susie debated several options to get through this conversation. His name was Eric and he was going to ask her out before the bus dropped her off. She beamed at the irony of knowing this, of knowing that there were several guys that she encountered over the past two months who were going to ask her out. The irony of once believing that no guys were interested in her – ever – wasn't true. She exhaled, saddened about all of the missed opportunities that she never saw because she simply didn't know what to do or say.

"What's the matter?" Eric asked, picking up on her exhale.

"Hmm? Oh, I just have a lot on my mind."

"A thinker, huh?" he asked, smiling.

Susie cringed inside. Dan had used a similar line when he first met her last year – only to be nothing more than the beginning of his elaborate plan to kill her. She knew Eric was going to say it, but actually hearing it invoked a more personalized emotion. She turned her attention completely on Eric – he had to leave her alone so she could focus on other things.

She turned to him and couldn't help but find him rather cute, boyish even. His eyes pierced her as he smiled – a smile that was a little goofy, but uniquely endearing. A solid blue T-shirt wrapped his lean, but sturdy frame. His dark brown hair was a bit messed up, having been caught in the rain, but it gave him a non-materialistic aura. His jeans were fraying at his ankles and he really wanted to buy a new pair; however, he was short on money – his greater attention was to take care of his mother, who was battling cancer for the past few years. Eric had no other help. His father died when he was younger and he was an only child.

Susie delved deeper into his past. She was looking for something to talk about that didn't interest him, but interested her. She dug deeper and deeper but couldn't find anything.

"You okay?" he asked.

"I'm sorry. I'm just a bit distracted."

"Ah, it's okay. I'll leave you alone."

Susie wasn't finished with Eric. The more she learned, the more she didn't want him to leave her alone. She looked at him and a delicate smile immediately peeked out from both of them at the same time. Her head turned towards the floor, but she wanted very badly to look at him again – it was almost as if she could feel the warmth radiating from his body. Out of the corner of her eye, she could see him lean an inch towards her – and she forced herself not to do the same towards him.

Susie had to let him go before anything could happen between them. She tussled with how cruel life could be at no fault of her own – she never asked for her full Polarity. She knew that is was unlikely that she would ever cross paths with Eric again. That's the way it had to be. The end game of being involved with anyone on a personal level meant that their lives would be in jeopardy because of *Them*. Saying goodbye to her mother and sister was hard enough and she didn't need to add more people to this list. Still, she played out a few scenarios – using her Polarity – to at least have a taste of what it would be like to be with Eric. He was a great kisser.

"Whoa," she said aloud.

"What?" Eric asked.

She put her left hand on her forehead and smiled ear-to-ear. "Oh nothing... nothing...," she said, stumbling through her words.

"Are you sure?" Eric asked, inching closer to her.

Susie turned and looked at him again. His eye contact seized her – she no longer had any desire to use her Polarity on him at all. She almost forgot she had it. The ambient noises from the bus's engine and the passengers disappeared. For the next few seconds, it was just Susie and Eric.

She snapped out of it and turned her head. What was she doing? She could never be with Eric. *They* would kill him just as *They* would kill her family – just as *They* killed Frank's family.

Eric was still a few feet away from her, but she remained motionless. She wanted to look at him one last time, but she wouldn't allow herself to do so. The bus finally arrived at her stop and she got off. The bus's doors closed and she slowly turned around to look up at the bus's windows. Eric was looking down right at her. He slightly waved his hand at her, a final goodbye. A tear streamed down her face as the bus drove away.

Her sadness, in an instant, converted directly into an erupting feeling of aggression. Adrenaline coursed unabated through her veins. Her breathing picked up and her body felt as if it was ready to pounce violently on the first thing that moved. Her skin was flush, red-hot. She was confused – mystified as to why she felt this overwhelming desire to attack without any reason whatsoever. She folded her arms, scared – hoping whatever was happening would end soon.

"So sad!" a man's voice behind shouted.

She turned around. It was Harold, one of *Them*. He was a few feet away, wearing a dark grey tailored suit and tie. His black shoes reflected the streetlights that lined the darkened neighborhood. His perfectly groomed, parted, greying hair gave him an outward aura of a model citizen – almost as if he was a politician ready to hold a baby for a photo-op.

"Oh poor Susie... poor Susie. That was so very touching. Crying in the rain is a bit cliché, huh?" he said.

She felt his Polarity seeping into her. She wanted to rip him limb from limb. Endorphins rushed through her body pushing her every thought towards causing his death. The last time she felt this way was when she was protecting her mother from one of her abusive, drunken boyfriends – but even then, this felt a hundred times greater and a hundred times more personal.

Harold chuckled, "Do *You* like getting close to *Us*?"

He walked a step closer to her. She leaned in towards him, like a reflex. She shoved her hands in her pockets out of fear that she may not be able to control their actions.

"Oh, I love feeling – the rush I get thinking about killing one of *You*," he said, closing his eyes, inhaling – as if he was savoring a succulent feast. "I know *You* can feel it, too."

Harold walked around her slowly, looking her over.

"Oh, come on now, Susie. *You're* almost 20 years old now. I'm 55. I'm way too old to survive an attack from *You*. I'm overweight...," he said grabbing his belly with both of his hands, "...and I'm stuck in a stuffy suit – not exactly survival gear."

"*You're* wasting *Your* time," Susie said and she started to walk.

Harold followed her. "What? Nothing more to say? No urge to attack me?"

Susie stopped and took her hands out of her pockets. She got right into Harold's face and stared him down. Her eyes kept on his for several moments. She could feel the evil seething from him.

"What are *You* going to do? Kiss me?" Harold asked sarcastically.

Susie leaned forward and kissed him on his right cheek. Harold stumbled back a step. Susie walked away.

"*You...*," he said, shocked.

"It's going to rain," she said over her shoulder as she opened her umbrella.

Rain started coming down a second later. Susie could hear Harold running for cover.

She was already familiar with the tactics of mocking between *Us* and *Them* – effective mocking is an effective distraction. She was upset at herself that she didn't pick up on Harold being there – she was distracted by Eric. However, she was quickly able to determine that she wasn't in any danger. Harold was only trying to work her up. He was there to tell her that *They* were going to kill her family.

Kissing Harold was the one thing he wouldn't have ever expected – and Harold was one of *Their* heavyweights, an overseer, Dan's overseer. It gave her a boost in confidence in using her Polarity to know that she was able to act before Harold was able to make a prediction – even more so because Harold was considered to be a revered master of his Polarity.

At the same time, it was troubling to her that she almost felt out of control in wanting to attack Harold. It was like trying to control a sneeze – it was wholly involuntary, but involved her entire body. This was the first time that she had ever come this close to one of *Them* without first preparing for it.

It took her a moment to get her composure back to safely deal with Harold – a moment that made her wonder what it would be like if her life would have been in danger. Despite all of the alleged disadvantages Harold pointed out to her, it was obvious to her that Harold was still much more fluent in his Polarity than she was. After all, he was able to approach her while she pined about Eric – a distraction that she brought on herself, but a distraction that Harold capitalized on. She was impressed that Harold knew that she would be there, presumably in that state of mind, at that very moment.

Susie made it to her mother's home and stopped at its front door, hesitating to knock – wondering if this would be the last time she would see her. However, she hesitated like this every time she came by to visit.

She knocked on the door and waited. A dog barked from within. Her mother didn't have a dog before. Susie saw back in time, earlier that day, her mother picking up the stray dog a few blocks from her home. Susie then predicted that a car would hit the dog in two days. She debated telling her mother this fact. The door opened.

"Susie! So glad you came over!"

"Hi Mom," Susie said, smiling ear to ear.

They hugged briefly, but Susie grabbed her mother again and hugged her hard.

"Whoa, Susie, you're full of hugs tonight."

"I love you, Mom," she said, still in embrace.

"Are you okay?"

"I'm fine… I'm fine."

Susie kissed her mother on the cheek. Her mother smiled tenderly. Susie looked at her tired, worn face. She reflected on all of the years of sacrifice this woman made for her – giving up countless meals so her and her sister could eat, wearing clothes until they were practically rags so her and her sister could have school clothes, and always being the bright point in their lives even when all else seemed to be at its darkest.

"Well, come on inside, dear," her mother said.

Susie walked inside and was immediately greeted by the stray dog. It jumped on her thigh and started licking her hands. She felt an instant connection with the dog. She remembered what Dan had once told her about animals and Polarity: Those with full Polarity can instantly influence animals by merely touching them – that they would become one with her Polarity. Animals are surrogates of Polarity and that's why they frequently acted like their owners.

As she petted the dog, she felt the connection. It was clear to her how pets and their owners had an inexplicable connection that was often experienced but never really explained, how animals could sense impending disaster just as easily as she could predict the future, and how animals seemed to sense things that most humans couldn't. The dog became an extension of her thoughts and will.

"Are you sure getting a stray off the street was a good idea?" Susie asked.

"Well, I think… Wait, did I tell you that I got this dog today? I can't remember," her mother answered.

Susie didn't say anything. Slipping back and forth between the real world and what her Polarity told her would still slip out from time to time.

"Hey, let's eat," Susie suggested, walking further into her mother's home.

"Oh sure… as soon as Karen gets here."

"She's not here yet? She should be," Susie said.

"Well…," her mother started.

Susie felt uncomfortable with this, so she let her Polarity take over…

Karen was still at her home, sitting on her couch crying. Karen's boyfriend was sitting on the floor against the front door with a bottle of whiskey.

"You're not going… You're not going anywhere tonight… you slut," the boyfriend said, tripping through his words.

"Please, I need to…," Karen said.

"SHUT UP!" the boyfriend yelled, throwing his now empty bottle at her, hitting her left arm.

94

Susie fast-forwarded five minutes later and watched Karen's boyfriend draw a gun and shoot her.

"I think Karen…," her mother continued, but before she could finish, Susie ran outside.

The dog chased after her, thinking it was a game. Susie stopped and grabbed the dog's head with both hands, remembering that with her full Polarity she could have complete influence over animals.

"I need your help," Susie said to the dog, peering into its eyes.

I need you to attack the man that I'm thinking of. Don't stop attacking him, she thought – in tandem communication with the dog.

The dog immediately calmed down and ran towards Karen's house, a few blocks away. Susie knew she wouldn't get there in time, but she knew the dog would – buying her more time by distracting Karen's boyfriend.

"Susie, what's going on?!" her mother yelled.

Susie continued running without looking back. She kicked off her pumps and ran full tilt barefoot on the urban sidewalk, unconcerned with whatever she might step on. She came to an intersection with cars passing from both directions in front of her. Without slowing down in the slightest, she ran straight through without looking. A car coming from the left slammed on its brakes. As Susie ran further, a car coming from the right didn't stop at all. Susie's left foot went forward in full stride, but as she picked up her right foot behind her, this car's bumper clipped it. Susie spun around and fell down on the sidewalk – barely making it across the street. The car stopped. Before the driver got out, Susie was already up and running.

It's just a minor bruise… must save Karen, she thought, panicking.

Susie turned a corner and could see Karen's home up ahead. The dog was almost there. Tears poured from her eyes as she tried to work out a suitable scenario for the future. She tried to work out a plan to save Karen. Hundreds of scenarios were thought of, but all of them ended with someone dying. She continued pushing herself to run faster, to buy just a fraction of a second of more time – anything to avoid someone getting hurt.

Susie approached another intersection and, once again, cars coming from both sides were blocking her path. She determined that she couldn't run through as she had done before without being mortally wounded. It was either stop or find another way across the street. She focused on each car passing by – at this moment and into the near future. There wasn't a way to gracefully stop any of these cars without a serious accident.

As she came to the intersection, she fell to her knees, crying.

"No… No… No…," she panted.

"Are you okay?" a man nearby asked.

"I need… I need to get across the street right now… it's an emergency," she answered between breaths.

"Leave it to me," he said.

The man walked out into the street and put up his left hand, palm out. A car slammed on its brakes and let loose on its horn.

HONK!

The man then motioned Susie to come across to where he was – she immediately did so. He then stepped into the next lane of traffic, which was coming from the other side. Once again, he put up his hand – palm out – stopping traffic and incurring the wrath of its many horns. Susie ran forward.

"Thanks," she said, barely with any breath left.

She continued to run, but briefly reflected on why she didn't consider the scenario – using her Polarity – of asking that man to help. This made her feel unable to help Karen; she wondered if she was thinking of every possible way to defuse the situation so no one would die.

The dog ahead of her made it to Karen's home. It jumped on the door and barked incessantly. A moment later, Karen's boyfriend opened the door and gave it a swift kick in its side. It yelped in pain but it promptly attacked his leg. He shook the dog off his leg and kicked it again, knocking it several feet away. The dog struggled to get up. It then limped its way back to attack again. Before it got within a foot of Karen's boyfriend, it was kicked squarely in its jaw, throwing it back and leaving it motionless on the ground.

Susie cried harder, realizing that she had sent the dog to its death. Her confidence in her Polarity dropped further. She couldn't help but wonder if she was going to make more mistakes in the few moments she had left to save Karen. She was within a hundred feet of Karen's home, still without a solution to avoid someone dying – herself included. Her gasps for air began to hamper her ability to concentrate.

As she burst through the front door, she was still without a plan. Karen's boyfriend was already pointing the gun at Karen, who was balled up on the floor fifteen feet in front of him.

"What the?!" he yelled.

Susie ran between him and her sister.

"Don't do it!" Susie yelled.

The man laughed a little bit and slurred, "And who… who are you?"

"I'm her sister. Just leave!"

The man's eyes rolled back, appearing to be on the verge of passing out. "I got lotsa bullets. I'll just shoot both of ya," he said.

He aimed at Susie. Susie charged him. The gun went off, barely missing her. She grabbed the gun with both of her hands, trying to overpower the much larger man. He punched her face once with his empty left hand – this forced her to the floor next to a pile of shoes and an umbrella. The man aimed the gun towards her. She didn't predict getting punched and it was then she realized that she wasn't using her Polarity at all – she was too caught up in the moment. She collected enough attention to use her Polarity. It guided her to grab the umbrella and open it – hiding her somewhat and blocking a clear viewpoint for the man to shoot.

He shot wildly at her. Through her Polarity, Susie skillfully dodged each shot, hiding behind the open umbrella. The man eventually stepped up and pulled the umbrella away from Susie. She lunged forward and swung her right elbow in his face, shattering the left side of his jaw and knocking him unconscious, falling to the floor.

Susie's attention immediately went to Karen – she had been shot in the stomach from the first bullet fired. She rushed over to her sister and held her up.

"Su… Susie," Karen whimpered.

Susie hugged her sister's head, trying to calm her. Karen was in bad shape, but she knew that Karen would live and would subsequently recover. Susie whipped out her phone and called 9-1-1 for help.

Karen's boyfriend was coming to. Karen pointed at him. Susie held her sister and sat still. He stood up, blinked a few times, held his jaw, and spit out some teeth. Blood streamed from his mouth. He looked at Karen's bloodied torso and looked down at the gun that was resting on the floor beneath him.

"Susie," Karen cried quietly.

"Don't worry Karen. Don't worry. We're gonna be fine," she said, gripping Karen's head tightly.

Karen's boyfriend picked up the gun and took a couple of steps towards them. He appeared somewhat sobered and very much troubled about what had happened. His eyes welled up and he gulped.

"I'm sorry, Karen," he said.

He then held the gun to his head. Susie shielded Karen's eyes. He pulled the trigger.

BANG!

Susie finished her call with the 9-1-1 operator and stayed with her sister until the police and ambulance arrived. She slipped away from them before they could ask her any questions, scurrying down the dark street as fast as she could.

Answers were needed because she hadn't predicted any of what had just happened. There was one person who could tell what she needed to know and she knew where to find him – he was waiting for her already. She turned a corner and went into an unlit park.

"Father Crane!" she yelled out.

Silence. She walked further in.

"Father Crane!" she yelled again.

"Yes," he replied in the darkness, stepping forward so Susie could see him better in the moonlight.

"YOU KNEW THIS WAS GOING TO HAPPEN, DIDN'T YOU!"

"Perhaps *We* should talk another time when you are able to think and not feel."

"No… wait," she implored.

"Good. Tell me, Susie… tell me what happened."

"*They* sent that man to kill my sister and *We* did nothing to protect her."

"Interesting. Do you really want to place blame on *Them?*"

Susie's head cocked back. "Well… I…," she started.

"I will give you five seconds to use your Polarity. You tell me if *They* had anything to do with this."

Susie closed her eyes and worked back through time – through Karen, through her boyfriend, and so on. She couldn't find any trace of *Them*. She reasoned that *They* were just clever.

"Do not even say it," Father Crane commanded. "Do not tell me that *They* did this when *They* had nothing to do with it."

Susie's lips tightened up. She squatted down, dumbfounded at this revelation.

"What? Are you surprised? Are you wondering how it was possible, even though you have been predicting the future for your sister and your mother since the day you received your full Polarity?" he asked.

She nodded slowly. "This wasn't supposed to happen. Karen was supposed to live another 57 years."

"Since you received your full Polarity, have you acted the same around your sister?"

Susie shook her head.

"Then your predictions for her are useless. Just by being in close proximity of her – and modifying your behavior – alters the future slightly… just like the slip up you had telling your mother about picking up a stray dog. She actually had to ask how you knew that. You upset those few seconds of her life – you changed her future slightly. Your changes in behavior, however subtle they may seem, alter the future. It accumulates in ways that are easy to place blame on *Them*."

Susie stood up. "Then why couldn't I predict the events of tonight earlier?"

Father Crane put his hands behind his back and began pacing around Susie. He didn't say anything. He simply looked forward.

"Well?" Susie asked.

"Well what?" Father Crane retorted sharply.

"I…," Susie began.

"USE YOUR POLARITY AND FIGURE IT OUT," Father Crane said adamantly, pointing his finger at her.

"I… I don't know," she replied.

Father Crane stopped pacing. "Whose idea was it to meet at your mother's house?"

"Mine."

"When was the last time you used your Polarity to predict your sister's fate?"

"Well… this morning… just before I asked her to come over," she said.

"Did you check her fate after you called her?" Father Crane asked.

"I don't think so. I try to do it as often as possible."

Father Crane stared her down, silent for three minutes that felt like an eternity.

"Would you have done ANY of this if you had your full Polarity?"

"Well… no…"

Susie grabbed the back of her neck, horrified. She began to realize that her own protective behavior of her mother and sister instigated this.

"Karen's boyfriend… he wouldn't have cornered her…," Susie gulped, "…if Karen hadn't been over to mom's house so many times… because of me. Karen was going to dump him in due time, but the frequent visits to mom's house made him believe she was cheating on him."

"And so Susie, this is all YOUR fault. If you would have acted as you did before you got your full Polarity, the tragedy of tonight would have never happened."

Susie cupped her faced with both hands, disgusted.

"Furthermore – and this is most severe – you interrupted the natural course of events that were to play out tonight. Karen was supposed to die and you stopped that from happening. You altered the future to suit YOUR needs. Only *They* do these kinds of things. *We* let humanity take its course. *We* do not let humanity be guided by *Our* selfishness."

"I… I…," she stammered.

Father Crane dug into her further, "And NONE of this would have ever happened if you would have simply acted naturally by letting nature take its course over the past several months since you received your full Polarity."

She shook her head. Her face went deathly pale. She knew what Father Crane was going to say – and she didn't need her Polarity to figure it out.

"If you would have just acted naturally for these couple of months then Karen would have lived another 57 years without getting shot tonight. And her boyfriend would be alive."

She nodded her head.

"You see, Susie, you killed her boyfriend. You have killed someone… finally," Father Crane said plainly and walked away.

Susie fell to her knees. Father Crane was right – everything that happened tonight was her fault. It all built up over the past few months. She could play it all back so clearly. She could play out what would have happened if she never looked forward into the futures of her mother and sister – that she would have acted naturally and none of this would have happened. It was time for her to truly let go. She knew that the best way to protect her mother and sister was to completely leave them alone, to never think about them again.

Chapter 8 – Being Frank

It was Sunday. The shooting incident with Susie's sister, Karen, quickly made the news. Vinny and Eddie picked up on this and decided to drive to the hospital where Karen was being treated for her stomach wound, hoping to have an opportunity to catch up with Susie.

"Sometimes I wonder if we're just wasting our time. This girl Susie isn't a criminal," Vinny said, leaning back, his eyes closed, and his seat halfway reclined.

"She's a person of interest," Eddie said.

"Interest of what? To who?"

"If an airplane crashes and no one knows why, then questions will continue until some answer is found. She got off that plane somehow – for some reason."

"Nah. She didn't do anything. The security cameras in the airport must have missed a spot or somethin'."

"Really Vinny? What's gonna happen when we finally catch up to her? Do you think she's gonna pull a gun on us?"

Vinny pulled his seat back up, sat upright, and said, "Eddie, in every case we've done together you always assume the worst in people. You always think everyone's a suspect. It's like you're itching to pick a fight – like you want to kill someone."

Eddie shook his head, "No Vinny. I just think it's best to be safe, that's all."

"Be a regular guy – that's the best way. Don't be so stuffy. Open up. Learn to relate to people."

Eddie glanced at Vinny and exhaled. "We've only been partners for three years. I've seen a lot of bad stuff before we got together."

Vinny was aware of Eddie's background mostly through rumors. Eddie had a history of finding trouble, violent perpetrators, and general mayhem – he was like a magnet to all things going wrong. Those at their field office saw him as good agent, but he had made other agents very uncomfortable – most avoided working with him. His exceptionally hot-tempered outbursts seemed to be of legend. He was forced to have several rounds of sensitivity training and anger management treatments. As a way of keeping the peace, his superiors specifically assigned him cases that had a low likelihood of violence.

Vinny saw bits and pieces of the darker side of Eddie over the past three years even though most of their cases were low-key, almost to the point of putting them to sleep. He saw Eddie oscillate frequently between seeming to care and then not care about his cases almost instantaneously. It was almost as if he believed that not caring would reduce his anger issues. Vinny reasoned that he was good for Eddie in this regard, that he helped Eddie be more light-hearted.

"Yeah, I'm sorry Eddie. I'm just a glass-half-full guy that's all and you – well you're the type who wonders who drank half your glass."

"Heh, yeah, you're all right, Vinny. Sometimes you get a little out there, but you're all right."

They pulled into the parking lot of the hospital and got out of their car. The many tall buildings of the urban backdrop surrounded them. A steady stream of noisy traffic came from all directions. They put on their sunglasses.

"Too bad Speed-O's aren't standard issue. I'm already burning up," Vinny quipped.

"I don't think we'd want them to be standard issue. Think about some of the other agents we have… ugh."

"Yeah, but it might encourage them to lose weight. You see…," Vinny winked, "I have answers."

Eddie cracked a grin – a rarity.

They walked into the hospital and went straight to an information kiosk. They presented their badges to the attendant there.

"Hello ma'am, we're Agents Kerwin and Lagetti with the FBI. We are looking for the young woman who was shot in the stomach and was admitted here last night," Eddie said.

"Oh, okay, just one moment," she said, gazing at her computer screen.

Vinny started wandering around the lobby, looking at the many pictures hanging on the wall and the many people going about their business. People interested him the most – they were all so very different, yet somehow managing to live together. All of society seemed so fragile to him.

"I think I found it," the attendant announced.

Vinny walked up to the counter and stood next to Eddie.

"I believe you're looking for the woman in room 210-B. That would be the second floor."

"Thanks, ma'am," Eddie said.

"Uh, wait a minute," Vinny said, "Did anyone else try to come by and visit her?"

"Is there anyone in particular?" the attendant asked.

"Do you mind if I come around and look at your records?" Vinny replied.

"Not at all."

Vinny went around the counter and began perusing the records. "Let's see if her sister, Susie, came by yet."

"You see, Vinny... you can be a good agent," Eddie cracked.

Vinny's eyes lit up.

"You see something?" Eddie asked.

"Yeah, I see that a Frank Moore was just released about 5 minutes ago from this very hospital."

"What?" Eddie asked, shocked.

"He was treated for alcohol poisoning overnight and was just released."

"You think he's still here?"

"Ma'am what exit would this man have likely used?" Vinny asked the attendant.

She looked at the screen for a few seconds and said, "This door – the same one you entered the building."

Vinny and Eddie ran out the front and looked around.

"Let's split up," Eddie suggested, "I'll go north up the street and you go west through the alleys. We may not cover everywhere, but we'll have a chance."

"Right," Vinny said.

They both ran their separate directions.

Vinny found a break in the traffic and jogged across the street, looking in all directions for Frank. He made his way into the alleys between the towering buildings. Dumpsters, bags of garbage, and some homeless people were peppered about. He approached a little old homeless woman pushing a shopping cart. He rifled through his pockets and presented her a picture of Frank.

"Excuse me, ma'am, have you seen this man?"

She squinted and smiled, "Why yes... yes I have."

"Awesome. Could you please tell me where he is?" Vinny asked, panting.

She smiled affectionately at Vinny, pointed in her empty cart, and said, "That's my boy, James. He's in my cart here."

Vinny tucked in his lips and said, "Thank you, ma'am."

He ran down one alley followed by another and another. He took out his phone and pressed a button, "No sign of Frank at all, Eddie."

"No sign here either. You wanna call it?" Eddie replied.

"Give me a few more minutes."

"Sure."

Vinny looked up to the sky and drew a deep breath. He felt that he should go down one more alley – the one a few yards away and to the right. Vinny walked to the alley's entrance and there, sitting against a rusty dumpster, was Frank. His arms were limp at his sides and his face had clearly been unshaven for a number of days. There was a brown paper bag nestled between his out-stretched legs. From the bag, an open bottle top was peeking out.

"Hey Eddie. I think I've found him," Vinny said over his phone.

"What's your 20?"

Vinny looked up at the building tops. "I'm between Salmon Bank and Miraco Insurance."

"Roger. I'll be right there."

Vinny walked up to Frank slowly. As he approached, Frank tilted his head up and weakly smiled at Vinny. He took a long swig out of his bottle and relaxed his chin onto his chest.

"Excuse me… are you Frank Moore?" Vinny asked quietly.

Frank laughed and took another swig of his bottle and, once again, rested his chin on his chest. Vinny blinked a few times and took another step forward.

"HEY!" Frank yelled, without making eye contact.

"Yes?"

"HEY!"

"Frank, I can help you."

Frank shook his head. "Nah... nah ya can't. No one... no one can. It was *THEM!*"

Eddie appeared in the distance behind Vinny and stopped about thirty feet behind him. Vinny turned around and motioned Eddie to come to him. Eddie shook his head – he appeared petrified. Vinny motioned him to come closer again. Eddie was motionless. Vinny sighed and turned back towards Frank, who was now holding a gun.

"Hey Frank, let's save the discussion about guns for another day, huh?" Vinny asked.

Vinny motioned Eddie to come closer again. He looked over his shoulder – Eddie didn't move. Eddie wiped his brow of sweat. He looked like he was about to run away in panic. Eddie then took a few steps back. Vinny mouthed to Eddie, "Come on man," but Eddie took another step back. Vinny exhaled and shook his head in disbelief.

Vinny took another step forward.

Frank pointed the gun at him. "Now... now how do I know you're not one of *Them?* I think you are!" Frank yelled.

"My name is Vincent Lagetti. I work for the FBI. I'm here to..."

Frank cocked the gun's hammer back. Vinny stopped.

"You know the world just isn't right. You come into it and you are born with blessings and curses. Sometimes you are given a blessing that turns out to be a curse. It's a curse because it's useless... you can't use it to save the people you love... you can only use it to be normal... to be stupid," Frank said, looking down.

"What happened Frank? Tell me what happened," Vinny said softly.

"*You* happened!" he said, pointing his gun towards Vinny, without making eye contact.

Vinny turned around and looked towards Eddie, who was still directly behind him. Eddie shrugged his shoulders, but was otherwise stiff as a board.

Frank put his gun down. Vinny took a few more steps towards him. He was within arms-length of Frank now. He briefly turned his head at Eddie again, frustrated that he wouldn't come closer. Vinny sat down in front of Frank.

Frank raised the gun at Vinny. Vinny didn't move. Frank cried, "My little kids are dead. My wife is dead. I will never see them again!"

"I'm sorry, Frank," Vinny said quietly.

"I was supposed to let humanity guide its own course. I was supposed to let things happen naturally. I was supposed to not interfere. And now... now I will never see another Christmas morning with them opening their presents. I will never see their eyes light up when the Tooth Fairy leaves them money. I will never feel the warmth of my wife's touch. And I will never forgive *Us* for letting this happen!"

Frank stood up, his gun still readied. Vinny remained sitting on the ground.

"Well then... maybe I just don't belong," Frank said stiffly.

Vinny slowly got up. Frank pointed the gun at his head.

"Frank, please give me the gun," Vinny asked.

"No... no... first I want you and your friend to throw your guns in this dumpster behind me."

Vinny slowly took out his gun from his jacket and threw it in the dumpster.

"Do it, Eddie," Vinny called out.

"DO IT!" Frank yelled.

Vinny turned around and Eddie was still frozen – now soaked in sweat and shaking.

Frank shot Vinny in his right leg.

BANG!

"Aaa!" Vinny yelled, falling to the ground, holding his leg.

Frank marched towards Eddie. With every step Frank took towards him, Eddie took one step back.

"Give me your gun! Now!" Frank demanded.

Eddie carefully took out his gun and tossed it the fifty feet to Frank. Frank picked up the gun and ran away.

"Eddie!" Vinny yelled. "Get over here!"

Eddie ran over to Vinny, pulled out his phone, and yelled, "I've got an agent down!"

Vinny groaned, "What... What were you doing just standing over there? Why didn't you do what he said?"

Eddie's eyes were glazed over. He held his head low.

"Eddie?"

"I... I froze up Vinny. The memories... the memories are bad...," Eddie said, hardly able to control his jaw's movement.

Eddie was a stalwart agent – freezing up wasn't possible.

"You? You froze up?" Vinny said, holding his leg, wincing.

Eddie squatted down and looked over Vinny's leg. "It's not bad... It's more of a nick really. It just hit the side that's all."

"That's all?" Vinny asked rhetorically. "How 'bout I shoot you the same way and we'll call it even, huh?"

Eddie stood up and put a hand on his forehead. "I'm sorry Vinny. I've... I've had some trouble in the past few years... coping."

Vinny looked up at Eddie and tried his best to conceal his pain. Eddie was opening up – something Vinny had never seen before.

"You okay, Eddie?"

He shook his head and furrowed his brow. "No. What happened back there just reminded me of an investigation I was part of about nine years ago. It was bad. It was really bad. I made some mistakes back then and I've... I've had a hard time."

Vinny panted a few more times and said, "It's okay Eddie. No worries."

*   *   *

Susie was walking the streets of downtown, using her Polarity to follow Dan and his activity. She saw Dan sitting in an Internet café reading a book – he had been doing so for a few hours now. Whatever Dan's plan was to destroy the evidence, it didn't seem to be on the forefront of his mind.

Why is He just sitting there? she thought.

She turned her attention to Frank – she couldn't help it. After having almost lost her sister, Susie was still mortified at the loss that Frank had. Her head perked up – she realized he was nearby. Frank was just a block away in an alley.

Susie stepped between the buildings and walked towards his location. She turned a corner in an alley and saw Frank sitting on a small set of concrete stairs leading into the back of a restaurant. He was holding a bottle of whiskey. She walked closer, but stopped about forty feet away from him.

"Hi Frank."

Frank looked up at Susie and stared. Tears began flowing from his eyes. He rubbed his nose and placed his head in his hands.

"I just shot a man," Frank said.

"I know. He's all right."

Frank looked back up at Susie. He patted the space next to him. Susie walked up to him and sat down. She was no longer worried about the repelling effects of having the same Polarity – Frank's Polarity was no longer full.

"I miss you, Frank. I miss the talks we had. I miss your company."

Frank began crying inconsolably.

"I can't do this anymore," he sniffed.

Susie looked over Frank's past 36 hours and saw the unfettered torment that had befallen him – heavy drinking, drugs, and violence.

"You don't have to."

"I know. My Polarity is gone. I'm useless to *Us*," he cried. "My life is useless."

"No Frank, you're not. You are a good man."

Frank sat up and wiped his tears away. "And what good is that? I've been the good guy all my life and it's caused me to lose everything that mattered to me. I have nothing. I have nothing because I was the good guy. I'm useless. I'm not needed."

"I need you Frank. You're my friend. Your neighbors – the Stewart family – they're your friends. Their children played with your children. Mrs. Stewart was your wife's best friend. She needs you. Mrs. Davis across the street from you – she never had children and she considers you her son. She needs you, too. You're missed at the police station – especially by Officer Nemec. He considers you a brother. I consider you to be a brother."

Frank gradually raised his eyebrows, "Yeah Susie – you are like the sister I never had. I do love the Stewarts still. Mrs. Davis... heh... she is cranky, but wonderful. Nemec – he always had my back. But that's... that's about it. I can't blame you for what happened. You're too new."

"You can't blame anyone," Susie said.

"The hell I can't!" Frank raged. "Father Crane, Spike, Melissa, Tommie, and...," he said, gnashing his teeth, "...and ...the rest of *Us* could have done something but *They* didn't!"

"It's *We*, Frank... not *They*. You meant to say *We*," she said cautiously.

Frank sniffed, blinked his eyes a few times, and looked down. "What's the difference?"

Frank stepped off the stairs, took a swig of his whiskey, and faced Susie. "*We* just let things happen. *We* don't know what's important. *We* are scared of the future. *We* hide from what might be. *We* believe in sitting back and watching everyone suffer. Why? Why Susie?"

"Well..."

"And don't give me any of Father Crane's crap about mankind can't take it. Mankind is resilient and it deserves better. It deserves to embrace what Polarity has to offer. Evolution has given us this gift to help push it along – not just let it sit there. What are *We* so afraid of?"

Susie wanted to say something, but she predicted that anything she said would cause him to resort to violence. She remained quiet.

Frank looked at the ground, his eyes shifting back and forth. He huffed a little and his face contorted in anger. He threw the bottle of whiskey to the ground, shattering it. He clenched his fists, pointed at Susie, and said, "You were always good to me, Susie."

He walked away.

Chapter 9 – Human Error

Later that day, Dan got up from his chair in the Internet café and placed his book into his backpack. He got in a line to the cashier to buy a bottle of water. In front of him were two young women chatting – Sarah and Melanie. Sarah was somewhat heavyset, had short red hair, fair skin, and was nearly six feet in height – a little shorter than he was. She was holding the exact book he was reading.

"Oh… that book," he said towards them.

They turned and looked at him.

"I'm actually reading that exact same book right now," he said as he pulled the book out of his backpack.

"Oh, is it any good?" Sarah asked.

"Oh yes, definitely. It's just getting a bit crowded in here so I thought I would read somewhere else. I like to get immersed as much as possible."

"Me too. A friend of mine recommended that book," Sarah said.

"Was it her?" Dan asked pointing to Melanie.

"Me?" Melanie asked.

Dan smiled.

She smiled back, answering, "No."

"I try to read as much as possible. Nothing beats a good book. Nothing," Dan said.

"Oh, I completely agree," Sarah said, "When a book is well written with a compelling story, it's wonderful."

"Yeah I think I go through about six books a month," Dan replied.

"Me too," Sarah said with solid enthusiasm.

"She is definitely a book worm," Melanie said, pointing at her.

"I'm Dan," he said, extending his hand.

"I'm Sarah," she said, shaking Dan's hand.

"I'm Melanie," Melanie said, also shaking his hand.

"Well, I admit that I've been accused of being the bookworm of all bookworms," Dan said.

Dan really didn't like reading, so he had to make the most of his Polarity...

"What's your favorite book?" Sarah asked.

"I don't know. What's yours?" Dan asked back.

"My favorite is still the whole Chronicles of Narnia."

"Why's that?"

"It's a bit old-school, but I love the mystique, the fact that children become unlikely heroes, the epic story of good versus evil."

"What's your favorite book?" Sarah asked.

"Oh there are so many to choose from, but I'm guess I'm a bit old-school. I still love the Chronicles of Narnia."

"I love that, too!" Sarah replied, brightly wide-eyed and smiling.

"Yeah, there's just something to be said about its mystique, the fact that children can be heroes, and – at least I believe – it was the classic epic story of good versus evil," Dan followed.

Sarah playfully slapped him on his chest, "Me too!"

"Ow! Careful now – I'm a fragile guy."

"You don't look it," Sarah said smiling, briefly looking at his broad shoulders.

"I could talk books all day long."

"Me too," Sarah replied. "Hey... I think I remember you coming in here a while ago... sometime this morning."

"Yeah I got in here before lunch."

"Wow, you've been here just about as long as we have. You are a dedicated reader."

Dan smiled sheepishly.

By now, Melanie was disconnected from the conversation between Dan and Sarah. She was facing forward towards the cashier waiting for her turn to be served. Dan saw that she was next in line. There was a small spill of a liquid next to her left foot that was – so far – completely harmless.

Time to get rid of the other one, Dan thought.

"Hey, Melanie?" Dan asked.

She turned around, "Yeah?"

Dan pointed to the food display case to the front and left of her, "Is that scone there blueberry or chocolate chip?"

Melanie took a small step forward and to her left, leaned down, and took a closer look. "It's blueberry."

Still leaning forward, she took a slight step back with her left foot – and planted it into the puddle of liquid. She quickly slipped and fell, slamming her left shoulder and head into the floor.

"Ow! Ow!" she yelled, holding her head, gasping.

Dan and Sarah huddled around her to help. The store manager ran around the counter. "What happened?" the store manager asked.

"My friend just slipped on your floor!" Sarah yelled. "She's hurt pretty badly I think!"

"I'll call 9-1-1," the store manager said and then rushed away.

"Are you okay Melanie?" Dan asked.

116

Melanie lay on the floor writhing in pain, holding her head, without saying a word. Paramedics arrived shortly thereafter. They spent several minutes examining her.

"We need to run some tests on her at the ER," a paramedic said as he and another paramedic lifted her onto a stretcher and put her in the back of an ambulance. "These kinds of falls can be deceptively bad. You're welcome to ride with us if you want to."

"Sure," Sarah said.

Melanie, lying down, simply gave a thumbs-up. Sarah jumped into the ambulance with Melanie and it drove away.

Dan noticed that Melanie's bag was left behind on the floor. He grabbed it, drove up to the hospital, and sat in the hospital parking lot for a few minutes. He didn't want to see Sarah and Melanie there too soon or else the timing wouldn't feel natural to them.

Dan hopped out of his car with Melanie's bag in-hand. To avoid registration, he trailed into the Emergency Room with another group of people. He approached a curtained area and peeked inside. Melanie was lying on her back. Sarah was standing next to her talking to her. Sarah turned her head towards Dan.

"Dan?" Sarah asked.

"Oh, Melanie left her bag behind," he said, holding up her bag. "Is she okay?"

"No," Melanie said. "My head is killing me."

"She probably has a concussion, a torn ACL, and a broken collar bone," Sarah said.

And a new brain aneurysm. She'll be dead in a month, Dan thought.

"Wow – poor thing," Dan said.

"I'll be fine," Melanie said.

"That was very nice of you to bring Melanie's bag," Sarah said.

Melanie gave a thumbs-up, still lying on her back.

The three of them continued talking for the next two hours. Melanie was taken away for several tests and this gave Sarah the opportunity to get to know Dan better. He shared his love of particular books with her – which was unsurprisingly aligned with the same books she loved.

"Wow, it's late. It's almost nine. Hey, you wanna catch a bite to eat?" Dan asked, looking at a clock on the wall.

"Sure, if it's okay with Melanie," Sarah replied.

"Have fun," Melanie replied. "And thanks for bringing my bag, Dan."

"No problem," he said to Melanie and then turned his head to Sarah, "I know a good bar and grill within walking distance. They have excellent burgers, but they have even better fried okra."

"Oh wow. I love fried okra. Let's do it."

The two locked eyes for a few seconds and they walked out of the ER.

"My last girlfriend hated fried okra," Dan said.

"Heh, my ex-fiancé hates it, too. Then again, I could never figure him out."

"How so?" Dan asked.

"Well… I don't know if I should say anything."

"Say whatever you want," he said, glancing at her.

She looked at him briefly and hesitated.

"You don't have to say anything if you don't want to," Dan said.

"Well… he broke off the engagement for no reason at all like around six months ago."

"Wow."

"Yeah, he just told me plain and simple that he didn't want to get married," Sarah said.

"As cold as a cop giving a speeding ticket," Dan quipped.

Sarah laughed, "He is a cop, and it was like that."

Dan laughed with her.

* * *

Susie had figured out Dan's plan with Sarah: Dan was going to convince her to call her ex-fiancé this evening and try to work things out. Her ex-fiancé would say he couldn't talk because he's working late at the police station. Angry, Sarah would go to the police station and get in a violent argument with him. In her rage, she would take a flash drive out of his hands and smash it with her high heels – the same flash drive containing the video evidence of the thugs sitting at the gas station before they assaulted Frank's family.

Susie grinned, feeling comfort in knowing she could look that far into the future. She felt confident it was Dan's plan. It explained why he sat in the café all day long – knowing that Sarah and Melanie would notice him there, thereby diminishing the suspicion that he was up to no good.

She hopped on a bus and headed to the restaurant that Dan and Sarah were going. This would be an opportunity to rattle Dan once again. She remembered that Spike had said that *They* were more emotional, that this was *Their* weakness that kept the balance between *Us* and *Them*. Derailing Dan's plan tonight would most certainly torque him.

She looked at her phone to check the time. It would take 24 minutes to get to the restaurant. That was plenty of time for Susie to get there – Dan needed another 43 minutes to convince Sarah to make the phone call to her ex-fiancé. It wouldn't be easy to find a way to stop Sarah from doing this because of the emotional nature of a broken engagement – Dan was very clever to pick her in this regard.

Susie took time to look at all of the events around Dan and the evidence, to make sure that there weren't any of *Them* helping

Dan. She focused on Harold, but it was clear he was not involved – he was staying the week at the White House. Harold was a friend of the President and was a big donor to the President's campaigns. Harold, being on the other end of the country, was not a factor.

Father Crane sent her a text that read, *All of Harold's operatives are busy with other things.*

Susie liked having Father Crane help her personally. She understood that part of his role, as an overseer, was to keep everyone focused. Her last interaction with Father Crane was exceptionally uncomfortable, but also exceptionally effective. He knew exactly the words she needed to hear in order to move on with life. The words were harsh. They hurt. They did the job.

Susie reflected on that night regarding the death of Karen's boyfriend. Her intentions were positive – she didn't want anyone to get hurt. However, she did alter the future very subtly and that ultimately led Karen's boyfriend to act the way he did. Strangely, it didn't bother her as much as she thought it would. She was able to pinpoint many instances of human beings – all with good intentions – leading people to their demise without knowing it. She thought about a woman who had won the lottery recently. The woman had bought lottery tickets with a $20 bill she found on the ground in a playground – dropped by a neighbor by accident. Soon after winning the lottery, she was killed by thieves. The neighbor didn't know that the woman died indirectly because of the lost $20. These kinds of things happened regularly and the only difference for Susie now was that she was aware of it.

She had a better understanding of "live and let live": There was no telling how many other unintended side effects *They* cause whenever *They* force suffering and chaos on mankind. *They* tirelessly work towards a single goal. *They* will create whatever mayhem necessary to make it happen – not fully realizing what other problems *They* have created along the way.

Susie got off at her bus stop and walked to the restaurant where Dan and Sarah were. She stopped at its front door. Susie's arms flared with goose bumps. Dan was nearby – she could feel his Polarity. Dan undoubtedly knew that she was there and she tried her best to discern his strategy. Looking into the near future, it was difficult to know how Dan would handle her interaction. Each time she tried something different, he seemed to have an answer.

Dan's effectiveness as an operative was, sadly, impressive. In the recent past, Susie would briefly browse at moments in Dan's life, causing her to choke up somewhat at just how many women he'd taken advantage of, how many people died, and how much pride Dan exuded from his work. *Their* other operatives envied Dan for his abilities and the favoritism that Harold bestowed on him. She still had difficulty envisioning the need to kill Dan and secretly wished that he would quickly die of natural causes – even though that was not to be anytime soon.

She walked through the front door and immediately spotted Dan sitting down with Sarah in a booth. Dan looked up at her, smiled, and waved her over to sit with them. Being nice? Waving? What was he up to? This wasn't part of any scenario she predicted. Sarah turned around and saw Susie standing there. Susie's Polarity told her that Dan was telling Sarah that he was motioning for his sister to come sit with them. Sister? Dan wasn't wasting any time throwing curveballs. Susie was having a hard time keeping up with his next moves.

Dan then caught the attention of a man sitting at the bar, adjacent to them. He motioned him to sit down with them. The guy sat down next to Dan.

Dan's going to try to set me up with that guy, she thought.

Susie stood still. Dan motioned strongly for her to come over – she had to do so. She had to stop Sarah from calling her ex-fiancé. Susie walked slowly to them, using her Polarity to play out every possible scenario that could be. With each scenario she concluded with, the exact same scenario would continually change to a different result – all thanks to Dan's through his Polarity.

Susie got to the booth and sat down – her opposing Polarity from Dan was difficult to ignore. She put her hands in her pockets and crossed her legs; the urge to rip Dan's throat out with her bare hands was very real and hard to shake.

"Sarah, this is my sister, Susie."

"Hello," Sarah said, extending her hand for a handshake.

Susie calmly took her right hand out of her pocket and spent all of her mental fortitude ensuring it would safely get to Sarah's hand for a simple handshake. Her hand passed over a knife resting on the table and Susie involuntarily considered picking it up and taking a slash at Dan.

"And this is my buddy, David," Dan said, playfully elbowing the guy who had come over from the bar.

"Hello," said Susie, waving with her fingers, still thinking about the knife.

She immediately put her hand back in her pocket.

"Can I be so bold to say that I think you're gorgeous?" David proclaimed with a confident smile.

"Thanks," Susie replied, averting her eyes to the table, thinking of a response to get rid of him.

"Can I buy you a drink?" David asked.

"I'm not 21," Susie said.

"I won't tell anyone," David winked.

Susie debated telling him she was a lesbian – only to have him come back with joking that he could change her. She debated telling him she had a boyfriend – only to have him come back with him saying he didn't care. Line after line had comeback after comeback. Dan was clever to have David on-hand, an unknowing pawn to keep her busy and away from Sarah.

Susie looked up at David and leaned toward him. David did the same.

"You know, David, I like confident men. It excites me," she said, biting down on her lower lip.

David smiled and cocked his head back slightly.

"I think you're hot. There's something about you," Susie said, looking him up and down.

David leaned forward more to her, "You wanna get out of here?"

Susie leaned forward more and replied, "Sure. Let's...," Susie said, but then started sniffing towards David.

SNIFF SNIFF... SNIFF

Her face shrouded with disgust and she coughed a couple of times. She feigned a slight gag reflex. "My God, you smell," she said, sitting back, waving her hand in front of her face.

David's eyes bulged and he smelled his armpits. He stood up and immediately left.

"Sorry about that," Susie said to Dan and Sarah.

Sarah's face was a bit blank, seemingly surprised at that exchange.

"Dan always tries to set me up with his friends. He really didn't smell, but telling a guy he smells is the best way to make him leave," Susie said.

Sarah giggled, "It worked."

"Wow, I'm so glad I ran into you, Dan," Susie said.

"Why's that?" he asked.

"I would have a chance to meet your girlfriend finally."

"Oh... no... we're not together," Sarah said.

Susie looked at Sarah and then at Dan. "Too bad. I think you'd make a cute couple."

"Well thanks, but we just met today... kind of hit it off with our love of books," Sarah said.

"Oh, Dan is SUCH an avid reader," Susie said, closing her eyes for a couple of seconds, smiling.

"Yeah, we're both fans of The Chronicles of Narnia," Sarah said.

Susie looked towards Dan. Dan stiffened up. "What's your favorite part of the series?" Susie asked him.

Sarah started, "Mine is..."

Susie interrupted, "Wait, you'll love Dan's answer to this. Promise me you won't say anything, nothing, nada, zip, zero... no matter what Dan says, don't say anything. His synopsis of The Chronicles of Narnia is almost poetic – he never stopped talking about it as a kid growing up."

Sarah perked up, waiting for a supposed melodious response from Dan.

Dan stared at Susie devoid of emotion. Susie knew the only way Dan could answer the question was to go forward in time and read the books or, at least, cliff notes. It would take him a full – and very uncomfortably long – eight seconds of pause.

Susie smirked at Dan.

"If it's all the same to you, sis, my mood has kind of changed out of respect for Sarah. She's been through a lot recently."

"Oh, what happened?" Susie asked her.

"Oh, my ex-fiancé... man problems... you know."

"Oh, how I know," Susie said looking at Dan, narrowing her eyes slightly.

"Yeah, well I want answers," Sarah said, stirring her margarita rapidly with her straw, frowning.

"You deserve to know, Sarah. You can't expect someone to walk away without giving some kind of explanation for a life decision," Dan said.

"No kidding," Sarah said, huffing.

"He moves on with life and lets you stew about it indefinitely," Dan followed.

"God… he's mocking me, isn't he Dan?"

Dan tilted his head and said, "I try to find the best in people, but I just don't know where to find it in this case."

"I have the right to know. I put my entire life on hold for him. I dreamt of having his children and growing old together… God, that sounds so corny now," Sarah said, burying her face into her hands.

"Call him," Dan said.

Sarah raised her head up.

"Call him," Dan repeated. "Ask him. It won't hurt, right?"

"I tried before and he never gave me an answer. He kept telling me that it wasn't right, that something was wrong with us."

Dan shook his head, "Well I think… uh… never mind."

"What?" Sarah asked.

Dan was silent.

"What?" she asked again.

"Does he have a girlfriend now?" Dan asked.

"Well… I…," Sarah said and stopped. She pounded her fists on the table, "He had another woman!"

"What are you going to do?" Dan asked.

Sarah dug through her purse and took out her phone. "I'm gonna call that rat – that's what I'm gonna do."

"Sarah?" Susie asked.

"Wait one sec," Sarah said, looking through her purse.

"Sarah, I'd like to ask you one question first… one woman to another," Susie said.

Sarah stopped and looked at her, "Yes?"

"Are you mad because you want him back?"

Sarah blinked a few times and looked down at the table.

"Do you still want to give him a chance to come to his senses and come back?" Susie asked.

Sarah's nostrils flared, "Yes and no."

"Do you need another drink?" Susie asked.

Sarah nodded, "Another margarita."

Susie motioned to their server. Within a couple of hours, Sarah was completely drunk. She was leaning heavily on Susie, who was sitting right next to her. Dan was across their table, nearly silent the entire time, coldly staring at Susie.

"Oh God," Sarah slurred, "I'm... I'm... I'm so drunk... and I've got work tomorrow..."

"What do you do?" Susie asked.

"Elementary school teacher... kindergarten... mostly five and six-year-olds."

"You like it?"

"I love it!" Sarah shouted. "I just know I'm gonna be... gonna be so hung over tomorrow."

"Call in sick," Susie suggested.

"I will!" Sarah shouted, smiling.

Dan got up and left.

"Where... where are you going?" Sarah asked him as he walked away.

Dan ignored her and kept walking.

"Pay no attention to him," Susie said.

Sarah shrugged her shoulders. "Oh God... I hope they don't... they don't call in that stupid Ms. Parmalee..."

"Who?" Susie asked.

"Oh... oh... this old woman with large, poofy grey hair... she's creepy. She's the substitute they usually call in... call in for us."

"So..."

"So she is TERRIBLE. She forgets to do things. She can't remember any of the students... or how many students she has for that matter... she's a complete nut job... irresponsible. She actually LOST students at a field trip one time," Sarah said, bobbing her head – appearing to almost pass out.

"Well I'm sure it will be okay. Here... let me help you home."

Susie helped Sarah outside and hailed a cab. Sarah spouted her address and Susie handed the cab driver $28 – she knew the cab's meter would land on $24.25 and so she reasoned that a $3.75 tip was appropriate.

She turned around – and not a second later – she felt *Them* nearby. It wasn't Dan. It was someone else. The feeling was coming from the restaurant and it was getting closer. She walked towards the door, but as she went to open it, Linus stepped outside.

She lost her breath, stumbling two steps backwards. Linus swayed his head around, stuck out his guide cane, and took two steps towards Susie. Being nighttime, his dark sunglasses added a unique sense of terror; it made him seem inhuman.

"Ah, it's the dear lady Susie!" he said, sporting a sinister grin.

Susie immediately began playing out the near future events – all of which seemed harmless. She closed her eyes and focused, trying her best to make sure she didn't miss something from Linus.

"Huh? This is Susie, right?" Linus sarcastically asked.

He walked up to her and touched her face. His fingers traced the contours of her cheeks. Susie's Polarity felt like an uncontained firestorm of energy. Her heart pounded. She wanted to claw into Linus and it took her great restraint to concentrate only on being defensive – she took Father Crane's advice in trying to avoid confrontation with him.

"Oh, forgive my hands if they are a bit dirty. I was digging holes earlier," he said and then let out a short laugh, "Or did I?

You won't check will *You*? *You're* scared… scared a little bit to get *Your* attention off of me right now, hmm?"

Susie gulped.

He lightly patted the side of her right cheek with his hand and leaned toward her face. "Good," he whispered.

She kept her focus; she wasn't going to let herself get distracted by him.

"So my dear lady… *You* seem surprised at my presence. *You* did not know I was here?"

Susie didn't move.

"Oh, don't worry. *You're* too stressed. I'm not here to kill *You*… yet."

He walked away, his guide cane waving out in front of him.

Susie's phone vibrated. It was a text message from Father Crane. Before she read it, she noticed that Father Crane had sent her several texts over the past couple of hours. She flicked through them all: *Linus is in the restaurant with you… Pay attention more… You need to be more aware of your surroundings!*

Susie closed her eyes and dropped her head. She gripped her phone tightly – mad that she was too immersed with Sarah and Dan when she should have at least spent some time focusing on other things around her. She could have, at the very least, had her phone out to keep in communication with Father Crane.

We need to talk, the last text message from Father Crane read.

*   *   *

The next morning, Vinny and Eddie drove up to Frank's old police station and parked their car. Now that Frank had shot Vinny, the FBI had jurisdiction to investigate Frank further – without Lieutenant Griffin or any other police officer impeding them.

"How's your leg?" Eddie asked Vinny.

"It hurts. It feels like a bad burn, but I'm okay. I can move around all right."

"Hey Vinny... I'm sorry...," Eddie said.

Vinny interrupted, "Not another word of it, Eddie. It's not a big deal." He whipped out his pen and began clicking it. "As payback, I'm gonna click this pen a thousand times and you're gonna pretend that you like it. You're gonna like it so much that you're gonna ask me to perform it at your kids' birthday parties."

CLICK CLICK CLICK CLICK

Vinny smiled and looked at Eddie. He clicked a few more times and stopped.

"Thanks, Vinny," Eddie said calmly.

The two grabbed their note pads and got out of the car. Vinny took in a deep breath. "Ah... love that smog. It's an acquired taste."

Eddie ignored Vinny and went to the backseat to get his bag. They began walking to the front of the police station. Vinny walked slowly, his face slightly contorting in pain with each step of his right leg. They entered the front door and walked to the nearest police officer.

They flashed their badges. Eddie said, "We're Agents Kerwin and Lagetti, FBI. Our office notified you that..."

"Yeah, we know," the police officer interrupted, "Come on in," he said pointing to a door on the right.

Vinny didn't expect a welcome committee. The FBI's interactions with local law enforcement always had a rivalry of sorts that pitted the supposed elite – the FBI – against the common sense know-how – the local police. Sharing information was usually a brutally slow process. The local police didn't want to spend any extra time helping the FBI, in a large part because they didn't have the resources; however, the unspoken belief was that they simply didn't want to help – they didn't need these elitist FBI agents telling them how an investigation was done.

The two of them went through the door and were quickly greeted by Lt. Griffin.

"Hello, gentlemen," he said pointblank.

They all shook hands.

"Hi Lieutenant," Vinny said.

Griffin waved another officer over to them.

"This is Sergeant Jason Nemec. He'll be with you today. Here's not here to help. He's here to make sure you don't mess anything up. Got it?"

With that, Griffin walked away.

Nemec was tall – a few inches taller than Eddie. He was medium-built with a short, blond, receding hairline. He looked completely spent, heavy-eyed. The three of them shook hands.

"Don't mind Griffin," Nemec said, "He's like this to everyone. What can I do for you?"

"Wow, you look pretty tired, Sergeant," Vinny commented.

"You can call me Nemec – everyone else does. And I'm dead tired. I've been here all night working the Frank Moore case – he and I both worked narcotics, pill mills… a lot of undercover. He was a good man. We were good friends. We're all taking this personally."

Nemec's phone rang. He looked at it and jerked his head back.

"You can get that if you want," Vinny said.

"No, I don't want it. It's my ex-fiancé… fiery redhead. I haven't talked to her in months and I really don't need the drama right now."

"I've been divorced four times," Eddie said, "You're better off this way."

Nemec rolled his eyes, "Tell me about it."

"Yeah, you probably heard that we caught up with Frank and – well, he shot me," Vinny said pointing at his leg.

"That is so unlike Frank," Nemec said, looking down at Vinny's leg.

"We have to find him and arrest him. No one knows where he is. We need any lead we can get," Vinny said. "So we need to take a look at whatever evidence you have regarding the case just to cover all the bases."

Nemec didn't say anything. Vinny sensed he didn't want any of the evidence touched.

"We won't touch anything," Vinny re-assured him. "You can handle everything yourself."

Nemec nodded, "Okay, come with me."

Nemec brought them to the back of the police station and into a large, brightly lit room. Computers lined the walls and there were large open tables in the middle. Large wheeled carts were found at various places, each sporting very large labels stating *EVIDENCE*. The three of them sat down in front of computer screen that was covered with dozens of photos of various men.

"I've been analyzing a surveillance video for the past hour or so – Frank and I busted a few narcotics rings recently so I figured I'd start with suspects that would be closest to those investigations first."

Vinny looked at the photos on the screen and pointed at one, "Wow that guy looks like a massively drugged out, large version of Napoleon Dynamite."

Nemec chuckled, "He's a small time pill-pusher... goes by the name Big Dynamite. He does have that afro going and those thick glasses. Generally a nice guy but just can't keep his nose clean."

"Moving on," Eddie interrupted.

Nemec looked back at Eddie briefly and then returned his attention back towards the screen.

"Back to the video... what's it a video of?" Vinny asked.

"Oh, well it appears to be the five men who killed Frank's family. Let me show you."

Nemec inserted a flash drive into the computer and started a video player. The black and white video showed five grainy figures hanging out in front of a gas station. Two of them were sitting on the hood. The other three were standing about.

"Now, this is 4 PM in the afternoon, mind you. They all look very casual and calm. The only thing that sticks out is that they're all wearing baseball caps. We never get a good look at their faces."

Nemec then fast-forwarded the video.

"Now see what happens at 4:14 PM. One of them gets a phone call and WHOOSH, just like that they all get in the car and go. Frank's family was dead within twenty minutes."

The video showed all five men quickly cramming into the car and speeding away. Nemec paused the video.

"Where is this car now?" Vinny asked.

"Your impound lot, I bet," Eddie said softly.

"Yeah – yeah it's in the impound lot. We've had a few people looking at it and they haven't found anything conclusive yet," Nemec said.

"Seems pretty coordinated," Vinny said as he wrote some notes in his notepad. "They got an order from someone to do this – that phone call and then sudden rush to get in the car makes it pretty obvious."

Eddie wasn't writing anything. He was just blankly watching the paused video, only breaking to pop a few heartburn pills.

"You want me to take notes for you, Eddie?" Vinny joked.

Eddie shook his head apathetically.

Vinny quickly sketched a stick figure sitting on a chair and showed it to Eddie, smiling, "Well, I drew this sketch of what you look like right now so we won't forget."

Eddie rolled his eyes.

"Okay, so your belly isn't to-scale, but I can work on that," Vinny said, grinning.

Nemec put his hand on his forehead, almost laughing.

"He's like this," Eddie said to Nemec, pointing his thumb back towards Vinny.

"Well, it's good to see some sense of humor," Nemec said.

"Yeah, right?" Vinny said. "Our jobs are stressful enough as-is."

"Moving on," Eddie said, getting impatient.

"Yeah," Nemec said, glancing at Eddie.

"Are we sure that's the same car that was parked in the front of Frank's house?" Vinny asked.

"What does this have to do with Frank shooting you?" Eddie asked.

"We gotta look at all of the angles. What would drive a cop to shoot an FBI agent? It makes no sense," Vinny said.

"Fair enough," Eddie said and leaned forward to the screen. "It looks like the same car."

"Yeah, it's the same make and model – a Chevy Monte Carlo," Nemec said.

"Do you have any stock pictures of Monte Carlos?" Vinny asked.

"We have a few but the angle that the video was taken doesn't match well with them."

"We can look online," Vinny suggested.

Nemec nodded.

"Well, Vinny, hop online," Eddie said, pointing at the computer.

Nemec moved out of the way and Vinny sat down. He perused a used car shopping site and quickly found pictures of Monte Carlos. He began downloading them – perhaps thirty pictures. The three of them spent the next half hour comparing pictures to verify the exact year of the car.

"2004 Monte Carlo," Vinny said, while writing down some notes.

"Looks right to me," said Nemec, looking down at Vinny's notepad.

Eddie sat still with his arms folded. He looked at his watch and said, "Okay, what else are you looking at?"

"Oh, well, lemme first put this flash drive away," Nemec said.

He pulled out the flash drive from the computer and a warning message appeared.

DRIVE MISSING. DO YOU STILL WANT TO SAVE FILES TO THIS DRIVE?

"Wait… wait… were you saving the pictures on this flash drive?" Nemec asked, horrified.

"I… I don't think so," Vinny said quietly.

Nemec shoved the flash drive back into the computer and confirmed that, in fact, the thirty or so Monte Carlo images were saved to the flash drive.

"You moron! You saved the pictures on the flash drive! This is evidence!" Nemec yelled.

Vinny closed his eyes. He knew what this meant; he knew that the flash drive couldn't be used as evidence against the murderers if they were ever caught. Now, as technicalities go, the evidence is tainted. A judge would certainly declare it inadmissible in court – the murderers would have an easier time fabricating alibis.

Vinny opened his eyes and stared inertly at the computer screen in front of him. He knew he was going to be yelled at by his bosses – perhaps even put on administrative leave. He turned to Eddie, who seemed indifferent.

Nemec pointed at the door and yelled, "GET OUT!"

The two of them got out of their chairs, left the room, and calmly exited the building. They walked to their car, opened the doors, and sat down. Eddie put on his seatbelt, but Vinny didn't move.

"We're dead, Eddie. I'm sorry. I'm so sorry."

Eddie replied plainly, "You've got nothin' to worry about Vinny. It was the cop's fault for leaving the flash drive in the computer. It's standard procedure that you never let anyone sit at your computer without first logging out – including removing all evidence. You're fine."

Vinny shook his head and tried his best to control himself from crying. He rubbed his face. "You sure? Really?"

"Yeah. This is standard stuff. Besides, that guy's been there all night long. This is easy peezy. It was his fault. I mean, yeah, it's gonna make it harder for us to work with them, but you're okay. Trust me."

Vinny ran his fingers through his hair. "God, I could use a drink. You up for a few?"

"I'll pass."

Vinny didn't expect a different answer from Eddie – he spent all of his off-duty time alone. Eddie was all but inaccessible during his off-hours. In the evenings, he never answered his phone and rarely responded to texts.

Chapter 10 – Proximity Problems

It was 7 A.M. Tuesday morning. Susie took a deep breath, waiting for Father Crane to speak. She held up her hand to block the rays of the morning sunlight from her eyes.

"You were too caught up in the moment at the restaurant. You made it easy for Linus. Furthermore, you did not follow up on the fate of the flash drive – you stopped tracking it once you thought you defused Dan's plan. It was a minor piece of evidence, but take heed in learning from this mistake," Father Crane said to her.

They were both sitting on the green hilltop once again. The wind was blowing somewhat stiffly and clouds were beginning to gather.

"I know. I was too proud of how I was handling Dan. I didn't see or feel anything else," she said.

"Polarity is not always at the forefront of your mind. Have you ever caught yourself staring blankly at something for minutes on end – not knowing why and not paying attention to anything else?"

"Yes. I think everyone does."

"The same is true for your Polarity. You can focus on something so greatly that you will not pay attention to any of your other senses."

Susie was motionless, ashamed of being so careless.

Father Crane tapped his fingers on his chair's armrest a few times. "Hmm," he mumbled.

Susie used her Polarity to try to figure out what he was going to say...

Stand up... lay down... sing a song as loud as you can... don't speak for another 37 hours... find a gun and shoot yourself in the head...

"Wait... you want me to shoot myself?" Susie asked.

Father Crane didn't say anything.

"What?" Susie asked, her head tilted.

"I never said that, but I planned on saying that. I was committed to saying exactly that. You predicted it but it never happened. If it were not painfully clear to you at the restaurant, whatever dialog you believe you will have with *Them* will be filled with commentary to throw you off. Why did you waste time asking me why I was going to tell you to shoot yourself when you knew very well I was not really going to do it?" he said, pointing at her, almost running out of air with his last word.

"But you said you were committed to saying it," she said.

Father Crane leaned forward and rested his elbows on his knees. "Tell me what you already know."

"Any plan... any plan I think of I must be committed in doing even if it sounds ridiculous. *They* will do the same. I need to learn to be smart about what needs to happen versus what is simply a distraction," Susie said.

Father Crane nodded, "Polarity is a great human sense, but it does not mean you should ignore common sense. You will find that it is sometimes better to not use your Polarity to truly discern *Their* plans. Knowing when to do this is what will set you apart from being a novice and being a master of your Polarity."

Susie's face tensed, "Father Crane? What did Frank... What did Frank go through when he lost his Polarity?"

"Imagine going blind and deaf at the same time. People will trust their intuition over what they see and hear all of the time – but with your full Polarity it becomes the dominate sense, the most important sense. If it were not enough that he lost his family, but losing his full Polarity – well, that is even difficult for me to comprehend. It would have happened in an instant – just as when he first received it. But having something so important and then losing it – that would be very overwhelming."

"What will become of him?"

"He is in a state of deep confusion. He has lost his full Polarity, but he has inside knowledge of *Us* and *Them*. He will not know when luck is truly random and when luck is because of *Us* or *Them*. He will increasingly become paranoid of everything that happens around him. He will go insane eventually."

"I didn't think it was possible to lose your full Polarity."

"It is very rare and it only happens when something snaps in your brain – usually something very traumatic, something your brain is not able to handle because it happens so quickly. Your intentions are then free to be negative or positive once again – you will be back to having the occasional Polarity just like everyone else in the world."

"Can... Can the same thing happen to me?"

"It is highly improbable. When it comes to gaining or losing one's Polarity, it usually takes events that are on the order of magnitude of seeing Satan or seeing God. Frank was not a complex man – it did not require much trauma to make this happen. Frank should have seen his family's fate; it was only a matter of time. If he allowed his brain to adequately prepare for this outcome, then he would have kept his Polarity. He did not."

"So he's powerless."

"He has lost his Polarity, but he knows what it feels like. He will be more attune to trusting his intuition, believing his déjà vu, and be more skeptical of people trying to convince him to do anything."

"Can *We* help him?"

"Why? It is not the best use of *Our* time. He is lost. Do not let your emotions distract you. Remember that *They* act with extreme subtly. *They* want you to think about Frank. It may be just a little bit of thought, but it adds up. It is all the little things *They* do that count, not the big things. Killing his family was effective in getting rid of Frank, but now it is paying off a dividend in distracting you. STOP THINKING ABOUT HIM."

"It's hard."

Father Crane stood up and walked to a nearby boulder. "Now, for another part of your training."

Susie stood up, but Father Crane motioned with his finger to sit down. Susie complied.

"I want you to focus on this boulder and tell me about its future."

Susie dropped her jaw a little, puzzled at the request. "How far forward should I go?"

"As far forward as you can. Millions of years if you must."

"Why?"

"Why stare at the boulder?" Father Crane asked.

"Yes."

"Two reasons: First, they are easy to predict. They will not make any sudden movement. They will not try to trick you and so on. Second, they are a great barometer in predicting truly earth-wide cataclysmic events. If something truly bad were to happen on a global scale – like a nuclear holocaust – it would be easiest to see on something that should not change for quite a while. A boulder is perfect for this. Inanimate objects are very valuable to *Us* in ensuring that *They* do not do anything that is truly stupid."

Susie focused on the boulder for a few minutes.

"Bored yet?" Father Crane asked.

She snapped out of her concentration and answered, "Very. How long must I do this? I've already gone several thousand years into the future — it's easy. It's just sitting here slowly moving with erosion."

"Another hour."

"What about stopping Dan?" she asked.

Father Crane stood up and said, "You need not worry. Dan's next stop is Mrs. Davis, the widow who lives across the street from Frank's house. He is looking for an angle to get to her dog, to tell it to kill her."

"What are you going to do?"

"The dog must die, unfortunately — it is a sure tactic for *Them* to use. I will do something that will lead to that end result."

Susie loved animals and hated knowing that Father Crane felt so cold about taking the life of an innocent dog. At the same time, she understood that all it took was for Dan or any of *Them* to simply tell the dog to kill its master, Mrs. Davis. The only thing that stopped them from doing it so far was that *They* could only safely get to the dog when she wasn't home — which wasn't very often. The dog was otherwise always at her side, reliably attacking anyone who came close to her. Susie knew these kinds of decisions occurred many times a day and she knew that Father Crane was going to say exactly the same thing.

"These decisions occur millions of times a day," Father Crane said and then he walked away.

Susie took a deep breath and focused on the boulder.

*　　*　　*

The FBI took care of the video for Us, Dan texted Harold.

Yes. Free will shows its ignorant head once again, Harold wrote.

Dan laughed quietly. Leading people to do his will was like herding cattle – he could lead them anywhere, even to their slaughter, and they wouldn't even know it. Sometimes, however, people just naturally do stupid things.

I will be back tomorrow. We need to meet. Continue as planned, Harold wrote.

Dan pocketed his phone and decided that it would be best to go after Mrs. Davis – the little old lady with the Rottweiler. She was going to call the police within the next 20 hours, so she had to be taken care of soon. He still had a couple of days to get around to destroying the car. Big Dynamite, one of the thugs that was going to turn himself in, was still holed up in his mother's home for at least a week. G-Man, the other thug, was just sent to jail for solicitation of prostitution. He would be out next Wednesday. Both men would turn themselves in together next Saturday.

Mrs. Davis never opened the door for anyone except Frank – the two were close. Simply knocking wouldn't work. Dan couldn't break in without the dog barking and alerting neighbors, whose sense of alertness was already heightened because of the murdering of Frank's family.

His attention turned to Susie, who he knew would be staring at a giant rock for the next 48 minutes.

"*He's* having Susie stare at the rock. What a moron."

He next turned his attention to Father Crane. He smirked, knowing that Father Crane was on his way to Mrs. Davis's house. Dan wanted to get there first, but he still was at a loss as to how he would actually get to Mrs. Davis's dog inconspicuously. He committed himself to different scenarios such as dressing as a pizza delivery man, posing as a phony charity volunteer, and even as far as befriending her neighbors. Nothing worked or anything that could work led to allowing *Them* to implicate Dan – a risk that he couldn't take. The only thing that could work was for him to dress as a Catholic priest and simply knock on her door – she was a staunch Catholic. He wouldn't have time to get the proper attire before Father Crane got there.

And this is why Father Crane has the advantage, he thought.

Dan was within a block of her home and he stopped, waiting for Father Crane to get there first. This wasn't going to be the time that he could get to her, so he would have to focus his attention on another plan.

*   *   *

Father Crane, wearing his black cassock and a fedora hat, walked up to Mrs. Davis's house. He could already hear her dog barking loudly from inside. He knocked on the door loudly because he knew she was hard of hearing.

KNOCK KNOCK KNOCK

He waited, knowing that she was cautiously looking through the door's peephole. Father Crane took a step back so she could get a good look at his entire body. The door slowly unlocked and it cracked open – with the door chain still latched.

"Yes?" Mrs. Davis asked.

"Oh, good day to you, Mrs. Davis. I'm Father Crane…"

"You'll have to speak up! My hearing isn't very good!"

"I'm Father Crane! I understand a terrible tragedy has occurred across your street and we, the Catholic Church, wanted to stop by and make sure that all of our parishioners in the area are okay!"

SNARL! SNAP!

The Rottweiler's snout shot through crack in the door with violent energy. The door chain held.

"Whoa there, grumpy!" Father Crane said to the dog.

142

"Oh forgive Bear, he's very protective of me," Mrs. Davis said softly and turned to Bear, "Mama is going to be fine."

"It's quite okay!"

Mrs. Davis turned to Bear and said, "Bear, we have company. You sit. Sit!" she commanded.

Bear sat down and kept quiet. She unlatched the door and opened it fully.

"Please come in, Father."

"Thank you," Father Crane said loudly, walking into her house and taking off his fedora hat.

"Can I get you something to drink, Father?" she asked politely.

"Oh, ice water would be very nice, thank you!" he smiled.

"I'll be right back," she said, shuffling into her nearby kitchen – out of sight of Father Crane.

Father Crane turned to Bear, who sat obediently still. He sat down on the couch nearby and smiled at Bear. He worked through a few hundred possible scenarios to earn Bear's trust. He settled on one. With his hands out and open he said, "Who wants a hug?"

Bear got up and walked to Father Crane, his nub tail wagging. Father Crane hugged him and said, "I have specific instructions for you..."

Very soon two men will come by and visit Mama. They will be called Eddie and Vinny. One will have an injured leg – you will smell his blood. You are to attack one of them. Go for the throat but do not draw blood. Understand?

Bear licked Father Crane's face once just as Mrs. Davis came back with ice water.

"Wow, I've never seen Bear be so friendly to a stranger before!" she exclaimed.

"He's a good dog!"

Father Crane spent the next twenty minutes chatting with Mrs. Davis – he had to spend the time to make his visit appear legitimate. Father Crane predicted that Vinny and Eddie would come by soon to question Mrs. Davis about what she saw. During the visit, Bear would attack Eddie, forcing Vinny to shoot Bear dead.

The conversation was easy. It afforded him ample attention to focus on Dan. He was outside waiting for him; Dan wanted to confront him. Father Crane thought about the possibilities of an ambush. He knew that this day would eventually come, but he also knew that Dan was very talented with his Polarity.

"So you see, Father, I am thankful that you've come over to check on me," Mrs. Davis said, finishing her conversation.

"It was delightful!" Father Crane replied loudly with a gentle smile. He looked at his watch and stood up. "Well, I must be running now, Mrs. Davis!"

Bear walked up to Father Crane and began licking his left hand.

"I just can't get over how much Bear adores you," Mrs. Davis said.

"Animals, by God's will, are mankind's companions! They've been with us through both peace and war! They have lived and died by our sides! They are divine!"

Father Crane went out the front door and put his hat back on, turning around momentarily to wave goodbye. Mrs. Davis waved back and closed her door. Father Crane walked to the sidewalk at the street and stopped to think, to focus more on Dan's plans. There would be a full eleven minutes to confront Dan in the open field behind Mrs. Davis's house without any witnesses. In eleven minutes, Eddie and Vinny would drive by and have a clear view of the field and would be potential witnesses to the expected violent exchange. This was a window of opportunity.

It is time that Daniel and I resume our chess match, he thought.

With that, he walked behind Mrs. Davis's home to a wide open field whose only prominent feature was the large power transmission towers cutting through its center. The field was nearly one hundred yards wide, flat, and its grass was a few inches tall. Its length stretched seemingly to the horizon – as expected for the long tract of high-power transmission lines it contained.

Dan was standing on the opposite side with his back turned to Father Crane at first. Father Crane took a few more steps into the field. Dan then turned around and walked toward him. They stopped when they were twenty feet from each other.

"Hello, Daniel."

Daniel cringed – Father Crane knew he hated being called that.

"*You* are here for another chat?" Father Crane asked.

Dan lifted his chin and scratched the back of his head. "I can feel now what I felt back then – way back then. Except... now I know what it is."

"I don't have to kill *You*, Dan."

"It's 'Dan' now is it?"

"Am I moving too quickly for *You*?"

Dan sulked. In return, Father Crane grinned slyly.

"Okay, we have no weapons on us. This is all fisticuffs," Dan said shaking his hands, loosening them.

Father Crane put his hands in front of him at his waist, interlacing his fingers to join them. The two walked slowly, side by side, deeper into the open field.

"You can stand down Dan, I will take care of *Him*!" a voice yelled out from behind Father Crane, somewhat to his left.

It was Linus. Father Crane didn't flinch.

Dan gritted his teeth and shook his head. He took a gulp and took a few steps back, coldly staring at Father Crane.

Father Crane then took a few steps forward towards Dan. Linus got within a hundred feet of Father Crane, smiling, "Heh... look at *You*! *You're* actually keeping close to Dan so I can't get close to *You*! Are *You* going to do this for the next nine minutes?!"

"It is the correct move to make, given the circumstances. Perhaps *You* would like to shake Dan's hand to wish *Him* luck?!" Father Crane asked over his shoulder.

Linus wiped his smile from his face. "There isn't much time to settle things here. It's a rare opportunity," he snarled.

"If this is a party then I'm in!" Spike shouted from a distance, behind Dan.

Dan turned around.

"I would have preferred to keep Spike at a distance – to avoid unnecessary proximity problems. But it seems we are at an impasse," Father Crane said.

Dan started walking towards Spike, who was standing still. Father Crane followed Dan. Linus followed Father Crane, who was still about a hundred feet away.

"*You've* got Linus at *Your* back and I've got Spike," Dan said to Father Crane. "Now how do *You* think this will go down?"

Linus started laughing. He began walking around Father Crane and Dan – in a wide semi-circle to avoid Dan's like Polarity to get to Spike. Dan stopped and asked, "Shall we make this one-on-one for each of us?"

Spike whipped out his switchblade and began to walk mindfully around the area where Dan and Father Crane were – he had to avoid Father Crane's like Polarity. He would eventually meet with Linus. Linus threw away his guide cane, took off his shirt, and twitched his over-sized chest muscles a few times.

Father Crane kept his focus on Dan, fully faithful that Spike would keep his focus on Linus.

Within a minute, Spike and Linus were facing each other, although still a good shouting distance away. About fifty feet on Spike's right were Father Crane and Dan – still twenty feet from each other.

Linus started hopping up and down, loosening his neck, ducking, weaving, shadow-boxing, and taking in deep breaths – just as a boxer might. "Oh, come on Spike! Mmm... yes! Come on!" Linus shouted.

Spike walked towards Linus slowly. Linus hopped a few steps back and then to one side – and then back to the other. Spike carefully kept his heading directly on Linus.

Father Crane focused – almost meditating – on Dan. He couldn't let the confrontation of Spike and Linus distract him.

Linus continued moving around to the left and right, not staying in one place for more than a second. "Oh, don't worry, Spike. I've prepared for this moment for years!" Linus reveled.

Spike kept walking cautiously ahead towards Linus.

"I will make *You* feel just as *Your* uncle made *You* feel on *Your* seventh birthday! *You* had a very penetrating experience, yes?!" Linus laughed and jumped a few feet to his right.

Spike stopped and opened his mouth slightly.

"I've got the same equipment that *Your* uncle did!" Linus yelled, grabbing his crotch before jumping back to the left.

Spike shook his head slightly and took a step forward, a tad to the left – only to have his right foot land cleanly into a narrow, but very deep hole in the ground. Spike tried to catch himself, but his right leg was already beneath the ground halfway up his thigh.

"Aaa!" Spike shrieked.

Linus stopped his movement completely. "Good. *Your* screams are like sweet music. This is *Your* end," he said.

"My ankle's broke," Spike gasped to Father Crane. "My foot... my foot is stuck. I'm stuck. I'm... I'm...,"

"*You're* dead!" Linus shouted, marching towards Spike.

Father Crane realized that Linus had dug that hole earlier, before Linus confronted Susie at the restaurant. He looked at Dan, who was now looking at Spike. He had to protect Spike from Linus, he also had to protect himself from Dan, and – at the same time – he couldn't get too close to Spike or else they'd both be rendered helpless because of their like Polarities. The only solution was to keep Dan between Spike and Linus without – somehow – getting too close to Spike.

Father Crane charged at the still-distracted Dan, grabbing him, and throwing him towards Spike – who was still about fifty feet away. Dan got up easily, just in time to lock arms with Father Crane. Father Crane had four very short seconds to get Dan close enough to Spike – to use Dan's Polarity to repel Linus. Linus began to run towards Spike.

Dan lifted his right knee straight into Father Crane's left ribs, breaking some of them – something Father Crane allowed so he could grab Dan's lifted right knee. He did so and then kicked Dan's left leg out from under him. Dan fell to the ground with Father Crane still holding onto his leg. Father Crane dragged Dan towards Spike with all of the energy he could gather. Dan tried his best to claw into the ground to hold steady. With one final heave, Father Crane swung Dan towards Spike – who was still fifty feet away but right in the forward path of Linus.

Linus sneered in anger, "You moron! Get out of my way!"

Dan got up, trying to run away, but Father Crane tackled him and rolled to the ground. Linus began to run to the right, trying to find an angle to get past Dan – Father Crane dragged Dan in lockstep with Linus's movements. Dan clawed at Father Crane, grabbed his left ear, and ripped it off. Father Crane did not make a sound, doing everything he could to keep focus on Dan's and

Linus's next moves – keeping up with both of their Polarities was very tasking.

Dan elbowed Father Crane in his jaw causing his eyesight to blur temporarily. Once again, Father Crane kept his concentration – just trying to hold on long enough, just trying to get through the next six minutes until the FBI agents would drive by. Dan jabbed at Father Crane's eyes with his fingers, but Father Crane – anticipating that exact move – punched Dan in the throat. Dan grabbed his throat and heaved his chest to draw in air. Father Crane grabbed Dan by his hair and repeatedly kneed him in the head, pulling him, leading him, to keep him in-between Spike and Linus.

In the middle of one of Father Crane's knees to his head, Dan pushed into Father Crane – and towards Spike.

"*You're* both dead now!" Linus yelled at Father Crane and Spike.

Father Crane dropped to his knees, acting as dead weight, right at forty feet from Spike. Dan then kneed Father Crane in his face, cleanly into his nose. Blood gushed out from it. Again, Father Crane grabbed Dan's knee, but this time leaned up and into Dan's body, stood up, and picked him up off the ground. With Dan on his right shoulder, Father Crane marched towards Linus.

Linus hurried back, frightened at Dan's closing proximity. "Get your thoughts together, Dan!"

Dan grabbed a pen from his pocket and began to repeatedly stab Father Crane in his back. The pen broke after twelve stabs, but was sufficient to draw a hefty amount of blood. Father Crane fell forward, throwing Dan forward and towards Linus. Linus began to run around to his right – leaving Father Crane and Dan to his left. Dan then moved to the other direction. Very soon, one of them would have a clean path to Spike.

Father Crane, exhausted, stood up, and promptly slumped back down. He slowly forced himself to stand up again, grinding his teeth through the pain. He was now certain that both he and Spike were going to die, that his gamble to save Spike meant they were both done for.

Dan laughed. Father Crane took a step towards Dan, swaying under his own weight.

"Goodbye to both of *You*," Linus said, now within twenty feet of Spike.

And then a woman's voice yelled out, "It's amazing the zoom features on phones these days!"

It was Susie. She was standing at the edge of the open field, her phone out and video recording the event. Linus and Dan stopped instantly, shocked. Father Crane looked at Susie, smiled, and fell to the ground.

"LEAVE!" Susie commanded.

"Susie, *You*...," Dan started to shout.

"Shut up and leave, Dan! No one wants to hear *Your* speeches!"

"*We* go," Linus said to Dan calmly. "*She* has the advantage. *She* can send that video anywhere before *We* will have a chance. *We* cannot kill *Them* safely. Let go of your emotion."

The two of them left.

Susie carefully walked towards Father Crane – stopping safely from his Polarity. Father Crane looked up at her. She looked puzzled. "I don't understand. I expected that you would let Spike die so at least you could live. The odds were against *Us*," she said.

Father Crane panted a few times, spit out some blood, took off his glasses, and wiped his brow. "Well... I love Spike... he is... he is like my son. Even I... Even I am not without faults," he said, breathing deeply.

Susie looked around to ensure that *They* were gone.

Father Crane panted some more and asked, "Why... why aren't you still focusing on the boulder as I instructed?"

"My intuition told me to come here. I'll get back to it later. I'm sure it will still be there."

"Something told me that your recalcitrant behavior would one day pay off."

Chapter 11 – Dog Fight

Eddie and Vinny pulled up to Frank's house – it remained cordoned off with police tape. A few police officers and forensics experts were there carefully examining every square inch of the property. The murders three days ago were the top priority for local law enforcement because it happened to a police officer's family.

Vinny was on the phone, talking to his boss. Eddie parked their car and waited for him to finish his conversation.

"I understand, yes," Vinny said solemnly.

His eyes began to fill with tears.

"Yes... yes. Yes. I... I understand," he said, struggling to speak.

Eddie sat motionless, staring straight forward.

Vinny finally hung up. He stared at his phone with contempt, wishing it would ring again, but with better news. He looked towards the car's ceiling. "I've... I've been written up for destroying the video evidence."

Eddie turned his head to Vinny, "But it wasn't your fault."

"No one got that memo, Eddie," he said quietly.

Vinny rubbed his eyes and then placed his hands on his cheeks. His head shook slowly back and forth. He wiped his forearm across his nose and sniffed.

"It wasn't your fault Vinny. I know the regulations."

"They said that they made it my fault to preserve the relationship with the police. And that... that I shouldn't be so stupid... that I made the FBI look stupid."

Eddie was silent.

"The FBI is everything to me, Eddie. I came in to make my brother proud of me. I want him to be proud of me, God rest his soul. My mother... it's all she talks about... says that she doesn't stop talking about how proud she is that I followed in my brother's footsteps."

A tear streamed down from Vinny's left eye. He wiped it away, grabbed his notepad, quickly opened his door, and got out of the car – but not without wincing from the pain from his injured leg. Eddie got out and put his arms over the roof. "Hey, uh, Vinny. We can take a break if you want. No big deal."

Vinny shook his head. "Nah... I need to get back into this."

Eddie raised his eyebrows and said, "Okay, where do ya wanna start? Frank's family was close to the Stewart family two houses down from him."

Eddie pointed down the street. Vinny looked down the street and then looked at his notepad.

"Or we can go talk with his neighbor across the street," Eddie said pointing behind him.

"Let's start with the Stewart family. I don't think the old lady across the street knew Frank too well," Vinny said.

"How do you know it's an old lady?" Eddie asked.

"I did a property check on all of the surrounding homes last night. Trina Davis, age 82, widow. No one else listed," Vinny said, looking down at his notepad. "We can get to Mrs. Davis afterwards."

"Sure you wanna walk?"

"It hurts, but it's not that bad."

They walked along the perimeter of Frank's house on their way to the Stewart family. Vinny looked at the home and felt its darkness. He watched the meticulous nature of the forensics experts analyzing the property.

"I wonder if we could ever get in there to take a look around," Vinny commented.

"Why?" Eddie asked.

"I just have a hunch that whoever killed Frank's family was somehow connected to our Susie. It's kind of odd that Frank goes out of his way to talk to her in the airport – and she fainted in front of him on the security video – let's not forget that. Susie somehow survives and she doesn't want to be found. And then... then these horrible murders happen. Whoever did this didn't want to kill Frank – they wanted to kill his family. The video on that flash drive showed that this attack was timed, that someone wanted it all to go down this way."

Eddie chuckled, "You're tying too many things together Vinny. Let's not waste our brains on circumstantial evidence."

"No, no, no Eddie... don't you ever trust your instincts?"

"All the time – maybe too much. It kind of got me in trouble in the past... it's kind of complicated. I just try to keep my mouth shut now."

The two of them got to the Stewart home and knocked on the door. Mrs. Stewart opened the door. She was in her mid-40's, petite, with long straight blonde hair.

"Can I help you?" she asked.

"Mrs. Stewart, we are Agents Kerwin and Lagetti with the FBI. Do you have a moment?" Eddie said, as both he and Vinny flashed their badges.

"Sure. Come on inside."

Vinny and Eddie walked inside her home. Every shelf, table, bookcase, and corner of the house was filled with crafts-works – ranging from homemade dolls to little rocking chairs to miniature homes made out of tree bark. There was a strong odor of pine and cinnamon. A sign posted on a ceiling support beam stated *NO, YOU'RE NOT AT A CRACKER BARREL.*

"We were told by the police that your family was close to the Moore family. We are trying to piece together some things and we thought you might help," Eddie said.

"Well, yes," she said with her eyes filling with tears. "We loved the Moore family. My children played with their children every day. They would play in the mud together, go to birthday parties together, play board games...," she sniffed. "It meant so much to us because our oldest, Maya, is disabled and is bound to a wheelchair. She's nine years old and doesn't have any other friends. The two boys, the twins, are six... and they were about the same age as the Moore children."

"Wow. That's amazing. Frank had twins and so do you."

"It worked out well – they played and played non-stop," she said, beaming.

"Frank seems like a good guy," Vinny said.

"Oh, Frank is a darling. He was always there to help if you needed anything. He never asked for anything in return. He never complained about anything. He adored his family. He adored my children... so kind and warm. My husband passed away from an illness a couple of years ago. Frank stepped in and immediately became my children's father figure. He would read to them alongside his own kids. They would have sleepovers in the middle of the week. My children call him Papa Frank. My children ask where the Moore children are and... and..."

Mrs. Stewart started bawling. Vinny hugged her and she strongly hugged back. Eddie was taking notes, his face completely stoic.

"I have some pictures," Mrs. Stewart said, reaching to grab a large framed picture nearby.

She handed it to Vinny and pointed at various figures. "You can see my kids… Maya… the twins Sammy and Mikey…"

"Whoa! They've got some blond hair," Vinny said brightly.

"It's almost white… all three of them," Mrs. Stewart proudly smiled.

Vinny looked over the children in the picture – the Stewart kids with the Moore kids. They were obviously very close. Frank's kids were crowded around Maya, the wheelchair-bound Stewart daughter, in the picture. They were hugging her while she sported the toothiest smile Vinny had ever seen.

"Wow, Maya looks very happy," Vinny said.

"She loved the Moore children. She can't say much but shouts and cheers whenever they were around."

Vinny and Eddie stayed for almost an hour. Vinny asked most of the questions while Eddie remained largely quiet. It was clear to Vinny that the relationship between Frank's family and the Stewart family was special. Frank hadn't visited the Stewart family at all since the tragedy and Mrs. Stewart didn't have any information that would appear to link Frank to Susie. They got up to leave.

"If you see Frank, tell him we miss him… tell him we love him," Mrs. Stewart said.

"I will, ma'am. Thank you for your time," Vinny said shaking her hand and then giving her a hug.

"Take care," Eddie said as he walked out the door.

The two of them walked back towards Frank's house.

"On to the little old lady's house now," Eddie said.

"Wow – that really tugs at the heartstrings."

"Let go of the emotion, Vinny. It's useless. You'll make emotional decisions and you'll screw up."

"Come on, Eddie. Are you really going to be THAT cold?"

"I'm not. We could have wrapped up that conversation in ten minutes, but you manage to drag out another…," Eddie paused to look at his watch, "…52 minutes. We have work to do. That was a colossal waste of time. I was pretty pissed off for most of it. We should have left as soon as that cursed cinnamon gave me that headache."

Eddie reached in his pocket and popped some pills.

"Jeez almighty, Eddie. It wasn't a big deal."

"Says you."

They made it to the front door of Mrs. Davis's house. Bear, the Rottweiler, was barking loudly at them, his head popping in and out of the curtains of the window adjacent to the front door. They knocked loudly to compensate for the loud barking.

KNOCK KNOCK KNOCK

There was no answer.

KNOCK KNOCK KNOCK

"Mrs. Davis, we're with the FBI. We need to ask you a few questions!" Vinny yelled.

Her door opened slightly. Bear's snout squeezed into its opening – the door's chain lock pulled tight, keeping the door from opening any further.

"Bear, sit!" Mrs. Davis yelled at the dog and then turned to the agents, "You'll have to speak up. My hearing's not so good these days."

Bear barked a few more times and sat down as Mrs. Davis ordered.

"We're Agents Kerwin and Lagetti," Vinny nearly yelled, as they flashed their badges.

Bear growled. Mrs. Davis turned to him and said, "No, Bear. Sit. Sit." She then turned back to the agents and unchained the door.

"Oh, well come in," she said.

"I like dogs!" Eddie commented as they entered.

Mrs. Davis smiled at him. "He's my Bear. He's my child. I love him and he loves me."

She walked over to Bear and hugged him. Eddie followed her. He petted Bear a few times. Bear growled at him.

"Bear, no!" Mrs. Davis scolded. "Be nice!"

Eddie turned to Vinny, who was still standing at the doorway and said, "Vinny, come over here and pet the dog. It helps earn trust."

Vinny slowly walked over to Bear and began petting his head with one hand – and then he knelt down and petted bear all over with both hands. Bear's nub tail wagged and he licked Vinny's hands and leaned up against Eddie's leg.

"Wow. What a powerful animal!" Vinny shouted and then stood up.

"Mrs. Davis, we'd like to ask you about Frank Moore! He lived across the street from you!" Eddie shouted.

Mrs. Davis turned to Eddie and opened her mouth to say something, but stopped. She put a finger between her teeth, biting down in thought.

"This isn't about the tragedy that happened. This is something different." Eddie said.

"What?" she asked.

"This doesn't have to do with the tragedy that happened across the street!" Eddie repeated.

"If there is anything you know about the tragedy, we would like to know, too!" Vinny added.

Eddie frowned at Vinny.

"Hey, why not, Eddie?" Vinny whispered to him.

"I see," Mrs. Davis said as she walked to nearby chair and sat down. "Please, sit."

Eddie and Vinny sat down on a couch across from her. Bear walked over to Mrs. Davis and sat down next to her. He growled a little bit.

"Bear, that's enough now. These are our friends."

Mrs. Davis let out a long sigh and looked down towards the floor. "Well… I wasn't sure who to talk to or even what to say. It was scary," she said.

Eddie and Vinny began taking notes in their notepads.

"What was scary?!" Eddie asked.

"Those… Those men who came by across the street," she answered.

"What did they look like?!" Vinny asked.

She gulped and didn't say anything.

"It's okay Mrs. Davis! Take your time!" Vinny yelled.

Eddie looked over at Vinny and frowned again. He shook his head and threw his notepad on the coffee table in front of him. "Look, I don't care about those men! I would like to talk about Frank!" Eddie yelled at Mrs. Davis.

Mrs. Davis stiffened up.

"Eddie, she wants to tell us about the men."

"I don't care about them, Vinny. Let's first ask about Frank and then you can spend a few minutes doing your own little experiment. I just don't want to waste any more time like we did down the street."

"Those men were…," Mrs. Davis started.

Eddie held up his hand, palm open, at Mrs. Davis, "Please ma'am! I would really like to talk about Frank and not those men!"

"Eddie, let her talk."

Eddie shook his head and he sucked his lips into his mouth. His face became flush. He turned to Vinny and pointed his finger at him, "Listen Vinny, I'm not going to sit through this again."

Bear growled.

"We wasted our time at the last house and we're gonna do things my way," Eddie said to Vinny, as quietly as he could, choking on anger.

Bear perked up and growled some more.

"I don't care what SHE has to say about those men, got it?!" Eddie said, now pointing at Mrs. Davis.

Bear barked at Eddie. Eddie quickly froze and put his hand up and out towards Bear. "Hey, lady… your dog is getting too aggressive," Eddie carefully – and quietly – said to Mrs. Davis.

Mrs. Davis was un-moved.

"I'm not sure if she heard you, Eddie," Vinny whispered to him.

"CALM YOUR DOG!" Eddie screamed at Mrs. Davis.

She popped back in her chair, wide-eyed.

"A bit too loud there, Eddie," Vinny said.

Bear snapped, his hackles going up.

"Bear, no. Sit. Sit!" Mrs. Davis shouted.

Bear's mouth began to froth.

"Whoa… whoa…," Eddie said, curling up into the couch.

BARK BARK BARK

Eddie stood up, pulled out his gun and pointed it at Bear. He yelled at Mrs. Davis, "Call him off!"

Bear charged at Eddie, but Eddie didn't have a clean shot at Bear – Mrs. Davis was right behind the dog.

"Whoa!" Eddie yelled, bringing his arms up to his face as Bear jumped on him.

Vinny tried to grab Bear, but Bear bit him, puncturing his right hand. Bear then resumed his attack on Eddie.

"NO BEAR! NO!" Mrs. Davis yelled as Bear bit down and pulled at various parts of Eddie.

Eddie screamed in pain. His arms began to bleed. Vinny pulled out his gun and pointed it at Bear – waiting for the instant he would have a clean shot at the animal without accidentally shooting Eddie.

"DON'T SHOOT MY BABY!" Mrs. Davis yelled as she got up from her chair.

Eddie was finally able to grab Bear's head with both of his hands and push Bear away from him several feet. Finally, Vinny had a clean shot. He pointed his gun and – just as he pulled the trigger – Mrs. Davis jumped in front of Bear to protect him. Mrs. Davis was shot in chest, falling limp to the ground. Bear ran away, scared of the gunshot.

"Oh my God!" Vinny yelled, rushing to Mrs. Davis. "Oh my God! What have I done?!"

Eddie tried his best to contain his pain as he took out his phone and dialed 9-1-1.

Vinny held the old lady in his arms, crying. "Oh my God, I'm sorry. I'm so sorry!" he sobbed.

"Calm down, Vinny."

Vinny looked up at Eddie, his face glistening with tears, and yelled, "Listen to me, you sociopathic animal! This woman is dead! I killed her! How can you just sit there and act like nothing happened?! How can you not care?!"

Eddie shouted back, "Vinny, calm down! I've seen it all. I'm just trying to calm you down that's all! This isn't your fault, you understand?! She jumped in front of you! Her dog was assaulting me!"

Eddie knelt down next to Vinny. Vinny's sniffing quickly turned into a quiet cry. His jaw wobbled as he hugged Mrs. Davis's head. "I'm so sorry," he whispered to her and then cried, "I'm so sorry!"

Chapter 12 – According to Harold

Harold gave his empty wine glass to the flight attendant as she walked by. He reclined back in his comfy first class seat and let out a sigh of relief. The video and the old lady were no longer problems – and Dan didn't have to do anything with their fate. Sometimes luck happens by *Us* and sometimes it happens on its own – Harold didn't care as long as the end result was the same. It now only meant that the car, Big Dynamite, and G-Man had to be dealt with.

Harold was due to land in Los Angeles soon. He cut his week with the President short so he could get back to other things. With Father Crane and Spike no longer serious factors, this was a moment for *Us* to make things happen. He expected Father Crane to assign an operative to help Susie now. One less of *Their* operatives meant a multitude of opportunities. Harold chuckled with excitement, thinking of the possibilities.

Time for something big, he thought.

He took out a sheet of paper; it was completely covered with scribbled writing in various colors – very little blank space could be seen. He began writing down ideas – not caring about writing through existing notes. His handwriting was completely unintelligible so no one else – including *Them* – could read it. He made a list of campaigns to pursue, debating the pros and cons as to what would impress his superiors the most.

> 1. Expose statewide police corruption through bombing families of local businessmen... 37 people will die... 128 injured. Will reduce wrongful prosecutions by 28% over the next ten years.
> 2. Leak newly invented electronics cleaner into water supply to expose its dangers that would otherwise go unnoticed for the next 11 years... 203 cases of terminal cancer... 128 children die. Will save 983 people over the next eight years.
> 3. Cause the First Medina Bank tower to collapse to bolster building codes against earthquakes... 7 to 723 people will die... Will save hundreds of thousands of lives over the next twenty years.

They all looked so promising. His mouth watered, almost drooling over the possibilities. Harold always told his employees at Beytern that they should enjoy their work so much that they couldn't believe it's a job – such words of encouragement made him an effective CEO.

Harold loved being the CEO of Beytern, but he loved his job as one of *Us* even more. To accelerate mankind's improvement while being able to destroy things in the process was his nirvana. Whatever follows is stronger than what it replaced – and he thought of himself as an unseen hero to the millions around him.

He laughed quietly – reveling at the notion that Father Crane was on ordered bed rest at his monastery and Spike was hobbling on crutches. Father Crane only had 30 other operatives that Harold knew of in the area – compared to Harold's 62.

Heh, Father Crane was practically three of Them by himself, Harold thought.

Shifting his operatives to work towards a new plan would be a challenge without interfering with existing plans. A good chunk of his operatives were busy executing a plan that was hatched twelve years ago – a plan that was important and ordered from above. He stuck the end of his pen in his mouth in thought – meddling with those operatives wouldn't be possible. There were eight other operatives on assignment to kill two un-suspecting men who were about to become *Them* – he didn't want to de-obligate those operatives either. Very few things were as important as killing someone who was about to become one of *Them*. Harold was still very upset that Susie wasn't killed in time, but reversing Frank helped him cope with that loss.

He drew in a deep breath and, as any good leader should, he thought about how to make the most with the people he had. Each of his plans – regardless of difficulty – required exceptional planning so *They* wouldn't interfere. Each of these plans would require thousands of actions to be taken by *Us* – some would lead to the selected plan's success while the vast majority were nothing more than decoys, distractions, and misdirections for *Them*.

"Hey, I know you," a man from behind said, tapping Harold's shoulder.

Harold turned his head and looked up. "Oh, hello Sully!"

"Ha! The last time I saw you was like…"

"Eight months, three days, two hours, fourteen minutes, and two seconds ago," Harold laughed.

"Ha! Yeah somethin' like that. I think you left out a few seconds though!" Sully laughed, slapping his knee.

"I'm sure I didn't," Harold said, grinning.

Sully slapped his knee again, laughing but then started coughing. Harold calmed himself and peered into Sully's life for a moment – realizing that this cough was something more serious, the beginning of Sully's end almost two years from now. Sully still sported his short pony-tail. His dark goatee was heavily contrasted against his greying hair. He was thin – thinner than he was the last time Harold saw him. Sully was penny-pincher at heart – he'd been wearing those same boots for seven years straight now. He was now worth $400 million and rising – a competent independent investor.

"How are the wife and kids?" Harold asked.

"Oh they're doing all right. I'm very proud of my kids – all hard workers. My wife and I are comin' up on our 35th anniversary. And you?"

"That's fantastic – congratulations. Well, my son graduated college and he's still looking for a job, but the economy is a bit tough right now. He hasn't asked me for a job at Beytern. I think he wants to make it on his own."

"That's a good fella you've got there. Nothin' wrong with proving yourself in the wild. Oh… hey, Beytern stock has soared recently."

"It's been good to us, yes," Harold said, bobbing his head.

"Any plans for Beytern you wanna tell ol' Sully about? And please don't tell me you're plannin' to step down as CEO. Beytern is climbin' to number one in market cap."

"Oh no, not any time soon."

Harold raised an eyebrow and realized that a new opportunity had presented itself. Sully's presence was indeed fortunate – and so was Sully's wealth. None of his three plans was the best right now. He needed more of Sully's time.

A dinging chime rang throughout the airplane's cabin. The intercom speaker bellowed, "Good afternoon everyone, we are approaching Los Angeles now. Could everyone please take your seat and fasten your seatbelts."

"Oh... Sully...," Harold said, fumbling through his wallet to pull out his business card. He wrote his direct line phone number on it. "If it's not any trouble and if you're available, do you mind stopping by Beytern headquarters some time this week? I have a few thoughts I'd like to pass off to you. The number I wrote is my direct line."

Sully grabbed the business card and said, "I still have the business card you gave me last time... sure no problem. I can give you a ring some time in a couple of days – got some other things immediately on my lap."

"That would be great," Harold said.

Sully went back to his seat.

Harold put his notes away and rested his arms on the armrests. One of his knees bounced up and down in excitement. Sully opened many opportunities for *Us*.

Harold looked back into Sully's past since they last met. He could see Sully searching online for him and his business dealings within Beytern. Sully had also investigated into Harold's past – almost to a point of stalking him. Hundreds of notes were taken about Harold. It was a fascination approaching idolatry and Harold saw Sully as ripe for the picking.

Sully's money was needed. Harold took the remainder of his 22 minutes of the flight investigating thousands of possible scenarios to get it. Harold need to do and say exactly what Sully needed to experience – it had to be perfect to get Sully to part with his life savings.

Sully will call in three days at 2:23 PM. I will have to cancel my 2 PM meeting then, he thought.

He briefly thought about Dan's progress, but he wasn't worried – Dan was his most reliable operative. More help wouldn't be needed. Dan would make sure everything would work out as planned – especially since he only had to contend with Susie. Harold saw Susie sitting in a restaurant by herself for the past 40 minutes doing absolutely nothing. He closed his eyes, reveling in how ineffective she was.

*   *   *

It was late afternoon. Susie sat in a booth of Luigi's, an Italian restaurant, aimlessly stirring her glass of ice water – thinking about the events recently: Two pieces of critical evidence against Harold were no longer, Father Crane was laid up in bed recovering, Spike was on crutches, and two FBI agents were pursuing her. Things weren't going very well. She had to protect the car, Big Dynamite, and G-Man, but it appeared that she – and Father Crane – weren't very effective at protecting anything.

Everything that Dan had done to destroy the evidence against Harold had failed, yet things were still going his way. She pondered if the natural course of events in life were merely being played out, that *Us* or *Them* really had no role in the flash drive being made useless or in killing Mrs. Davis – sometimes accidents do happen. Susie's only surprise was that *she was surprised* that she didn't predict Mrs. Davis's death – it made her question her death as being merely an accident.

So far, the only common factor was the two FBI agents, Eddie and Vinny – and all they wanted to do was to talk to her about surviving the plane crash two months ago. Did she have control over what was going on? There was no fate. There was no free will. Both are jockeyed back and forth by *Us* and *Them* – to result in somewhere in-between. If *They* aren't involved, then nature simply carried out its natural course of events unabated. She wished she could talk with Father Crane to get answers.

She peered into the lives of Eddie and Vinny to see how, if at all, they could be playing a role. Going back days, weeks, and even months – there was no indication that either was influenced or had anything to do with *Us* or *Them*. Everything that happened appeared to happen without any ripple in the natural course of events. The two FBI agents were, in fact, unlucky.

Just to cover her bases, she looked into the future to re-examine what would happen to the car and the two thugs, Big Dynamite and G-Man. With each examination, Dan was somewhere in the mix. She re-played the future several hundred times – with each time varying her approach to nullifying Dan. In most instances, Dan skillfully succeeded in destroying the car and killing the thugs. What would become of these things was still within her influence, but Dan would make it very tough for her.

She held her head low, wishing she had more help. Admittedly – and as much as she didn't want to admit it – Dan had more control of his Polarity than she did. He had the advantage against each and every plan she hatched.

To make matters worse was Linus – she had no idea what role he was playing. She could only reason that Linus was sent to ensure Spike wouldn't be a factor. At this moment, she saw Linus working out in a gym – he even had a personal trainer helping him with his exercises. Susie wondered if Linus was targeting her next. She debated if it was better to simply protect herself and ignore Dan.

"Are you ready to order, miss?" a waitress asked.

Susie looked up, downcast.

"I'll give you more time," the waitress said and walked away.

Susie, sensing a sneeze, grabbed a napkin. She sneezed into the napkin and crumpled it up. She went to grab another napkin – sensing another possible sneeze – and noticed that there was a nickel sitting underneath the napkin dispenser. She picked it up and looked at it – its date caught her attention.

"Heh, the same year as when my mother was born," she said and then she pocketed it.

Susie got up from the booth and left $5 on the table for the waitress for her trouble and for the nickel that she took – perhaps a misplaced tip. She walked out the front door and stopped, wondering where she should go next. After four minutes of indecisively standing still, she took the nickel out of her pocket and flipped it.

Heads I go right and tails I go left, she thought, wondering if luck would matter for her.

Heads. She went to the right. She reached an alleyway.

Heads I go into the alley and tails I keep going straight.

Heads again.

She took a few steps in the alleyway and saw a homeless man laying down under some newspapers about fifty feet in front of her to the right. She cautiously walked forward – a precaution if *They* had set an ambush. After all, a coin flip was very easy for *Them* to predict. She used her Polarity to ensure her safety...

Susie took five steps further and she began to feel weak. She took another step and collapsed to the ground, trying to catch her breath. She was dizzy and her vision went blurry. She quickly crawled backwards a few yards and returned to her senses.

"Don't do that again, Susie," the homeless man said as he sat up.

It was one of Us. He was terribly dirty and disheveled – long matted beard, soiled white baseball cap, a long-sleeve shirt that had several holes in it.

"Who... Who are you?" she asked.

She used her Polarity to trace this man's life but there was nothing outwardly remarkable about it. There wasn't any apparent activity that would even hint he had his full Polarity.

"Stop that. Stop that now," he said to her. "You won't find anything on me. You or no one under Father Crane don't know anything about me. Don't try to use your Polarity at all on me. It'll get you nowhere."

"All right," she answered skeptically.

"Thanks for meeting with me," he said.

"Meeting? It was luck."

"Look at the nickel... look at both sides of it."

Susie pulled it out and saw that the nickel had heads on both sides. She used her Polarity to trace the 27 exchanges of hands it took to get to be under the napkin dispenser – a full five weeks.

He coughed and said, "Very few things involving luck ever happen to Us or Them. Everything is deliberate. Everything is planned."

"You put the nickel there?"

"Kind of, yeah. This was one of the possible outcomes I predicted. The nickel would have made its way there even if you never stumbled upon it."

"One of many possible incomes? But...," she started.

He interrupted, "Fully committed. You gotta fully commit yourself to any of your possible plans – didn't you listen to Father Crane? When I first put the nickel out five weeks ago, I knew there was a good chance it wouldn't be needed – but here We are. It's all about being effective – your actions shouldn't always be a bunch of decoys with just one single, true plan. You should make it a point to kick off several actions that will also end up giving you a good result. Don't be so one-dimensional. If you wanna defeat Them, you gotta master this."

"Have several different plans that will yield the same result?"

"Yup."

"Who are you?"

He stood up and brushed off his pants. Clumps of dirt fell to the ground and a hazy dust cloud formed below his waist. "I haven't been asked that question in nearly three years. People seem to avoid me."

He brushed off his shirt sleeves and took off his hat briefly – just to re-adjust his hair – before promptly putting it back on.

"Please. Tell me," she implored.

"My name is Max. Let's just say that Father Crane isn't at the top of the totem pole."

"You're his overseer?"

"Sometimes I am. As you move up Our hierarchy, the trail is more carefully concealed. There is more communication done through Polarity alone. I usually don't get involved with lower-level activities."

"Then why are you here talking with me?"

"You need help and We don't have anyone to help you. My time is very… well very committed to other things We are doing on a much bigger scale. I can't help you as an operative. I can only help you with my guidance."

Susie stayed silent.

"My guidance is that They have most likely put more than one plan into place that will yield the same result."

"It isn't just Dan?"

"I'm not sure. I've spent the past thirty minutes looking over millions of possibilities. The tell-tale sign of detecting someone with Polarity – without getting close to them – is to see if the future is altered by Their actions. I'd see ripples of change occurring. If those ripples are happening, they're very small because nothing jumps out at me," said Max.

"I haven't been able to see any changes at all. Everything just appears to be bad luck," Susie said.

Max smiled and shook his head. "Well, you're new with your Polarity. You're very good with it but you still need training so you can work with other people. When it comes to something as important as putting Harold behind bars, this isn't just luck. You can look back in time and see every event, but what prevents you from understanding everything?"

"There has to be context. I won't understand languages I don't know. I can only understand as if I were a fly on the wall," she answered.

"Beyond that, you gotta look at the details. Just because We can see into the future doesn't mean that We won't miss details – you gotta pay close attention. You stopped Dan at certain points but it doesn't mean that They don't have other actions in play," he said and briefly paused. "Oh, also,

171

make it a point to focus on two things: Your survival and stopping Dan. I wanna stress your survival. You don't have the same protection as you did before."

He coughed a bit and started to walk away.

"Where are you going?"

Max pointed forward and yelled over his shoulder, "Do NOT follow me. I must remain hidden from Them. I've gotta go. By the way... Dan is creating a surprise for you."

"Dan is what?" Susie asked, but Max ignored her.

Susie watched as Max lay motionless on the ground, snoring. Could Dan have more than one plan in place? Father Crane has an overseer? She turned around and decided to walk back to the Luigi's, the restaurant she just left, to ponder what Max had said.

She opened the front door and walked towards the booth she was once sitting at – she could see the top of someone's head sitting at her booth.

"Oh, I'm sorry. I thought you left," the waitress said, stopping as she was about to walk by Susie.

"That's all right," Susie responded.

"I can seat you somewhere else... and... here's your $5 back," she said, handing her the bill.

"Oh... keep it...," she said and then trailed off because she now noticed who was sitting in her spot.

It was Eric, the man from the bus. This was too coincidental – this felt like meeting Dan all over again. She narrowed her eyes and said, "No, I will sit with this guy."

"Oh, okay," the waitress said.

Susie promptly sat down in the booth across its table from Eric – he was reading a newspaper. His eyes darted up and his head immediately jumped.

"Well hello," he said.

Susie stared at him coldly, wondering exactly how *They* set him up for this. "Hi," she replied.

"Is… Is everything okay?" Eric asked, putting his newspaper down calmly.

"I think so," she answered.

"We saw each other on the bus…"

"Yeah… the other night."

He smiled and nodded his head, "Yeah, yeah that's right."

"Yeah," she said with a quickly fading smile.

Eric stared at her and began to fiddle with a drink coaster. She stared back. Eric blinked a few times and finally said, "So… uh, what brings you to my table?"

"I don't know. I left here maybe… I don't know… five minutes ago. I was at this very table. Something told me I should come back."

"Oh," he said, tripping over a grin, "Well… you're welcome to join me if you want. I'm Eric," he said extending his hand.

"I'm Susie," she said as she shook his hand.

His grip was strong, confident, but not over-powering. His hand was warm to the touch, causing Susie to want to hang on just for a second longer than she probably should.

"I love coincidences. What brought you here?" she asked.

"Oh, a family friend owns this place. The food is great and they kind of give me a family discount – somewhere around 100%," he said, playfully rolling his eyes.

Part of Susie wanted him to say that he found money in his pocket and his favorite restaurant burned down – it would make it a bit easier to pin this coincidence on *Them*.

"Not bad," she said, as she put her elbow on the table and rested her chin on her hand.

The waitress put a glass of ice water in front of her. "What can I get ya?" she asked Susie.

"What's he having?" she asked back, pointing at Eric.

"Scooter is having the spaghetti," the waitress said with a straight face.

"Scooter?" Susie asked, holding back an endearing laugh.

Eric put his hands over his face. "Yeah, I've been called that my whole life."

"He's always been Scooter to us," the waitress said. "When he was a baby he didn't crawl. He would just sit on his little butt and scoot around the floor... so we just called him Scooter."

"That's funny... but in a sweet way," Susie said.

"It's a name that I don't think I'll ever shake," Eric said.

"We'll never let ya," the waitress said, patting him on his shoulder.

"Susie, this is Margie," Eric said motioning a hand at the waitress. "She's been working here for..."

"For as long as you've been alive," Margie said, again patting him on the shoulder and then turning to Susie, "Did ya want anything?"

"I'll have the spaghetti, too," Susie said, shining.

"Gotcha," the waitress said and walked away.

"That was awkward," Eric said, tilting his head down somewhat.

"Nah – don't worry about it," Susie said.

"Margie's like an older sister to me."

"She's sweet."

"Yeah, I was actually on my way over here the other night when we saw each other on the bus."

"Wow... I really was a mess that night – I got splashed by car that hit a puddle, my hair was everywhere, and I think I was coming down with something," Susie said.

"Nah, you looked okay that night," he said slowly, smiling softly. "And you look okay now."

Susie looked into his brown eyes and melted. He was still the same Eric that she saw that night – still caring for his sick mother, still scraping by financially, and still a nice guy.

Wait a minute. What was she doing? She was enjoying his company – this can't be allowed.

"Excuse me for a minute," she said, standing up. "I've got to go to the ladies room."

"Sure," he said gently, looking up at her.

She walked briskly to the bathroom and looked in a mirror. This was the second time she's run into Eric and the second time she let herself dive into him – albeit just a little bit. Did Dan influence Eric in some way? Part of her wished Dan had – it would make walking away from Eric very easy. Susie searched the past – at all the little nuances that Eric encountered – to see if there was anything that could have led him here. There was nothing. It was true that Eric ate at that restaurant often; the owners were childhood friends of his mother. They've let him eat for free his entire life.

It doesn't matter if this is serendipitous or not – I have to walk away.

He's either a pawn that was cleverly sent by *Them* or he was just Eric, a man that she couldn't take a chance on because *They* would certainly hurt him. She scratched the back of her neck and took a deep breath.

She knew it, but didn't want to accept it: She was going to be alone forever. Her heart felt heavy and emptiness invaded her body, consuming her. She wasn't going to have a chance for a family. No boyfriend. Nothing. It pained her to think that she would never have a chance to experience love because of this ironic gift – this Polarity – she would never have a chance to grow a relationship with someone like Eric. The only people she could have any measurable amount of a relationship with was with *Us* – and she couldn't get any closer than forty feet because of Polarity's restricted – or more precisely, *repulsive* – nature. Her face became barren of emotion, and it was crystal clear why the lack of emotion dominated the faces of Father Crane, Spike, Frank, and others of *Us*. It was unbearably lonely.

"There isn't a way, is there?" she said into the mirror.

Her phone beeped. It was a text from Spike that read, *there's a way... we got to talk.*

Susie's heart skipped a beat. She jammed her phone back into her pocket and took a few deep breaths.

"Okay, Spike, tell me. Use your Polarity to tell me. I need to know. I REALLY need to know."

Her phone rang. She took her phone out again, trembling with excitement, almost dropping it on the floor. It was Spike again.

"Hello?!"

"You can only have future conversations with someone usin' your Polarity if it's possible for that future to 'appen. If that future can't 'appen then neither can the conversation that you want to 'ave," he said.

"What do you mean?"

"Use your Polarity and tell me if you will live longer than the next ten minutes," Spike said and hung up.

Susie focused ten minutes into future – the restaurant was going to be robbed. Eric would bravely act up and get killed. The robbers would then kill anyone else they saw to get rid of any witnesses – including Susie. She quickly traced the robbers back to Dan – he had persuaded them that there was over $100,000 in the restaurant's safe. This was untrue, but the robbers were convinced and committed.

Susie ran out of the bathroom and whooshed by Eric, but stopped quickly a few feet beyond him. She turned around, ran to him, gave him a kiss on his mouth, and then ran out the front door.

"Susie?!" he shouted.

"I'll have to catch up with you later!" she yelled over her shoulder.

Once outside, she ran to the left, along the sidewalk outside of the restaurant – she knew the robbers would be coming from that direction. She fast-forwarded into the future and quickly devised a plan. It would work but then – without any measurable thought – she jumped forward a few feet. She felt the slight wind and heard the quiet flutter of an air conditioning wall unit drop by her as it plunged into the sidewalk, right where she was just standing.

CRASH!

Susie looked around, mystified. A few passers-by noticed this and pointed, but no one bothered to ask her if she was okay. She looked across the street and there was Dan, shrugging his shoulders before calmly walking away.

She had skipped too far forward into the future to see that coming. It flustered her, but she shook it off and returned her focus to the next nine and a half minutes. She took a deep breath, turned slightly to her right, and looked up towards the top of a 10-story apartment building across the street. Going on her tiptoes, she put her hand up over her eyes to shield the sun.

"Please don't tell me what I just saw," she said as two women walked by. "PLEASE DON'T."

The two women stopped and one asked, "Is everything okay?"

"I hope so... I think I saw a small child playing on the roof of that apartment building over there," she said, pointing to where she was looking.

The two women looked up with her. They, too, brought their hands up to shield their eyes from the sun.

"I don't see anything," said one woman.

"I don't either. The sun's right in my eyes," said the other.

"No… I'm sure of what I saw. It was a boy tiptoeing on the ledge."

"That's horrible," one woman said.

A man and his wife walked by the three of them. They, too, stopped and looked up at the top of the building – also shielding their eyes from the sun.

"What you guys lookin' at?" the man asked.

"There's a little kid at the top of that building playing on the ledge," said one of the women.

"That's awful!" the man's wife gasped. She got her phone out and dialed 9-1-1.

The police won't get here in time, Susie thought.

"I'm gonna go up there," Susie said. "Please keep an eye down here if you see him."

"Yeah, the sun's right in our eyes. It's kinda hard to see, but we'll try," the man said.

Susie ran across the street, dodging the traffic. She ran into the apartment building and let her Polarity guide her to get in the elevator and stop on the ninth floor.

Six minutes.

She ran down the hallway on the 9th floor to the fourth door on the right. Knowing it wasn't locked – and that no one was home – she opened the door, and ran to a bedroom that belonged to a toddler. She grabbed a pair of toddler shoes, pants, and several shirts. She ran into the kitchen and grabbed a roll of duct tape sitting on top of the refrigerator.

Five minutes.

Susie ran out of the apartment and to the end of the hallway to a staircase that led to the top of the building. Along the way, she grabbed a fire extinguisher that was hanging on the wall. She ran up the couple of flights of stairs to the chained door leading outside to the roof. She dropped the toddler's clothing, lifted the fire extinguisher over her head with both hands, and slammed it down on the door's chain, breaking its links.

Bursting through the door, Susie immediately squatted down and began stuffing the toddler pants with the shirts, but kept one shirt out.

Two minutes.

She duct-taped the shoes to the bottom of the pants. The top of the pants were then duct-taped to the fire extinguisher. She ran towards the building's ledge, carefully squatting so the people below wouldn't see her.

One minute.

She flung the shoes over the ledge, but kept the fire extinguisher on the roof; it acted as a counterweight to the dangling pants and shoes. This caused an instant reaction from the slowly growing crowd below – convinced that a toddler was now dangling from the ledge – although the sun still obscured their vision.

"OH!" she heard people yell in unison.

Still ducking, she wiped the fire extinguisher clean of her fingerprints with the one shirt she kept out. This caused the dangling "legs" to wiggle some and this elicited more shouting from the crowd below. She ran back inside and went back to the ninth floor apartment where she borrowed the items. With the same shirt she kept, she wiped the doorknob clean of her fingerprints, closed the door, and calmly went back downstairs. She left out the back of the building, not returning to the crowd. She used her Polarity to verify that her plan was to work…

The robbers arrived a half-block from the restaurant, but stopped because of the ever-growing crowd of onlookers in front of the restaurant. Police sirens can now be heard and their blaring was getting louder with each passing second. In a panic, the driver of the car holding the robbers attempted to U-turn in the middle of the street. Unable to see through the throng of people that was gathering, he unknowingly turned into the path of an approaching police car — causing a small fender-bender between the two vehicles. Before the robbers had a chance to react, another police car pulled up behind them. The robbers left their car behind — including their guns — and they were all captured within two days for existing, outstanding warrants.

Chapter 13 – Hell Hath No Fury

Susie gritted her teeth – she had enough of this, of not having better control over Dan. It was time to go after Dan directly and make his life a bit more complicated. She took out her phone and dialed the direct number to Officer Nemec.

"Nemec," he answered.

Susie only let her breath be heard at first.

"Hello?" he said, speaking louder.

"Uh," Susie softly spoke.

"Who is this?"

"I… I think you're the right person to talk to," Susie said, trying her best to make her voice shake a tad, to feign nervousness.

"Talk to about what?" Nemec asked.

"Those murders… the Moore family."

Susie counted to four in her head – for a dramatic pause – and then said, "I know who did it."

"Who is this?" Nemec asked.

"I'm… I'm a nobody. You can call me Linda."

"Okay, Linda. I'm interested. What do you know?"

Susie cried a little bit, but was careful to make sure it didn't sound too forced.

"It's okay… it's okay," Nemec said.

"I'm just so scared."

"Come on down to the station."

"I can't do that," Susie immediately answered, almost cutting him off.

"Why?"

"Because they… they are watching me."

"Can I meet you somewhere?" Nemec asked.

Perfect – as expected. Susie wanted Nemec to offer this. She needed bait to get Dan interested.

"O'Shay's Pub… tomorrow at 7:17 P.M."

"7:17 P.M. That's a bit specific," he said.

Susie bit her lip, realizing that her Polarity caused her to slip outside the bounds of what others would expect.

"My window of time will be very short, so I need to make sure that you're there on time and realize that minutes do matter."

"This better not be a hoax – that's a felony, you know."

"You once lost a $5 bet to Frank that you couldn't eat 20 cupcakes in 20 minutes," Susie replied confidently.

"Okay, I'm sold. I'll be there at exactly 7:17 P.M. tomorrow."

Susie hung up, but kept her phone out. She played back the video that she took of Linus, Dan, Father Crane, and Spike. She froze a single frame that showed a clear headshot of Dan. She saved it as a picture on her phone. She then walked a block up the street to an office supply store.

She entered the front doors and walked over to a set of shelves that displayed bright fluorescent colors. After a few seconds of thought, she grabbed a 100-pack of cardstock paper that was fluorescent orange on one side and white on the other. She looked at the picture on her phone and she compared it to the paper – the paper was large enough to support four pictures of Dan per page. This suited her plan.

There was a long line at the main checkout counter, but Susie ignored it. Instead, she went to the back of the store towards another checkout counter. At the moment she got there, another clerk had just manned its register. He announced over the store's intercom, "I can take people here in the back."

Susie put the stack of paper on the counter and showed the clerk the picture of Dan. "I need to copy this picture on the white side of each of these sheets... four to a sheet... for all 100 sheets."

"Oh, I'm not sure if our copier can print from your phone."

Susie paused for two seconds and responded, "It can. That's the newest Kriytol copier. We just need to sync our Bluetooth."

She had only played out 27 scenarios before realizing that it would take at least another eighteen minutes for the clerk to get help from a manager who would tell him the same thing. It was just easier – and far faster – to tell him what he was going to know anyway.

"I would have never guessed – you sure know your copiers," he said.

"It's a long story."

*   *   *

Dan stood, leaning on a building not too far away from where the air conditioner almost landed on Susie. There was a slim chance it would have killed her, but he was delighted to see her reaction. The absence of Father Crane and Spike greatly simplified his life. It was a relief.

"I wonder what *She's* up to," he said quietly.

Dan used his Polarity to follow her movements. She was in a nearby office supply store writing on hundreds of white cards with fluorescent orange backsides. Each message she wrote was different.

Looking for a good time? Come to O'Shay's Pub tonight! said one.

You're my kind of girl. Come to O'Shay's tonight and see me, said another.

I'm not gay but I am curious. I'll see you at O'Shay's tomorrow night, said yet another.

It was odd that this last card said tomorrow night instead of simply "tonight" like the first two. He looked at the 28 she had already completed and they all had similar messages – with the only obvious variation being an indication of *when* to go to this place, O'Shay's. Dan then rewound time to catch the phone call that Susie had with Nemec. Was she was trying to get people to come to O'Shay's tomorrow night for her meeting with Nemec?

She's trying to get people to go there. She thinks she'll be safer in a more crowded place, he thought.

This made sense – O'Shay's was never really busy. Dan looked into the past 40 nights in a row and the place was mostly empty every night. It would go out of business in three months. He also reasoned that the differences in time stated on the cards were to account for the time it would take for the cards to get to people – some would get there today and some would get to them tomorrow. When they eventually got to the right people, it would influence them to all go there tomorrow night. Why she used his face on these cards was obvious to him: He was a good-looking guy and he was a great model to catch the attention of women and men alike.

Too easy.

Dan fast-forwarded time to tomorrow night to confirm his thoughts about Susie's plan: Sure enough, O'Shay's pub would be crowded. He then looked ahead three hours from now – Susie would be carrying a hefty bag of these cards. One card would be put under a windshield wiper blade of a randomly parked car.

The owner would see it six hours later and discard it to the ground. A three-year-old child will pick it up a half hour later. A half hour after that, the child's mother will take it and throw it on the ground again – only to be continually picked up and dropped by a few more people over the course of many hours. The card eventually ended up in the trash can for good. That particular card was a decoy, a convoluted distraction – Susie had 399 more cards to go.

What a noob. She's not very good at setting up decoys, he thought.

Just to be certain he was reading things correctly, he followed that first card again. However, this time Susie put the card under the windshield wiper of a different car – Susie was mixing things up on him. He groaned, brimming with anger. He went forward in time, again and again – each time the fate of the first card was different. He still had 399 cards to go.

God, I hate her.

Dan was worried. It would take Susie twenty hours or so to place all 400 cards around the city. He was at an impasse. He had to continue his mission to destroy the evidence against Harold but, at the same time, he couldn't ignore what Susie was doing. The only way he could be certain as to where the cards would end up would be when she actually placed them in real time. He decided he would only follow the first 50 of the cards to their ends. If any of them produced something of interest then he would take action. However, if none of them did then he would just let the rest go. It was a calculated risk.

Dan was certain that he could counter whatever she had planned for him the split second before it would unfold – whatever it could be. Besides, if Susie did indeed spend the next 20 or more hours distributing these cards, then she would certainly be too exhausted to adequately defend herself when she would meet Nemec – and probably for another day afterwards. She was killing herself and he really didn't have to do anything.

Susie wasn't trying to fill O'Shay's with people for her protection – the most probable plan was that Susie wanted Dan to waste the same 20 or more hours following him, so he could be just as exhausted.

Through his Polarity, Dan followed Susie for the next two hours in real time – until the first 50 cards were actually passed out. He saw her place each card in various spots around the city – some she even threw directly into garbage cans. He fast-forwarded time with each and every one of them: Each ended up in the landfill, chewed by animal, or biodegraded over the next several months. They were harmless.

He was right – she wanted him to waste his time on her, to make him just as exhausted as she would become. It was clever to some extent, but he wasn't going to fall for it any longer. He decided to retire for the night. Letting her continue passing out those cards was the best way he could beat her. Let her make herself exhausted. Let her think she was fooling him.

*   *   *

Through the night and through the next day Susie was still distributing the fluorescent orange cards that sported Dan's picture on one side and a customized note on the other. She kept herself on a constant feed of black coffee. It was nearing 7 P.M. She was three blocks away from O'Shay's and she only had one card left to distribute. She knelt down to tie her shoe, placing the card Dan-side-up on the sidewalk. She quickly took a few steps forward and stopped to look across the street aimlessly. Within a few seconds, two women turned a corner heading towards her. One noticed the card on the sidewalk and bent over to pick it up.

"This guy looks familiar," she said to the other girl.

"Oh?" the other girl said.

"He looks like that guy that Renee dated for those months… you know THAT guy."

"THAT guy?" she said wide-eyed, grabbing the picture. "Yeah, it does look like him. Let's call her."

The two women continued walking. Susie then walked to O'Shay's – getting through the front doors at exactly 7:17 P.M. She scanned the room. The place was full and very loud. Officer Nemec was sitting at a table in the middle of the floor wearing plain clothes. Susie walked over to him and sat down, facing the front entrance.

He looked up and said, "Are you…"

"I'm Linda," Susie said, raising her voice over the ambient chatter.

"Well, I hope I can help you," Nemec half-yelled.

Susie leaned closer to him and said, "I wanted to choose a place that had a lot of people in it… to keep lots of witnesses if something bad were to happen… to me."

Nemec raised his eyebrows and looked around, "Well, you chose the wrong place… well, normally this place is a ghost town. This place is packed tonight – very oddly, it's mostly women. It's VERY loud, too."

Susie's face was blank.

"Are you okay? You look really tired," Nemec asked.

She wobbled her head, answering, "Yeah. I haven't slept in over a day."

A waiter came up to their table, asking Susie, "Can I get you anything?!"

"Coffee! Black!" Susie shouted.

"Sure thing!" the waiter said and walked away.

"Well, I've gotta go to the bathroom. Excuse me," Nemec said, getting up from his chair.

Susie watched Nemec weave his way through the multitude of women and make his way into the bathroom. The second the bathroom door closed, she turned her head to the entrance of the pub. Dan walked in. Her eyes met his. With each step Dan took into the pub, the noise level of the chatter went progressively down. By the time he got to Susie's table, it was almost dead quiet. Dan sat down, leaned back, and put his hands behind his head – apparently not noticing the change in atmosphere.

"Hello, babe," he said.

Susie didn't respond.

"I see *You* were busy for the past day and night... wasting *Your* time," he cackled.

Susie's head dipped down and she kept silent.

"I'm not going to let *You* get to Nemec. I've got a plan and *You're* too mentally dead to keep up with me," he said, with a cocky smile.

"Well, *You're* right," Susie finally said.

"Yes – I am right. *You* don't have any help. Just give up on me and let Harold go. *You* lost this one."

"I won't. *Your* overconfidence and *Your* smug laziness is the best help I can get."

"What? Those stupid orange cards *You* were passing out? Harmless. I stopped caring about them at around 50. *You* wanted me to follow *You* for all 400 just to waste my time... wasn't going to happen. I had other things to do."

Susie raised an eyebrow.

"What? Wondering why I told *You* how far I went?" Dan leaned in towards her and continued, "I want *You* to know just how incompetent *You* are. *You* aren't as good as *You* think."

"Oh?"

"I'm glad *You're* still alive. This is fun watching *You* try so hard."

"The first 280 were decoys. The last 120 were legitimate."

Dan's body immediately tensed. He blinked a few times. He slowly looked around the room. Everywhere he looked, there were women looking directly at him. All of them had sharp, fermented anger dripping from their faces. Some were holding those same fluorescent orange cards in their hands. Dan's breathing hastened, nearing panic.

"I invited 120 of *Your* closest friends… well, ex-girlfriends really. Oh and those two ex-boyfriends… and I really didn't peg *You* as bisexual. But, yeah, they're here, too."

The front door opened and a group of women – all holding fluorescent orange cards – entered the tightly packed room and immediately put their attention on Dan.

Susie stood up and whispered into Dan's ear, "And there are 22 more to come. I need some sleep. I think *You* know what kind of impact *You've* had on their lives and they would like to show *You* some impact, too. Of course, for them, this was serendipitous. For *You*, however, it's just unfortunate."

Dan was motionless. Susie began crying inconsolably, "Dan… you said you loved me!" she shouted, covering her face with her hands. "You were my only love, my first love, and you just USED ME!"

The audience was silent, captivated. Susie started a slapping motion at Dan. Instinctively, Dan grabbed her wrist before her hand struck his face.

"OH NO YOU JUST DIDN'T!" one woman yelled – followed by another and another and another.

Dan looked around and cowered as three women immediately attacked him. One broke her beer mug over his head as he was brought to the floor. More women joined the foray – clawing, kicking, punching, pulling out chunks of his hair – all in the name of 120 pawns unknowingly used in the past for Dan's bidding and amusement. Dan was quickly under an ever-growing dog pile of distilled wrath as Susie quietly left.

Dan would live, but he would be in the hospital for almost two days. Dan was out of the equation for now and this would provide some time for Father Crane to recover.

*   *   *

Susie met Spike the next day in a parking lot of a sports arena. A basketball game was going on inside the arena – the lot was full and no one else was around. Susie was behind the bed of a pickup truck, resting her arms on its bed's sidewalls. Spike had crutches, but opted to sit on the hood of one of the cars while he smoked.

"A kid danglin' from the ledge of building… pretty clever, but it was too close of a call," said Spike.

"You seemed pretty casual about it when we talked on the phone. Why are you worried now?"

Spike gasped, "I didn't predict you were going to kiss the bloke… that made it too close with that air conditioner droppin' – it was supposed to miss you by a mile."

Susie didn't expect she was going to kiss Eric either – it was the only thing that came to mind when she had to leave him in such a hurry. She beamed thinking about it and she played back that moment dozens of times, exactly as it happened – a rare blessing from her Polarity, given all of the curses it imposed.

"I'm supposed to be unpredictable, right?"

"Yeah, yeah… ya did good," he said, his cigarette hanging out of his mouth. "And the bringin' the crowd together like that… I saw it comin' but it was still quite a show. And to have this end with them all bein' arrested – I didn't see that comin', strangely."

"I did after I kissed Eric… the five second delay caused the police sirens to be delayed by five seconds – and that was all it

190

took for them to decide to turn down that street and then be cornered."

"Kissin' him was foolish, I'm afraid. Timin' is everything. Time is nothin'. Be a bit more careful. Mistakes like that are easy for *Them* to pounce on. You 'ave some talent with your Polarity, but your use of it is just ghastly sometimes."

"About Eric or anyone for that matter… Tell me how it's possible to… to be just a little human with my full Polarity… to not be alone forever. Tell me how it's possible without putting their lives in danger because of *Them*."

Spike took a long drag of his cigarette, "Well, this fight *We* have with *Them* – it's pretty overwhelmin' for both sides. 99% or so of what either side does is a distraction, a decoy – to throw the other side off to waste the other side's time… just like those cards you 'anded out yesterday and the day before – that was brilliant, by the way."

Susie was unmoved by his compliment.

Spike nodded and followed, "So with that 99%, you can do pretty much whatever you want just as long as your actions indicate that you aren't personally attached to it. Dan didn't waste *His* time with the remainin' cards you passed out because *He* probably felt it was a waste of *His* time."

"But the point is… I *want* to have that personal attachment with someone someday," said Susie.

"Flings are a better idea – *They* love the idea of you wastin' your time with someone and it usually isn't worth the risk for *Them* to go after that person."

"I guess there's no chance or hope for something a little more meaningful."

"Oh there is, you just can't really show it. Remember that Polarity doesn't allow *Us* to read people's minds – with it you can only deduce in what is witnessed through sight, sound, and touch. Smell, by the way, is not included… Father Crane can go over the biology of the brain with you some time, if you can keep awake through it."

"I can love someone, but I can't show it? What's the point? How can I be expected to blend in and act human if I can't be human?"

Spike shook his head and flicked his spent cigarette away, "You can show it but you 'ave to be careful to make it appear that it's just a decoy. There's a very fine line."

"I... I don't want to think that all of my relationships are nothing more than decoys that will last less than a day – a fling, just like you said."

"God, I wish Father Crane were 'ere to explain this better," Spike said putting his hand on his forehead. "You should always be creatin' decoys. Some are used for short-term plans – like those cards you passed out – while others are used for long-term plans. You can have long-term decoys."

"How will I know what long-term plans I need to use decoys for?"

"THAT'S THE BEAUTY OF IT! *They* won't know either. *They* won't know why you do everythin' you do. *They* will get suspicious about everythin' but will do *Their* best to decide what's real and what's a decoy. You can make up whatever you want – and it will surely piss *Them* off pretty quickly. I'm certain Dan was pretty ruffled at 'aving to follow you just through those first 50 cards."

"Yeah, *He* was," she grinned.

"The other thing is that – whatever you do – you cannot use your Polarity at all for things like this. *They* are very attuned towards detectin' small disturbances in what should be. If *They* detect that you're changin' the future – however slight – to protect someone then *They* will pick up on that and know what your true intentions are."

Susie stared ahead in thought to digest what this meant for her. She could be with Eric, but she couldn't make it look like he genuinely meant anything to her. Furthermore, she couldn't use her Polarity on him at all.

Spike reached in his pants' pocket for his pack of cigarettes, "Oh...," he said, trying to reach in his pocket without moving his injured ankle too much, "...forget about that Eric fella – you're done. *We* 'ave to assume *They* are monitorin' *Our* conversation at this very moment. There's no way you can pass him off as a decoy."

"Yeah, that's no problem."

Spike cocked his head back and brought his hands up into the air, "That's it? I thought you were practically head over heels for 'im."

"Well, I was caught up in the moment and I really don't think he's my type – he's not careful enough with his money, he doesn't seem to be motivated to do anything with his life... he's better suited for someone else. I'm sure he'd be fun for a bit, but he's not a keeper."

"Suit yourself... you're takin' this much better than I...," Spike trailed off, stared pensively at Susie for a few seconds, and raised his eyebrows.

Susie locked her eyes on Spike, motionless – not so much as blinking. Of course, she wanted to be with Eric, but she had to have Spike play along. She couldn't give him any overt clues towards her desire – just in case *They* were watching this conversation. Spike drew a new cigarette from the pack, put it in his mouth, and narrowed his eyes a little. He took out his lighter, but stopped short of lighting his cigarette. He stared at her for a few seconds more – she was still motionless. He finally went back into motion and lit his cigarette, cracking a brief smile.

"You... you're very well-suited for your Polarity."

"Thank you."

"One last thing."

"Yes?"

"Remember that even decoys can be mistaken as being *real* from time to time. If other people are involved, *They* may still hurt those people if *They* feel it's worth the time and risk. Killin' Frank's family took careful plannin' and look where it is now for *Them*. It's a huge mess."

"Oh… okay," she replied, caught up in the thought of keeping Eric.

Spike started to slide off the car's hood. He shuddered in pain as he grabbed his crutches and positioned them under his armpits.

"Well, I best be off. Linus is finishin' *His* workout and *He'll* be out to kill me today – just as *He* does every day."

"Can I help?"

Spike shook his head, "No – not under any circumstances. Keep your focus on what Father Crane instructed. I can handle Linus – it's a bit taskin', but I can manage."

Chapter 14 – Harold's Death?

It was Friday morning. Vinny sat on a chair in his supervisor's office, waiting for her to return with his fate regarding the Mrs. Davis shooting. Eddie sat to his right. Vinny hunched forward with both elbows planted on his knees and his face buried in his palms. He gently rocked back and forth. He could hear Eddie biting his nails.

"You bored, Eddie?" Vinny asked.

"A little. Why?"

"You always bite your nails when you're bored. Aren't you nervous?"

"About what?"

Vinny sat up and looked at Eddie. "About what... About what...," Vinny said quietly, shaking his head.

"Vinny, how many times do I gotta tell you that this wasn't your fault: The dog was assaulting me, we took every measure to ask the owner to get control of the dog, your weapon was already drawn, and – by the way the logic goes – Mrs. Davis was going to let the dog attack me again."

"You seem so sure," Vinny replied feebly, hanging his head.

Eddie rolled up his sleeves and revealed large bandages covering his forearms. "Look at this Vinny," he said. "I've got stitches up and down my arms because of that dog. It would've killed me if it had the chance."

"I... I just can't believe I killed someone."

"It ain't an easy thing to live with," Eddie said.

"I just thought if I was going to kill someone – ever – it would be a criminal... not some poor old woman."

Eddie shook his head, but didn't say anything.

"Eddie, I'm just amazed at how calm you are at this."

"This is pretty plain and simple for me, Vinny – you didn't have a choice."

Vinny heard footsteps behind him approaching; their supervisor walked into the office.

"Gentlemen, I presume you're Agents Lagetti and Kerwin?" she asked.

The two men stood up.

"I'm Special Agent Willis – I'm still new here, so please be a bit patient with me."

"Not a problem, ma'am," Eddie said.

They all shook hands before Willis sat behind her desk, facing the men. Eddie and Vinny sat down as Willis rifled through several papers on her desk. Vinny couldn't help but notice that she looked young, maybe thirty-years-old – but it was hard to tell through her glasses and bunned-up light brown hair.

"Hmm... okay, Agent Lagetti?" she said, looking down at her papers and then at Eddie.

Eddie pointed at Vinny.

Vinny raised his hand up. "That's me."

"Oh, sorry... In most cases like this, we put you on administrative leave with pay until everything can be sorted out. Most cases that end tragically like this, for example – accidentally shooting a civilian in a crowd when chasing after a perp or an unsub – we would have to go through interviews of all the witnesses and collect quite a bit of other evidence to make an unbiased assessment. We've looked this over..."

Vinny closed his eyes.

"And we've decided to keep you active. Agent Kerwin here was the only witness to talk to and all of the evidence points to a tragedy that wasn't your fault – you acted in accordance with protocol. However, you are required to undergo several counseling sessions and we will give you the option to take a paid leave of absence to give you... time. These things are never easy."

"No... no I can't take leave," he said somberly, looking up towards Willis. "I'd drive myself nuts thinking about this with nothing else to do."

Willis sat back in her chair, "Are you sure?"

"Yeah... yeah I'm sure."

"I am required to follow-up with you at least once a week towards the progress of your counseling," she said.

"Sure," Vinny replied.

Willis stood up and said, "Well then, there's nothing more to discuss for now."

Vinny and Eddie stood up.

"You gentlemen have a good day."

*   *   *

Harold was sitting on a dark leather couch in his office at the Beytern headquarters building, sipping some wine. He admired the recent renovations that extended his old office; it now occupied the entire top floor. The board of Beytern was very happy with Harold at its helm – it was now in the Fortune 5 when it wasn't even in the Fortune 500 eight years ago. He again sipped his wine, prideful at how adept he was at making the right decisions for his company. He was even more prideful for making his decisions look like sound judgment – and not give any hint that they came from his Polarity.

His office was filled with expensive scotches, handcrafted furniture, antique map collections, special cheeses flown in weekly from Europe, and several gold-plated trashcans. He didn't waste his Polarity on what others thought of it – no one questioned his purchases because no one questioned his decisions; he was always right. However, when it came to priorities, Beytern was always a distant second – the will of *Us* always came first.

He looked at his gold watch – it was 2:23 P.M. Sully was going to call now. He walked over to his desk.

RING RING

"This is Harold," he answered.

"Hey Harold, this is Sully from the airplane."

"Oh hey, Sully! How are you?!"

Sully chuckled, "Doin' fantastic. I'm just callin' ya like ya asked me to."

"Yes, thank you for doing so. Are you still in town?"

"I sure am – through Monday mornin'."

"If it's not any trouble, I've got to cut this call short – but I'd like you to stop by here for lunch tomorrow, if you can. I realize that tomorrow is Saturday, but I'd sure like to have some of your time."

"I can do that. What's the subject?" Sully asked.

"A business idea."

"Hey, I'd like that."

"Is 11 A.M. too early for you? I like to eat sooner in the day."

"Ha! I do, too! There's not as much traffic on the road…"

"…and you always have the best parking when you get to lunch," Harold continued.

"…and you never have to wait to be served!" Sully laughed.

"Just stop by my office. I'll see you tomorrow," Harold said.

"See ya!"

Harold hung up and rolled his eyes – Sully was a little too rough around the edges for him to tolerate, but Sully's money would make just about anything tolerable for him. He walked over to his large, solid teak desk to review his notes. Two dozen pages – each completely covered with scribbles in different ink colors – canvassed his desk. The pages were placed flush, on-edge against each other – a necessity to keep his train of thought.

He looked at his watch again and thought, *Time to meet with Jennifer*.

Harold went to the center of his office to the elevator – it was always there because it was for his personal use only. He went down to the building's service basement and, among the many pipes and valves, stood Jennifer. Harold approached her but stopped some distance away.

"Why did you get rid of your long, beautiful, blonde hair?" Harold asked.

"I got tired of the men hitting on me. It was becoming difficult to keep track of *Them*. Besides, I still have the face," she said, pointing at her face.

"You ever thought getting fat or getting a breast reduction?"

"This was easier," Jennifer said with a tinge of aggravation.

"You're a little more uptight than you usually are. Why?"

Jennifer shifted her head to her left, "Well… you're pulling me from a mission that I've been working very hard to contain. I'm just worried that…"

"No need to worry," Harold interrupted. "The software convention you were targeting will no longer get the H1N1 virus outbreak."

"No?"

"No… they are now – at this very minute – being exposed to the H5N1 bird flu. I handled it personally through some other means. *They* were caught off-guard."

Jennifer smiled, "And more people will die – the effect will be huge."

Harold nodded and smiled proudly, "Profound. Public outcry will be huge, millions will be poured into research, and an effective vaccine will be developed six months sooner – we'll save thousands of lives."

Jennifer lowered her head, flaring her nostrils.

"Don't worry Jennifer – I was certain your plan would have worked. This other plan was a last minute thing so I could free you up."

"Okay… what do you need me to do?"

"I need you to kill me in a manner of speaking. Get the rumor out on social media, news outlets, and so on. I need to be dead – on a global scale – by 11 A.M. tomorrow morning," Harold said.

"You got it."

The two walked away from each other.

Harold went back up to his office. He took a fresh sheet of paper from his desk's drawer and aligned it edge-on against a couple of his existing note-ridden papers. He illegibly wrote 'SULLY' in the middle of the sheet. Then, as quickly as he could move the pen, he drew hundreds of lines connecting this word to other notes on the other sheets of papers. His hand trembled with delight as he wrote illegible paragraphs of thoughts to accompany several of these connecting lines.

He didn't go home that night and slept no more than four broken hours. His office had its own shower and wardrobe, so continuing into the next day was seamless. Throughout the morning, he continued cramming notes onto the single page – and as usual, different colors of inks were used so he could write over existing notes without harming their content. The once-new sheet of paper was now completely coated with ink.

Harold finally put his pen down – he went through several pens that night. He stood up and looked down at the sheets of notes covering his desktop. From his tired face emerged a broad smile. "God, I'm good," he said with his arms out-stretched.

He turned his head to the right and briefly glanced at his emails; they had been piling up since he last talked with Jennifer. There were 427 new messages. Using his Polarity, he read them in a matter of minutes.

"All right. Let's just do this," he grumbled.

He systematically replied to each and every one of his emails over the next two and a half hours. He answered all emails personally – it didn't matter if they were from the lowest level Beytern employee. Harold was very popular in this regard. Every employee knew they could reach out to him – he would respond within a day. It gave his employees a feeling that he was with them no matter what. He didn't particularly like responding to all of his emails each day, but this tactic kept his employees closer to him. Unions were less likely to strike and Harold's decisions were more likely to be followed without question.

He finished his last email just as 11 A.M. hit. His desk phone rang and he answered via speakerphone.

"Hello, sir. Mr. Sullivan is here to see you," a woman's voice said.

"Thank you, Jane. Please send him up," Harold responded.

Harold hung up and turned his attention to his computer screen. He opened various websites – all reporting in one way or another that Harold I. McGee, the CEO of Beytern, died. Some said he committed suicide, some said he had a heart attack, and one even said that he was killed by a drunk clown.

"Ha! A drunk clown," Harold laughed, beating down on his desk. "Oh Jennifer, that was good!"

He received a text from Jennifer.

I thought you'd like that one, it read.

The elevator doors opened and Sully emerged. Harold looked up at him and motioned him to come over towards his desk.

"Hey, Sully! Please come and sit down!"

Sully slowly walked through the thick opulence of Harold's massive office. His head turned frequently at the various artifacts that adorned the walls and many display tables.

"This is one nice office, Harold," Sully said as he neared Harold's desk.

"Life is beautiful and you should treat it beautifully."

"I agree," Sully replied extending his hand to Harold.

Harold stood up and shook Sully's hand.

"I'm sorry if I appear a little disheveled… apparently the world thinks I'm dead."

"What?" Sully asked.

Harold motioned Sully to come around to his side of the desk. Sully walked around and Harold began clicking through the many screens on his computer.

"Heh… you really are dead, aren't ya?" he chuckled.

"This one says a drunk clown killed me," Harold said, showing the website to Sully.

Sully laughed and slapped his knee a few times, "My God! Who comes up with this stuff?! This is a hoot!"

"It's one of those 'Why me?' moments," Harold chuckled, shaking his head.

"What can ya do?" Sully asked rhetorically.

"Well I have to do something – our stock price is dropping in weekend trading. It's already down 7%."

Sully face fell pale. "Say what?" he gasped.

He lost $6 million, Harold thought.

"Yeah," Harold continued, "An Internet prank that's taken a life of its own… I've been trying to put out this fire all morning.

I've called news outlets to let them know that I'm alive... What a weird conversation that is."

Harold clicked to CNN's website and refreshed it. A headline read, *BEYTERN CEO IS ALIVE – INTERNET HOAX GONE WILD.*

"There... it only took all of two hours for them to finally get it."

"What kind of damage will this do?" Sully asked.

"Probably none. These things happen from time to time – mostly with celebrities."

The stock price will take three weeks to fully recover.

"Isn't that kind of thing illegal?" Sully asked, fixated on Harold's computer screen.

"It doesn't really matter. Who knows where these things start? This was probably just a few people who made me dead. Can you imagine what it would be like if a government was behind it – like the U.S., China, or Russia? They could convince the world of anything because whatever they say would be bombarded six ways from Sunday."

"It's scary," Sully said, raising his eyebrows.

Harold nodded, "Just imagine the power that comes with this... if it were possible for just a few people to do it."

"No kiddin'."

"Our stock price dropped 7% in a flash because of this silly incident. I wonder what kind of damage would be done if it were something more serious – like an allegation of environmental pollution or corruption."

Sully's eyes were still locked on Harold's computer screen, "I'm surprised no one's doin' this to their advantage."

"How so?"

"I dunno... like sayin' that a company invented something – like a cure for some disease – and the stock prices would rise."

Harold sat back in his chair and put his hands behind his head. "It would be interesting if someone had this kind of power, but used it for more valiant causes."

"Like what?"

"You could steer entire populations of people towards one cause. For example, Crohn's disease runs in my family but there's roughly forty different organizations trying to find a cure. None of these organizations has enough money to make any progress because all of the money is split forty different directions. Politics and advertising keeps the inefficiencies in place. But with a power like this, you could choose one of those organizations and steer the entire world towards it."

"Hmm, my wife has Crohn's disease – that's interesting. But don't you think the truth will come out eventually?"

"It's hard to say. I wonder how many people out there will continue to think I'm dead for the next year or more. The impact is there and the world seems to believe whatever they see on the Internet without so much of ten seconds of research. If this were done on a larger scale, there's no telling how much power you could wield."

"Well, you also don't want to be caught with your hand in the cookie jar."

Harold furrowed his brow, "Oh no, Sully, we at Beytern would never do anything like this. It's unethical and unnecessary. We have too many people watching us."

Sully looked at Harold and smirked, "Well I wasn't implyin' that Beytern do this."

Harold closed his eyes and laughed.

"What?" Sully asked.

Harold shook his head, "Ah, never mind."

Sully smiled, "What?"

"Well there is a way to make this happen – my mind wanders from time to time. I get some really shady people from questionable organizations pushing ideas like this to me."

Sully stood up straight, "I'm curious."

"Forget it. There isn't a cause that's valiant enough to overcome the questions of ethics. Besides, everything is far too expensive."

"Aw… all right."

Harold looked at his watch, "Oh, lunch… do you mind if we eat up here? I have to make sure that all will be well in putting out this hoax. I can order food up here."

"Not a problem."

For the next hour, Harold and Sully had lunch in his office. There was nothing Sully said that Harold didn't already know long in advance.

"I can tell ya that I've done well for myself, but what really matters is family. No amount of money can replace them. I'm a blessed man," Sully said.

"I completely agree."

"I know I won't live forever. I'm gonna leave my wife and kids everything. They've made me feel richer than any amount of money could ever make me feel."

Harold grabbed a framed picture from his desk and said, "My son, Garrett, means everything to me, too."

"He gonna follow in your footsteps?"

"Nah. And you know… I really don't want him to. He's a brilliant kid. He'll find his own way."

"You married?"

Harold averted his eyes and said, "No. My wife died a few years back."

Sully put his hand on Harold's shoulder, "I'm sorry. I truly am. My wife is my best friend and I would be devastated without her."

"I appreciate that. She was my best friend, too."

Harold looked at his watch, "Well, I'm going to have to move on to other things. We never had a chance to talk business – I'm sorry."

"That's all right. After all, you've been a bit busy trying to prove you're alive."

"We'll have to get together again sometime. Please reach out to me if you're in town. It's hard to make friends with my lonely job."

"Absolutely," Sully said, extending his hand.

Harold grabbed Sully's hand with both of his and firmly shook his hand. He then gave Sully a brief hug – and Sully reciprocated.

"Take care and have a good weekend."

"You, too. I'll find my way out. Don't worry about me," Sully said and winked.

Harold watched Sully get into the elevator and leave. As soon as the elevator's doors closed, he took out his phone and crafted a text to Jennifer, *Take care of his family. Leave his wife in a state of constant reminder for him. Need this by next Monday no later than noon.*

Consider it done, she replied.

Chapter 15 – A Duel

It was Sunday morning. Susie was in a hotel room, lying on her bed, looking up at the ceiling while she debated her next move against Dan and Harold. The car and the two thugs were still on course to link Harold to the crimes by the police.

She looked into Dan at the present. She laughed – Dan was missing patches of hair and was forced to wear a baseball cap. He couldn't shave his head because it had several lines of stitches sewn into it. Bumps and bruises covered his body. Susie relaxed a little knowing that this would make Dan's life a bit more difficult.

She received a text from Father Crane, *I can move around somewhat, but my help will be limited.*

This was better than nothing. Even though Dan would be hindered, she still had Linus in the mix. Her Polarity showed that Linus spent all of his time either working out or setting up death traps for Spike. What was even more bizarre was that Linus never altered his plans – he never had any decoys. It was exceptionally easy to predict his movements. Spike had no trouble evading him.

Then there was Eric – she grinned. Spike's advice to avoid her Polarity to track Eric was mostly adhered to – this was deeply reinforced with her experience with her sister's now deceased boyfriend. She tried to hold her Polarity back so she wouldn't see him, but she couldn't keep complete control over it – she would see glimpses of where he was and what he was doing.

I wish I could just forget about him.

She couldn't get enough of him and the small moments she had with him cruelly teased her. He was easy-going and she reflexively relaxed when she saw him through her Polarity. There were serious issues in his life and – if it weren't for her Polarity – she would have never known it, based on his demeanor. He was comfortable. Being near him made her feel uncomfortably comfortable. She imagined him being next to her in bed, smiling at her. She could almost see his head next to hers – spending a lazy, cozy day together.

She sat up in bed, looking forward – it dawned on her: All of the methodical constraints she put in her life kept her from ever having a chance of feeling this. Her life was nothing more than self-imposed, sustained, controlled stress – all in the name of preventing unpredictable stress that would naturally come along. It wasn't just a matter of "live a little" – it was a matter of actually feeling good about life.

She looked at her purse sitting on the nightstand next to her. She grabbed it and took out her small accounting ledger. The ledger kept all of her budget entries for every transaction she made up until about four months ago – shortly before Dan put her on that doomed airplane. Some entries had small errors that, after having been detected, were scratched out and written with the correct values – complete with many exclamation points and underlining.

Dear God. I was actually yelling at myself for making simple errors.

She tossed her ledger onto the floor and took a deep breath. Vinny and Eddie would be stopping by in less than ten minutes. Dan had given them an anonymous tip – he just wanted to keep her moving. It was still the late morning and she would prefer to rest longer and to spend more time thinking about Eric.

*   *   *

"I betcha no one will be there," Eddie said to Vinny as they walked up to Susie's hotel room.

"I don't care. I didn't sleep well last night," Vinny said softly.

Eddie stopped a few feet from the door and grabbed Vinny's shoulder. "Hey, snap out of it. You gotta have some thicker skin for this job."

Vinny sighed, "I don't think there is anything that could be adequately done to prepare anyone for that. Give me a little time, huh? In a way, I envy you."

"Why's that?"

"You're cold. You've felt cold since the day I met you."

"I'm not as cold as you think. It's just a matter of balancing care and apathy," Eddie said and then popped some pills in his mouth.

Vinny saw Eddie as a time bomb waiting to go off. Four failed marriages, kids that he never sees, and a career filled with violence and tragedy – all of these took a continual toll on him although he rarely talked about them. Eddie seemed to turn to apathy whenever he could.

"You gonna focus?" Eddie asked.

"Yeah, yeah… Who knows? She could be here, right?" Vinny said.

"I'm not counting on it."

Eddie knocked at the door – upon doing so, both of them instinctively stepped to the sides of the door so the peephole wouldn't give their identities away.

KNOCK KNOCK KNOCK

They stood waiting. While they waited, Vinny checked his email on his phone.

KNOCK KNOCK KNOCK

Still no answer.

"Well, they found your gun, Eddie."

"What now?" he asked, rubbing his temples.

"Email was forwarded to me by the boss – your gun you threw to Frank was used in a string of robberies yesterday."

"Jesus," Eddie closed his eyes as Vinny continued to read the email.

"Testimonies by witnesses show that all but the last robbery was done by the same masked man – all fit the body shape profile of Frank. However, the last robbery was done by a teenage boy who is the same size, shape, and race of Frank. Get this: The teenager told police that he was given the gun by someone who fits Frank's description."

"Frank robs a few places and pins them all on this boy. Pretty clever."

"What? Do you actually admire what Frank did?" Vinny asked.

"To a degree, yeah… it was pretty clever," Eddie said as he stopped short of knocking the door again, "Look, the girl's not here. We can't open the door without a warrant. Twenty bucks says that she left without checking out."

"Hmm."

"Maybe it's just our bad luck that she's never around," Eddie said.

"No… no I don't think so anymore," Vinny said. "I'm beginning to think she is truly avoiding people. This has gone on too long. She knows something. And everything that's happened to Frank... there's something else going on. She has to know something."

Eddie chuckled, "So now you want to get her? A minute ago you didn't seem to care."

"I always care. I don't believe in apathy."

"Apathy is great when it's used properly. Try it sometime. It keeps you out of trouble. It keeps you numb – you only care about the things you need to care about."

"That's the easy way out. Forget it," Vinny said.

"All right. Fine. I'll play along with you a little on this. Where do ya wanna go next?"

"Well, we go back to the police station and see what they've found and what kinds of leads they have."

Eddie smirked, "They're gonna love seeing us again."

"I ruined their flash drive – I expect them to still be upset. But, as you said, it wasn't my fault and we have a job to do."

*   *   *

Susie, across the street from the hotel, watched Vinny and Eddie drive away in their car. She foresaw them getting to the police station and leaving without any surprises – specifically no damage to the thugs' getaway car, which was still being held in the impound lot. The car was scheduled to be moved to a police headquarters lot later that day – Susie saw no issue with this either. The car would get there safely.

"It's time to go on the offensive," Father Crane said, calling out from behind her.

Susie turned around. Father Crane was standing upright and was just as stoic as ever – no sign that he had broken ribs, had been stabbed twelve times, or that his left ear was stitched back onto his head.

"Harold has too much confidence in Dan – even with Dan's injuries," he said.

"What should I do?"

"Kill Dan."

Susie gulped.

"Do it. Do it or *He* will continue doing *Their* will, *Their* bidding."

Susie remained motionless.

Father Crane exhaled and wiped his brow. "Dan will directly kill at least a hundred people over the next two months. *He* will indirectly kill another two hundred more – mostly the elderly for the plots *He* is to be involved in once this little thing with Harold's mess is over. *He* will do so and enjoy it. *He* will enjoy it because *He* is addicted to destruction. *He* will be exalted by *Them* for the pain *He* will cause and the overcorrection mankind will impose to hastily improve itself."

"Isn't there…"

"There is NO ONE ELSE… except you," he said and then took a knee on the sidewalk. "For every plan that I devise, not only does *He* nullify it but – more often than not – *He* counters it with my demise. *He* is injured, but not as badly as I am. The pain from my wounds… the pain is very distracting."

"What about…"

"The rest of *Us* in the area are busy – barely holding on – to undo some of *Their* major movements that have been in progress. Do you really want that overpass to collapse? Do you really want that chemical plant to explode? Do you really want that terrorist group to finally get their nerve gas?"

Susie shook her head – she saw all of these plots, and many more, in progress. "*We* have to be more optimistic or, at least, less pessimistic."

"Optimism… Pessimism… these are words invented by people who did not like the word 'realism'. *We* are dealing with reality. Fictional outlooks will not impede *Their* decisions to harm others."

"But can't *We*...," Susie began.

Father Crane interrupted, "YOU are it. Linus is busy with Spike – it is pretty clear that is why *He* is here. Harold is always busy with something, but *He* is pretty detached from Dan. It is just you and Dan."

"I... I can't do it. I can't kill someone even though I already have. I can't knowingly and willfully do it."

Father Crane slowly stood up, grimacing. "Well...," he said, pausing briefly to breathe, "...this was a waste of *Our* time. I cannot convince you of what you must experience."

"Are you angry with me?" Susie asked.

"No. Anger is nothing more than convincing oneself into believing that force is a rational option. I cannot force you to do this."

He started to walk away. Susie followed him. "You can't just walk away."

"Walking is a pretty generous term... it is really more of a hobble," he said over his shoulder.

"Aren't you going to help me with Dan?"

"By killing *Him*, yes – and I am going it alone."

"I thought you said that you couldn't do it... that Dan would not only get away but you would end up dead."

Father Crane turned around, "I would gladly give my life trying to save the people that Dan will eventually kill. It is my one life and their hundreds, if not tens of thousands later. Even permanently crippling Dan will have some efficacy. I will not sit idly by knowing what is to come. I had an opportunity to dispose of Dan years ago and... and I should have done it then."

Susie couldn't believe this. Father Crane was just trying to use reverse psychology on her to get her to go.

Father Crane's eyes widened, "Use your Polarity and tell me if I am bluffing. Tell me if I am just trying to trick you into going."

Susie saw forward and – no matter how many times she examined the events to come – Father Crane was wholly committed to going forward to attack Dan.

"Do not interfere – your hesitation will be my undoing. Just keep away."

*   *   *

Dan was on the edge of the city, lying down in a motel room, still recovering from his injuries. He saw this exchange through his Polarity and welcomed Father Crane's attack – it was unfinished business from their last encounter. He agreed with Father Crane – he had a distinct advantage because he was in better physical shape. His wounds from the women at the bar were still a hindrance and it was clear that this next encounter would involve far less direct physical interaction.

Go, a text from Harold said.

Dan smiled – he was glad that Harold was also paying attention to this. He was confident that Father Crane was going downtown – every scenario he played out had zero alteration towards that fact. It was as if Father Crane wanted Dan to be at a particular spot. He didn't want to underestimate Father Crane's ability, so he had to have a plan that would introduce some complexity.

Dan arose from his bed, put on a black baseball cap backwards, went outside, and hopped on a dirt bike that he stole earlier. He pulled out his phone to check the time. He paused a few seconds and said, "Time to leave."

He carefully drove the speed limit through the sub-burbs and into town – the dirt bike wasn't street-legal in California, so he didn't want to draw unwanted attention. A big box retail store at the corner of a busy intersection caught his eye. He drove behind the store and slowly got off his motorcycle next to a dumpster. There was a set of concrete stairs next to the dumpster – they led to a back door of the store. The top of these stairs was roughly at the same height as the top of the dumpster, but a few feet away.

There were piles of cardboard boxes and several dozen wooden pallets nearby. He began throwing several cardboard boxes in the dumpster – and threw a few more in after a couple more seconds of thought. He then lifted one of the wooden pallets and laid it down to create a bridge between the top of the dumpster and the top of the concrete stairs.

Dan got back on his dirt bike and drove to the front of the store. Inside, he bought several items: a bright red shirt, a bright yellow baseball cap, sunglasses, and cigarettes – although he didn't smoke. He walked outside, back to his dirt bike. He slowly took off his black baseball cap – the pain from the various stitches on his head stung sharply – and put it in a storage compartment on the side of the dirt bike. He then put the bright red shirt on over his existing shirt, carefully put the bright yellow baseball cap on backwards. Finally, sunglasses, and he was ready.

Ready, he texted.

Let's do this, the reply said.

He zoomed through the streets of the city, recklessly speeding and cutting through traffic. This quickly caught the police's attention and they gave chase. Dan smiled as the sirens roared. Throttling his dirt bike, popping a wheelie – doing everything he could to draw as much attention from the surrounding pedestrians and motorists. As he entered the thick of downtown, he slowed his speed so the police wouldn't lose sight of him in the lines of traffic. Cars behind him did their best to pull out of the way of the pursuing police cars.

Dan pulled up next to a stopped car whose driver-side window was down. The driver – a woman – was rummaging through her purse for something. Dan reached into her window, grabbed her purse, and threw it and its contents all over the ground. The woman screamed as Dan quickly sped away. Dan looked into his rearview mirror and – at that moment – the woman got out of her car to collect her things. The leading police car slammed its brakes, but it didn't stop in time to avoid the woman – the police cruiser crashed into her, slamming her into her car's open door. This woman's death would certainly grab the attention of every police officer in the vicinity.

Dan then took a right at the next block and stopped. He counted to seven and continued speeding along – just as more police cars turned the corner to follow him. He popped another wheelie, keeping it as he drove straight through a red light. Cars coming from both sides hit their brakes and swerved violently to miss Dan – one car spun near Dan, only missing him because he kept his wheelie. He looked into his rearview mirror again and was delighted to see the twisted mass of wrecked carnage behind him.

He kept shooting straight down several more blocks, knowing that more police cars would appear, coming from his sides – they did so, as expected, one after another. Block after block, Dan took turn after turn, collecting as many police cars as he could. He laughed at the shoddy roadblocks they tried to set up. As soon as Dan predicted he had collected as many police cars as he could, he headed back in the direction of the big box retail store he came from.

As soon as he got to the store's property, he immediately drove through the parking lot – forcing the police cars to drive more slowly in their pursuit. Once Dan cleared the parking lot, he sped to the back of the store. He drove his dirt bike up the concrete steps and across his makeshift wooden pallet bridge – landing softly on the many cardboard boxes inside the dumpster.

He immediately took off his bright red shirt, leaving his black shirt on that was underneath. He took off the bright yellow hat and sunglasses. The sirens were getting closer. The police were twelve seconds from turning the corner to come his direction.

He took his black baseball cap out of the dirt bike's storage compartment and put it back on his head facing forward. He climbed out of the dumpster and shoved the impromptu wooden pallet bridge to the ground. The pain from his injuries gripped his attention, but he willed himself to scamper up the concrete stairs, sit down, and light up his cigarette, coughing a few times. Just then, a mass of police cars turned the corner to come behind the store. Several drove by him, but one stopped.

"Have you seen a man on a motorcycle drive by here?" a policeman asked.

Dan pointed the direction the police cars were driving, "He went off that way."

"Thanks!"

Dan walked to the front of the store and into its parking lot. He looked over the many parked cars and smirked. He walked up to a much older blue sedan and opened its unlocked door. He sat down in the driver's seat and lifted the hatch on the center console – keys were there. He started the engine and glanced at the clock on the dashboard.

52 minutes until Father Crane.

He drove off back into the city.

* * *

Vinny and Eddie arrived at Nemec's police station and parked.

"You think they're gonna be at lunch?" Vinny asked.

Nemec walked out of the front doors of the station, catching Vinny's eye. Vinny waved at Nemec and he stopped, averting his eyes and visibly grumbling.

"Oh, he's happy to see you," Eddie quipped at Vinny.

"Time to put on the friendly face," Vinny said, walking confidently towards Nemec.

Nemec looked up and folded his arms. As Vinny got closer, he could see him cursing under his breath.

"I got in a lot of trouble because of that flash drive idiocy," Nemec said to them.

Eddie walked straight to Nemec and got right in his face – just a few inches away. Eddie's broader stature dwarfed that of the much lankier Nemec. Eddie huffed a few times, but didn't say a word at first – his eyes locked on Nemec's.

"Insult my partner again. Do it. Please do it," Eddie said calmly.

Vinny cut between the two and separated them. "Hey, come on. It was my fault. I am an idiot. I screwed up. This is completely unnecessary. Once this case is over, we can all be rest assured that we will never have to see each other again. Until then – Nemec can call me idiot. I deserve it."

Eddie stepped back a few steps without saying anything else.

"I'm heading out to oversee the transfer of the perps' car to our forensics lab in town at HQ – they have better equipment there to examine stains and collect DNA evidence," Nemec said.

"It's being moved now?" Vinny asked.

Nemec pointed to his right – a short distance away, a tow-truck was entering the police station's impound lot. "That tow-truck is taking it. I'm escorting it. You can catch up with me tomorrow morning."

Nemec's phone rang. He looked at the caller ID and his face went red. He picked up the call and yelled, "LOOK, stop calling me! You wanna know why I dropped our engagement?! Let me tell you the many reasons…,"

Nemec walked away.

Vinny looked up into the sky and said, "We gotta follow him."

"Why?" asked Eddie.

"My intuition tells me we should."

"Intuition? Oh please. You don't believe in that, do ya?"

Vinny turned to him and said, "Yes, I do. I would do the same for you if you ever said your intuition told you to do something."

Eddie stared at Vinny for a brief moment and said, "Sure. Whatever. Let's go."

Several minutes had past. Finally, Nemec's police car pulled out of the police station with the loaded tow-truck right behind him. Vinny and Eddie followed the tow-truck.

"You think something's gonna happen to the car?" Eddie asked.

"I don't know. I really don't know what to expect…," Vinny said but then was distracted by the massive traffic backup ahead, "Whoa, look at this backup… must be an accident or something."

Vinny saw Nemec turn on his sirens so the tow-truck could plow through the traffic less impeded. Nemec's police car took a right turn.

"That's not the fastest way to their HQ. He should be going straight," Vinny said.

"It's probably faster than getting through this – this ain't going anywhere," Eddie said, sitting up higher, trying to see further out, "And I don't see any movement ahead. The lanes are closed."

Eddie turned on the local police scanner in their car – a good portion of the chatter centered around the many accidents caused in the area by a man on a dirt bike.

"Let's turn around and go another way. I don't like this. I don't like it at all," Vinny said.

"Really?"

"Did you hear all of the locations of the other accidents? Nemec's headed to yet another one right now. He's gonna have to take another detour," Vinny said.

"He's probably on his phone still, not checking his scanner… He looked pretty pissed. I don't know if we should follow…," Eddie hesitated.

"Where's your apathy when I need it?" Vinny asked.

Eddie chuckled, "Okay – I found it. I don't care what we do right now, so let's go."

* * *

Dan was nearing his destination to confront Father Crane in the heart of downtown. He pulled into a gas station to pick up a few supplies. A fuel truck was parked at the side of the station – a large tube from it was filling the gasoline reservoirs below the surface.

Perfect, as expected.

There were several beds of rocks nearby – a usual substitute for grass in the arid southern California environment. He squatted and examined several of them, eventually settling on one that was about the size of a walnut. He stuck it in his pocket and stood up. Dan sported an uncontrollable smile and walked straight over to the driver of the truck.

"Wow!" he said to the driver.

The driver looked up at him.

"That's a DOT 406 AL Brenner petroleum tanker with a Volvo ACL64 cab," Dan said, taking in a refreshing breath.

"Yeah," the driver said, without any enthusiasm at all.

"I sure miss workin' on these babies. I loved them… it was like a sick hobby."

"You a mechanic?"

"Used to be," Dan said, sighing.

"Why did ya quit?"

Dan paused for a second, admiring the beautiful machine, "Hmm? Oh… I got married and the wife wanted me to get a real job."

"Heh, my wife is giving me crap about that right now," the driver said.

"Happy wife. Happy life. Go with it," Dan said, shrugging.

"Oh I will… If you wanna take a look around, go ahead. I ain't goin' nowhere for a few more minutes."

"That would be awesome. You mind if I pop the hood?"

"Be my guest."

Dan fist-pumped and said, "YES."

"I've never seen anyone get so excited about my truck before."

"Well, it's a long story."

"The cab's door is open – just pop the trunk with the lever…"

"…on the left side just below the parking break," Dan said.

"You got it," the driver smiled.

Dan nodded and walked to the cab door – discreetly taking the rock from his pocket as he approached it. He opened the door, leaned in, and placed the rock underneath the brake pedal. He pushed down on the brake pedal with his hand – the rock stopped the pedal well short of the floor.

Perfect.

He then moved the rock a few inches from the brake pedal and nudged it – it rolled a few inches with little resistance.

Perfect.

He then moved the rock far to the left of the brake pedal and immediately pulled the lever to pop the hood of the cab – just as the truck driver walked up to him. He walked around to the front and opened the hood. He smiled in amazement; Dan usually had to think of past "conquests" in order to conjure this kind of convincing show of emotion. In this case, he thought of a time that he convinced two women to leave their husbands and children just so they would have a chance to fight over him – literally.

"Good times," he said and then slammed the hood shut. "Well, thanks. I gotta go."

"Sure, man," the driver said.

Dan got back into his car and texted, *Truck is set.*

He drove into town and parked his borrowed car deep in the city. His Polarity predicted that Father Crane would be unwaveringly heading down a street a few blocks away. This didn't surprise him: When it came to a serious duel between a member of *Us* and a member of *Them*, making sure both sides were at a predictable location was required. The manipulation of surroundings was the weapon.

Dan approached a few men in their early 20's – they were playing hip-hop music and were occasionally laughing. They turned to him once he was a few feet away.

"Jay, we need to talk," Dan said.

One of the men, who was exceptionally tall and large, nodded his head. "Hey, I gotta take this," he said to the other two.

Dan and Jay walked about ten yards away from the other two men. Dan had to remind himself that his name was 'Michael' to Jay – he helped Jay dispose some members of a rival gang.

'Michael' even helped him get access to weapons and drug sources. Jay was an up-and-rising star in his gang and would do anything for Dan.

"Jay, I really need your help."

"Anything Michael. You're tight with me."

"I need you to take care of a priest."

Jay cocked his head back, "What?"

"He's not really a priest, but he dresses like one."

"What did he do?"

"It's a bit embarrassing… he… he did some things to me when… when I was child," Dan said, glassy-eyed.

Jay put his hand on Dan's shoulder and said, "Brother, you ain't got nothin' to worry about. The priest is gone. Where is he?"

Dan gulped and pointed north, "I've asked him to meet me down the street over by the police headquarters way over there. He'll be wearing all black, glasses, and one of those old-fashioned fedora hats. He'll be around here sometime soon… just keep an eye out."

"We ain't getting near the police."

"I understand… I don't expect you to," Dan said.

"We gotcha covered. If we see him, we'll be the last thing he ever sees."

"Thanks."

They shook hands and Dan walked away – he headed north towards the police headquarters. He travelled two blocks before passing by a garbage can that was in front of a bakery. With no effort, he picked out a scratched-off lottery ticket and dropped in on the ground right at the front door of the bakery.

"Hmm," he mumbled, staring down at the useless ticket.

He stepped on the lottery ticket and scraped it a few more feet towards the street.

The bakery's door was within a few feet of a door of a clothing store outlet. Dan entered the clothing store and saw several stacks of black polka-dotted shirts on a display rack. Dan looked them over and re-arranged the shirts so that the largest ones swapped places with the smallest ones.

Delayed four seconds... need a delay of six, he thought.

He then knocked the stack of shirts over on their side.

That will do.

He walked back outside and continued trekking north. There was a sporting goods store on his left. He stopped in front of it, looking at the ground in thought. After a few seconds, he started walking again – only to stop again once more. He nodded once, turned around, entered the store, and walked over to the medicine balls.

A bowling ball would be better, but this will do.

Dan chose the 25-pound medicine ball and brought it to the register, placing it on the countertop.

"Hold on one second," Dan said to the cashier.

He raced back into the store and grabbed a tube of curing oil from the baseball glove section. He ran back to the register and placed the oil with the medicine ball.

"You're not planning on catching that big medicine ball with a baseball glove are you?" the cashier joked.

"You got me," Dan said, trying his best to grin without losing focus on his plan.

"That will be $75.34," the cashier said.

Dan provided a gift card for that store. The cashier ran the gift card. "Wow, you had exactly $75.34 on that card. What are the odds of that?"

"That is pretty amazing, yeah," he answered, then looked at a pile of coupon booklets next to the register. "Oh, can I have one of these?"

"Sure," the cashier said, handing Dan a bag with the oil in it.

Dan grabbed three of them and put them in the bag. The cashier raised an eyebrow at this.

"I have friends that might be interested in the coupons," Dan said.

"Oh."

Dan left the store, supporting the medicine ball on his right shoulder and holding the bag with oil and booklets in his left hand. He walked further north and stopped in front of a large scaffold covering the front of jewelry store. He took a few steps back from the scaffold – almost walking off the curb to the street. He knelt down and put the medicine ball on the street, resting it against the curb. There would be people capable of watching him for the next 37 seconds so he faked re-tying his shoelaces. As soon as the 37 seconds expired, he immediately took the oil out of the bag and lathered the medicine ball with it. He then ripped several pages from the coupon booklets and covered the ball.

Dan continued walking north and turned into an alley. There were a few rats sniffing through some garbage nearby. He picked them up one by one and gave them the same instruction: *You will attack a man that I point at. Stay nearby, but out of sight.*

Dan waited for Father Crane. He knew exactly where he was: five blocks south. He looked around and focused on his immediate environment to make sure that neither Father Crane nor any of *Them* had put a trap into play. He turned around – the police headquarters were a block to the north of him. Everything was set.

*   *   *

Vinny and Eddie pulled into an open parking space across from the police headquarters.

"Do you think Nemec already beat us here?" Vinny asked.

"It's hard to say. Let's go inside and find out," Eddie replied. The two of them went inside.

*   *   *

Father Crane proceeded walking north towards Dan. He held a large bag in one hand and a newspaper in his other. He wore his black cassock and fedora hat – not hiding was part of his plan. He casually walked towards Jay and his two friends – they were still listening to music, but this ended quickly.

"Hey," he heard Jay say to the other two men, "That's the priest. That's him."

Father Crane continued walking towards them – now only 30 feet away – as they walked towards him. A gust of wind blew his hat off and he knelt down to pick it up.

SCREECH!

A car pulled up along the street, slamming its brakes. Guns pointed out of its open windows and began to fire on Jay and his two friends. Father Crane kept perfectly still in his knelt position. In a matter of seconds, it was over. The car zoomed off and people in the immediate area were in a panic – some ducked for cover as others ran away hysterically. Father Crane stood up and continued walking, knowing that Jay and his two friends were dead.

Father Crane ignored the chaos that was behind him and approached the bakery, his eyes affixed on Dan, several blocks further north. He stopped a few feet short of the store and put his bag down, still holding his newspaper. A few seconds later, an older woman walked out of the bakery and noticed the lottery ticket on the ground. She squatted to get a closer look at it. When she did so, two chatty women walked out of the clothing store. One was holding a black polka-dotted shirt in one hand and a steaming hot coffee in the other. The woman holding the shirt immediately tripped over the squatting woman, causing her coffee to spill towards Father Crane – just when Father Crane widely opened his newspaper. The hot coffee harmlessly splashed the newspaper's pages.

Father Crane closed his newspaper and helped the woman up.

"I'm so sorry about the coffee… I didn't see her… I…," she said in shock.

"It is quite okay," Father Crane said, balling up his soaked newspaper, and throwing it 30 feet – perfectly – into the garbage can that Dan originally fished the lottery ticket.

Father Crane approached the jewelry store with the scaffold, his bag in-hand – still keeping his eyes on Dan, now two blocks away. As he got closer, he took off his fedora hat. He then reached into his bag, pulling out a hard hat while he walked. He put it on his head and, a few steps later, a large truck pulled in to park alongside the street. Its large tires pinched the slippery medicine ball out from the curb, shooting it towards Father Crane like a cannon ball. He shifted his body back slightly – barely dodging the medicine ball; however, the ball made a direct hit on the scaffold, causing it to collapse. Father Crane stepped out of the way as it collapsed, hearing a man from above scream.

"Aaa!"

Father Crane then stepped forward, catching the man before he fell to the ground – but not before a hammer landed squarely on top of his hard hat. Father Crane tightened his lips from the immense pain catching the man caused his existing wounds, but pressed to keep somewhat of a smile.

"OH MY GOD! Oh my God!" the man yelled.

"You are okay," Father Crane said, handing him his hard hat. "Have this – it can save your life."

The man nodded, but was still in a disoriented panic.

Father Crane put his fedora hat back on and continued walking north. Dan was a hundred feet away – Father Crane could see him shaking his head, rolling his eyes. He then saw Dan point at him. A half-dozen rats appeared from the alley and ran towards Father Crane – but all of them were immediately swooped up by an equal number of owls.

Father Crane strolled up to Dan and stopped a few feet in front of him.

"Owls? Really? *You* used owls?" Dan asked.

"When I told them to attack, all they could ask is 'who?'"

"*Your* jokes were always dumb."

"*You* seemed to enjoy them at the time."

"Yeah – I was locked in a freakin' monastery. Anything other than that stupid monotony was entertaining."

"I am bit underwhelmed with *Your* efforts to kill me. No complexity. No decoys," Father Crane said.

"*You* think *You're* always right," Dan snapped back.

"No. I just need to be right more often than *You*."

"Whatever. *You* think *You* know me that well?" Dan asked.

"So *You* expected this outcome? *You* did not really want to engage in combat?"

"No. I just wanted to make sure Susie wasn't going to be here – and *You* gave that to me."

Father Crane's eyes kept at a dead stare – he knew what was about to happen and there was nothing he could do about it. Had Susie come along, there could have been a chance. Father Crane walked away.

*　　　*　　　*

Vinny and Eddie walked out of the police headquarters.

"Well, Nemec isn't here yet. Boy, he must have taken the slowest route possible," Vinny said.

"You just wanna wait in the car?" Eddie asked.

"Sure," Vinny said, but then looked down the street to the west. "Hey wait, there's Nemec and the tow-truck right now," he said, pointing.

They stopped and waited. As the tow-truck got closer, a loud horn from the east was heard. Vinny turned around and saw a large fueling truck careening out of control. It was coming closer – heading right toward Nemec and the tow-truck.

"Oh my God, that truck can't stop," Vinny said under his breath.

"This ain't gonna be pretty," Eddie said in monotone.

The fuel truck flew in front of the police headquarters, keeping its path towards Nemec's car. Nemec's car accelerated quickly and moved out of the way; however the fuel truck clipped his car's back end. The fuel truck then rammed with most of its energy into the passenger-side of the tow-truck, causing the fuel truck to spin somewhat clockwise. The heavy fuel tank in the back of the truck began tipping over and it fell on the pavement with a loud crash.

Vinny started to run to the accident, determined to help somehow. He saw the tow-truck driver stumble out of the truck and walk away. Nemec appeared unhurt, rushing to help the tow-truck driver. Vinny ran past them, hopped onto the bed of tow truck, and pulled a lever to lower it.

"Come on! Come on!" he yelled at the tow-truck. "Hurry!"

The car's steering column had already been popped open to allow free movement between the gears of the car – a standard procedure for vehicles that don't have keys. Vinny moved the gear from *PARK* to *NEUTRAL* and let the car roll off the bed and into the street. The car had enough momentum to carry it at least 100 feet away, allowing Vinny to do a somewhat decent job of parallel parking it alongside the curb.

Eddie and Nemec ran up to him and yelled, "What are you doing?!"

Vinny reply, "The fuel tank overturned…"

"And…," Eddie said, panting.

"Aren't you guys worried about…," Vinny began.

"It exploding?" Nemec asked.

Vinny didn't say anything. Eddie and Nemec started laughing. "Vinny," Eddie said, trying to contain his laugh enough to speak, "Fuel tanks don't do that. It takes a lot to bust them open. This ain't the movies."

"Did he seriously just do that?" Nemec asked, laughing.

Eddie sighed, popped a few pills, and walked away.

Nemec continued laughing – to the point of crying. Vinny walked back to his car without looking back, his head hung low. He could hear Nemec yell, "BOOM!" behind him, followed by a boisterous laugh.

Chapter 16 – Agent Revelation

Heeding Father Crane's directive, Susie left Dan alone. It was about as close to a vacation that she could expect – Father Crane was dealing with Dan while Spike had Linus in check. She sat on a bench in the art museum – the same place that Dan had taken her many months ago to demonstrate Polarity. The quiet atmosphere was nice. However, there was a part of her that wondered if she should feel guilty for spending time on herself – and not helping *Us*. It was obvious to her just how unrelenting *They* were.

However, she felt no guilt at all. In her old life – before she received her full Polarity – she remembered how meticulously she kept every aspect. She wanted to have complete control of everything. With her full Polarity, she saw just how impossible that was. Everywhere she looked, there were flaws. Every person that walked by her was full of flaws.

That woman has gone on and off diets for the past 22 years. That man has quit smoking twelve times in the past three years. That woman spikes her water with vodka at work but tells everyone she's quit drinking. That...

She stopped herself and looked deeper into their lives. She realized that she admired them because they were doing the best they could to change their lives for other people. The overweight woman wanted to be able to do more with her children and grandchildren. The man who couldn't quit smoking wanted to quit because he wanted to be alive long enough to see his newborn child grow. The woman who spiked her water wanted to quit drinking because the alcohol made her detached from her children's needs.

Improving oneself for someone else is the most impressive form of love that one can express.

She brimmed with happiness – a new kind of happiness that she never felt before. She thought she was happy when she made good grades – and she was; however, the kind of happiness she felt now had no way to be measured. She didn't have to wait for a test result to be happy. Her body filled with warmth and she felt tingling all over her body.

"Well, hello again. Funny seeing you here," a man's voice said from her right.

She looked – it was Eric. "Oh, hi," she smiled, patting a spot next to her on the bench.

He smiled back. Her heart pounded a little harder – she could almost feel the heat of his body as he sat down next to her.

"Sorry about...," Susie started.

"The kiss?" Eric asked.

Susie raised her eyebrows, still smiling, "No – rushing out the other day."

"Oh," Eric said. "Was everything okay? I mean there was quite a scene outside."

"Well… it's kind of a long story, but everything's okay."

"Is it?" Eric asked.

Susie nodded, smiling, looking into his eyes, "Yeah. Definitely. So what brings you here?"

"Oh, I come here pretty regularly. I've never seen you here before," Eric said.

"I've been here once before. I just thought I would stop by again to collect my thoughts."

"It's good for that. The art takes me to a different place – removes me from the city. This place gets beautiful pieces walking in just about every day...," he said looking at her, but stopping short, "I... I mean the artwork... I didn't mean..."

"I know what you meant," Susie said, giving him a playful elbow into his side.

Eric looked down shaking his head, blushing bright red.

Susie leaned a few inches towards him, "I wasn't sorry about the kiss."

"Yeah... neither was I," Eric said, looking back up at her.

God, what am I doing? They could be watching. How do I pass this off as a decoy?

Susie took out her phone and checked the time. "Well, I have to go," she said, standing up.

"Hey?" Eric asked.

"Yes?"

"Is it okay if I take you out sometime? I would kinda like to have more than two minutes with you."

Susie looked him over – she wanted a lot more than two minutes, but she had to be better prepared to fool *Them*. She took a pen out of her purse and wrote her number on his forearm.

"Sure. Call me."

"I will," he said.

Susie walked away with her pen in-hand. She looked at it closer – it was the same pen she used for her schoolwork. It was the same pen she used to yell at herself in her accounting ledger. As she walked by a garbage can, she threw it away.

Dan remained standing a block away from police headquarters. He saw every bit of this exchange between Eric and Susie. He was puzzled that her visit with him was suddenly cut short – but she seemed like she enjoyed it. He decided he would deal with Eric later.

Dan looked towards Nemec and Eddie – they were sitting down, talking about Nemec's narcotics work. Police officers had already poured out of the police headquarters like an army of ants – descending on the wrecked tow-truck and fuel tanker. It was chaos.

Dan then looked towards the thugs' getaway car. It was still parked where Vinny left it. The only people paying attention to it were the two men working to steal it – common car thieves with years of experience in and out of prison. Dan was ready to steal the car himself – chaos was the most effective form of distraction to steal in broad daylight. Since the steering column was already open, hotwiring the car was easy. He kept his distance, happy to let the thieves do the job for him.

*   *   *

Vinny sat in his car waiting, looking blankly forward, deciding how he could recover from such an embarrassing show of novice and stupidity.

"God, I'm so stupid."

He banged his head on the dashboard once, but decided that it was best to keep moving forward. He decided to embrace the humor he had brought to Nemec – certain it would melt the ice between them.

Vinny got out of the car and looked around for Eddie. He looked towards the parked getaway car – it was being driven away.

"The car! The car is being stolen!" Vinny yelled, but neither Nemec nor Eddie had a chance of hearing through the swarm of people between them.

Vinny ran full tilt back to Nemec and Eddie, who were still sitting down. Nemec looked up as he approached.

"Did you forget to turn off the headlights?" Nemec quipped.

"NO! The car!" he pointed, "The car's been stolen!"

Eddie and Nemec popped up off the ground. Nemec put his hands on top of his head, "NO! NO! NO! This can't be happening!"

Eddie watched with a hollow face.

Nemec turned around and walked up to Vinny. He stopped short of saying anything, but his eyes were aflame with rage. Vinny didn't say a word. A few seconds later, Nemec walked away.

"Christ... what the hell is going on?" Vinny said, bewildered.

"Bad luck," Eddie said. "This is bad luck. It happens."

Vinny turned to Eddie, "THIS bad? How much more can I take?"

"Apathy. Apathy is the miracle drug for anger management and disappointment about life in general. You can get it without a prescription. Use it. Use it now," Eddie said, popping a few pills.

Vinny shook his head and squatted down. "I... I don't know where to go from here. It almost feels like there's something else pulling the strings. Let's suppose we get the car back..."

"The car's gone, Vinny. We ain't ever gonna see it again – at least, not in any shape that forensics can use. It will be tainted evidence at best. It will probably be found burned or something – it seems that most stolen cars end up that way."

Father Crane was talking with Susie and Spike in the middle of a large park as the sun was setting.

"The car thieves took the car for a short ride and determined there was nothing in they could steal. They drove it to an abandoned lot and they set it on fire – just a few minutes ago," Father Crane said.

"It's not Linus. I've spent all of my time watchin' that bloke. *He's* rather boring, but I can't underestimate *Him*," Spike said.

Father Crane turned to Susie and waited for her to speak.

"I wasn't watching Dan… when you told me to step away. I was… I was…," Susie said.

"You were at the art gallery. I know. Is there anything that Dan has ever done since Frank's family was killed to even hint that *He* has something to do with… with THIS. Think hard… the flash drive corruption, Mrs. Davis' death, and now the getaway car. None of what has happened was predicted – not in the slightest. Dan's involvement, at best, has only been on the periphery."

Susie shook her head, "I'm doing my best… I'm trying."

Father Crane nodded – he was asking a lot from a novice.

"Could it be Frank?" Spike asked.

Father Crane put his hands behind his back and paced. He thought, in great detail, about Frank's behavior since his family was killed. He tried to understand every angle of this short period of time to try to gather any shred of Frank's involvement. A tear came down his face.

"Are you okay?" Susie asked him.

Father Crane took off his glasses – cringing from the pain from his stitched left ear – and wiped his eyes. "Frank has been through a lot recently. He heard about Mrs. Davis' death and his mental health has degraded badly – she was like a mother to him and she treated him like a son. He has become violent and reckless. It is hard to watch this happen to a once fine, young man and be powerless to stop it."

"There's Officer Nemec, the FBI agents, Harold, Jennifer...," Spike started.

"There is a whole network of Harold's operatives that could be helping," Father Crane interjected. "And perhaps the mistake is believing that Harold is not using any others – that Dan is working this alone. I never saw it in the future that the car would be stolen until I confronted Dan."

"Why... why not?" Susie asked.

Father Crane exhaled, "Whoever is involved has many mechanisms in place that are set in motion only when all of *Us* are distracted – and they are set in motion only at the last minute. I cannot confidently trace the origins of those car thieves – they were to be at that exact spot regardless of the events of today."

"Maybe it was just bad luck then?" Susie asked.

Father Crane stared at her coldly, "The term 'luck' is for those who are too lazy to consider the possible."

"I'm sorry."

"Do not apologize. Just learn."

Father Crane stopped his pacing and looked toward the sky. "Spike, you must continue your full focus on Linus. *He* is waiting for you to let your guard down. *He* will kill you. *We* need you to heal and return to *Our* ranks in good health," he said.

"Right," Spike said.

"Susie, you are to continue monitoring Dan. Stop *His* plots just as you have cleverly done so far. Although our backs are against the wall right now, *His* plots would have surely succeeded without your intervention."

Susie nodded.

"I… I will keep on thinking about this. *We* still have Big Dynamite and G-Man alive – they will turn themselves in very soon for killing Frank's family. They need *Our* protection," said Father Crane and then looked down to the ground, "Whoever is behind this is a true master of Polarity – someone who acts with such exacting precision that they need not use it hardly at all. This ability is the hallmark of someone special. I will go and find this person or persons."

"How?" Susie asked.

"I just need to get close. At around a hundred feet or so one can pick up *Their* presence if you are paying attention. Of course, the closer one gets, the much stronger the attraction gets. Once revealed, though, this person will take the gloves off and it will get ugly – no more hiding."

"But this can be anybody," Susie said.

"If you have a better idea, please let me know. This cannot go on any longer," he replied and then walked away.

*   *   *

Vinny and Eddie were eating dinner at a quaint diner in town. Vinny had a coffee in front of him that grew cold while Eddie made short work of a plate of lasagna.

"This is just so bizarre," Vinny said, tapping his fingers on the table. "I know that I've been a little clumsy on previous cases, but this is pretty messed up."

Eddie wiped his mouth with his napkin, "Bad luck happens."

"Like this?"

"Yeah."

"Eddie… all of the evidence to find the murderers has fallen through. The police have no leads at all."

"There's Frank – he has to know something. He's avoided everything. He hasn't even claimed his family's bodies at the morgue yet. He's never talked to the police either – not once. I'm beginning to believe that Susie may know something, too – just like you said. Odd behavior can be the smoke that leads to the gun," Eddie said.

Vinny took a sip of his coffee and promptly spit it back in his cup, "Yuck."

The waitress walked by and asked, "Is everything all right?"

"Yeah – my coffee's cold that's all."

"Can I get ya another?"

"Sure, and throw in some apple pie, too. I need some comfort food."

The waitress winked at Vinny, "Sure thing."

Eddie reached into his pocket, took out a prescription pill container, opened it, and popped a few pills in his mouth.

"Heartburn gettin' ya again?" Vinny asked.

Eddie nodded, "Something like that," he said and then sipped his water. "We gotta find Frank or Susie. This whole thing has been too embarrassing – it's the only way we can save face now. Even my apathy has its limits."

"Well, the only lead we have with Frank is the Stewart family."

Eddie sighed.

"I know, I know – you don't want to go back," Vinny said, dropping his shoulders.

Eddie shook his head, "No, I think you're right this time. Mrs. Stewart would probably be the only person who'd know anything about Frank's habits and where he could be. We should pay her another visit and ask more specific questions."

The waitress returned with a fresh coffee and a slice of apple pie.

"Thanks," Vinny said to her.

"Uh huh," she replied.

"Well, tomorrow's Monday... you wanna stop by the Stewart house tomorrow morning?" Vinny asked Eddie as he dug into his pie.

"Yeah."

Vinny chomped and grimaced slightly, "Wow, this pie is a bit stale."

"Don't eat it. It's probably old. It'll make you sick or something."

"I'll manage. It's good enough."

*   *   *

The next morning, Father Crane waited outside a baseball park dressed in his black clergy shirt, black trousers, and fedora hat. He was waiting for the Stewart family to show up to watch a ballgame – Frank was going to meet them there. Mrs. Stewart kept the children out of school for the chance to see their beloved Frank. Father Crane wanted to get close to the Stewarts – including the children – to pick up on any opposing Polarity they could have.

"Hmm," he mumbled, realizing that Vinny and Eddie were trailing the Stewarts' car – they had arrived at the Stewart house just as the Stewarts were leaving. This would be a good opportunity to get close to Vinny and Eddie as well.

He closed his eyes and tilted his head up towards the sky, pondering how much of a wild card Frank could be – Father Crane knew that Frank would be violently angry towards him for letting his family die.

The baseball game was nearly devoid of fans so it would be easy for Frank to spot him. He looked into the future and didn't foresee any ripples in what events were to happen. Everything was simple: The Stewart family would watch the ball game with Frank, Vinny and Eddie would notice Frank's presence, Vinny and Eddie would call for backup to try to apprehend Frank, and Frank would leave before the backup would arrive – escaping, once again, from the agents.

Father Crane stayed put for twenty-eight minutes and then walked towards a set of bathrooms. As he approached, he saw Eddie standing outside a bathroom door, leaning on a wall with his arms folded. He looked at Eddie keenly, trying to pick up on any mannerisms that would suggest that Eddie had his full Polarity – such as incessant note-taking or random facial expressions of surprise. He took a few steps closer – about sixty feet away – and Eddie looked up directly at him. One step more – Father Crane felt a slight, but distinctive sense of opposite Polarity – the hairs on his arms raised. One step more – Father Crane felt a small surge of violent energy beginning to trickle through him. He stopped.

"So… it's *You*," Father Crane said to Eddie, almost shouting.

Eddie looked at Father Crane, then looked around, and then back at Father Crane – no one else was around.

"*You* play the perfect part – FBI agent by day, prescription pill-pusher by night, and the occasional wrench thrown in to disrupt *Us*."

Eddie's eyes widened and he said nervously, "What?"

"Eddie Kerwin. FBI agent. Mid-level drug dealer – *You* are *Your* own best customer, but *You* play it off as heartburn problems. 46-years-old. Divorced four times. Violent past filled with intense psychotherapy. You have a penchant for prostitutes – redheads, to be precise. And – most importantly – *You* slip through life undetected. And now here *You* are exposed to the rest of the world. *Your* days are numbered."

Eddie's face went red, "Don't threaten me. Priest or not – it won't matter. Don't push me into a corner, because I'll come out shooting. I got nothin' to lose. No one threatens me. NO ONE."

The bathroom door opened. Vinny emerged with his back to Father Crane and Eddie. He fanned his hands towards the bathroom area. "I feel sorry for whoever has to go in there. I don't know what crawled up my butt or maybe it was that apple pie, but Lord have mercy...," he stopped as he turned toward Father Crane.

Father Crane kept his eyes on Eddie.

"Oh, sorry," Vinny said to Father Crane. "I didn't mean to use Lord's name in vain... uh, Father."

Father Crane turned to Vinny and said, "It's quite all right."

"Is everything okay?" Vinny asked.

"Everything is fine. I was just having a chat with your partner, Eddie. He has caught my interest."

"Oh," Vinny smiled and pointed his thumb at Eddie. "Don't worry about Eddie – he's a good guy. He's a devout Catholic. He goes to mass at least a couple times a week."

"Yes, I know. Good day, gentlemen," Father Crane said and then walked away.

Father Crane immediately walked into the stadium and climbed the stairs to the highest seats. He walked along the top row until he was behind the Stewart family and Frank, who were sitting in the first row. He went down the stairs and got closer and closer to them – never detecting anything out of the ordinary. Within thirty feet, there was still no sense of Polarity emanating from them. Father Crane left, feeling satisfied with his findings.

*   *   *

Susie stood a few blocks from the baseball stadium, waiting to catch up with Frank – he would be leaving in the next nine minutes after having eluded the FBI. She kept her attention on Dan, but Dan was spending time with one of his six somewhat regular girlfriends. Monitoring Dan was very difficult for her – all of the precise compliments, the girlfriends' naïve receptiveness, and the very graphic sex.

"I wonder what it would be like if someone was watching us right now," Dan said as he made love – as if he expected Susie to be watching.

Susie gagged. Dan would be with this girl for the next hour – and she couldn't stand to watch any more of it. Her phone rang. It was Eric.

"Hello," she said.

"Hey, it's Eric."

"Oh, hi!"

"Hey, I wanted to know if you were free tomorrow night. There's a comedy club I'd like to take you to."

"Oh, sure. That sounds like fun."

"How's 6 P.M.?"

"Sure."

"Okay, where should I pick you up?"

Now that was an interesting question. Susie really didn't live anywhere. She was effectively a transient with money – sleeping in a different hotel every few nights.

"How about I meet you at your friend's restaurant again?"

"Oh… okay. Oh… also… I don't have a car. Are you okay with a cab? I mean, if you want, we can take the bus," Eric said with a tinge of nervousness.

"I don't mind," Susie said.

"Great. I'll see you there."

"Great. Take care," she said.

"Bye."

Susie hung up her phone – she knew that *They* could be watching this. She had to misdirect her intentions with Eric.

"Well, there goes tomorrow night," she said plainly, hoping *They* were paying attention.

Inside, however, she was giddy. She had trouble keeping herself from smiling. Eric's voice excited her and she wished she could speak to him longer. She just wanted to be near him. Without any thought, she began to play out what tomorrow night would be like using her Polarity.

"NO," she said.

She couldn't allow herself to use her Polarity while she was with Eric – doing so might prompt her to alter the future ever-so-slightly. These slight alterations would be picked up by *Them* and then *They* would certainly know that her intentions with Eric were genuine – it would put Eric at risk just as she did for her sister, Karen. Susie shook her head, clearing it of running away into the future.

She looked towards the baseball stadium – Frank was jogging her direction on the sidewalk. He was wearing new clothes that he bought with stolen money. His hair was matted somewhat and he had grown the beginnings of a beard. He ran right up to her and stopped.

"So," he panted, "So, are you now sending the cops after me?"

"No – *We* wouldn't do that. It will work itself out on its own."

"Oh Susie…," he huffed, "You are so programmed by *Your* kind, aren't you?"

Susie felt something different from Frank's presence. She couldn't put her finger on it. In an obscure way, she felt unsafe near him but – even with her Polarity – she wasn't sure why.

"Are you okay Frank?"

Frank nodded – still breathing heavily to catch his breath – and laughed. "Sure – I mean, no one's out to kill me anymore, right? *They* don't seem to care about me anymore. It looks like

I'm free of this stupid *Us* and *Them* thing and... and all it took was killing my wife and kids."

Frank collapsed to the ground and began to sob. Susie knelt down next to him. He leaned towards her and wrapped his arms around her. She hugged him firmly and whispered to him, "I will always be there for you Frank. I care about you."

Frank cried, "Oh, but you can't... none of YOU can. *They* kill whoever you care about."

Frank let go of Susie and sat on the sidewalk. Susie remained kneeling. He gulped a few times and wiped several streams of tears from his eyes.

"I... I want *Them* to end me. I want *Them* to end me so I can end this. I don't have the guts to do it myself."

"Frank, please don't say that."

"Susie... *They* took everything from me. *They* keep taking everything from me. My wife... my kids... sweet old Mrs. Davis...," he said and then stood up yelling to the sky, "WHO WILL YOU TAKE NEXT?!"

Susie shook her head. Frank looked down at Susie and squatted, to look at her eye-to-eye.

"Susie, you have to promise me that you will protect the Stewarts. I know they're next. I just know *They* will... will..."

"Frank, *They* are not going after the Stewarts – *They* are trying to cover *Their* tracks for... well, you know."

"Promise me that you will protect them."

Susie was at an impasse – the truth was that she couldn't spend the time to protect the Stewarts. Furthermore, none of *Us* were assigned to protect them, but she felt she had to tell Frank what he wanted to hear. Besides, it would be a huge risk for *Them* to attack the Stewarts – especially when it served no purpose to help cover Harold's tracks. Frank needed to hear words of comfort.

"Ok Frank. *We* will try."

"No – promise me."

"I promise."

Frank stood up and said, "That Father Crane won't go along with this – I know it. But I have your word and I guess that's all I can hope for."

"Frank – I want to help you if I can."

"How? I'm a criminal now, remember? I've done some really bad things."

"We can get you counseling."

"Ha! That's not going to bring back my wife and kids. Do you really think someone can talk me out of reality? NO," Frank said and then pointed at his chest, "These are my raw emotions pouring out, needing an outlet, and being the bad guy is a great distraction. If I'm lucky, someone will shoot me."

Susie was silent.

Frank smirked, "Ah, nothing to say. I guess that I won't get my wish and get shot, huh? Well, I guess I gotta go amp it up a bit."

Frank began to walk away.

"Frank... you know you can talk to me whenever!" Susie shouted to him.

Frank didn't reply.

*   *   *

Dan lay in bed under the sheets with his girlfriend of the moment, Amber – a petite, fair-skinned brunette in her early 20's. He saw this exchange between Susie and Frank. He stared towards the ceiling while Amber lay on her side, stroking his bruised chest.

"You still thinkin' about that gang that jumped you?" she asked.

"No. I have some friends that are in trouble. I just worry."

"Babe, you worry too much. I can make you forget," she said, softly kissing his chest.

Dan ignored her. He peered into Susie's near future and foresaw the date she was to have with Eric. It would be too soon to kill Eric – he would prefer that Susie develop deeper feelings for him first. This would take time. However, it wasn't clear to him if Susie's intentions with Eric were real or just a decoy. He also wondered if she was just using Eric as part of a greater plan. Besides, killing Eric would require careful planning to ensure that he could get away with it. He already had enough on his plate by helping dispose of Harold's mess. It wasn't worth the time or the risk just yet.

Dan groaned.

"What's the matter, babe? You don't want some more of me?" Amber asked, sitting up.

"No. Actually I think I'll leave."

"What?" Amber scowled.

Dan got up slowly and said, "I'm leaving."

"When will I see you again?"

Dan shrugged his shoulders with indifference while he put his pants back on.

"Why do you do this every time we get together?"

Dan shrugged his shoulders again.

"If you leave, I won't take you back," Amber said.

"Don't say that. You know that you're the only one for me. I just don't want to have my troubles invade your life."

"I just think that you don't want to stay with me."

"I'll be back," Dan said.

"You can tell me anything, babe – you know that."

"Maybe, but not right now," he said as he put on his shirt.

"Why do I get the guys that treat me like dirt?" she asked rhetorically.

"I'm not gonna play that game. If you want me to leave for good, I will."

She shook her head.

Dan left Amber's apartment. He received a text from Harold. *Look what Father Crane discovered*, it read.

Dan turned his attention away from Susie momentarily and focused his Polarity to look into the recent past of Father Crane. He saw the exchange between him and Eddie.

Interesting, he wrote back.

Exploit it, said the reply.

Dan stopped outside of Amber's apartment and closed his eyes. He focused more on Father Crane and whatever plan he was devising. The difficulty in doing so was enormous – Father Crane was expertly changing dozens of details by the minute. It was clear, though, that Father Crane's focus was on Eddie – more specifically, killing Eddie. Killing Eddie wouldn't be easy because of Eddie's position in the FBI. Killing law enforcement meant it would get more attention from investigators – it would make it easier for Dan to lead investigators to evidence to implicate *Them*. This would certainly occupy most of Father Crane's attention.

Some of Father Crane's plans included Big Dynamite – whom was only days away from turning himself into the police. Dan could see Big Dynamite talking with Eddie over the past few days; Big Dynamite hustled prescription drugs and Eddie was his supplier. Dan predicted that Eddie and Big Dynamite would be spending more time together over the next week. *They* wanted to kill Eddie, but *They* also had to protect Big Dynamite – Dan grinned at the added complexity this caused *Them*.

Big Dynamite needs to die. Whatever happens to Eddie is Eddie's problem, Dan thought.

Dan opened his eyes and walked to his car in a nearby parking lot. He unlocked it and carefully sat down to help ease his pain from the beating he took from the bar. His attention returned to Susie – she was on her way to meet with Father Crane again. He focused on their conversation, but he felt a presence. Linus was about sixty feet away on his left, walking towards him. Dan rolled down his window.

"I didn't expect you!" Dan yelled.

Linus smiled, but didn't say anything as he continued walking towards Dan. He stopped about forty feet away from him.

"My dear friend Spike is rather boring – *He* is keeping on the defensive all the time. I worry that I'm getting rusty just waiting on *Him*."

"*He's* killed too many of *Us*," Dan said.

Linus licked his lips. "Yes... I can feel the pain *He's* inflicted... the suffering... the death. I can almost feel *His* neck in my grip," he said, holding his right hand out, clenching it, and then wiping some drool from his mouth.

"Have you come to help?"

"Why yes!" Linus shouted, smiling widely. "Your sad addiction of women has cost you your ability to operate properly. Even diminutive little Susie is outmatching you."

"Well, I...,"

"You are stupid," Linus cut him off, straight-faced.

Dan was petrified, too afraid to say anything – Linus answered to no one. Even Harold had no power to direct him. Linus only answered to those of *Us* who were somewhere near the top – and Dan had little insight into those above Harold. Dan had deep admiration for Linus and wished he could be just as disciplined as he was.

"You need to take care of Susie."

"But, Harold wanted me...,"

Linus put both hands on the top of his guide cane and slammed its end into the pavement. "Your questions will not change my directive."

249

Dan nodded.

"Do you understand?"

Dan nodded again – temporarily forgetting that Linus was blind – and then answered, "Yes, I understand."

Linus smiled and took a deep breath, "Let's go have some fun."

*　　　*　　　*

Susie met with Father Crane outside of his monastery in a field of cabbages. There was a light drizzle, but neither she nor Father Crane cared.

"So Linus has directed Dan to focus on you and not Big Dynamite or Eddie."

"It's just a decoy," she said.

Father Crane shook his head, "I do not think so. I believe that Linus wants to avoid having Dan and Eddie get too close to each other. Eddie can take care of Big Dynamite on *His* own. This also explains why *They* did not appear too interested in Big Dynamite – Eddie always holds him close. I do not think *We* will be able to get to Big Dynamite to save him. Eddie appears to have abilities that far exceed *Our* own – including me."

"Something doesn't feel right about this."

Father Crane raised an eyebrow, "Is your Polarity telling you something that has not been considered?"

"No. It just seems too contrived. I don't know… it's like Linus is telling *Us* what to do."

Father Crane paced slowly back and forth with his hands behind his back.

"I guess I should just keep tabs on Dan," Susie said.

Father Crane stopped pacing, "No. I will."

"Why?"

"I need to take some time to focus on Dan. I will not elaborate."

Susie didn't want to ask any more questions in case *They* were monitoring the conversation. She reasoned that Father Crane just wanted to throw *Them* a curveball – switching Father Crane to Dan would cause *Them* to re-assess *Their* strategy.

"Okay, what should I do until then? Keep on G-Man, the other thug? He won't be out of jail for another two days – on Wednesday," Susie said.

"Focus on Linus – I am not certain what *His* true purpose here is. I am afraid that Spike has become too bored with *Him* and he is missing details – the fact that Linus instructed Dan was unexpected. G-Man is safe in jail. It will be either Linus or Dan who will take care of him once he gets out. Just monitor Linus. Do not confront *Him*."

"What about Harold?"

Father Crane exhaled, took off his glasses, and massaged the bridge of his nose. "Harold is, of course, hatching some new plans. The best plan *We* can have is to take *Him* down through the murder of Frank's family."

* * *

Harold was in his office sitting on a firm, hand-crafted, fine leather couch sipping on a glass of 30-year-old single malt scotch. He looked at his watch, put his glass down, and picked up his phone from the marble end table at his right. The phone rang. It was Sully.

"This is Harold," he said.

"Harold!" Sully shouted, panicking.

"Who is this?"

Harold could only hear heavy breathing with intermittent crying. He leaned forward to reach his laptop on the coffee table in front of him. He refreshed the news site on his web browser to reveal the headline: *NEW YORK MILLIONAIRE INVESTOR'S FAMILY TRAGEDY* – *Three children dead. Wife in critical condition.* Another headline read *Hurricane Pummels East Coast.*

Harold smiled. "Hello?" he asked.

"This is… This is Sully," he said through tears.

"Sully – are you okay?"

Harold read through the news article while he waited for Sully to regain some composure. The article explained that his wife and kids were traveling together in an SUV that was hit by a passenger train.

It was freight train, but close enough, Harold thought.

"Sully?" Harold asked again.

"Harold… my kids… my kids are dead. My wife… she's… she's…,"

"Oh my goodness, Sully – is there anything I can do?"

"I don't know," Sully sniffed.

"If you're in town, come on over. I'll clear my schedule for you."

"Thanks. I'll be right there."

Sully hung up. Harold picked up his scotch and toasted. "Good work, Jennifer."

Within twenty minutes, Sully was in Harold's office, sitting next to him on the couch. Harold had given Sully his bottle of scotch – and Sully drank directly from it. "I can't fly out east to see my kids because of the hurricane that's hitting the east coast. I'm stuck here in L.A. and I have nowhere else to go."

"You're always welcome here," Harold said, patting Sully on the shoulder.

Sully stared blankly forward. "My wife has head injuries and they think she won't ever wake up." Sully took a swig of the scotch and said, "I've got nothin'. There's nothin'."

"For what it's worth, Sully, I went through hell when I lost my wife. I know that it's tough. I know that everyone has their own personal hell."

"This is it," he said, taking another swig.

"It took me some time to recover. You, too, should take time. As your friend, it pains me to see you suffer."

"What did you do when you lost your wife?"

Harold sat up and said, "Well, I… I went through an amazing transformation. It was almost as if I was a completely different person. As hard as it seems to fathom, I found myself more focused. I know it's easier said than done – but at that moment, I decided to do what I thought my wife would want me to do."

Sully turned to Harold, "What's that?"

"Everything I can to make the world better. I imagined my wife being with me and I never wanted to let her down. I gave everything I had – and I still do – to honor the short time I still have on this planet. Even at this very moment, I want her to be proud of what I'm doing as if she was here watching me do it."

"We could all be dead tomorrow," Sully said, staring toward the floor.

"Yes, that's right."

"And what would we have to show for it?" Sully asked, turning his head toward Harold.

"Yes."

Sully put the bottle on the coffee table in front of them and stood up. "I have $400 million and I'd gladly give it all just to have another minute with my kids and wife."

"I would do the same for my wife, but…"

"But it's just a fantasy," Sully interrupted.

Harold stood up, picked up the bottle, and returned it to a glass shelf in his bar area. "What would your wife and kids want you to do?" he asked.

Sully turned around towards Harold and said, "They would want me to make a difference."

"Like cure Crohn's disease?"

Sully nodded, "Yes – that's what they would want. Their poor mama went through so much suffering from it. All of my money was going to go to them, but now I think something that this is probably the best place to put it."

"I know it's not easy to see through the pain."

Sully shook his head, "No – I can see through it. I need to take action. My wife and kids wouldn't want to see me cry myself to death."

"Well, what do you want to do?" Harold asked.

"Do you donate to any of the Crohn's charities?" Sully asked.

"Yes, I donate nearly fifty thousand a year to one, but... well..."

"Well what?" Sully asked.

"I just don't think it does much good, considering that there are 39 other charities also focused on Crohn's."

"Just like we talked about last week," Sully said, sitting down again.

"Yes – it's really a shame. I really wished that just one of them would get all of the funding. It's just there's so much politics keeping them all alive."

"You talked about some pretty shady stuff though. You talked about how it would be possible to steer the world... to force the world to look at the problems that mattered most."

"Well, I talked about how easy it was for the world to be convinced that I was dead – it was just a few people most likely."

Sully turned to Harold, stiffened his posture, and said, "You talked about what would happen if the U.S., China, or Russia was behind something like this... and how it would be unstoppable."

Harold perked up.

Sully pointed to his head, "I remember these things."

"Oh, well, I don't think you can buy off those countries."

"You also said that you knew of some other ways to make it happen... some that are more shady... that some people already approached you before."

Harold nodded, "Yes, but it's a question of ethics."

"Ethics? Where are the ethics of people wasting their money forty different directions ensuring that Crohn's will never be cured?"

"Sully... I can't have Beytern...,"

"Screw Beytern. I got money. I got nowhere to spend it."

Harold was silent.

Sully leaned towards Harold, "Please. Please tell me."

Harold looked down, closed his eyes, and gulped with dramatic flourish.

"Please," Sully implored.

"Well, okay... Okay, Sully...," Harold said and sat down. "There are very tiny nations that most people don't even know exist. These nations are so small that they are referred to as micro-nations. One of which is the Principality of Sealand. It's literally just off the coast of England – basically just a platform the size of a football field."

"What makes it special?"

"Well, it's rumored to house Internet servers for business that's not approved internationally. Because it is its own nation, it can do whatever it wants and no one can stop it. Crime syndicates in other countries are rumored to route all of their transactions through these servers and there's nothing – not a thing – anyone can do about it."

"What do I have to do?" Sully asked.

Harold shook his head.

"Tell me. Please, tell me."

"Buy the little country and all of its Internet servers with it. Hire cheap labor by the thousands from third world countries.

Have this cheap labor use these servers to inundate social media and the rest of the Internet with a particular cause. Also, hire black market hackers to live in your new country to crack whatever institutions stand in your way. You can make the other 39 Crohn's competitors become irrelevant overnight. Money towards Crohn's will finally have a focus."

Sully's eyes widened.

"I told you that it was unethical."

Sully shook his head, "No… no… that's brilliant. How can I make this happen? You mentioned that you were approached by people about it."

Harold inhaled deeply. "I will give you a phone number. Call it. Tell the person who answers that you're interested in real estate off the coast of England. They will help you with everything else," he said.

"I will."

"One more thing."

"Yes?"

"I will deny this conversation ever happened."

Sully shook Harold's hand.

Chapter 17 – Night Out

Susie took Father Crane's instruction and focused on Linus. The monotony of his movements was basic and boring: Work out, followed by trying to kill Spike, and then repeat. Linus didn't have more to his life at the moment, apparently. There was nothing for her to do until tomorrow night – when she was to go out with Eric. This was an opportunity for her to bolster her display that Eric meant nothing to her.

Time to go out and find a guy or two, she thought.

Why not? Other than tracking Linus, she only had to ensure her own safety. In a strange way, this would be a vacation. Even though it was Monday, there was always something going on in L.A. With her Polarity she could go into any club or celebrity party with very little questioning, so she grabbed her purse, caught a cab, and went straight to a discount clothing store to buy clothes. She already knew that she would be widely noticed at these chic events for her choice in apparel – the clothes she would wear would be so foreign to the partiers that they would assume that she was on the leading edge of fashion.

Less than forty dollars later, Susie was in a burgundy halter top, white cuffed shorts, and matching four-inch stiletto heels. It wasn't what she wanted to wear – or what other women would praise her the most for wearing; it was what she predicted would get solid attention from guys.

She hailed a cab as one drove by. It pulled over and she got in.

"Where ya going?" the cab driver asked.

"100858 Mulholland Drive, Beverly Hills."

"You know someone there?"

"Rico Nevos," she answered.

"Wow."

"It's a long story."

Rico Nevos was the latest 20-something Hollywood hunk to break into the movie scene. He held large parties every night at his home. There were so many people showing up, he would have no idea who was invited and who wasn't.

He will be broke in four years, Susie thought.

The cab pulled up to the entrance of Rico's estate. The front gate was wide open and cars were parked across his vast lawn. Music was booming over the large gathering of people inside – and nearly over-flowing – from his house. All three stories were bursting with energy.

Susie entered the house and briefly thought about whom she should talk to first. She spotted Demetri – he looked like her type. He was wearing a Polo shirt and jeans. He was almost six feet tall and had short, dark hair. His biceps would peek from his sleeves whenever he lifted his hands. He was talking to two other guys, looked happy, and animated. She let her Polarity take it from here…

Susie walked up to Demetri and said, "I'm new here. Can you show me around?"

258

"Sure," Demetri said and grabbed her hand.

He led her upstairs and opened the door to a room. Inside, there were three couples already in there – most of their clothes were already off.

"Is this okay?" he asked.

That was fast – a bit too fast. She spotted another guy, Scott, who was further inside the house...

Susie walked up to Scott and said, "Have any of you seen Rico?"

Scott said, "Yeah, I can take you to him."

"Thanks."

Scott grabbed Susie's hand and allowed her to move in front of him. They walked forward, but a group of people in front of them immediately choked up their movement. Scott put his hand on Susie's lower back and gently pushed her forward through the group. His hand slowly started sliding down. Susie perked up, not sure how to react. She grabbed his hand and held it as they maneuvered through the group. Susie looked back at Scott and smiled at him. He narrowed his eyes and returned a confident grin.

"Is Rico upstairs?" Susie asked.

"What?!" Scott yelled over the noise of the group.

Susie turned around and asked again, "Is Rico upstairs?"

"I don't know. Sure. Why not?" Scott answered confidently.

He grabbed her waist.

Susie went through similar scenarios with six more guys – each one of them made short work of leading her to sex. She was surprised that she was actually surprised about this. Ten more guys, ten more similar results. She used her Polarity to go to a different party and, unsurprisingly, she got the same results.

In the corner of a large room was a full bar complete with a dedicated bartender – an older woman who was 47. Susie worked her way through the crowd of people to get something to drink.

"Can I have a bottled water?" Susie asked.

The bartender ducked down and popped up with a bottle of water.

"Thanks," Susie said.

"You're welcome."

"Can I ask you a question?" Susie asked.

"Sure."

"Why is it when I talk to a guy all he ends up doing is leading me to sex?"

The bartender smiled, "That's probably the most rational question I've been asked since I got here." She looked Susie over, leaned forward, and quietly asked her, "You're a virgin, right?"

Susie didn't budge.

"Whatever you do with that is up to you, but no matter what you never talk to the guy first – ever. You do and he'll get right to the end real quick."

Susie took a sip from her bottle.

The bartender continued, "Every guy wants sex and there's nothing you're gonna do to stop it. You don't want to stop it. Trust me – at my age – you don't want to."

"Okay."

"The trick is this: Guys want sex, but it doesn't mean they want you. It doesn't mean they'll stick around. But – more importantly – you gotta decide if YOU want the guy to stick around. This is for YOU – not for HIM. I've seen too many girls convince themselves to stick with the wrong guy."

Susie thought about this for a brief moment. "That's good advice, Delores," she said.

"Oh, how did you know my name?"

"Well… you look familiar somehow."

"Maybe we knew each other in a past life," Delores winked.

Susie laughed, "Well, thanks."

Delores winked at Susie, "Take care, hun!"

With that, Susie went back towards Demetri and walked by him. She caught his attention and his eyes traced her body from top to bottom. She smiled and stopped.

"Do I know you?" Demetri asked.

"You're Demetri. You're Martina's brother."

"You know my sister?"

"Sort of."

Knowing Demetri's sister meant that Demetri would be on better behavior. He didn't want to hurt his sister's friend – he would never hear the end of it from her.

"Oh, well… welcome to Rico's party. It never stops," Demetri said, then took a sip from his bottle of beer.

"It doesn't look like it."

"This has been going on for like five days in a row," Demetri said.

"I wanna dance," Susie said, pointing to the living room area where people were dancing.

"Sure," Demetri said.

Susie grabbed his hand and took him to the dance area. She wasn't sure how to dance without looking stupid, but she also knew that no one else cared – especially Demetri. Just as long as she somewhat moved her body, legs, and arms to beat then she would be fine – all credited to her Polarity.

Thank you Polarity, she thought.

Demetri held his beer in one hand and danced with Susie. She grinned, knowing that Demetri was just as bad of a dancer as she was.

"You have a great smile!" Demetri shouted.

"Thanks!" she replied.

More people joined the floor – Susie and Demetri were forced closer to each other. Over the next twenty minutes the two danced to every song that was played. It was exciting to see his body move – it was sensual and inviting. Demetri's physique was hard for her to ignore – every movement he made caused her to want to grab him. Susie couldn't remember if she ever had a more exhilarating twenty minutes in her life and, by the end, Susie had already got close enough to Demetri that he had his arm clutched around her waist.

"You're very beautiful," he said.

Susie bit her lower lip and pulled him to her. She put her arms around him. He leaned in and they kissed. Demetri's hands wandered to the front of her body and up towards her chest, but before he could go any further, she brushed them away.

"I'm shy," she said.

"That's okay."

*   *   *

Dan watched Susie on and off late into the night while he lay in bed with April – another girlfriend. He preferred April the most because she never hassled him about staying, so he stayed whenever he could. Staying at different places made it difficult for *Them* to ambush him. He slowly got out of bed.

"You okay?" April asked.

"Yeah, just gonna go watch some TV."

"All right. I'm just gonna lay here and relax."

Dan walked into her living room and turned on the TV. He kept the volume low so he could think more clearly about how to set up G-Man's ambush. Father Crane or Susie stymied any plan he put together.

"It would be nice to have Jennifer's help," Dan said softly.

His phone beeped. It was a text from Harold.

No, it read.

Dan sat down and stared at the ceiling. He had to get Susie or Father Crane out of the equation before Wednesday's release of G-Man. Susie would be far easier since she was still new with her Polarity. Susie was with Demetri tonight – deep kissing at the moment – but she would be with Eric tomorrow.

I wonder how much she cares about Eric, he thought.

Dan didn't like the idea that Susie wasn't being stressed at the moment. He didn't believe that she could wholly ignore him – he was too important for her to ignore. He had to get her attention back to him and putting Eric's life in danger was the right plan to accomplish this. Besides, if she acted to protect Eric then Dan would know that she actually cared about him – and then he would have a true target to disrupt Susie's state of mind. To add the most drama, Dan would ensure that Eric's near demise would happen when Eric was with Susie.

Dan got up and left April's apartment without saying anything to her – he had left many times before like this, so he wasn't worried about her reaction. He got in his car and drove nearly an hour out of town to a landfill. Parked alongside the landfill was a row of garbage trucks.

Using his Polarity, he picked out the garbage truck that serviced Luigi's restaurant – the Italian restaurant that Eric frequented – and the surrounding area. The passenger's side was unlocked. He opened the door and spent a few minutes looking over the wide variety of objects strewn about the truck's cabin – empty soda cans, crumpled up pieces of paper, a few dozen balled-up plastic grocery bags, empty fast food containers, and other random pieces of junk that were clearly once someone else's garbage.

Dan picked out one of the empty soda cans and carefully crushed it in his hands until it was nearly flat in its middle. He placed it under the garbage truck's brake pedal – a perfect fit. He then set the crushed soda can on top of the passenger's seat – knowing that it would be knocked to the floor on the driver's side at the needed moment. Like the fuel truck earlier, causing vehicles to go out of control by forcing objects under the brake pedal was a favorite method used by *Us* – the public would never look any further than bad luck as the cause.

Dan took a few of the grocery bags and got out of the garbage truck. He picked out several broken light bulbs, a badly soiled towel, and small piece of plywood from the garbage nearby. The broken light bulbs were put on top of the plywood and then covered with the towel. He stomped down on the towel, freeing up all of the loose glass from the light bulbs. The stomping continued until all of the shards were smaller than grains of rice. Once completed, he carefully poured the fine broken shards into a grocery bag.

Okay… next is the grease.

He closed his eyes to focus on the mounds of refuse piled around him – he was looking for grease. His Polarity found empty containers of axel grease, ball bearing grease, and motorcycle chain grease in several locations. All of these containers were buried to varying degrees under the tons of trash – he settled on ball bearing grease because its container was the easiest to reach. Dan picked up a nearby wooden plank and walked to a trash mound about thirty yards away. He used the wooden plank to dig through several feet of trash – the odor made him gag. Finally, he found the mostly empty container of ball bearing grease. He put the container in an empty grocery bag, walked back to his car, and drove off.

Dan had spent so much time at the landfill that he was certain that this would catch Susie's attention. However, she was still dancing and kissing the night away with Demetri – seemingly unmoved by his actions.

Dan headed to Laughy Hour, the comedy club that Eric and Susie would go to the next night. It was nearly midnight and the last show had just finished. Patrons were pouring out of the exit. Dan got out of his car with his bags of broken glass and ball bearing grease. He approached the doorman.

"Hey, I think I left my wallet in there earlier. Is it okay if I go in and look?" Dan asked the doorman.

"Yeah, go ahead," he said, waving his arm towards the inside.

"Thanks."

Dan walked inside. There were several dozen tables scattered about. Each of the tables had several chairs propped upside-down on them – a man nearby was sweeping the floor.

"Have you seen a black wallet?" Dan asked the man.

The man looked at Dan and scratched his head, "No, I haven't... hmm... but let me go ask our manager if anyone's turned one in."

"Thanks, man."

As soon as the man walked away, Dan took the ball bearing grease out of its bag. He unscrewed the lid and scooped up a finger-full of grease. He scraped the grease on the feet of one of the upside-down chairs that was near the stage. The grease's color was transparent enough that it was barely noticeable. Once finished, he quickly wiped his greasy finger across the backside of his pants. A moment later, the man returned.

"No one turned in a wallet. I'm sorry."

"Really? It couldn't have ended up in a lost and found box or something?"

"We do have a lost and found box. You're welcome to look through it. Come on, I'll show ya," the man said, waving Dan his direction.

"Thanks."

Dan followed the man into a hallway that led into the club's kitchen. He opened a door to a closet in the hallway, revealing a large cardboard box full of coats, sunglasses, hats, and other mostly clothing items.

"Here ya go," the man said.

Dan groaned, "It's worth a shot."

"Knock yourself out. I gotta get back to sweepin'," the man said and left.

Dan rummaged through the cardboard box until the man was no longer in sight. He then quickly walked into the kitchen and grabbed a large bag of sugar. He dumped nearly all of its contents into a nearby large metal bowl. He then dumped the tiny shards of glass into the sugar bag with the small amount of sugar he left behind. He shook the contents a few times and looked inside.

Perfect.

He then dumped the sugar in the bowl back into the bag and carefully put the bag of sugar back where he found it. He jogged over to the cardboard box and put his hands on his head. "Where is it?" he asked aloud.

"What are ya lookin' for?" a woman walking into hallway asked.

"My wallet. It's gone. This really sucks."

"Yeah I wouldn't expect many people to turn in a wallet. I'm sorry. If it makes you feel any better, I can give you a free pass for a future show."

"Thanks," Dan said softly.

Susie is on her way home. Father Crane is asleep at the monastery.

Dan wanted to return his focus back to Big Dynamite or G-Man, but he dared not disobey Linus. He went back to April's house and – having a key to her apartment – went in and joined her in bed.

Chapter 18 – A Date

It was late Tuesday morning and Susie awoke alone in her hotel room – she left Demetri at the party when he excused himself to go to the bathroom. She uncontrollably smiled – she could go out like that every night. She briefly thought about the dullness of her life in the not-so-distant past. It felt so distant. She had never felt so full of life.

"You knew that Linus would be easy to watch. You knew that I would go out. You wanted me to experience this. You wanted me to learn to relax. Is that right Father Crane?"

She received a text from him that read, *Ask me again in two minutes.*

Susie sat up in bed. Her body filled with negative energy. Her heart raced and her mouth began to water. A click was heard at her door.

CLICK

The door opened and Linus entered. Susie jumped off the bed and scooted back to the window.

"Relax, dear lady. I have no intention to kill *You*… yet."

"LEAVE."

Linus shook his head. "*Your* words are not so convincing."

"Why are *You* here?"

Linus walked up to her. Susie couldn't help it – she began to swing her fists wildly at Linus. Linus dodged each swing effortlessly. Susie eventually stopped.

"*Your* control of *Your* Polarity is pathetic. *You* should also consider more physical training to have a chance with *Us*," Linus said, adjusting his black sunglasses.

"Why are *You* here?!" she yelled.

Linus got in her face and said, "Did I rattle *You?*"

Susie didn't move.

"Good," he said and walked away.

Susie shook uncontrollably. Her heart pounded fiercely. She was but a half-thought away from destroying everything around her – a deadly mix of anger and aggression – all driven by a million different ways she replayed the last minute with Linus through her Polarity.

A moment later, she was able to regain her focus. She walked over to her bed, picked up her phone, and scrolled through her previous texts. Over the past hour, Spike had sent her a number of texts warning her about Linus's visit. Once again, she missed the texts because she was too caught up in the moment. She clenched her fists – angry that she wasn't able to handle herself better with Linus. However, she slowly calmed herself down knowing that the confrontation could have been far worse. Father Crane's previous advice about allowing oneself to make mistakes so one can better react to them was priceless – she had to embrace it fully and Linus's visit was proof. Mind games were a tool both sides used to distract one another – she had to recover.

Any joy that Susie felt from her night was instantly refunded back to the reality of the world of Polarity. She felt unnerved about dropping her guard just a little bit this evening with Eric, pondering if *They* would try something. She was tempted to use her Polarity to predict Eric's fate but stopped herself – she didn't want to feel tempted to change future events and reveal that she cared about him.

I will watch for my safety and I will watch Linus – just as Father Crane asked me to.

She couldn't help but think briefly about Dan. Through her Polarity, she saw Dan eating brunch in the restaurant of her hotel. She tried to track him forward, but she couldn't make out exactly where he would be throughout the day or evening. G-Man was due out of jail tomorrow, Wednesday, and it didn't appear that Dan had anything concrete in place for him. She looked into G-Man's future and saw that he would easily make it to the police by Thursday morning to turn himself in. There were no surprises.

Susie took a shower, got dressed, and went downstairs. She saw Dan sitting at a table, slowly sipping coffee. He was wearing a baseball cap and he still had some visible cuts on his face. He looked up at her as she approached him. She sat down across from him.

"*You* had quite a night," Dan said.

"It was all right," she said, yawning.

"I didn't know *You* had a slutty side."

"I'm a bit too groggy to react to whatever *You* just said."

"Have some coffee," he said, motioning his hand at the coffee pitcher in front of him.

She shook her head, "*You've* poisoned it."

Dan smirked, "Just a little."

Susie folded her arms and sat back in her chair.

"What? Frustrated?" Dan asked.

"No. *We* found out about Eddie."

"Eddie's an interesting guy. Good luck with him."

"*He's* coming by here with *His* partner in a few minutes to look for me."

"Well, Eddie's got to play his role."

Susie leaned forward and said, "*He* can't hide anymore. Big Dynamite and G-Man will make it to the police alive."

"Nah. Eddie's got his ways. I really don't think any of *You* can keep up with him – *You* haven't so far."

Susie got up and walked away.

"Oh, have fun with Eric tonight," Dan said.

She kept a straight face and didn't stutter in her walk, trying her best to ignore any thoughts about Eric.

"I'm gonna have fun with him today!" Dan shouted.

Susie didn't bother to use her Polarity to determine an appropriate response to Dan – she reasoned that saying anything would make Dan more inclined to believe she cared about Eric. She was resolute to ignore Dan if it appeared that he was to have anything to do with Eric. She had to focus on Linus, just as Father Crane instructed.

*   *   *

Vinny and Eddie drove away from Susie's hotel.

"And we miss her again," Vinny said, defeated.

"Yup."

"Do you suppose we have a rat?" Vinny asked.

Eddie looked briefly at Vinny and then returned his attention to driving, "You think someone on our side is tipping her off?"

"Yeah. It's like that same someone is tipping off Frank, too. It's just beyond me how close we always come to getting them and they always get away."

Eddie shrugged his shoulders, "I suppose anything's possible. You got any suspects?"

"No, but it's the only thing that makes sense. I mean, who has something to lose with this whole thing?"

Eddie shook his head.

"I wonder, if we caught Frank or Susie, whether we would be led to find out who killed Frank's family and why," Vinny said.

"That's a stretch, Vinny."

"You got anything better?"

Eddie took out some pills and popped them in his mouth.

"You should get a second opinion about your heartburn – you pop pills like you have some crazy addiction."

"Let's just get over to the Stewart house," Eddie said.

"Sure."

The two didn't say a word for the fifteen-minute drive to the Stewarts. They parked their car in front of the house and knocked on the door. Mrs. Stewart answered.

"Oh hello, I wasn't expecting you again," she said.

"Oh, we're sorry to bother you again, but we'd like to ask you a few more questions if that's okay," Vinny asked.

"Sure. You're lucky to catch me at home – I'm normally at work, but one of the twins is home with the flu. I only have about twenty minutes to talk – my other twin is having problems with his substitute teacher and I have a parent/teacher call. I don't know where his usual teacher is – it's been like this for about week. His substitute is a disaster," she said, placing her hand on her forehead.

"Well, any time you can spare is appreciated."

A boy walked up to the door and stood behind Mrs. Stewart.

"And who's this?" Vinny asked, smiling.

"This is Sammy – he's the one with the flu."

"Wow, he does have blond hair," Vinny said, crouching down, smiling at Sammy.

Sammy hid behind Mrs. Stewart's leg.

"Don't mind Sammy – he's shy."

"Ma'am, have you seen Frank recently?" Eddie blurted.

Mrs. Stewart tilted her head up and her mouth opened slightly. "Why… yes. We went to a baseball game the other day. He left early."

"Do you realize that Frank is a wanted fugitive – burglary, armed robbery, attempted murder?" Eddie added.

Vinny closed his eyes, wishing Eddie wasn't being Eddie at the moment.

"Mrs. Stewart," Vinny interjected, "We're letting the police handle those issues. We just wanted to know if you were aware of any of Frank's activities outside of work or family."

Mrs. Stewart shook her head, "No… no I can't think of anything. He worked pretty late from time to time doing investigative work. Sometimes he'd be gone for a day or two."

"Anything unusual in the past year?" Vinny asked.

"Well, he seemed to have a rough time about a year ago. He looked tired… dirty… really worn out. It was for many weeks. It was like he had a nervous breakdown or something. He was on medical leave from work for a couple of months. It was just the stress that came with the job."

Sammy began to vomit on the floor.

"Oh honey… oh my poor baby. Excuse me, but I've got to take care of my son," Mrs. Stewart said, hugging Sammy.

"Thank you for your time," Eddie said.

Vinny and Eddie got back in their car and drove away.

"Did you have to dig into her like that?" Vinny asked. "We could have got a lot more out of her if we would just be nice."

"Nice isn't my thing – I hate it when people knowingly help the bad guys. I don't care what the reason is."

*   *   *

Dan left the hotel and drove a block away from Luigi's restaurant. He parked his car and walked towards the restaurant. Along the way, he picked a fast food bag out of a trashcan. A garbage truck drove by.

Right on time, he thought, watching it drive by.

He strolled toward Luigi's and stopped at the edge of its building. He looked out of the corner of his eye and saw Eric hauling full garbage bags from the back door to a dumpster about fifteen feet away. Dan groaned – Susie would have done something by now to save Eric. He slowly walked up to the front door and placed the fast food bag on the ground in plain sight. He walked back to the building's edge and – a few seconds later – he caught a glimpse of a woman from the restaurant picking up the fast food bag he left behind.

"Hey Eric!" the woman yelled outside. "I've got more garbage for you hun, if you don't mind!"

Eric was halfway to the dumpster with a garbage bag in-hand. He turned around, took a few steps back towards Luigi's, and yelled, "What?!"

CRASH!

A garbage truck plowed through the fence behind the dumpster and knocked it forward, narrowly missing Eric. Eric jumped back, falling to the ground.

Dan immediately turned his attention to Susie to see if she was paying attention. She was painting her toenails.

"Really?" Dan said, aghast.

*   *   *

Susie was in a new hotel. She finished painting her last toenail and briefly turned her attention to Linus – he had just executed a plan to set Spike's house on fire, but Spike easily foiled it. She then looked into her future for the next few hours – it was uneventful with no variation whatsoever. Father Crane sent her a text.

We will meet tomorrow morning. Do not alter your course, it read.

She had nothing to do until her date with Eric. She began to worry that boredom may cause her Polarity to stray towards Eric, Dan, or her family. She received another text from Father Crane.

Doing nothing is not easy, but it is sometimes the correct answer, it read.

She turned on the TV.

*   *   *

Dan walked along a sidewalk away from Luigi's, wondering how it was possible that Susie seemed so disinterested in the events that were to unfold during the date with Eric. Was she calling his bluff? Dan re-considered killing Eric in front of Susie, but he wasn't sure if he could completely get away with it – there were plenty of witnesses of his visit last night at the comedy club and there were security cameras that could implicate him. Dan's Polarity couldn't accurately predict how Susie would react to Eric's death – in each scenario she cried hysterically, but he wasn't sure if the crying was genuine or just a show for those around her. In any case, it was obvious to Dan that Susie was ignoring him.

Dan then peered into Father Crane's activities. Father Crane focused only on G-Man and Eddie – it didn't seem like he was interested in anything else.

Dan got in his car and drove across town. He stopped in front of a postal collection box at the corner of a busy intersection across from the city's Natural Science Museum. He put on a utility belt and a hard hat that he had bought earlier. He then got out of his car, but not before grabbing an orange pylon from his back seat. He set up the pylon near the postal collection box, took a wrench from his utility belt, and proceeded to loosen all of the bolts securing the collection box to the ground. Passers-by ignored him.

*　　　　*　　　　*

It was 5:32 P.M. Susie turned off the TV and went outside the hotel just as an available cab was approaching. She hailed it and got in, instructing the driver to take her to Luigi's restaurant so she could meet up with Eric. She beamed, in anticipation of the evening with Eric, but she quickly rubbed her face to hide her emotion from *Them*.

Susie continued to keep her Polarity focused on Linus and herself, for her own safety. However, she knew that once she was with Eric this also meant that she would see his future whenever he was with her. She concluded that she wouldn't look ahead any further than five minutes into the future when she would be with him – she would always be a target by *Them* and she couldn't keep her guard completely down. This "five minute rule" was a reasonable compromise. She wasn't entirely sure if she would be able to ignore any eminent danger that Eric may face within that five-minute window.

Her night with Demetri helped shrug off any perceived importance that Eric – or anyone else – would have in her life. She just had to keep *Them* guessing. Passing out the 400 cards with Dan's picture taught her that *They* won't spend all of *Their* time watching her – that *They*, too, have to make judgment calls as to when to ignore what she was doing.

The cab pulled up to Luigi's. Susie got out of the cab and noticed there was a large tow-truck there pulling away a garbage truck. Eric was standing outside with a few people watching – one of them was Margie, the waitress that served them earlier.

"Hey," Susie said, walking up to him.

He turned around and smiled. Oh yeah – she liked him. His gaze was potently addicting.

"Oh… hey!" he said, brightly smiling, and then looked down at his clothes – there were a few stains on his shirt. "I'm uh… I'm a little behind. There was an accident here."

Susie was a few feet away and said, "An accident? What happened?"

"That garbage truck just came out of nowhere and plowed through that fence," he said pointing behind him. "It knocked this dumpster forward. It almost hit me."

"You were lucky," Margie said.

"Tell me about it," Eric said.

Don't think about it, Susie thought.

"Are you okay?" Susie asked.

"Yeah. I'm a little dirty, though. I was holding a bag full of garbage and it spilled all over me. I'm sorry… I don't have another shirt with me."

"You're not looking for an excuse to take off your shirt, are you?" Susie joked.

Eric laughed, "I swear I'm not. Everything happened exactly like I said."

"You're fine. Besides, I don't think anyone will notice," Susie said.

"Thanks," he said, looking her over. "Those clothes look nice on you."

"Thank you."

"Oh – where are my manners?" Eric said, looking around at the several people nearby. "Everyone, this is Susie. Susie, this is everyone."

"Hello," they all said, somewhat in unison.

"Hi," Susie waved. "I already know Margie."

"That's right," Margie said. "Eric, you get out of here with this nice young woman and show her a good time."

"I will," Eric told her.

A cab then pulled up.

"Oh, there's our cab," Eric said and then turned to Susie, "After you."

Susie walked towards the cab and Eric briefly put his hand on her back as she walked by – it sent shivers through her body. They got in the cab.

"We're going to the Laughy Hour Comedy Club," Eric said to the driver – a scruffy, jovial man in his late 60's.

"Out for a night of fun?" the driver asked.

"Yeah," Eric said.

Susie cut out of the discussion briefly to check five minutes into the future – nothing stuck out at her.

"We'll have to try one," Eric said to Susie.

"Huh?" she asked blankly.

"The driver suggested we try Laughy Hour's homemade ice cream," Eric said.

"They make it fresh – cream, sugar… the whole nine yards," the driver said. "They do it in a matter of seconds by dipping the ingredients in liquid hydrogen or something. It's unlike any ice cream you'll ever have."

"Oh, that does sound good," Susie said, locking eyes with Eric.

Eric held out his hand. Susie held it – heaven. It then occurred to her that her feelings towards Eric were too obvious. She had to do something that she wouldn't do. What would Demetri do? Susie leaned in towards Eric. Eric leaned in and gently kissed her lips.

"That was nice," she told him.

"It was almost as good as the first," he said.

He put his left hand softly on her right cheek and kissed her again. Susie's heart pounded – she wanted more, she couldn't get enough of it. She blushed.

"I'm glad you could make it out tonight," he said.

She smiled briefly and then her face lit up in surprise, "Oh, do you mind if I send a text out real quick?"

"No, not at all."

Susie took out her phone and typed, *Demetri – This is Susie from last night. I can't stop thinking about you. Will you be at Rico's tonight?*

YES, the response said, a few seconds later.

*   *   *

Wow. She fell off the deep end – all good girls do, I suppose, Dan thought, waiting a block away from Laughy Hour.

*   *   *

Eric and Susie were dropped off at Laughy Hour. They held hands as they walked inside. An usher greeted them.

"Reservation?"

"Yeah – two for Eric," Eric replied.

"Ah, up front at the stage. You sure you want to sit there?" the usher asked.

"I called ahead for the best seats. Comedians tend to heckle those sitting up front – if you're okay with that."

"I don't mind," Susie said.

"You'll have a great time," the usher said.

They sat down and a waitress immediately tended to them, "The show will start in about fifteen minutes. Can I get you something to eat or drink?"

"Susie, what would you like?" Eric asked.

"Water, please," she replied.

"And for you?" the waitress asked Eric.

"Oh – that ice cream that I heard about…," Eric said.

"Laughy's Brain Freeze?" the waitress asked.

"Yeah, you make it fresh?" Eric asked.

"Yup. Large or small?"

"I'll go for a large – if it's that good, it has to be large. Oh, and a water for me," Eric said.

Susie felt *Their* presence nearby – her body tingled, detecting opposite Polarity. She saw nothing in the next five minutes that would cause her harm. Her blood ran hot and she cracked her knuckles.

"Are you okay?" Eric asked.

"Oh, I just forgot to do something. No big deal."

"If you need to take care of something, go right ahead."

"No it's okay. It'll be fine."

Eric grinned, "The comedians tonight are supposed to be really funny…"

Susie kept her eyes on Eric but continually checked five minutes into the future to evaluate how much danger she could be facing. Finally, in her Polarity, she saw Dan tripping over a waitress and then walking towards her. She immediately ignored her Polarity – Dan wouldn't risk hurting her or Eric in person with so many people around.

"Nothing is better than a good laugh," Susie said.

"Nope," Eric said.

"It's good to take a break and do this."

"So… what do you do? Work? School?" Eric asked.

"Yeah, I'm in school – well, not this semester. I'm taking a break. What about you?"

"I take a few classes and work as a valet – my weekends are usually shot because of that. But the tips are usually good and it frees up my days."

∗   ∗   ∗

Dan was already in Laughy Hour, sitting in the back. He kept a watchful eye on Susie to see if there was any hint that she was picking up on Eric's imminent danger. The conversation she was having with Eric was boring him, but she seemed engaged.

Three more seconds and I'll stop it.

Dan counted to three, stood up, and walked towards the kitchen area. As he approached, he faked tripping over something and he rolled into the legs of Susie and Eric's waitress – the contents of her tray fell to the floor.

"Whoa!" Dan yelled. "Sorry about that. I tripped on something," he said, standing up.

"Oh… it's all right," the waitress said, putting her hands on her hips, sighing. "I need to go get a mop."

The noise had caught the attention of many people in the mostly crowded room – including Eric and Susie. Eric, who was turned around in his chair, returned to facing Susie to resume their conversation. Dan walked towards them slowly. He watched Susie's fists tighten up as she put them under the table.

Dan could hear Eric say, "Well, excuse me. I have to hit the restroom."

As Eric stood up, he immediately slipped – but just as he was about to fall back on his head, Dan was there to catch him.

"Easy there," Dan said.

Eric caught his breath.

"It looks like there's grease or something on the floor here – it's everywhere," Dan said, pointing at the ground. "You should tell someone about it."

"Wow… thanks. That all happened so fast," Eric gasped.

"No problem, man," Dan said.

Eric walked away towards the restroom. Dan sat down in his chair.

The waitress walked up to their table and told Susie, "We used our last bit of sugar on your Brain Freeze – and it just ended up on the floor. Excuse me, I need to help clean it up."

"It was my fault," Dan said, playfully raising his hand but keeping eye contact with Susie.

The waitress walked away.

"I should have killed him," Dan said.

"With all the trouble *You* went through to set things up – it sure seems like a lot of wasted time to not go through with it," Susie said.

Dan raised an eyebrow, "It's not like *Your* kind to be so cold towards humanity. *You're* hiding something."

"Are *You* playing psychotherapist again or can't *You* recognize sarcasm?"

"Oh shut up – *You* can comfort *Yourself* with words. I believe *You're* failing pretty miserably in protecting the evidence against Harold."

"All of this time, Dan – all of this time that *You* spent on me. Wow. Do *You* really think it was worth it? What do *You* think *Our* plan was? How much do *You* have set up to kill G-Man? Nothing, is it? *You're* more interested in my love life. I'm sure Harold will be really happy with *You*."

Dan stood up and walked away.

Oh my God that was close, Susie thought, trying her best to keep an even composure.

Chapter 19 – Timing Everything

It was Wednesday morning. Vinny walked into a breakfast diner alone, carrying his laptop bag.

"Just one?" the hostess asked.

"Yeah," he said.

"Come with me," she said as she grabbed a menu and led him into the dining area.

Vinny looked across the room and spotted Nemec. Nemec noticed Vinny and waved him over.

"Oh ma'am – I'll be joining the guy over there," he said, pointing at Nemec.

"Oh, okay," she said and walked away.

Vinny walked over to Nemec, his head tilted low.

"Hey, Vinny. What are the odds I'd see you here? You can join me if you like."

"You sure? I'd be really pissed if I was you."

"Oh I am, but at the end of the day we're not the police or the FBI – we're just people. I admit that I have my emotions wrapped tightly in Frank's case... I just wanted to help him so badly," he said and then took a sip of coffee. "I've been told to take him in dead or alive now. It's... it's hard to accept."

"My God. I'm sorry," Vinny said, sitting down and putting his laptop bag on the floor next to him.

Nemec shook his head, "Bah – Don't worry. I'm choosing to let the case go. I don't think I could hurt Frank. I guess that makes me a bad cop."

"It makes you human," Vinny said.

"Well, maybe, but philosophical conversations aside – where's your partner?"

"He called in sick – didn't leave many details."

Nemec's phone rang. He pressed a button to dismiss the call.

Nemec closed his eyes and swallowed a knot. "That was my ex-fiancé. She lost her job and she's asking me to help her with money problems. I just think she's looking for a way to get back together."

"She bothers you a lot?"

"I can tolerate a lot – she bothers me non-stop. Most of it is drunken gibberish."

The phone beeped.

"And she left me a voice mail. Listen to this," Nemec said, pressing a couple of buttons and setting his phone face-up on the table.

"This is... this is Sarah... I'm sorry about... about what happened between... between us. Please... please... GOD, I HATE YOU!"

The phone call ended.

Vinny, wide-eyed, said, "Wow, she has a temper."

"Fiery redhead. I'm razor-close to filing a restraining order on her."

"I would."

The waitress came back and asked Vinny, "What would you like?"

"Oh geez – my stomach still isn't right. Just a coffee for now, thanks."

The waitress walked away.

"What are your plans today?" Nemec asked.

"Frank," Vinny said.

"Frank… of course."

"And Susie," Vinny said.

"Susie… she's that girl that you're looking for, right?"

"Yeah," Vinny said and paused before saying, "We believe she has connections to Frank."

"How so?" Nemec asked.

"Well, Frank went on medical leave for a few months last year, right?"

"Yeah."

"Why?" Vinny asked.

"He said he had some personal problems – nothing specific," Nemec said.

Vinny took out his laptop and turned it on. While it booted up he said, "I'm gonna show you a video that was taken the day that horrible plane crash happened – you know… the one that was going from L.A. to Detroit."

"Yeah. Everyone died," Nemec said.

"Maybe not. We believe Susie was on that plane and lived somehow. But right before she got on it, she met up with Frank."

Nemec put his elbows on the table and rested his head in his palms. "I'm not gonna like this, am I?"

"You tell me," Vinny said.

The laptop was booted. Vinny clicked a few icons and a crystal-clear black and white video began playing.

"This is surveillance video from the airport – there isn't any audio, so we don't know what was said," Vinny said and then pointed, "You can see Frank standing over here on the right."

"Yeah – that's Frank. He's always had a goofy posture."

"Okay, in about ten seconds, a young woman appears on the left. That woman is Susie."

Ten seconds later, Susie appeared in the video.

"Hmm, she looks familiar."

"Yeah?" Vinny asked.

"I met with a woman recently that looks like her, but her name was Linda."

"Oh?"

Nemec leaned in as they watched Frank approach Susie. Frank was struggling as he got closer to Susie, gripping his face and holding his hand out towards her. When Frank was about ten feet away from her, she fainted. Frank then scurried away.

Nemec's jaw dropped, "What was that? What did Frank do to that woman? Why did he go away like that?"

Vinny closed his laptop and said, "We don't know. But we do know it happened while Frank was on medical leave. And then – here we are a short time later – and Frank's family is dead. He's become a criminal practically overnight and he's avoided everyone from the beginning."

"Yeah – he hasn't even contacted us," Nemec said, staring down at the table. "Have you been able to talk to this woman… Susie?"

Vinny shook his head, "No – it's like she knows when we're coming. We've missed her – I don't know – countless times."

"Frank and I worked closely together. It would surprise me that he had anything else going on."

"Was there anyone that you guys busted that could have a grudge?"

Nemec chuckled, "Every drug hustler in the greater L.A. area."

Vinny sighed.

"Okay, lemme think," Nemec said and began to stir his coffee.

The waitress came back with Vinny's coffee.

"Thanks," he said to her.

"Uh huh," she replied and walked away.

"Okay," Nemec started, "Just before Frank went on medical leave, we busted up a small ring of pill-mill pushers. They were pissed – Frank was undercover and had them completely fooled. We busted six or seven guys – all went to jail or prison. Do you remember that guy, Big Dynamite, from the pictures you saw back at the station?"

"Yeah."

"He was one of them," Nemec said.

"It wouldn't hurt to find him and ask him a few questions, would it?"

Nemec looked down at the table, silent.

"Hey – no big deal. If you don't wanna go after Frank anymore, I understand," Vinny said.

Nemec tapped his fingers on the table for a few seconds and said, "I gotta know what happened to Frank. It's been eating at me."

"What do you wanna do?" Vinny asked.

Nemec stood up and threw a five-dollar bill on the table. "Let's go to police headquarters and find Big Dynamite's known addresses – they have more information than my station. We'll start there. I'll drive."

*　　　*　　　*

"G-Man will be released from jail in less than an hour from the police headquarters, one block away," Father Crane said to Susie. "I cannot foresee any difficulties with his safety – yet.

Eddie is at *His* home waking up from a minor drug overdose – I have never seen one of *Them* so uninvolved before."

The two of them stood apart from each other in an empty parking garage. Susie exhaled and shrugged her shoulders, "Do you think Eddie is just stringing *Us* along? Like *He* knows *We* are watching, so *He* doesn't do anything."

Father Crane inhaled slowly and said, "That is a possibility. Now that *He* has been exposed, *They* could have others targeting G-Man and Big Dynamite. Victory of this game played between *Us* and *Them* is unequivocally decided by who reacts the most effectively in the shortest amount of time. Still, there is the strategy of long, drawn-out patience. Convincing someone that you are doing nothing should not be ignored."

"What's the plan?"

"Keep your focus on Linus."

"Still? I thought you just wanted to make things easy on me so I could live a little."

Father Crane frowned, "I recall that Linus walked right into your room. If THIS is what you call easy then I would ask you to re-assess your abilities. You have improved on many fronts with your... well, diversification of activities. You will learn from your mistakes with them and you will get better at recovering from your mistakes as they happen."

"But I can help with G-Man's safety, can't I?"

Father Crane closed his eyes briefly. "Very well. I will give you thirty seconds to look into G-Man's future."

Susie closed her eyes to concentrate. G-Man was to be released from jail, go home to his mother, confess to her of his murders tomorrow morning, and then turn himself into the police with Big Dynamite on Saturday. She opened her eyes, "It's... it's very simple."

Father Crane said, "Officer Nemec and Agent Lagetti are going to the police headquarters at the moment. As they enter the building through the left front doors, G-Man will exit through the right front doors – they will never see each other. That is the only event that is even remotely interesting."

"Yeah, but all of it just seems so straight-forward... so..."

"Do you believe there is more?" Father Crane asked.

"I don't know."

"It is mankind's nature to investigate something only deep enough to confirm what was already believed beforehand; searching deeper may conflict with that belief, so the searching is stopped unconsciously once self-validation is attained. It is not any different for *Us* or *Them*. Mistakes are made because of this. If I missed something, please tell me," he said.

"There's nothing to miss. This just seems so..."

"Uneventful. No matter how many times I look into G-Man's future, it does not alter. The only conclusion I can make is that *They* do not intend to kill G-Man until sometime later. Even I have tried several hundred decoys – just to see Eddie or any of *Them* move in the slightest. I even altered the police record on Big Dynamite to make it easier for the police to connect him to Eddie. But, no, the future does not change."

"So there's nothing *We* can do?"

"There is nothing for *Us* to act on – yet. Eddie has timing that appears exceptionally refined. I have looked back in the past and it is difficult to discern, exactly, where *We* went wrong."

"I wish there was more I could do."

Father Crane began to walk away, "*We* are done here. Keep your focus on Linus."

*　　　　*　　　　*

Vinny was in the passenger seat of Nemec's police car on their way to police headquarters. His phone rang. Vinny looked at the caller ID.

"Hey, how 'bout that. It's Eddie," Vinny said, smiling.

"Oh," Nemec said.

Vinny answered the phone, "You feelin' better, big guy?"

"Yeah – just a bit stuffed up."

"You sound terrible."

"I'll be fine. What are you doin' right now?" Eddie asked.

"I'm with Nemec. We're headed up to police headquarters."

"Why's that?"

"There are a few guys he and Frank busted in the past that could know more about Frank and Susie – we just wanted to look up where they might be living and whatever other leads we can find. Who knows? Maybe it'll be that freaky guy who looks like Napoleon Dynamite. That would be funny."

Eddie was silent.

"Hello?" Vinny asked.

"Yeah, I'm still here. I'm just thinking."

"No apathy?" Vinny asked, smiling.

"No. I'll be right up there."

"You sure? You don't sound too good."

"What are you, my mother? I'll be there in ten minutes."

"We're about ten minutes away right now, so we should see each other."

Eddie hung up. Vinny looked at his phone. "Sometimes I can't figure that guy out," he said.

"What's up?" Nemec asked.

"Eddie is either fully engaged or he's fully apathetic – it's really peculiar and really unpredictable."

*   *   *

Father Crane was talking to a newlywed couple at the edge of a park – they were asking him about his past because they rarely saw Catholic priests so out in the open. Father Crane obliged but tried to keep the conversation brief.

He put his hand over his mouth, shocked.

"What?" the husband asked.

"I'm sorry, but I must go," Father Crane said and walked away, still hampered by his injuries.

Eddie wasn't supposed to go to police headquarters – it wasn't part of his predictions. He already knew that Eddie would call Vinny, but the phone call was supposed to end with Eddie staying at home for the rest of the day. He cracked his knuckles, realizing that Eddie's change in path occurred at the moment he was talking with the newlyweds. The slight distraction – just a few seconds – was all *They* needed.

Father Crane walked briskly towards police headquarters, uncertain as to what he should do. His injuries slowed him down considerably. His Polarity showed that Eddie would arrive there at the same time as Nemec and Vinny. However, from that point forth the future was constantly changing...

Nemec will notice G-Man as he is leaving jail and G-Man will run away...

Nemec will notice G-Man as he is leaving jail and G-Man will grab his gun...

Nemec won't chase after G-Man after he runs away...

Nemec will shoot G-Man with Vinny's gun...

Scenario after scenario filled Father Crane's head – it consumed him. He spent a full five minutes trying to make sense of it all. Finally, there wasn't enough time for Father Crane to discern what would happen – Vinny and Nemec had already parked in the back of police headquarters. Father Crane tried to run, gritting his teeth through the immense pain. He stopped, bent over, and planted his hands on his knees – there was nothing he could do. It was clear to Father Crane that Eddie's purpose for going to meet them was to ensure they wouldn't connect him with Big Dynamite and, now, to end the life of G-Man. *Their* timing was perfect and Eddie was seemingly unpredictable in every possible manner.

*   *   *

Vinny and Nemec were approaching the concrete steps leading up to the entrance of police headquarters.

"Hey guys!" Eddie yelled from across the street.

Eddie lightly jogged through a break in traffic, straight to Vinny and Nemec.

"Hey you're lookin' all right," Vinny said to Eddie.

"Yeah," Eddie said, gasping for air. "I just had to get moving."

"Well, we're happy to have you. Let's go inside," Vinny said.

Nemec lightly back-handed Vinny on his chest and pointed up at the doors of the building. "There's G-Man," he said.

Vinny saw a shorter man, covered with various tattoos, a deathly pale face, and a shaved head. The man stared at the ground while he walked lethargically forward.

"Who's G-Man?" Vinny asked.

"He's one of the guys Frank and I busted in that group."

Vinny walked up the steps as G-Man walked down. "Excuse me, sir," Vinny said to him.

G-Man stopped, "Who are you?"

"I'm Agent Vincent Lagetti, FBI. Could we have a few words with you?"

"FBI? Why?" G-Man asked and then looked behind Vinny, seeing Nemec and Eddie standing there.

G-Man's chest noticeably began heaving in and out.

"It's about Officer Frank Moore," Vinny answered.

G-Man shook his head rapidly, "I don't know who that guy is."

Eddie and Nemec walked up the stairs and stood next to Vinny. G-Man looked at them and he quickly averted his eyes, blinking them several times.

"Hey, what are you so nervous about?" Nemec asked him.

"You know something, don't ya?" Eddie asked him.

"You," G-Man said, pointing at Nemec.

"Me?" Nemec asked.

"Yeah, you busted me a few months ago, right?"

"I make lots of busts," Nemec said.

"No – you busted me. You're the only one I recognize here."

G-Man took a step towards Nemec. Nemec put his hand on his gun and unsnapped the holster that secured it.

"Whoa, man. Easy. I just wanted to tell you something," G-Man said.

"You're acting a little aggressive right now," Nemec said.

"Me? Aggressive? What? What did I do? I get out of jail and the next thing I know I'm surrounded by the FBI for Christ's sake."

Nemec took his hand off his gun and – just as quickly as he took his hand off – G-Man grabbed the gun from its holster. He pointed it at Nemec and yelled, "I'm not going back!"

Eddie fainted. As Eddie dropped to the ground, G-Man watched. Vinny drew his gun and fired one shot right in the head of G-Man.

BANG!

G-Man dropped to the ground as other policemen rushed out the front door to investigate.

Nemec took his gun back from G-Man's lifeless body and said, "Thanks, Vinny. That was quick thinking."

Vinny knelt down to help Eddie sit up. "Eddie – man, are you all right?"

Eddie stared listlessly ahead and then turned his head towards G-Man's body. "What happened?" he asked.

"You fainted or something," Vinny said.

Eddie looked up at Nemec. Nemec nodded.

"I'm sorry... I... I don't react well to situations like this. I'm embarrassed... I've been through too much of this. I have a hard time coping."

"It's okay, Eddie," Vinny said, "You distracted him perfectly. You saved Nemec's life."

"That was quick thinkin', Vinny. I'm glad you didn't hesitate," Nemec said, squatting down, examining G-Man's body.

"Thanks... I guess," Vinny said, downcast.

"You okay?" Nemec asked.

"Yeah – it just hasn't sunk in yet. It felt so automatic."

"That's good training. Sometimes there's no time to think. You just have to react."

"I guess," Vinny said, staring at the ground, unfocused.

Eddie sat by himself on the concrete stairs about twenty feet from Vinny and Nemec.

"Is he all right?" Nemec asked, looking towards Eddie.

"Eddie has been through a lot – he's been in the middle of some pretty bad shoot-outs. He shot and killed a child by accident a couple of years ago and, ever since then, he freezes up whenever guns are around."

"Dear Lord," Nemec said.

"Yeah, he's been getting help, but he's far from okay."

Chapter 20 – Setup the Setup

Susie sat in the art museum, pondering the events that had just unfolded. She regretted obeying Father Crane's directive that she only focus on Linus, but she wasn't sure what she could have done to save G-Man. She had enormous respect for Father Crane's abilities and felt uncomfortable doubting his judgment. In less than ten minutes, she would have to leave the museum to go meet with him back at his monastery. However, she wanted to meet with Eric again first – he said he'd have some time during his lunch break to see her.

She looked at her phone to check the time – he was twenty minutes late. She dared not use her Polarity to check on him, but the idea of him getting hurt kept gnawing at her.

"Hey, Susie," Eric said from her left.

Susie turned, smiled, and gave him a quick wave.

"Sorry I'm late – I had a pretty demanding customer with valet parking," he said as he sat down on her left.

"Hollywood movie star?"

"No – family of eight and a mother-in-law."

Susie giggled, "I don't know why that's funny."

Eric grinned. "It is. I guess from your perspective it would look hilarious… kids running around everywhere, juice boxes being thrown at me, dad yelling at me not to scratch the minivan, the mother-in-law yelling at the dad about his low-paying job…," he said and then chuckled. "Thanks – that took the edge off the stress."

"It's not an easy job."

"Yeah, I'm a pro," Eric said, opening his wallet showing a thick wad of one-dollar bills, "Look at all of these one's."

"Showing a bunch of one's isn't exactly the best way to impress a lady," she said.

"Well, I also get a bunch of spare change," Eric shot back, jiggling his pocket.

"No – you need to go up with the money, not down," Susie smiled.

"God, I wish I had some paper to write that down. So THAT'S where I've been going wrong with women," Eric said.

Susie loved Eric's sense of humor. Susie wanted to touch him – anywhere – but she had to restrain herself. She received a text from Demetri.

"Excuse me," she said to Eric.

Were wer u last nite?????? the text read.

Susie rolled her eyes and wondered exactly how she should respond. She was able to give some degree of leeway for correct grammar and spelling when it came to texts, but she felt prompted to write back and tell him to learn how to write at least at a third grade level. The pushiness of the extra question marks, the lack of tact altogether, the… she pocketed her phone. She was enjoying the moment with Eric and she didn't want to spoil it – she spent a lifetime of spoiling moments by getting hung up of nit-picky things, expecting perfection. The moment she had with Eric was perfection and letting go of the crass text was much easier than she thought it would be.

"I need to leave in a minute," she told Eric.

"Yeah – I'm sorry again about being late. Maybe we can get together again sometime?"

He scooted a few inches closer to her and grabbed her hand. She stood up, wondering if *They* were watching.

"I can't be late," she said.

Eric stood up and said, "I'll call you later."

"Sure," Susie said, walking away.

She exited the museum and hailed a cab. It pulled up. Susie approached the door and opened it. Before she got in, she checked her future to ensure her safety. She stepped back from the cab and said to the driver, "I'm sorry, I forgot something," and then closed the door.

Her Polarity showed her that the driver would suffer a heart attack during their drive – causing the cab to crash, killing her. Dan had influenced the cab by making a few phony pick up requests and then, finally, taking the cab himself to be dropped off up the road – just so the cab would be positioned to pick up Susie at that moment.

That was too easy. Is He even trying? she thought.

She expected Dan to hatch a more elaborate plan than this. It then occurred to her that she almost died. She felt oddly at peace – knowing that she was quite able to use her Polarity to counter *Them*. Spike had told her earlier that she would get used to this. She was beginning to believe him.

About an hour later, Susie was sitting in a chair in the cabbage field next to Father Crane's monastery. Father Crane was forty feet away from her, also sitting. He was staring at the ground ostensibly somewhere in-between the two of them. He rested his elbows on his chair's armrests and kept his hands up, touching fingertips to fingertips. Unless her eyes deceived her, it was as if he were about to cry.

"I've never seen you look so sad," Susie said to Father Crane.

Father Crane's eyes darted up at her and he put his hands down. "I cannot recall the last time I felt this confused. I have had my full Polarity since I was eighteen – and I have never once felt this frustrated."

"I'm sure *They're* loving seeing you like this."

"Let *Them* waste *Their* time reveling. There is no reason for *Us* to care. There is no reason for you to care – do not let *Them* distract you with *Their* ways."

"Is all lost with getting Harold?" Susie asked.

"*We* are tragically close. Oh, what a victory it would have been to put Harold behind bars. *We* have invested everything I can spare."

"What about… What about asking for help from another overseer?"

Father Crane didn't say anything.

"You already have, haven't you?" Susie said.

Father Crane nodded once and said, "They outnumber *Us* two to one. *They* dedicate an enormous amount of energy trying to kill *Us*. The few people *We* have are literally saving thousands of innocent people by the minute around the world, using whatever spare energy is left to defend *Us*. *We* only go after *Them* if the opportunity is plausible. All of the evidence against Harold at the beginning…," Father Crane paused and then said, "This should have been easy."

"Now it's not."

Father Crane shook his head, "No. The other overseers feel this is a lost cause now – Eddie undoubtedly has Big Dynamite at arm's length. Big Dynamite is all *We* have left."

"Then why has Eddie waited so long to kill him?"

"To keep our attention dispersed – killing Big Dynamite would have kept more of our attention on the other evidence. Killing Big Dynamite early on would have made it easier for *Us*."

"Then why is Big Dynamite still alive?"

"That, I do not know. I can only surmise that *They* are taunting *Us*, but I cannot help but consider that there is something else at stake – it feels as if *They* are trying to draw *Us* in to him."

"Using him as bait," Susie said.

"For what purpose? What else is there to accomplish? Regardless, this will not last much longer. Big Dynamite found out about G-Man's death and he was quite unsettled by it. He will be turning himself into the police earlier than originally predicted – tomorrow, Thursday, at 1:17 P.M., if he lives long enough. It is either *We* save him or *We* give up now and walk away."

"And he dies?"

"Yes. Eddie will shoot Big Dynamite at 11:04 A.M. in what appears to be an accusation that Big Dynamite was skimming profits from Eddie's pill business – my Polarity, of course, cannot tell me what is actually going on in Eddie's head. The bottom line is that Eddie is on track to kill Big Dynamite before Big Dynamite can turn himself in."

"A gun? All *We* have to do is lead the police to where Eddie will be and they'll catch *Him* in the act," Susie said.

"And if *He* did run away, it would be easy for *Us* to lead police to the weapon, the ballistics data, the witnesses *He* bought it from, and so on – none of this makes sense. Guns are too easy to counter. Neither *Us* nor *Them* use guns very often. It makes no sense."

"You sound like you've given up hope," Susie said.

"*We* never rely on hope. Hope is a euphemism for surrendering one's fate to someone or something else's will."

"Well, *We* have to try. Let me take care of this," Susie said.

Father Crane raised an eyebrow.

"*They* know you too well. Maybe it's time I mix it up," she said.

"Very well. I will keep watch on Dan. Also, your cab is here," Father Crane said.

Susie returned back to the city and slowly walked the sidewalks while she thought. Big Dynamite needed be saved sooner, if possible. Susie wanted to force Eddie's hand to move as soon as possible – she didn't want Eddie to wait until the last moment to change things on her. Eddie was currently with Big Dynamite in an abandoned brownstone apartment. They were re-packaging a new shipment of prescription drugs into various containers and plastic bags for re-sale. They would be together continually doing so until the moment they stepped out of the apartment building at 11:02 A.M. tomorrow – two minutes before Eddie would shoot Big Dynamite in an alleyway.

She played out several scenarios using her Polarity...

Tip police off about their drug operation. The police show up. Eddie shoots Big Dynamite and claims that he was undercover busting a prescription ring. Eddie gets away with it.

That was no good. She considered...

Tip off Vinny that Eddie is a mid-level drug dealer, but no matter what is said, Vinny won't believe it.

That, too, wasn't good. She considered...

Convince Big Dynamite's mother to call him, but Eddie won't let him leave.

No matter what Susie tried, Eddie was going to kill Big Dynamite at 11:04 A.M. tomorrow. Her only legitimate chance was to have Vinny see for himself who Eddie really was – it would be at the exact moment when Eddie would point the gun at Big Dynamite. At that moment, Eddie wouldn't be able to use the excuse that he was undercover – Vinny would be in earshot of Eddie yelling at Big Dynamite for skimming money. Big Dynamite would live; however, she also predicted that Vinny would let Eddie go. Not only was his heart too soft to bust his partner, but he was also afraid of Eddie's unpredictable behavior. Someone else had to be with Vinny so he would go through with busting Eddie.

She found a mobile phone sitting on a windowsill of a bakery – its owner was already on a flight to leave the country. Susie borrowed it and called Nemec.

"This is Nemec," he said.

"This is Linda... remember... from O'Shay's?"

"Yeah I remember. I went to the bathroom and came out to a poor guy being roughed up by a hundred pissed off women. How can I forget... and you disappeared."

"Yeah – sorry about that. I'd like to meet with you again."

"Sure. When and where?" Nemec asked.

"Tomorrow at 11 A.M. in the alleyway between the HalfStack Textile building and West Coast Palm Apartments. Use the weather service's time to ensure you're not late."

"A stickler for punctuality again... got it."

"One other thing," Susie said.

"Yeah?"

"My name isn't Linda... it's Susie," she said and then hung up.

Susie knew that Vinny was with Nemec at police headquarters – Eddie was at home "sick".

*　　　*　　　*

Vinny noticed a look of amazement strike Nemec's face at the end of the phone call.

"What?" Vinny asked.

"That was Susie."

"My Susie?"

Nemec nodded, "Yeah – I knew that girl in the video you showed me looked familiar."

"What did she want?" Vinny asked.

"She wants to meet with me tomorrow at 11 A.M. down in alleyway in a pretty shady part of town."

"I have to go with you," Vinny said, "Let me call Eddie and see if he's feeling better."

"No… wait. We don't want to spook her away. She seems pretty insistent on details and I don't think she would want someone to be with me."

"Can I at least circle around the both of you, so I can make sure she doesn't give me the slip again?"

"Yeah. That should be okay."

Vinny picked up his phone and dialed Eddie. He was instantly sent to voicemail. Vinny hung up.

"I get his voicemail again. He'll probably be out tomorrow, too. He didn't take that shooting too well."

*   *   *

Father Crane sat on a simple chair, shirtless at the monastery while another monk changed the bandages on his back.

"Your wounds are healing nicely," the monk said.

Father Crane didn't respond. He was deep in thought, evaluating the outcome of whatever Susie was putting into play. He could see Dan at a restaurant flirting with a set of twin girls who had just turned eighteen – they didn't appear to have any relevance to Susie's plan. Dan would be busy with them through the night. He could see Harold playing racquetball with a Congressman. Harold appeared carefree – Spike hadn't had a chance to kill him since he broke his ankle. Spike normally attempted to kill Harold at least once a day. Linus was at a nutrition store buying body-building supplements. Jennifer was flying with Sully to the Principality of Sealand – Sully was out to purchase it. Jennifer was there to ensure that Sully was unknowingly influenced in accordance with *Their* needs. Father Crane had already reported to his superiors this activity with Sully and left it in their hands as to how to proceed.

Father Crane grunted – another one of *Us* had just been killed by *Them*. It was Melissa, a 42-year-old librarian. She had been one of *Us* for nearly nineteen years. Replacing her would be quite an undertaking. Melissa was assigned to help a young man survive – the young man was on the cusp of becoming one of *Us. They* would certainly be able to kill that young man now. He received a text from Harold.

You lost Frank, you lost Melissa, and now… aw… poor baby, it read.

He was down to 29 operatives. Maybe it would be better to let Harold get away with it and cut the losses. Susie's life was at risk pursuing Eddie. Father Crane worried that he could lose her, too. Susie was keeping her distance – and that was the only thing that kept Father Crane comfortable.

*　　　*　　　*

Susie was about to begin setting decoys for Eddie even though she predicted that none of them would cause him to alter his course in the future. She contacted Demetri promising a "night of fun" and asked him to pick her up in front of her hotel – she just needed a ride to help her put her decoys into play. Hanging out with Demetri also gave her detachment from Eric more plausibility.

She had about 25 minutes before Demetri would arrive. The extra time coaxed her into checking on Frank – he was nearby.

She walked a block north and found Frank sitting on a bench at a bus stop across the street from a bank.

"Hi Frank," she said.

"I'm gonna rob that bank," Frank said, looking across the street.

"You'll get $32,315 if you do… but you'll be caught."

Frank turned to her, "Will I get killed?"

"Nope. You'll be sent to prison. You'll come across a few of the guys you busted there. They will rape you regularly over the next 12 years before you get out."

"Oh – well that's no good," Frank said slowly as he sunk on the bench. "It's harder to get people to kill me than I thought it would be."

"Please stop hurting yourself."

"How are the Stewarts?" Frank asked.

"They're fine. Sammy's been sick all week with the flu."

"He's a good little guy," Frank said, smiling.

It was the first real smile Susie had seen in Frank since his family was murdered.

"How's Maya?" Frank asked.

"Good. She'll be seeing a specialist day after tomorrow. The doctors think they can get her out of that wheelchair with some new treatments."

"She has a good soul. She couldn't say many words – but it seemed that my kids understood everything she said. She was their favorite part about visiting them."

"And what about Mikey – Sammy's twin?"

"He's doing well. He's been talking non-stop for the past two weeks about going to the science museum on Friday."

Frank slowly produced a tired smile and said, "Yeah – that sounds like Mikey. He's the little scientist."

"The Stewarts are fine, Frank."

"Thanks, Susie. Thanks for taking care of them."

"I'm trying."

Susie stood up.

"You leavin'?" Frank asked.

"Well – you know how it goes with *Us*."

Frank frowned, "I don't ever want to hear that word said like that again."

"Okay, Frank," she said and walked away.

Susie walked back towards her hotel to wait for Demetri. She was about a hundred feet away from her hotel when she stopped. A street-sweeper truck was slowly driving by cleaning the curbside. As it passed by, a small metal clinking sound was heard. At the spot where she was to step next was a half-inch roofing nail that had landed face-up. She realized that Dan had set this roofing nail on the street six days ago – it would have severely wounded her foot. She picked up the nail and threw it away in a nearby garbage can.

It bothered her to know that Dan knew that she could possibly be at that exact spot at that exact moment in time. Dan was very capable with his Polarity, but considering how much that had taken place over the past six days, this was extreme. It gave her a very uneasy feeling that everything that had happened to date was planned precisely – and it also meant that everything that was to happen has also been planned to the same precision.

She thought about her earlier experience with Max and the two-headed nickel. Max had several viable plans in place well in advance. This roofing nail matched that line of reasoning. Max, being Father Crane's overseer, would point to one of *Them* of his equal caliber helping Dan pull this off.

Eddie, she thought.

She still had a hard time imagining herself killing someone knowingly. Eddie, Harold, Dan – *They* seemed unhuman to her. *They* had no issue killing Frank's poor wife and kids. *They* couldn't be reasoned with – all of the destruction, pain, and hurt *They* had cast on the world. Susie was slowly believing she could kill one of *Them* if she had to.

Demetri pulled up alongside her and rolled down his window.

"Hey babe! Get in!" he yelled at her.

Susie stopped and looked at him, forcing a smile. He was driving a new Porsche – white with tinted windows.

"Like my ride?" he asked with a cocky smile.

It belongs to your father, who is over $2 million in debt, she thought.

"It's all right," she said.

Compared to Eric, Demetri seemed vilely disgusting. The two were the same age, but Demetri still had the maturity of a middle-schooler. She got in the car and looked him over – trying to find at least one redeeming quality that would help her forget about his immaturity. His hair was slicked up with hard sculpting paste. He wore a few heavy gold chains. His cologne was strong, but not strong enough to mask the residual stench left behind from his smoking. He wore a tight, painted-on designer shirt – he had a great physique and that helped Susie cope with the experience.

"You like this?" he said, pointing at a tattoo on his inner forearm.

It read *EDUCATED BUM* in large, bold letters.

"Nice," she said, trying to keep from laughing.

"I got it last night. It says what I am – laid back and smart."

She felt nauseous – she remembered that she was making out with him just a few nights ago. She rubbed her face with both hands so she could have a chance to cringe without him – or *Them* – noticing.

"That's sexy," she said, biting her lower lip.

Demetri winked at her and sped off.

"I wanna show you my place," he said.

"Sure, but can you help me with a few things first?"

He patted her right knee a couple of times and said, "Yeah, Stacey."

"It's Susie."

He turned and winked at her and said, "Yeah, Susie."

For the next four hours, Susie had Demetri drive her all over town – making several stops along the way. They went to various stores to buy a variety of random objects ranging from tennis balls to dryer sheets – only to have those objects spread randomly throughout the city. Whenever Demetri was on the verge of complaining, Susie would kiss him briefly and thank him for being such a good guy.

Throughout it all, Susie couldn't foresee any changes towards the fate of Big Dynamite or Eddie. Nemec would arrive just as Eddie would draw his gun at Big Dynamite. Vinny would arrive at the same moment as well, but from the other entrance of the alley. Eddie would give up and explain that he was undercover – only to be convicted shortly thereafter for drug trafficking. Big Dynamite would live and testify against Harold.

Susie spent all of this time creating decoys without any results – nothing in the future would change. She didn't believe that *They* would allow Eddie to be caught and Big Dynamite to live, but there was nothing to indicate that *They* were doing anything about it.

"Hey babe, let's go do something or you can go home," Demetri said to her.

She grabbed his inner thigh and whispered in his ear, "You're gonna have to work a little harder to get me."

Demetri looked her up and down and said, "Hard to get, huh?"

"Oh no, I'm easy. I just like to make you work a little first."

Demetri leaned in and kissed her. To his credit, Demetri was a great kisser. The kiss seemed like it wouldn't end and – at the moment when Demetri was about to put his hands on her chest – she gently pushed him away and said, "I think I'll go home."

"Seriously?"

"I'm worth it."

Demetri groaned. He drove her back to her hotel. As she got out of the car, Demetri asked, "You stayin' here?"

"Nope. I live nearby. Thanks for the good time tonight."

"Yeah. Whatever."

Demetri drove off. Susie watched as he weaved through traffic, barely missing several much slower cars. A few blocks up the road, a car in front of him stopped unexpectedly and Demetri rear-ended it.

"His father's gonna kill him," Susie said and then walked into the hotel.

Chapter 21 – Spilled Coffee

Susie awoke the next morning having not slept well the night before – the realization that this was *Our* last chance to nab Harold wore heavily on her mind. It was 9 A.M. and the fate of Big Dynamite and Eddie hadn't changed. She saw Dan heading to a coffee shop that was just a block away from where all of the action would happen. Susie quickly got dressed to meet him there. She wanted to keep him close so he wouldn't be able to alter anything.

She walked into the coffee shop and saw him sitting at a table near the store's large front window. He waved her to come over. As she walked towards him, she shoved her hands in her pockets – the urge to kill him was becoming tamer but it still felt uncontrollable. She tightened her face and sat down.

He took a sip of coffee, "Ah… that's good."

Susie was silent.

"I love the look on *Your* face. It's anger. It's hatred. It's just like *Us*."

"Well, *You* can be right or *You* can be happy."

"But being right makes me happy," Dan said, taking another sip. "Come on… we can be civilized people just for a moment. I'm not doing anything. You're not doing anything. Look… I didn't even stress the word *you're*. Relax."

Susie shook her head.

"Fine. Be a ball of stress," Dan said, taking another sip and looking out the large window, disinterested.

"I'm not letting *You* out of my sight."

"Well… there's still Harold."

"*He's* playing golf," she said.

"There's Linus."

"*He's* at the gym."

"And, my God, what a gym rat he is. That guy has image issues," Dan said flippantly.

"Jennifer is overseas," Susie added. "The rest of Harold's crew is busy with the rest of Father Crane's."

"*You* lost Melissa yesterday. *Our* guy Billie took care of *Her*," Dan smirked, briefly pointing at Susie.

Susie didn't say anything.

"I'm just sayin' *We* have another guy who doesn't have anyone to focus on anymore."

Susie gritted her teeth.

"Oh – that's right. Billie is out killing the man Melissa was protecting. *You* won't be adding anyone to *Your* roster any time soon. Wow. Too bad."

"*You* won't break my focus," Susie said.

"If *You* insist on following me, *You* had better bring a lot of coffee. It will be boring but I'll try to keep it interesting for *You*."

Dan stood up and took a sip of his coffee, tilting it nearly upside down.

"On second thought," he said, "I'm predicting that *You'll* be boring. I better get another coffee."

Dan walked to the cashier and ordered another large coffee. Susie followed Dan out of the coffee shop. She continuously peered into the various points of time into the future to see what plans he had.

"Why are *You* going up to the roof of this building?" she asked.

"Am I that predictable?" Dan asked rhetorically. "Hey, if *You* follow me then *You* can't do anything down here, right?"

Susie stopped. Dan stopped with her.

Dan continued, "At the same time, I could just be leading *You* to the roof to push *You* off. Fifteen stories is quite a drop."

"No – *You* can't do that. There are too many witnesses. This building is shorter than most of the other buildings here. There will be at least eighteen people who will see *You* do it from the taller buildings' windows."

Dan walked up and opened the door to the lobby of the building. "Are *You* coming with me or are *You* staying?"

Susie followed him inside. They both entered a nearby elevator. Her eyes kept glued to him.

"It isn't polite to stare – besides, do *You* really think staring is making a difference?"

"If it annoys *You,* then it makes a big difference," Susie said.

"It's a little creepy, yes," Dan said and then took a sip of his coffee.

The elevator opened its doors at the top floor. The two of them got out and headed to the end of the hallway to a door leading to the service stairs. Dan gave a swift kick to the door – its rusty chains buckled and the door swung open. They went up the single flight of stairs and onto the roof.

Dan walked over to the edge and looked down on the streets below. Susie stayed away from him.

"Still think I will throw *You* off the building? Don't *You* trust *Your* Polarity at all?"

Susie took a few steps towards him, but stopped about five feet away.

"The city is ripe – so many people to hurt, so little time to do it in," Dan reveled, looking over the vast cityscape.

"I know about *Your* past, Dan," Susie said, hoping to strike a nerve with him.

"Good for *You*," Dan said, still looking outward. "We've got a few more moments before the police officer and FBI agent arrive. Are *You* giving it one last good push to rattle me? If so – that's just amazing. I'm way up here and *You're* wasting *Your* time with me."

"I know that *You* were raped by an escaped convict when *You* were six."

Dan took a sip. He appeared unmoved.

"I know that *Your* first set of foster parents sold *You* out as a child prostitute."

"Yep," Dan said.

"I know that *Your* last set of foster parents tortured *Your* pets – even *Your* favorite puppy."

Dan nodded, turned around, and got into Susie's face. "Six months ago I drugged *Your* sister and had my way with her for ten hours straight."

Susie's eyes widened in horror.

"It would have been more interesting if she wasn't unconscious through it all," he said.

Susie swung her right hand at Dan, but he blocked it with his left arm – which also had his coffee. The coffee flew out of his left hand and went over the side of the building.

"Oh no," Susie said, hurrying towards the building's ledge.

They both looked down just before the coffee made impact on the windshield of a white SUV below.

"Well, this changes everything. They'll be twenty seconds late and that's an eternity," Dan said and then turned towards Susie. "And *You* still care about *Your* sister. My, that's interesting."

*   *   *

Vinny and Nemec were walking by the coffee shop with the large front window when they heard tires screeching.

SCREECH!

Vinny and Nemec jumped backwards just as a white SUV narrowly missed them and barreled into the large window of the coffee shop.

CRASH!

"Whoa!" Vinny yelled.

"Christ, that was close!" Nemec yelled.

They entered the coffee shop to help anyone who needed it. The driver of the SUV was shaken up, but he was otherwise fine – his airbag protected him.

"Something… something landed on my windshield. It was a drink… a coffee… or a soda," he panted.

Vinny looked around. No one appeared hurt.

"Vinny, we have to keep moving. Susie insists on being punctual," Nemec said.

Vinny looked around some more and nodded. "Okay," he finally said.

They exited the coffee shop. Vinny began to jog. "I'll run around to the other side of the alley."

"Okay," Nemec said.

Vinny ran a half-block to the left of the alley Nemec would go. He took a right into an alley running parallel to Nemec's alley. He got halfway up the alley and took a right to a passageway that would get him behind where Susie was expected to be found.

Vinny turned the corner just as Eddie was shooting Big Dynamite. Big Dynamite's cries for help were easily heard over Eddie's silencer.

"POLICE!" Nemec yelled from Eddie's left – about sixty feet in front of Vinny – drawing his gun.

Eddie turned and opened fire on Nemec, hitting him in the shoulder. Nemec dropped his gun. Eddie continued firing at Nemec, hitting him multiple times, causing him to fall to the ground. Vinny took out his gun, carefully aimed, and pulled the trigger – a clean shot, right into the back of Eddie's head. Eddie dropped like a ragdoll.

Vinny panicked as he ran towards Nemec. He took out his phone, pressed a button, and said, "I gotta...," he started crying, "I gotta agent down! AGENT DOWN!"

He ran by Eddie, briefly slowing to ensure his wound was lethal – bits of brain were scattered about. He then ran to Nemec and crouched down over him. Nemec struggled to breath.

"Oh God! Oh God!" Vinny yelled, his hands on his head, unsure as to what he could do to help him.

Blood streamed from Nemec's chest in several places and he gasped for air. He turned to Vinny and said, "Vinny... You're... You're all right."

Nemec's body when limp.

"SOMEONE CALL 9-1-1!" Vinny yelled. "SOMEONE HELP!" he shrieked, crying.

Chapter 22 – Making History

The next day, Susie was with Father Crane and Spike. They were standing in a mostly empty parking lot near a construction site.

"Harold gets away, but Eddie is dead. It was not a total loss," Father Crane said.

"I didn't think it would end this way," Susie said, despondent.

"Neither you nor Dan can predict your emotions. When it comes to *Us* and *Them* – emotions are the wild card."

"Somethin'… somethin' just feels fishy to me," Spike said.

"There is something that is not right – Eddie did not have to shoot Big Dynamite. I can only surmise that Eddie was ordered from above to give *His* life to protect Harold, if it were required. Eddie most likely was not expecting your emotional coffee outburst – quite frankly none of *Us* did either. In the past, *He* appeared to wait until the last instant to change *His* plans, but you changed the course of events at just the right moment. *He* had no other choice but to finish Big Dynamite and expect *His* own demise."

"It still feels artificial," Susie said, her eyes shifting in thought.

"Do not dwell on this much longer. *We* have the future to protect. Move on," Father Crane said sternly and then walked away.

Susie thought about how Frank would handle Nemec's death. She decided it would be best to tell him about it personally so she could explain better how it all happened. She knew Frank was sleeping on a bench at another bus stop, recovering from a heavy night of drinking. She took a cab to meet him.

"Where to?" the driver asked.

"The Science Museum," she said – it was the closest landmark to where Frank was.

The cab drove off and Susie ran through thousands of scenarios to find the most perfectly crafted set of words that Frank would want to hear. Several scenarios she predicted resulted in Frank blaming her for Nemec's death – she wanted to avoid that.

The cab drove by the coffee shop whose window had been destroyed indirectly by her coffee. A large blue truck holding several very large windows on its sides was parked in front of the shop. There were several men carefully installing one of the window panes where the old one used to be. This reminded her of the possibility that she almost killed both Nemec and Vinny – and Eddie would have cleanly killed Big Dynamite. It made her wonder if Dan knew she would knock the coffee out of his hand but, perhaps, his timing was a little off – he didn't have any other reason to go to the top of the building.

She looked into her near future and didn't see anything alarming. Dan was at an electronics store hitting on a woman who just turned 40 years old – she wasn't even close to being attractive. It looked as if Dan had already moved on to his next mission. Linus had packed his brown bag and had arranged for a taxi to take him to the airport. Harold was back in his office running Beytern. Jennifer was still overseas with Sully. It seemed that *They* already moved beyond the events of yesterday – just as Father Crane suggested that *We* do the same.

The taxi stopped at an intersection that was right around the corner from where Frank was. The traffic light was out and a police officer was directing traffic around the needs of a repair truck – a truck that had a large human-sized bucket at the end of its large, telescoping boom. The repair truck was parked halfway on the sidewalk, between a telephone pole and a large blue postal drop box. A technician got into the truck's bucket console and was soon moving up high towards the traffic light in need of service. Susie had accounted for this delay already and she mouthed out the words of the taxi driver as he spoke, "Are you kidding me?"

She put her hands firmly on the back of the seat in front of her to brace herself. The taxi began to move forward as soon as the police officer directed, but the repair truck moved out in front of taxi. The taxi slammed it brakes, but Susie hardly reacted except to mouth out along with the taxi driver, "Learn to drive that thing!"

She looked at the police officer as they turned the corner – it reminded of her when she first met Frank. Now, Frank was unrecognizable in that regard and his recent life of crime set him a world apart from the man he used to be. Susie wiped a tear away from her eye – she saw, in an instant, Frank's life before he was one of *Us* and the stark contrast of what it was now.

The taxi pulled up at the Science Museum. Susie paid her fare and got out. She saw Frank lying on the bench across the street. A newspaper covered the upper half of his body.

The police will catch him tomorrow and he will be sent to prison.

She walked up to him and said, "Frank, it's Susie."

Frank sat up – the newspaper slid off his chest. His eyes were bloodshot and heavy. His short beard was full of crumbs of food. He blinked a few times and squinted at Susie.

"Hey," he said.

"A man was killed yesterday – *He* was one of *Them*. *He* had a hand in your family's murder. *He* was in a shoot-out with your former partner, Jason Nemec."

"That's good. Thank you," Frank said.

"But…"

"But what?"

"But Jason didn't survive either."

Frank dropped his head, "*They* just couldn't stop taking from me, could *They*? *They* took my best friend and none of *You* thought about saving him."

Susie let Frank vent.

"I hate Father Crane."

"Frank, let me get you some food. There's a snack vendor across the street."

Frank rubbed his eyes. He stood up. "What time is it?"

"Almost 10 A.M. You've been here for almost twelve hours. You're badly dehydrated."

"Oh," he said lethargically.

Susie held Frank's hand as she guided him across the street. On the other side, she stopped – she felt *Them* nearby. Just ahead, she saw Linus being helped across an intersection by a woman who was also pushing a girl in a wheelchair. A young boy with near-white blond hair was helping his mother push. It was the Stewarts. Susie's mouth opened – they were only thirty feet away.

"Thank you for helping me cross the street, dear lady," she heard Linus say.

"You're very welcome," Mrs. Stewart said.

"Hey, I know that voice," Frank said, turning to his right. "It's Tammy Stewart and a couple of her kids."

"The Stewarts?" Susie asked rhetorically, still in shock, wondering what was happening.

"Yeah," Frank said.

Mrs. Stewart looked at Frank, leaning forward, squinting.

"Hey Tammy!" Frank shouted and waved.

Mrs. Stewart put her hands on her chest and smiled ear-to-ear. "Hey kids, it's Papa Frank!"

Maya bounced up and down in her wheelchair and clapped. Sammy ran up to Frank and hugged his leg.

Susie's Polarity was giving her a mountain of information to sort through – Linus wasn't supposed to be here. Where was Dan? Dan was getting out of a red minivan across the street near the repair truck that was working on the traffic light. He was with the 40-year-old woman from the electronics store.

"What brings you here?" Frank asked Mrs. Stewart.

"Maya has an appointment with a doctor a block away. They're going to try a new treatment on her. And, well, Sammy – he's been sick all week but he's getting better, so it was a good chance to get him outside."

Frank bent down and kissed Maya on her cheek. She clapped incessantly. Sammy kept a hold of Frank's leg.

"Okay Sammy, Papa Frank has had enough," Mrs. Stewart said.

Sammy came back to her and latched onto her leg.

Linus walked up to Susie and bumped into her – his strong Polarity distracted her from keeping her concentration. "Oh sorry," he said.

"Whoa there, sir," Mrs. Stewart said to Linus. "Do you need help?"

Linus turned around towards Mrs. Stewart and said, "Thank you, but I'll be fine, dear lady." He then turned to Susie and said,

"Please excuse my clumsiness. Sometimes my movements aren't so easy to predict."

Susie's Polarity showed that Linus was about to push Sammy on the street into on-coming traffic. The prediction quickly changed to him pushing Frank on the street. Then it was Mrs. Stewart. Then it was Susie herself. She froze.

She turned to look at Dan – who was now holding hands with his woman as they were walking by the traffic light repair truck.

"Mikey?" Mrs. Stewart said, surprised.

Susie turned towards Mrs. Stewart. Her other twin son, Mikey, wandered up to her.

"What are you doing here? Shouldn't you be in school?"

Mikey pointed at the Science Museum. "We went to the museum today!" he squealed.

"Oh, that's right… but where is your teacher?"

Mikey shrugged his shoulders and said, "I don't know." He then hugged Frank's leg quickly before running to his twin brother.

Mrs. Stewart rolled her eyes and told Frank, "He has an awful substitute teacher…," she stopped and raised herself on her tiptoes. "There she is now – Mrs. Parmalee," Mrs. Stewart said, pointing towards the Science Museum.

"Mikey!" Mrs. Parmalee shouted, pointing at the Stewart child.

"Wow, that's the poofiest grey hair I think I've ever seen," Frank said.

"If that was her only problem, then we would be okay. She forgets EVERYTHING. Now she forgets about my son," Mrs. Stewart said.

Mrs. Parmalee stormed towards Mikey, shouting, "Mikey, get back over here!"

"First of all, you don't YELL at my son," Mrs. Stewart said sternly.

Susie drowned out the ensuing argument between the two. There were too many things going on right now. Her heart raced. She gripped her head, pulling her hair.

"I must be off," Linus said as he walked away.

Nothing? Linus was here to do nothing? She turned to Dan, who was whispering something in his woman's ear – the woman's face quickly went sour and she slapped Dan. The police officer turned his attention to Dan – ignoring the on-coming traffic. Dan fell backwards and into the large blue postal drop box.

Then it hit Susie: Dan had unbolted that same postal drop box earlier.

Dan's fall into the postal drop box pushed it, causing it to tip over onto the street – just as a large blue truck was cruising through the intersection.

"That's the same truck that was repairing the coffee shop window," Susie said in disbelief.

The large panes of glass on the truck's sides were unmistakable. It should have been stopped at the intersection by the now distracted policeman. It swerved hard to miss the postal drop box – so hard it began to overturn onto its right side.

Without any time to warn anyone, Susie grabbed Frank. She pulled him several feet towards the Science Museum and tackled him onto the ground. At that moment, the glass truck overturned completely – right in front of where Susie was just standing. The large panes of glass shattered on impact. Thousands of pieces of glass shot forward to where Frank was standing.

Screaming was heard from all around.

Susie got up and saw the horrible aftermath – the entire Stewart family was pelted with a countless number of glass shards. Mrs. Stewart was on the ground, blood streaming from all over her body. She barely breathed, holding the hand of a lifeless Sammy while trying in vain to reach the motionless body of Mikey. Maya was slumped over in her wheelchair. Mrs. Parmalee lay on the street twitching.

Frank got up, walked a few steps, and collapsed on the ground next to Stewarts.

"I... I... I...," he stuttered, rapidly shaking his head. "God no... no..."

Susie took a step towards him.

He quickly turned around towards her and yelled, "YOU WERE SUPPOSED TO PROTECT THEM!"

"Frank, I tried to...," Susie started.

"You saved ME! You should have saved THEM!" he yelled, pointing at the Stewarts. He then gripped his head and yelled in broken, high-pitched agony, "IT SHOULD HAVE BEEN ME!"

Susie's blood went red hot. Adrenaline shot through her veins. Negative energy pierced her body. She shoved her fists into her pockets.

Frank was now one of *Them*.

Susie gasped and stumbled backwards, uncertain as to how she should react. She ran across the street and right into the arms of Dan.

"Hey there," he said, smiling.

"What have *You* done?!" she yelled.

"What have I done? What have *I* done?" he laughed and said, "Tell me Susie: Who got Sarah drunk and eventually forced Mrs. Parmalee as the new teacher, causing Mikey to get lost? Who ordered the dog to jump on the agents, causing Mrs. Davis to be shot? Who sent the coffee on the windshield of that car, causing Nemec to be sent to his death? Who caused the window to break at the coffee shop guaranteeing the truck full of glass to be here at the perfect moment? Who promised Frank to protect the

Stewart family? It wasn't me. If I recall – and I'm sure I do so perfectly – it wasn't me. Most of it was specifically *You*, Susie."

Susie fell pale and choked in disgust.

Dan got in her face and said, "Do *You* really think any of THIS was about protecting Harold?"

Susie's eyes widened.

"Frank has made history – he is the first to ever make a full reversal – and *We* couldn't have done it without *You*," Dan cackled.

Susie grabbed Dan's shirt with both hands and pushed him backwards – he laughed as she did so. "*You* and me Dan. *You* and me tonight. 9 P.M."

"Sure. I'll be there," Dan said, straight-faced. "I look forward to killing *You*."

Dan and Susie parted ways.

Susie hadn't walked more than two blocks when she saw Father Crane in front of her on the sidewalk.

"To the park!" he shouted.

A few minutes later, the two of them were standing in a park.

"You must get a grip on your emotions. You will not survive against Dan in your duel. Dan is injured but *He* is still physically able to dominate you," Father Crane said.

"*He's* a monster – what *He* did to those poor people… what *He's* done to so many people," Susie said, tears forming in her eyes.

"Yes, Dan is a monster."

"Why didn't you kill *Him* when you had the chance – a long time ago at the monastery?"

Father Crane put his hand on his brow and shook his head, "That was, perhaps, the greatest blunder I have ever made. When the time came and *He* was on the cusp of getting his full Polarity, I faltered – I could not kill my friend. My long history with *Him* begat a love that a father would have for his son. I let *Him* go hoping, in error, that *He* would not do *Their* will."

"It's hard to picture Dan as ever being loveable."

"Anyone can be loveable. Love is only a good advisor if you are certain that the love is genuinely reciprocated. In my case with Dan, I thought incorrectly."

"*He's* hurt so many people. *He's* killed so many people – women and children. No more. I won't let *Him* do it anymore," Susie said.

"Please do not go through with this tonight. Your death will mean that *We* will be weakened terribly. *We* cannot afford to lose another."

Susie closed her eyes briefly and said, "Now that Frank has his full Polarity back, *He* will know the truth as to what happened. *He* will know that I did what I could. *He* will know that I will still do what I can."

Frank Crane held out his hands and pleaded, "Susie – Frank is one of *Them*. I once thought the same with Dan. *They* cannot be reasoned with. Frank will gladly see you die – *He* would gladly do it *Himself*. Do you really believe that Frank will see your reasoning?"

"Are you asking me or are you telling me? I don't think any of *Us* would know," Susie said.

Father Crane put his head in his hands and said, "If you are to go through with this, you must know that both sides won't send anyone else to interfere. If one side does, then the other sends one to balance the fight. This is carefully done because both sides recognize the inherent dangers that come with close proximity."

"I don't expect anyone to help me," she said confidently.

"Don't bring any weapons or else Dan will bring weapons – and vice versa. Choose a place that has objects that you can use as impromptu weapons – like rocks, wooden boards, or dirt you can throw in the eyes. Be wary of animals such as rats, stray dogs, and stray cats – as animals can provide a decisive advantage. Do not hesitate to enlist the help of animals if you are able to find them there."

"How do I know *They* haven't already influenced animals?"

"Ever since the moment you challenged Dan, both sides have paid particular attention towards any contact with animals from both *Us* and *Them* – none have been touched, none have been influenced. All eyes from both sides will be on the two of you."

Susie was silent.

"The duel you have with Dan will take your very best efforts."

"I won't let Dan hurt anyone anymore. If I die, but I've injured *Him* then it's worth it," Susie said and she walked away.

"Re-consider. Please re-consider!" Father Crane shouted.

Chapter 23 – Showdown

Susie headed to an industrial building complex as 9 P.M. approached. She stopped in an area that was rectangular in shape, about the size of a basketball court. Four-story buildings formed three sides of the area. The fourth side consisted of a line of dump trucks – this was where they parked at night. No one else was in the area.

Various rubble scattered the ground from whatever spilled from the dump trucks during their daily grind. Susie looked over the baseball-sized pieces of asphalt, random mounds of sand, and hand-sized pieces of glass scattered about the ground. Piles of garbage bags next to several over-flowing dumpsters dominated the entire wall of the building in front of her. The other two sides of the area were nothing but the bare walls of the other buildings. She felt it best to keep the garbage bags behind her so Dan wouldn't have access to their contents.

She felt Dan's presence. She turned around. He entered the area with a slow but confident strut. Susie felt the presence of his Polarity grow stronger with each step. A small part of her was frightened – not of Dan, but of losing control of herself. She could not foresee Dan's strategy, so she focused on her own. She fully committed herself to talk to Dan and get him riled up about his past and his failures – particularly how he failed to kill her. This was what Father Crane taught her. She carefully crafted the right words that she thought would distract him the most.

Dan, still walking, was within four feet of her when he said, "So, Susie...,"

Susie clawed at his face with her right hand – digging into him with her fingernails, instantly drawing blood. She leaned in and struck across his face with her right elbow. Dan stumbled a little to his right, but Susie continued her furious onslaught – she kicked him in the face with her left foot and he spun to his left, hunching down. Susie raised her right foot, cleanly connecting with Dan's jaw – knocking him backwards, causing him to fall to the ground. As he struggled to get up, Susie charged at him. Dan's eyes made contact with her just she punched him in the throat followed by a knee to his groin. Dan fell to his knees, choking, as Susie picked up a large rock from the ground and hammered it onto the top of Dan's head.

Dan shook off her attack. He plowed into Susie, picked her up, slammed her to the ground, and jumped on top of her. Susie swung the hand with the rock at Dan's face, but he blocked it and followed with a head butt to the side of her face – narrowly missing her nose. He then punched her in the face with his right fist, followed by his left. Susie grabbed his groin area, squeezed hard, and pulled down.

"Aaa!" Dan yelled.

Susie, still underneath Dan, grabbed his head and pulled it to connect his jaw with her forehead – a solid headbutt. A tooth flew out of Dan's mouth. Susie pushed him off her.

*　　　*　　　*

Harold walked on the rooftop of the building with the garbage bags and dumpsters underneath it. He had a folded chair with him and a bag of popcorn. He unfolded the chair, sat down, and watched the spectacle below – delightfully eating his popcorn.

"Come on, Dan!" he cheered.

He watched below as Susie and Dan exchanged blows. He enjoyed the live violence – it made him feel invigorated. He stood up as Susie successfully knocked Dan back to the ground with a knee to his face.

"Come on! Come on!" Harold shouted.

As Susie went to kick Dan in the face, Dan grabbed her foot and tackled her to the ground.

"YES! KILL *HER*!" Harold thundered.

Dan punched her in her ribs several times. Susie's mouth was very bloody and her left eye was swollen shut. Dan punched at her another time; she grabbed his arm and bit down on his wrist. Dan screamed in pain as he pummeled the back of her head with his free hand. Dan finally used this hand to free the one that Susie was biting down on – and Susie was able to break free from him, pushing him back to the garbage bags. Susie was kneeling, trying to catch her breath.

Harold was still standing while shoving popcorn in his mouth. "Oh, he's got *Her* now," he said, brimming with excitement.

Dan quickly found a brick in the rubble and threw it at Susie – she rolled over and it missed her. Dan grabbed another brick and charged her. Susie picked herself up off the ground, her knees beginning to buckle. Dan swung at her several times with the brick – Susie dodged each swing. Susie's knees finally buckled and she fell to the ground. Dan smiled, recoiled his arm back, and swung at the side of Susie's head – just as Susie was getting up and throwing a handful of sand at Dan's face. Dan's brick connected with a glancing blow to Susie's temple. She took a few crooked steps backwards and slammed into one of the dumpsters behind her. She slumped to the ground, her eyes closed, motionless.

"KILL HER!" Harold yelled.

Dan rubbed his eyes frantically trying to brush away the sand, "I can't see!" he yelled.

"Don't use your eyes! Use your Polarity!" Harold yelled.

WHACK!

Harold felt a sharp pain to his left kneecap, causing him to fall down.

WHACK!

Another sharp pain came down on his right collarbone.

"Aaa!" Harold yelled.

He looked up. Standing over him was Father Crane; he was holding a baseball bat.

"*You* know how it goes, Harold: If *You* bring someone then *We* get to bring someone," Father Crane said.

"So... *You* are finally going to kill me," Harold cried out, writhing in pain.

Father Crane grabbed Harold by his injured leg and started dragging him. "Fortunately for *You*, Harold...," he said, struggling, "This is a rare case in which *You* are worth more to me alive than dead."

Harold tried to grip any part of the rooftop – trying in vain to stop Father Crane from dragging him any further. He looked to his left below and saw Dan with his eyes mostly closed, but his movements more stabilized. Dan was about thirty feet from Susie when he picked up a broken piece of glass from the ground – then he started running towards her helpless body.

Father Crane pushed Harold off the top of the building and onto a pile of garbage bags below – right next to Susie. Dan, only five feet away from Susie, collapsed immediately, vomiting blood and bile. Dan grabbed his throat, struggling to breath. Harold's chest heaved up – it felt as if all of his organs were imploding. Harold's injuries prevented him from moving – he could only rely on Dan moving away from him before they both died from their like Polarities. Harold's eyes began to blur as he watched Dan struggle to get away from him. Harold sweated profusely and his breath began to shorten until it gave him no air whatsoever. Dan scraped at the ground and was able to roll away from both Harold and Susie. Harold began to improve with every inch that Dan moved until – finally – Dan was a safe forty feet away.

"NO!" Dan yelled, standing up. "NO!" he frothed at the mouth. "SHE WAS MINE TO KILL! MINE!"

Dan fell to his knees and pounded the ground violently.

Harold saw Father Crane looking down on them. "Is someone mad?" Father Crane asked Dan.

Dan looked up, pointed at Father Crane, and yelled, "*She* was lucky!"

"There is no luck. There is only *Your* lack of sufficient skill. The police will be here in one minute and six seconds. I am certain they would like to talk to *You*," Father Crane said.

Dan shook in anger. He walked away.

Harold closed his eyes.

*   *   *

Susie awoke several days later in a hospital. A nurse was taking her blood pressure.

"Oh, look who's finally awake," the nurse said. "I'll go get the doctor."

Susie had a terrible headache. She felt pain all over her body. There was an IV taped on the top of her hand. She sat up slowly, still feeling anxiety left over from her duel with Dan even though it felt as if it happened weeks ago.

A doctor entered her room with the nurse. "Ah – you're awake," she said.

Susie blinked her eyes a few times. "Can I go home now?"

The doctor shook her head and said, "Oh heavens no – you're in bad shape. First things first, though, we need your name."

"Susie."

"Susie what?"

Susie paused for a few seconds and slowly said, "Is it okay if I just take a walk down the hall first. I need to wake up a little."

The doctor smiled and said, "If you think you can walk, then it's okay. Your IV is mobile – it has wheels on it. Don't go too far, though."

Susie nodded. The nurse tried to help her out of bed but she refused the help. "I got it."

She began to walk forward, holding the mobile IV.

"I'll be right back," Susie said.

"We'll be here," the nurse replied.

Susie walked out of her room, across her floor, and out the door leading to a long hallway. She ripped out her IV and entered a stairwell with a sign labeled *EXIT* over it. She took a deep breath and slowly went down the three flights of stairs. With each step, she felt angrier and angrier about how Dan got the better of her. She replayed their duel several times and she re-lived the energy she felt that night. Her adrenaline began to release through her body as she reached the bottom of the stairs. Wait – this wasn't her re-living the other night – it was one of *Them.*

An object pressed against Susie's throat – it was a sharp, but badly rusted knife. A man behind her said, "Greetings, dear lady."

"Linus," she whispered.

Linus moved closer – his head was beside the left side of her face. He turned his head towards her. She could feel his breath on her neck.

She focused, using her Polarity to determine what to do. No matter what she tried, everything she saw within five minutes was pitch black. If she tried to move, Linus would kill her – pitch blackness was invariably seen. Blackness was her future – this was her end, but she had no fear. Any remnant of fear that was once in her body was beaten to a pulp by Dan.

Linus slowly licked the side of Susie's face with the tip of his tongue. "It is sweet... *You* have probably determined that *You* have no way out. This is *Your* end. Rust doesn't leave fingerprints – there will be no evidence against me."

Susie steadied her breath and shifted her eyes to the left to look at Linus. His black sunglasses were off. His eyes were completely missing – his deep, pitted eye sockets seemed to stare at her. He licked his lips a few times.

"Do *You* want to die?" he asked.

She felt an instant calmness to his question as if she knew exactly what Linus wanted to hear.

"People die all the time – it's just a matter of how, when, and where," she said.

"And 'why'," Linus said.

"No. A reason isn't needed to die. People die all the time for no reason at all."

"Then why should people live?" Linus whispered.

"All that matters is *why* – a purpose – big or small. Most people aren't born with a purpose. History's most profound figures found purpose on their own – it didn't matter where they lived, when they lived, or how they lived. Anyone can have a purpose if they so choose to. *Why* someone lives is the only aspect of their life that they have the most control. People should live so they can fulfill the purpose that they find on their own. That is the definition of humanity."

Linus put his knife down and said, "Yes, since the beginning of time."

Susie turned to him and said, "*You've* had many opportunities to kill me, but *You* never did. There's a reason why *You* let me live."

"I was sent here to aid in the last few minutes of Frank's reversal. More importantly, though, I was sent to assess *You*."

"Assess?" Susie asked.

"If I wanted Spike dead, then it would already be so. I just needed to keep *Him* busy enough so *He* couldn't help *You*. I wanted to know what *You* could on *Your* own," Linus said and began to walk away.

"Why?"

Linus put on his sunglasses and opened the exit door, but stopped when he was halfway out. He turned around and said, "Nearly all of *Us* gave *You* less than 32 seconds to live against Dan – including me. Only one of *Us* precisely predicted the outcome exactly as it happened – one day *You* will meet her. Fortunately for *You*, she told me not to kill *You*... yet."

Chapter 24 – Patron

Harold was riding on a motorized wheelchair on a sidewalk that circled his favorite lake. He always found it relaxing to feed the pigeons there. His left hand controlled a joystick that directed his wheelchair's movements. His right arm was propped high in a cast because of his broken collarbone. His left leg was propped straight out, also in a cast.

As he approached his usual park bench, he noticed someone else was already there. He got closer but stopped forty feet away. It was Vinny.

"Aren't you worried about *Them* seeing *Us* together?" Harold asked.

"Crane will have figured it out within the next hour anyway – I shouldn't have had to touch the dog," Vinny said, staring towards the lake.

"Well I…"

"You took something that was supposed to be easy," Vinny said and turned towards Harold, "And you managed to make a mess out of it."

"But you never broke character once – not once. And you were always at the right place at the right time and…"

"Shut it. This isn't about me. This is about you. You're lazy and clumsy. You left it to Dan to fix what should have never been broken. He went through great pains to hold it all together while you sipped fine wine."

Harold gulped.

"Also, your experiment with Sully wasn't authorized," Vinny said and then stood up. "*We* will deal with you later."

"Yes, sir."

"Dan no longer reports to you. *We* are moving him up."

"Yes, sir."

Vinny walked away.

www.ingramcontent.com/pod-product-compliance
Lightning Source LLC
Chambersburg PA
CBHW050921250626
47155CB00001B/328